THE
NOT SO MERRY
ADVENTURES
OF
MAX CREED

THE
NOT SO MERRY
ADVENTURES
OF
MAX CREED

THE MODERN-DAY CHRONICLES OF MAX CREED

MATT COST

LEVEL
BEST BOOKS

To those who seek justice in a world that does not always provide it.

Chapter One

Long Beach Island, North Carolina

I t was not a physical ailment that plagued him at night. Rather, memories tattooed to his soul consumed his senses with a fervent and insistent prodding.

Max Creed was a man of desires. He lusted for sex, craved brown liquor, and was drawn powerfully to the poker table. As it was, he now allowed himself none of these things. He'd turned his passions toward a more devout pursuit.

Sleep commonly eluded him from two a.m. until first light, when he allowed himself to rise from bed and begin the day. He found those small hours to be essential to the crafting of who he was. A block of time in which there was nothing to do but ponder life should be required of every single human being on the planet, he thought, as light began to illuminate his bedroom window with the arrival of the rising sun.

He opened his eyes to the sight of his most trusted companion staring back at him with eager eyes. Soter was a chocolate Lab with deep brown eyes that possessed all the optimism that Max was lacking. It was time to eat. That was plenty of reason for excitement. This took Soter about ten seconds, and he was forced to wait as his master pulled on a pair of jeans, T-shirt, and sweatshirt. No socks or shoes.

Max paused at the mirror. He saw a man staring back at him with sad blue eyes. He was just six feet tall, had brown hair, a jagged nose, and an incredibly fit body, the result of four years of training. The time was near to put the training to use; he could feel it in the air, on the wind, in the sounds of the seagulls, and resounding with the crash of the waves.

He and Soter lived in a two-bedroom bungalow on the beach of a barrier island in North Carolina. It was a modest affair for someone of his means. Off the back deck, over the dune, and onto the beach they went. The sun was an orange ball of fire rising into the sky to the east, pulled by Apollo and his chariot, bringing a new day to the earth.

There was a chill in the air on this January morning. Max stepped off the steps of the home on stilts and into the icy sand in his bare feet. He embraced this sting to the senses, this jolt to his nerves, this message that he was still alive. Soter had already bounded over the dune, hoping to surprise some morning bird unaware. He was happy to chase, but on the few occasions he'd come close enough to catch, he'd slowed his roll to allow the feathered creature to escape. The game was in the chase, not the capture.

Max paused on the dune to appreciate the rising sun, the start of another day, not just one more rotation of the earth, but one more revolution of the sun for Max, for today was his birthday. Today he was forty years old. A milestone for some, just another day for him. Kinsley would've made the day one to remember. That is, if she hadn't been killed on their wedding day almost five years ago. The smell, the sounds, and the emotions of that sunny June afternoon swirled in his mind with the graphic images that he could never banish completely.

His thoughts led him to the man who had Kinsley killed for the purely selfish pleasure of causing Max pain and suffering. Winthrop Gould. Max had a different name back then. He was Milo Sharp and was a private detective, investigating a case of heroin smuggling. He'd connected enough dots to realize that the operation traveled downhill from a billionaire who'd made his money in Big Pharma. Already crossing the line in shady business practices, Winthrop Gould had turned his access to fentanyl into a full-blown drug business, flooding the East Coast with the deadly mix of his manufactured drug with street heroin.

Milo had found indisputable proof connecting Gould to the drug smuggling operation. Following Milo's tip, the police had caught the man red-handed at one of his illegal heroin facilities. Milo then supplied other damning evidence, and eventual testimony, that should've seen the man go away for the rest of his life. Over the course of a year, the team of lawyers for Winthrop Gould had stonewalled, fought with dirty tactics. Milo suspected massive bribes had been handed out, as witness after witness recanted. The case was eventually thrown out, and Gould walked free, not that he'd seen the inside of a jail cell since the day he was arrested.

Gould had easily paid the bail, and the trial was little more than an inconvenience for the man, though his drug empire had been dismantled, split up among other cartels, and the spotlight was on him for any future improprieties. Hence his hatred for Milo Sharp and everything near and dear to him. That had been the last time that Milo had underestimated the depths of heinous malevolence that a seemingly normal human being could harbor.

Unable to stop the vision, the wedding day appeared before Max as if on some cosmic projection screen. The movie screen of Long Beach switched from the courtroom and Winthrop Gould to be replaced by an idyllic grassy lawn on a cliff over the Atlantic Ocean on the coast of Maine. Chairs were filled with friends and Kinsley's family. Their very good friend was officiating. The sky was a perfect cerulean blue, illuminated by the sun, a special wedding gift delivered to them on that perfect summer day.

Kinsley, grinning her wicked and mischievous smirk, with eyes that were filled with love and promised carnal delights. The screeching heckles of mocking seagulls and crashing waves below. And Max, for just the briefest moment, a nanosecond almost too short to recognize, felt that absolute and unblemished happiness, quickly replaced by the dawning realization of what was to come as he heard the shot, and then it did. The red dot on her chest, that grew into a mess of blood, bone, and skin. Her eyes, now desperate, her grin fading, her mouth trying to speak, and then she was dead.

Returning to his North Carolina beach haven with a sigh, Max, no longer Milo, chose to go right today, or Soter did, and he followed. There was nobody braving the beach at this hour in January, and they were the sole owners of the sun ascending behind them. Forty minutes out, turn and return, four miles. Pelicans traveled in formations, skimming the waves, looking for breakfast. Sometimes there were dolphins, not this morning, and the occasional perfect shell which never made it into his pocket.

It was these minute aspects of everyday existence that Max focused on as he prepared to move on with his life. Or so he hoped, now that he'd avenged Kinsley's death and compromised with his demons, taking one step at a time, moment by moment, the slow tick of the clock marking the passage of time. Later, on the sunset walk, there'd be more people, some who'd say hello and he'd reply, but none that he knew by name.

When he got back to the cottage on the beach, John Little was sitting on the back deck, serenely watching the waves. John was an enormous man with a bald head, wide smile, and eyebrows that looked like twin mustaches. He was also the man who'd mentored Max through his darkest days.

John was a master of many kinds of hand-to-hand combat, boxing, wrestling, stick fighting, and someone whose practice of mixed martial arts incorporated pieces of Kun Khmer, Sanda, Judo, Karate, and Kung Fu. These he'd trained Max in over the past four years, all combined with a healthy dose of meditation, perhaps the most important piece. Max wouldn't say that he'd gained peace in that time, but he had at least a compromise with the darkness.

Soter bounded up the stairs and thrust his head into John's lap, his tail wagging, butt wiggling, ecstatic to greet his friend. It'd been John who'd suggested Max get a dog, and he was like the favorite uncle to the canine, one who always had a treat at hand to share, and one who brought comfort everywhere he went.

After Kinsley had been murdered on their wedding day and Max had avenged her death, acquiring more money than he could ever spend along the way, he'd run across John Little, and their lives had intersected, merged, and begun to move forward on a single, shared path. John had trained his body and mind, sixteen hours a day, seven days a week, interrupted only by the weapons training provided by another professional-turned-friend,

Scarlett.

"Nice spot you have here." John stood and embraced Max in a bear hug.

"It's good for the soul."

"That's important."

Max sat down in a rocking chair as John settled back into his. "Is this just a social visit?"

John laughed, an eruption from deep in his belly. "After you told me you needed time on your own? No. I think we found somebody."

"Who?"

"A woman by the name of Sevyn Knight."

Chapter Two

Dhaka, Bangladesh

Four Years Earlier

Milo Sharp sat on the stool at the end of a barroom in Dhaka. He was fairly certain it wasn't a legal drinking establishment. A hand-painted sign tacked over the door had some symbols that might've been hieroglyphic for all he knew, and underneath, it said *Duba Bāra*. Dive Bar.

He wasn't sure how long he'd been here. On this stool. In this bar. In Dhaka.

Of the twenty or so people in the room, only three were of the female persuasion, but they looked like they could kick the ass of any of the men, Milo included. Most of them were Bengali, or so he figured, either not Muslim or weak in their belief.

Nobody professed to speak English. He knew almost no Bengali. That was fine with him.

Milo had plenty of *taka*. Enough money to get him killed in a place like this. The lights were dim, the glasses were dirty, and his feet stuck to the floor. The men spoke in low whispers, their eyes flitting nervous glances around the room, and kept one hand close to their belts, behind which, most likely, a weapon was tucked.

What Milo most liked about this place was that the bartender, a one-eyed pirate with a glass eye, had produced a bottle of whiskey when enough *taka* had been brandished. Sure, you could get good liquor in the hotel, but Milo had no desire to go to one of those sanitized, cookie-cutter bars where ranks of Euro trash mixed with rich locals being vaguely naughty. Here, at the *Duba Bāra,* was where he intended on getting drunk. Day after day. Which was what he did. And still, the pirate bartender produced new brown liquor every day, for how long, Milo had no idea.

All three of the women had come up to him, flirted with him, propositioned him—but he'd not turned to look nor spoken in return. After a bit, they went away, and the men began to eyeball him, wondering who he was, a Westerner, an American, unless they were mistaken, who didn't want a woman, didn't ooze the Westerner's normal compulsion to tell those nearby why he was so great. He was an enigma.

They were each working their way up to picking a fight with the *Mārkina,* the American in their midst, relieving him of the wads of *taka* in his pockets, when that opportunity was taken from them. Milo had stumbled from his stool to take a piss, a slight stagger to his step, and bumped into a rugged individual of no small proportions. The man was bald, his pate shaven smoothly clean, his shoulders wider than most doorways on a body that towered a good five inches over six feet.

The man bumped him with an elbow and hip, sending Milo stumbling into the wall, the shock shaking the entire establishment.

Milo righted himself and stepped menacingly toward the huge man. "Watch where you're going, you fucking moron."

The man smiled. "My apologies. I shouldn't have gotten in front of your drunkenness."

Milo paused, the English words in an American accent, perhaps from New Jersey, cutting through his fuddled brain. It was no matter. He was not here to make friends. He stepped past the man to the door of the one-hole pisser and shitter.

"Sorry, friend, but I was here first." The man held up a massive forearm to block egress.

"The hell you were." Milo shoved the man. He did not budge.

"Just wait your turn and be a good little shaver."

Little shaver, Milo thought, anger flaring again like a fire poker stuck into his mind. He hooked his foot around the man's ankle and spun, and as the man stumbled, his elbow cracked into his chest, and the man stumbled back against the wall, threatening to tumble the entire edifice to the ground.

Milo followed, swinging a roundhouse blow that was knocked from the air by a move he didn't even see. Then something crashed into his chin, and that was all.

When Milo came to, he was propped with his back to the wall, and the man was putting a damp cloth of cold water to his face. He turned his face, spat blood on the floor.

"I didn't even see you hit me."

The man smiled. "I am trained in many forms of fighting."

Milo ran his tongue over his teeth. They appeared to be intact. "Yeah? Like what?"

The man shrugged. "I started with boxing and wrestling, then it was on to the sticks. Over the years, I have apprenticed in many a dojo, Japan and Korea, yes, but also Cambodia, China, Hong Kong. I ended up borrowing from Kun Khmer, Sanda, Judo, Karate, and Kung Fu, mixing them together into my own unique style."

Milo chuckled. "I guess that beats my expertise in schoolyard spats and barroom brawls."

The man held out his hand, and Milo took it, allowing himself to be pulled to his feet. "The restroom is yours. I took my opportunity while you were napping."

"What brings you to Dhaka?"

"Spiritual retreat was the purpose, or so I thought."

"Or so you thought?"

"I now believe that it may have been you who brought me to Dhaka. There is something in you that I sense has drawn us together with all the force of gravity. That our meeting is karma. Kismet. You name it. I feel that our destiny lies together. What is your name, stranger?"

"I am Milo Sharp."

CHAPTER TWO

The man held out his hand. "John Little."

* * *

It took some time. Milo had continued to imbibe in brown liquor from early to late over the course of the next week, but each day, John Little came in and sat with him. The hulking mass of a man would have one whiskey and sit for hours speaking with Milo about his own search for existence and purpose, his desire for expanded spirituality matched only by the tangible results of his study of various hand-to-hand combat mediums.

The second week, Milo began to cut back on the booze, intrigued by this man, John Little, as they began what would become a daily ritual of walks through the back streets of the crowded city. He wanted to hear his stories and remember. His voice was like a balm on Milo's tortured soul. Things like the Hindu belief that all things are eternal gave him cause for hope. The Buddhist tenet to abstain from sensual overindulgence gave him pause for consideration. And these messages were mixed in with colorful tales of the travels of John Little to all corners of the earth in search of understanding.

Milo Sharp might've been just one more tale on the nomadic search for meaning if they hadn't connected in a way that neither of them fully understood. The third week, Milo gave up alcohol, and they found a practice room with mats and gear. The fourth week they began to train in fight methods together. The fifth week, Milo shared with John that he was a very, very wealthy man.

They shared a connection to Dhaka, and the two stayed there for a year. Milo learned the basic elements of some of the various martial arts of John's fighting style, though he was sure John wasn't pushing him to the very edge of his abilities. Not yet. He learned to box, taking many a beating in the ring with the massive man who weighed in at 270 pounds. They fought with sticks. Wrestled. Day by day, Milo grew stronger, both in body and spirit.

* * *

It was on the one-year anniversary of their meeting that John came to Milo and told him it was time. Time to put the training to the test.

Dhaka was largely run by gangs, some eighty in number, who controlled every sort of debauchery there was, and had their fingers in the government, the police, the tourist hotels, and every segment of society.

John had pegged one such gang as a target for Milo's graduation. He didn't expect his student to wipe them out, but just to demonstrate his new abilities by breaking a few heads, with the fighting style Milo had jokingly started calling Jo-Lit.

Tik Kishor. A teen gang involved in human trafficking, mostly women and young children. Their leader was a nineteen-year-old thug named Mukta, and John had spent some time watching how he went about his business. John theorized that without his leadership, this gang would dissipate, leaving a hole, however temporarily, that someone else would surely fill. He was no idealist and knew that it was only a drop in the bucket, a temporary solution, and that the space would be almost immediately refilled by another. But it was time for a real-life assessment of Milo's skills and also time to leave Dhaka.

They made their move on a Saturday evening just before midnight. The Tik Kishor gang's routine was to share their acquired victims over the course of the week with paying customers before shipping them off down the Padma River to the Bay of Bengal and on to their final destination. Of course, there were a few kept aside—special orders from those who paid a pretty penny to have their merchandise unsullied.

John and Milo carried no weapons. Their cover was simple. Drunk Americans looking for underage women. A cover as old as time.

Once inside, they were brought to a room, and the available merchandise was brought out and paraded past them, quivering young girls, sobbing children—a sight that inflamed the ire of Milo to a volcanic rage that he barely kept in check with the calming deep breathing John had taught him for use in just such a situation.

John did not do as well with his own practice and preempted the go-easy strategy by slashing his palm into the neck of the teenage boy standing insolently next to him, holding a rifle of some sort. The boy dropped as if pole-axed. Milo spun on his heel and kicked the other gangbanger in the jaw, followed with a jab and a cross to the already broken chops.

There was a hallway to the back, which they took instead of going out through the heavily guarded front of the building. It would also take them past the lair of the boss, Mukta. John led the way, Milo doing his best to herd the six children in front of him and at the same time convey that he meant them no harm. "Bandhu. Bandhu," he repeated, Bangla for friend.

Again, John deviated from the strategy, kicking in the door to his right, which turned out to be Mukta's office, instead of continuing out the back door. Milo cursed under his breath and then touched the arm of the oldest girl, maybe twelve years of age, "Thākā." He believed that this was the word for stay, but his limited Bangla skills allowed for no more explanation as he brushed past the children and into the room behind John.

John had a Bengali teen by the neck up against the wall. The young man had a thick shock of black hair styled to the side, a thin mustache to match his face, and various tattoos spotting his exposed skin. His feet dangled a foot off the ground. It was Mukta.

Another young man held a pistol toward John and was moving to the side so the bullet wouldn't also kill his boss. A third held a knife and was stepping forward with it raised high above his head.

Milo had to make a choice. There wasn't time to stop both of them, and he chose the one with the gun. He took one step and kicked the weapon from the boy's hand, elbowed him in the back of the head, and turned toward the knife-wielding youth. The blade was buried in the area between John's shoulder and back, the highest point the budding hooligan could reach. He was currently trying to tug the steel from the corded muscles with little luck.

As Milo took several steps to aid, the boy looked at him with wide eyes, fearful, unsure of what was happening. The look was not a gangbanger, but a frightened youth, a boy who should be home, tucked in bed at this time of night, not trying to pull a knife from the back of a giant as another man crossed toward him with malicious intent.

Just before Milo struck the boy, he heard a snap, Mukta's neck breaking, and then his fist struck the delinquent punk in the nose, showering everything close in blood. John dropped the lifeless gang leader's limp body to the floor. Another tattooed lout came through the door, saw Mukta's dead body, Milo's gun, and John's fierce face, and exited in a hurry. They waited a few minutes, then left the way they'd entered; an eerie silence having descended over the whole compound.

They brought the children to a charitable organization, not the police, who couldn't be trusted. John and Milo then disappeared, first up into Tibet, and then down to the port of Mumbai, where they gained passage on a freighter to South America.

It had been, after all, time to leave.

Chapter Three

New York City

Present Day

The Bryant Park penthouse office took up the entire top floor of the building. Windows stretched the entire circumference of the 55th floor from floor to ceiling. The boardroom was in the corner facing the Empire State Building, with Brooklyn just beyond, Queens to the left, and the Hudson River to the west. From the north side of the building, especially at night, the lights of Times Square illuminated the city in their glow.

Early on, what Milo had taken to calling the working group had jettisoned the concept of rigid seating around a table, in its place choosing comfortable armchairs with side tables on wheels that could be easily rolled in front of each if there was paperwork to be reviewed or filled out. Or, more often than not, to serve food and drink. There were thirteen such Haverty Aviator Recliners in brown leather circling the room.

Max sat with his back to the Empire State Building. He'd changed his morning attire to meet the prospective client and now wore an off-white cashmere Kiton jacket with burgundy hues and black cotton jean trousers of the same brand. He was beginning to take on the role that he'd soon be playing for real, much like an actor getting into character in a movie, for Max Creed was going to immerse himself in the world of the ultra-wealthy.

His bank statement said he was a billionaire, but his soul told him he was just a man, so acting would be required to easily pass as just another of the rich and famous.

In a circle, to his left were John Little, Marian Zhang, Tucker Friedman, Scads Miller, and Scarlett. As far as Max knew, she had no other name, like Cher, or that magician, Teller. Scarlett was a Black woman, Brazilian, who had intimate knowledge of every sort of handheld weapon ever devised by mankind, or so it seemed. She was one of those people who could kill you with a spoon.

Scads Miller was the stereotypical computer whiz kid white-boy nerd. He might've been twenty-two years of age, was slight of frame, several days unshaven, with square black spectacles. He wore a red Flash T-shirt, with the yellow lightning bolt through a white circle. It was acceptable to be eccentric when your forte was technology, even when convening with clients. As well, Scads would not be meeting face to face with the elites as Max soon would be.

Tucker Friedman was a Queer Jew with a slightly rotund body, broad face, and a friendly smile. He was also a financial magician, capable of transforming lettuce into moola, and had doubled Max's worth in just four years' time. This was considerably easier when you were already starting with a stack of currency, but all the same, he was better than most, and in Max's opinion (or so he'd been told), the best money mind in the world.

Marian Zhang was not quite five feet tall, but what she lacked in height she made up for with energy and vitality. As a matter of fact, she was currently out of her seat, the only one on her feet, pacing the room as she updated Max on the legal implications of creating the non-profit mental health program for veterans, which was in the works, but which was progressing slower than Max would like. She wore her hair in a choppy and flipped style that reached her shoulders and complemented her dark flashing eyes.

John Little had taken on the responsibility of business manager. It seemed that the skills of hand-to-hand combat transferred over smoothly to discerning the difference between friends and foes, an important factor in both a fight and a boardroom power meeting.

Max's cell phone buzzed. It was the receptionist, Dale Allen. Dale was the latest hire and was not really one of the band, but more the public face of the mysterious group that Max had put together to tip the scales of justice. He was ten inches over five feet, with sandy hair that was always carefully styled, a nice smile, and was the perfect face to meet the public, deflecting unwanted attention away from the potential borderline-legal activities of Max and friends.

The client, Sevyn Knight, was here. He told Dale to bring the woman back to the boardroom. Tucker turned off the television monitor, which had been hyping that night's basketball game between the Spurs and the Nets. He was an avid Brooklyn fan and had been making disgusting sounds that Durant was still out, and Kyrie had just been scratched from the lineup.

Dale buzzed his way into the room and led a woman across the room to an empty armchair opposite Max. She towered several inches over his six-foot frame, had high, striking cheekbones, and her head was shaven smoothly bald. Her eyes were a chilling blue, and her eyebrows were light in color. A dragon tattoo in red and black swirled up from the cleavage between her breasts and around her neck.

She looked far from a powerless victim, Max thought, struck by the force of her presence. "Miss Knight. Welcome." He stood and held out his hand. Her grip was firm.

"You must be Max Creed."

He nodded. "Please. Sit."

"Please, call me Sevyn."

"I am Max. This is John, Marian, Tucker, Scads, and Scarlett. They are my band of equalizers when the scales of justice need some weight on the side of right." He didn't mention that this was their first foray into the field. The working group's mission statement, if they had one, might have read: to right the miscarriages of justice writ large, stepping in to use whatever means possible to defend those who'd been abused by the ultra-rich, the one-percenters, those who existed in another dimension in which laws didn't apply. "Dale was the gentleman who brought you into the room. He will be your contact person."

"I'm not sure what this is all about," Sevyn said. "Only that he," she nodded at John, "knocked on my door one day and asked if I'd like a chance at handing Rupert Hastings his comeuppance. I said, fuck yes."

John chuckled. "I read about what happened in the newspapers and then followed up a bit more. It seems that your father got the raw end of the deal."

"He got fucking shanked is what he got." The raw emotion pouring forth from Sevyn was blinding. "Rupert Hastings dicked him over, and there's nothing anybody can do about it."

"Will you share the story with all of us?" Max spoke gently. "We think that we might be able to help."

"Why?"

Max sighed, sat forward. "Because we believe in a justice that is not always provided by the government, the courts, or public opinion. We believe in what is right. And what is wrong."

"Who are you? I mean, I know your names and all, but who are you really?"

"Think of us as if we were the Justice League of America," Scads said.

Sevyn furrowed her brow. "You mean, like the comic books?"

Scarlett scoffed. "Ignore him. His adolescent mind has been addled by Marvel."

"We are a band of people with the ability to help," Max said.

"Help? Can you bring my father back to life?"

Max shook his head no. "But we can make sure that Rupert Hastings can't ruin other lives."

"Can you tell everybody what you told me?" John asked. "It will help to hear your account firsthand."

Sevyn sighed. "My father, Tom Knight, was a third-generation cabinet maker, only he no longer made the cabinets, but had a factory for this purpose. His father, my grandfather, expanded from woodworker to business owner. My dad, Tom, grew the business for thirty years until it was one of the premier cabinet and furniture producers in America. If Goldman Sachs was moving into ten floors of One World Trade Center," she gestured out the window, downtown, "the office project manager would likely call Knight in for everything not attached to the floor."

She stopped, caught her breath, as Tucker stepped forward with a tissue for her.

"Go on," Max said.

Sevyn took a deep breath. "It was a multi-million-dollar business, and the sky was the limit. Especially when Knight Custom Cabinets & Closets landed a huge job. To outfit all the rooms of a new casino in Las Vegas. The Castle Casino & Hotel."

"Owned by Rupert Hastings and completed four years ago," John said.

Sevyn nodded. "My father completed the job on time. He'd been paid the first two installments, but the final bill came to almost five million dollars."

"For which he wasn't paid?" Tucker leapt to his feet, a unique agility for a man his size, and began shifting from foot to foot in agitation.

"No. He was not paid. Not a dime of that bill was ever paid."

"What reason did the Hasting Corporation give for not paying?" John prodded gently.

"They said that the work was not up to standard. Nothing more than that. But Knight Custom Cabinets & Closets is renowned for their quality, and their installation team is the best in the world. It was just bullshit."

"What did your father do?" Max asked.

"At first, he was patient, but I could tell he was becoming more and more agitated when I spoke with him, which I fear," Sevyn sniffled, took a deep breath, "was not nearly as much as I should have. My parents' home is in Lincoln, Nebraska, and I was living here in the city, but I should've called more, gone to visit. My mother told me how upset he was, and I could tell, I could hear, I knew that he was struggling, I was just so involved in my own life, so selfish, but I...." She started crying, silently, tears running down her cheeks.

Nobody said a word, nor made a sound, as the seemingly strong, confident woman broke down.

After a couple of minutes, she dabbed at her cheeks with the tissue. Max noted she must not be wearing any makeup as there were no smudges or rivulets. He guessed that when one had skin like a marble goddess, there was no need for alteration.

Sevyn blew her nose, shook her head, and was again the defiant woman who'd entered the room. "After a year, my father filed a civil lawsuit. Hastings had a roomful of lawyers. My father was paying every cent he had for his own lawyer. And he won. The judge ruled that the Hastings Corporation was in default and ordered them to pay what was owed. But Rupert Hastings' lawyers appealed, they knew what they were doing. They knew that they didn't have to win, they just had to outlast my father, to outlast his money, which was dwindling away to nothing."

Tom Knight walked out of the courtroom with the spryest of steps he'd possessed in quite some time. Maybe this horrible debacle could finally be put to rest, put behind him, a distant memory that left a bad taste, but no lurking menace.

Tonight, he and his wife, Janice, would celebrate. A fancy dinner, a fine wine, maybe even splurge and screw the diet and have dessert. Maybe they'd take a trip to the city, visit with Sevyn. This ordeal had hurt him, his family, but now it was over. Maybe the three of them could take a trip together, a cruise, or go to a beach and drink frozen drinks?

He stepped into the men's room and went to the urinal to piss. As he was washing his hands, the door opened, and Rupert Hastings came into the room. This was one of the few times the man had been in court, leaving it to his lawyers and underlings to clean up his shit.

"Ah, there you are, Tom," he said. "I was hoping to catch you before the next time."

"The next time?"

Rupert stepped up to the sink next to him and turned the spigot on. "You don't think this is over, do you?"

Tom chuckled. "The judge just ruled in my favor. She has ordered that you pay the money owed plus compensation for my time. I'd say it's over."

Rupert guffawed. "It's not over until the rich man sings, and this billionaire don't sing, so don't expect to see one red cent. My lawyers will appeal. I am prepared to drag this out until you have to whore your goddamn wife out to pay the light bills. Do you have any idea who I am? You think you can beat me? I pick the food out of my teeth and wipe the shit from my ass with toadies like you."

As Tom stared, mouth agape, shocked by the blatant viciousness mixed with narcissism, Rupert dried his hands, sneered, waved, and walked out of the restroom.

The room was again quiet. After a minute, Max leaned forward. "And then what happened?"

"About a year ago, my father declared bankruptcy. This was the biggest job the company had ever taken on, and they couldn't survive not being paid. They owed people, you see. My father had to pay for the materials that went into the product, had to pay his workers, and he tried. He paid every damn cent he could. His retirement, my mother's, the houses, it all went. But, in the end, he couldn't withstand a five-million-dollar default of payment, and he had to declare bankruptcy."

"And then what?" John said.

"And then he killed himself." Sevyn sighed. "But it was Rupert Hastings who pulled the trigger. Not my father. That bastard killed him as sure as if…And why? Just to add to his billions? Just because he could? Just to make clear that he was a god who could do whatever he pleased, simply because of his wealth?"

"He thinks he's above the law," Marian said.

"And he is," Sevyn said. "There is nothing that anybody can do."

"That's where we come in," Max said.

"How?" Sevyn almost spat the words out. "What can you do?"

"First," Scads said, "we will find out everything there is to know about Rupert Hastings. I will dig so far into his life that I will soon know him better than he knows himself."

"Second, "Tucker said, "we will bankrupt him and introduce him to poverty."

"And third," Marian said, "we will take him to court and prosecute him for every transgression he has ever made."

Max looked over at John and Scarlett, their triangulated glances transferring a silent communication. Those silent, unspoken words rang in his head and hung in the air between them. *Fourth, if necessary, we will beat him within an inch of his life, and fifth, if merited, we will kill him.*

Chapter Four

A Jet in the Sky

The day was gorgeous as only a summer day in Maine can be. The sky was a brilliant blue, the sort of day you wanted to reach up and see if you could poke holes in the heavens, a few wispy clouds streaking the empyrean to further bring out the rich color. The sun had crossed over to the west and begun its descent, even if it'd be light for hours to come. Waves crashed on the rocks as the tide worked its way forward, powerful and relentless.

The music of a three-person band wafted forth on the breeze, an acoustic guitar, a harp, and a flute. Milo was an orphan and had no family there, but Kinsley had parents, siblings, cousins, and they both had a smattering of friends, making a grand total of forty-one people in attendance. A small and intimate gathering to witness the nuptials that would unite Milo and Kinsley forever.

The music stopped.

"Welcome, family and friends. We are gathered here today to witness and celebrate the marriage of Kinsley and Milo. This is not the beginning of a new relationship but an acknowledgment of the next chapter in their lives together."

Milo had thought this day would never come, and that he was destined to live his life alone. He'd never known a family and didn't have the first idea how to go about the entire process. Before Kinsley, he'd never been in a relationship with a woman for more than six months, and now, here he was, getting married.

"Milo, I promise to cherish you always, to honor and sustain you, in sickness and in health, in poverty and in wealth, and to be true to you in all things until *death alone shall part us."*

"Kinsley, I promise to cherish you always, to honor and sustain you, in sickness and in health, in poverty and in wealth, and to be true to you in all things until death alone shall part us."

A seagull flew low overhead, squawking 'ha-ha-ha'.

"A ring is an unbroken circle, with ends that have been joined together, and it represents your union. It is a symbol of infinity and of your infinite love. When you look at these rings on your hands, be reminded of this moment, your commitment, and the love you now feel for each other."

Kinsley had come as if a gift from the heavens and taught Milo how to love. She was witty, mischievous, tender, tough, and had a keen intellect that amazed him every time he was with her. As Milo placed the ring on her finger, her skin smooth and cool and warm all at the same time, he worried that this might just all be a dream, that it was too good to be true, that no human being had ever existed as fine as Kinsley Smith, soon to be Sharp.

"Before these witnesses, you have pledged to be joined in marriage. You have now sealed this pledge with your wedding rings. By the authority vested in me by the great State of Maine, I now pronounce you married!"

No matter how many times Max replayed it in his head, he couldn't be certain whether he first saw the red circle blossom on Kinsley's chest like a late-arriving rose, or whether he heard the gunshot ring out. He knew that a bullet travels at a rate twice the speed of sound. So, there was no doubt that it had already struck Kinsley before he heard the crack of the high-caliber rifle from five hundred yards, but did he see the blood and then hear the shot, or did he hear the shot and look down to see the blood?

Milo had been preparing to kiss his new bride. His mind was fuzzy with the wonder of it all. Their mutual friend, ordained just for the purpose of marrying them, had just pronounced them married. The sound or the blood? He looked up from the spreading crimson on her white wedding dress, a pool of glowing red, to her face.

Kinsley's lips made a perfect circle, having no idea what had happened, more shocked than he. Her eyes were liquid pools of mixed love and surprise. She put her hand on his shoulder. "Kiss me," she said.

Max shook his head to banish the early morning memory that had bedeviled his existence for 1,655 days now. Goodbye, Kinsley. Goodbye, Milo Sharp. Max rolled from the bed and looked out the window of his private jet. There were streaks of light. Apparently, back behind, to the east, the sun was preparing to rise. That meant that he'd be landing in Las Vegas shortly. He used the master bathroom and then grabbed a cup of coffee from the pot that he'd set to brew the night before.

He grabbed his leather backpack, and coffee in hand, went to the Club Suite to review what Scads would certainly have sent him over the course of the night. The jet, a Bombardier Global 7500, was the most expensive private plane on the market and had been bought largely to impress those Masters of the Universe who needed such impressing. One of Max's favorite features was the *Nuage* seats, *nuage* being the French word for clouds, and they truly were like sitting in the fluffy comfort of a cloud.

His laptop was a Scads Miller original, encrypted, in his words, so that it was safer than Hillary Clinton's email server. Sure enough, there was a download of information on Rupert Hastings, the Hastings Corporation, and the Castle Casino from Scads waiting for Max to review.

> Rupert Hastings was born in 1978 on Long Island and grew up in the Hamptons. His father, Bill Hastings, was worth $500 million that he inherited from his father. To his credit, he did not squander it, even if it did not grow (a tough act to not turn that much money into more).

Max smiled. He wondered if that last statement was aimed at him and his own personal fortune, recently acquired, and doubled in size. He'd tried hard not to screw people, and yet it still grew, and now he was ready to start building foundations to give the money back to those who needed it.

Scads had been a college dropout, hacking government agencies for the lark of it, but living in near poverty in Chicago, when Max had found him. Max took this as a sign that the nineteen-year-old had chosen to not use his gift to steal from the rich. Not until Max came along, anyway, and made him a thief.

> He attended Choate, Harvard, and then Wharton. When he graduated, Dad gave him fifty million dollars in seed money to get started (my dad might've done the same if he hadn't been killed along with my mother, and the government confiscated all their money).

Max wondered if it was more difficult to be an orphan or have a father who was a dick. For Scads, at least, it appeared his father had been a dick *and* was now dead. At least Max could idolize his parents, put them on a pedestal, even if he'd never see them again. Not in this world, and he doubted, in any world. He and Scads were alike in the lack of parents, as was the entire band he had assembled.

> Note: Rupert claimed that his father never gave him anything, but there was a trail of money from Father Hastings that appeared in Rupert's accounts right at the time of his graduation. Upon graduation, in 2003, Rupert also became the president of his father's real estate company, which consisted of mostly low-rent apartment buildings in New York City.

Max felt the shift in the jet and realized they must've begun their descent. As if on cue, the copilot, Darius Landon, buzzed to let him know. Max finished his cup of coffee and went back to reading the report on the laptop.

> In 2007, Rupert parted ways with his father's real estate business, and, while he has publicly claimed it was his decision to strike out on his own, rumors suggest otherwise, and the fact is that Rupert and his father no longer talk. Sources suggest that their relationship is acrimonious at best. Rupert used his seed money and position to open a casino in Atlantic City. This appears to be his first business venture on his own.

Max made a note to follow up on this. What, he wondered, could've caused a split between the golden child who'd been given the keys to the kingdom and his daddy? Power, money, and sex sprung to mind as reasons that the royal offspring had their ties to succession cut.

At the same time, he left his father's business and opened a casino, Rupert also became a consultant for Johnson Whales, who was found guilty of a half-a-billion-dollar Ponzi scheme in 2008, one of the reasons for the collapse of big banks, and the recession that followed. Rupert was indicted but was turned loose. Innocent of all charges.

Interesting, Max thought, very interesting indeed.

Since branching off on his own, companies owned by Rupert Hastings have faced sixty-three lawsuits that I have found so far, ranging from non-payment to breach of contract. Some of them settle out of court, reportedly for pennies on the dollar, while many of them are tied up in litigation until the smaller company owed money is no longer able to continue, much like what happened to Knight Custom Cabinets & Closets, litigation which has now been dismissed.

Max was well aware that if there were sixty-three documented cases, easy to find, then the true number was probably ten times that. What of the people and businesses that just wrote it off as a dead loss and walked away? What of those who tried but couldn't even get in the door of the courtroom?

In 2012, Rupert opened a modeling agency that employs only women aged eighteen to twenty-two years of age. At that point, the ladies 'age out'. Photo shoots often take place at his private island southeast of the Bahamas, but also in exotic locales all over the world. The models are often transported on his own private jet.

What a world, Max thought, in which anybody would age out of their career at twenty-two. But he supposed that was true of many athletes. Personally, Clay had always liked a more mature woman and was not a fan of the rail-thin runway models who appeared to be the current fascination of today's male.

> He has publicly supported cryonics and has stated that upon his death, he will have his head and his penis frozen (Both heads, that is). It seems he might want to come back and view the world he plans on populating. He is a huge fan of eugenics and has postulated the notion of impregnating as many women as he can in order to pass on his superior DNA.

Max personally knew what could be done with immense wealth. Just about anything that you wanted. The man who'd paid an assassin to kill Max's wife had been the same man Max had put in jail back when he was a PI in Maine. The case against him had been foolproof. The man had used the cover of his Big Pharma firm to build a thriving street trade based on illegal heroin laced with fentanyl, an operation that Max had put the kibosh on. He had this billionaire dead to rights on the drug operation as well as a string of murders. And still, the rich man had walked. And then paid a sniper to kill Max's bride on their wedding day.

> In 2015, Rupert Hastings claims to have started a financial management company that caters only to people with over one billion dollars in assets. There is no proof of whether he has any clients of this stature, but I will keep digging. This might be your in.

As the jet touched down on the tarmac, Max nodded his head. This very well might be his way in. For he did have a billion dollars.

Chapter Five

Las Vegas

Max knew that you were supposed to travel with an entourage when you went to a casino carrying the hefty bankroll he had in his bag, but that wasn't his style. He'd always been a lone wolf. That was what had pushed him out of being a cop in Boston for the more solitary career of being a private dick in Maine. And then Kinsley changed that. Only temporarily, as it turned out.

Besides, he thought staying in the King Richard penthouse suite should be statement enough at thirty-five thousand dollars a night. Tucker had assured him that it was a necessity to garner the attention of Rupert Hastings, gain street cred with the other rich and powerful, and he could afford it. As Tucker was always telling him, he had something like a million dollars a day in investment income to spend at this point.

The Castle Casino was exactly that, a medieval castle theme permeating the outside and inside alike. As Max stepped out of the limousine, he took a moment to appreciate the stonework, the turrets at each corner that rose high into the sky, taller, he imagined, than any actual castle.

Atop each turret, archers stood at the ready, and as Max watched, each raised his crossbow, pointed it to the sky, and released the string, one of a hail of arrows, winging toward the strip. Halfway to the target of pedestrians and traffic, the arrows checked up, attached to strings, and the archers reeled them back in. It was eight in the morning on the dot, suggesting that they did this on the hour.

Max shook his head in wonder and moved forward across the drawbridge that led from sidewalk to castle, crossing over the moat that had sharks cruising within, their motion lazy and deadly at the same time. He imagined that feeding time for the sharks attracted quite a crowd, and idly wondered if anybody had ever fallen into the water below, perhaps plied with too much drink.

A knight in armor stood on either side of the entrance, immobile, a huge battle axe in one hand and a shield in the other, with the logo of Rupert Hastings as the royal crest inlaid upon it, the capital R woven into the capital H below. Max wasn't sure whether or not the knights were real, but guessed that they were, and perhaps engaged in some performance of their own at a given time.

Inside, the ceiling, from which hung massive chandeliers, rose easily a hundred feet. Halfway up, all around the interior, balconies protruded with a single maiden upon each, wearing sheer white silk dresses, hair braided on their head, dancing erotically. Max counted twelve such balconies and maidens circling the gaming room.

He entered a maze of slot machines, glowing monsters with one arm, blinking, beeping, and speaking. *Spin the wheel. Wild card. Jackpot.* Beyond he could see the tables, craps, blackjack, baccarat, pai gow, on and on, stretching endlessly.

The waiters were dressed as jesters, he noted, in purple and yellow tights, while the waitresses were wenches, with skirts that barely covered their special parts and only made it three-quarters of the way over their bottoms. The tightly corseted tops threatened to release their bosoms at any moment in an explosion of flesh. Max thought that in this day and age, wenches was probably politically incorrect, but then again, this was Vegas, right?

He had the distinct impression that the clerk at the registration desk was quite surprised that he was Max Creed, checking into the King Richard suite. Maybe that was because he was in his travel clothes of jeans and T-shirt, or maybe it was his unshaven face, but most likely, it was that he was alone, a garment bag over his arm, and a rolling suitcase in his other hand, checking into a room that was going to cost over a hundred grand for the three nights that he was there.

* * *

The first night at the Castle Casino, Max started on the high-stakes blackjack table on the floor, spending several hours betting two thousand dollars a hand, before being invited to an upstairs room where the limit was ten thousand dollars a hand. He also sipped on very expensive bourbon, hence breaking two of his restrictions, gambling and boozing, but, as he told himself with a chuckle, it was the role he was playing.

The second night, he was invited to the high-stakes poker table, but it was not *the* high-stakes poker table. The fellows at the table were the whales and cheetahs, their rooms comped, their VIP status intact. But Max knew that there was a level that he'd not yet reached. The cards were favorable, and he was not afraid to lose, a healthy combination landing him, after two nights, up four million dollars.

He assumed that this was why the man in charge of operations personally stopped by his room to let him know that the stay was free and to deliver an invitation to Rupert Hastings' poker game that evening at ten p.m.

There were five of them at the table, including Max. Rupert Hastings was immediately on his left, followed by three others he'd been introduced to as Larry, Jeff, and Taytum. He recognized Larry Gilbert and Jeff Beal as part of the world's elite multi-billionaire club. The woman, Taytum Liu, was a mystery to him. His own two billion dollars was a drop in the bucket of wealth held by the others at this table. Max figured he best be awfully careful, or he'd walk out of this room with nothing but the shirt on his back.

The game was poker. Max was introduced to the unique chip values, with the top one being pink, worth a hundred grand apiece. He got his first taste of what no limit meant when Taytum Liu raised him a million dollars playing five-card draw. Ten pink chips, pushed gently to the middle of the table. He folded, it being too early to read the other players yet, though the casual manner of the bet suggested that she had the hand.

Rupert looked to be in his fifties, but the notes from Scads said differently, that he was only forty-four. He was thin, but his belly protruded, suggesting a drinker's gut, and had well-gelled hair combed back on his head. There was a bit of a permanent smirk to the corner of his mouth and a glitter to his eye like that of a hawk. He was brash, plunging forward and attacking, especially when he was bluffing, but this could be a reverse tell, setting up for the big sting later on in the night, though it was hard to tell, never having played with any of them. When he had a monster hand, it was almost as if all the air went out of him, leaving him feeling deflated and quiet.

Max felt the pull of the man's charisma, a rise of spirit just being in the orbit of this man exuding confidence—that mixed with a faint thread of danger. This charisma Max perceived was somewhat leavened by revulsion at what he knew of Rupert. All together, this made for a confusing cocktail in his mind.

Larry was a tight, patient player, who was happy to sit back, folding out of most hands, waiting for that big score. Max noticed that, before betting large on his powerful hands, Larry would give the slightest of sighs, as if to calm himself so as to not give away his excitement. He wore a fedora, drank whiskey, smoked a cigar, and looked as if he'd watched too many 1950s gangster movies.

Jeff never rushed a thing, slow playing every card, every bet, all the while carefully watching everyone else, reading their eyes, noting their body movements, and creeping into each player's inner being before making, matching, or raising a bet, and even longer when he folded. He had round spectacles and a narrow, balding head.

Taytum was the one who Max had trouble pinning down. She seemingly had no routine, no tells, and never bet the same way twice. She had a pleasant smile, long black hair, and wore what looked to be a racecar jumpsuit zipped down to her belly button, showing ample cleavage to her advantage.

It was an hour before Rupert started digging into Max. "What is it you do, Max? I'm surprised I haven't seen you before. You obviously have money and a penchant for the cards. Why is this the first time I've run into you?"

Max did have a penchant for the cards. He could feel the thrill of addiction whistling through his veins. "I dabble with this and that," he said. "Most recently, I was in Macao. There are very few rules there if you have money."

Rupert smiled grandiosely. "There are few rules anywhere if you have money."

Max flipped over his hole card, a jack, matching two others on the table, and raked in the pot. "Money does open many a door."

"Where did you come from?"

"A tale as old as time," Max said.

Rupert looked at him, shuffled the cards, called stud, one down, four up. "But not as old as time. As far as I can tell, you didn't exist until four years ago."

Max looked at his hole card. An eight. Rupert was right because Max Creed hadn't existed until two years ago. Until then, he'd been somebody else. Then his life had changed, and his name along with it. As far as where his money came from, it was a tale as old as time, truly, but what he had omitted was that he meant that he stole it.

"Five years back, my uncle died," Max said. "He'd done well in the tech industry and left me a chunk of change and some advice, which I followed, and attached my inheritance to a few companies that did well, especially with the pandemic."

"Don't tell me you got in on Zoom early."

Max shrugged. "Five years ago, I was working a dead-end job bringing home enough money to put a roof over my head. I liked going down to Atlantic City and Foxwoods on the weekend as my big excitement. Now I'm in Vegas, having come here from Macao, and before that I was in Monte Carlo."

"No family?"

"Had a wife back in the day. Called me a loser and ran off with the neighbor. I bet she regrets that now. Never had kids. And now? Can't see why I'd tie myself down to one woman when there are so many willing and nubile young ladies excited to be in my company."

Rupert nodded. "There is something to be said about nubile girls."

Max cringed inwardly. It'd been difficult enough to say 'nubile ladies', but 'nubile girls' was a step that made his insides tighten and his toes curl. "What about you?" he asked. "You've done okay for yourself."

"I do appear to have the Midas Touch," Rupert said. "And I didn't have the luck of a wealthy uncle. As a matter of fact, I have a financial management company if you're ever interested."

"I might be. I just might be. Maybe we can discuss that at another time."

Max knew Rupert's words were not quite the truth. The man had received a graduation present of fifty million dollars from his father, and quite possibly, had embezzled a great deal more from the man before he was found out and cut out of the family. Still, he appeared to have done quite well for himself. Surprisingly well, had been the comment from Tucker after reading the latest information Scads had gleaned from the internet.

At four in the morning, Max had lost back the four million he'd won thus far in Vegas and added a couple more on top of that for good measure. He'd also had one too many Bowmore scotches, the fifty-year-old at a price tag of forty-two thousand dollars a bottle, if he wasn't mistaken. Max figured he'd drunk about thirty thousand dollars worth, money that could've been better spent feeding a hungry child. But he was doing it for a good cause, playing a part, making a difference in the world. At least that's what he told himself, though in truth, he wasn't sure that his role justified him drinking down five glasses. He might be enjoying the role a bit too much.

Max had the diamond down in the hole that matched straight for the other three cards on the table of the same suit. There was one more to come, the last card being down. Betting had been cautiously aggressive thus far, Rupert pushing it the hardest, throwing chips into the pot with disdain, as if the money didn't matter, or that he was so certain of victory that he was doing them all a favor by not betting more.

The interesting part was that nobody had dropped out. Even Larry was sitting tight, probably because he had three aces showing, Max thought, knowing the man would've been long gone with anything but a full house. He was staring at Max with his penetrating eyes of chill blue, trying to pry into his brain, read what his hole card was.

Jeff was fiddling with his chips, seemingly lost in thought, contemplating matching Rupert's bet. The easy conversation of the past six hours was no longer. This was the time. This was the moment.

Taytum leaned forward over the table, closely inspecting what everybody had showing and in turn, giving Max a generous glimpse of her breasts, her skin smooth and clear, the flesh calling to him, the third thing he'd given up and not yet succumbed to on his current mission as he played the role. Sex. Max could feel the desire burning in him, the mix of gambling and brown liquor, and the scent and sight of this beautiful woman next to him suffocating him in his craving.

Get ahold of yourself, Max thought. Or better yet, use it to your advantage.

"Aces bet," Rupert said.

Larry gave that almost imperceptible sigh and pushed a stack of pink chips into the center. "Two million."

Jeff threw his cards down in disgust.

Taytum took a long moment to call the bet and raise a million. She had two kings and a queen showing.

Max allowed her to catch him staring at her breasts. He blushed and hurriedly called the bet.

Rupert pushed a stack toward the center. "I raise you five million." He had three sevens showing.

Larry eyed him slowly and matched the bet.

Taytum called.

Max followed suit.

The last card came around, down. Max didn't look at the card. Rupert bet five million again. Larry sighed and matched.

Taytum eyeballed Rupert, then Larry, and finally Max, who'd allowed his desire to leak into his eyes, a lust borne of celibacy, triggered by cards and brown liquor. She smiled at him. Raised two million.

It was seven million dollars to Max. He pulled the last card to the edge of the table and peeked at it. Breathed ever so slightly in through his nose, something he'd done all night every time he'd bluffed.

"I'll call and raise ten million," he said.

"No way," Rupert said loudly. "No way that a flush is going to win this hand."

"How about a straight flush?" Max asked. Again, ever so slightly, he breathed in through his nose.

Rupert pushed ten million, in pink chips to the center. "Going to have to show me."

Larry grunted and threw his cards down.

"You know that diamonds are a girl's best friend, don't you?" Taytum said. She caressed Max with her eyes. "They speak to me. And right now, they're telling me that you're bluffing." She pushed a stack of chips in. "I call."

Max flipped over the down cards, revealing the four, five, six, seven, and eight, all diamonds, for the straight flush. Rupert laughed, a hollow booming sound. Taytum's eyes narrowed angrily.

"That's going to do me for tonight," Max said.

Rupert nodded. A man came to tally Max's chips. He didn't even wait for the total, rising and walking from the table and the room as if he didn't care about the almost hundred million dollars he'd just won playing five-card stud. At least that was the impression he hoped he was leaving. Money was just money. But gambling, booze, and sex were things worth living for. He just wasn't sure that he was ready to live again. Like that, anyway.

Max made it to his room, every bit of him craving another drink, another bet, the touch of a woman like Taytum Liu, her hot breath on his neck, her teeth nibbling at his ear. He closed and locked the door and sank to the floor, gritting his teeth.

It might've been a minute or an hour later when there was a knock at the door. Then again. Insistent.

Max stood, smoothed his jacket and pants, took a deep breath, and opened the door. Two young women, very young, very beautiful, stood there. One of them was holding a bottle in her two hands. She had blond hair that floated around her eyes, tumbled deliciously down her back, and blue eyes that shone with the pleasure of being young. The other woman, girl, female—had short black hair, swirled around her face, with dark eyes that burned intently, mischievously.

She held out her hand. "Rupert asked us to bring this to you."

Max took the piece of paper. It was a marker for eighty-three million dollars.

The blond held up the bottle. "He thought you might also like a nightcap."

It was the Bowmore fifty-year-old. Held by an eighteen-year-old if she were a day. She giggled and brushed past Max on her way into his suite, followed by the brunette.

Chapter Six

Jets in the Sky

The girls left just after seven in the morning. Within fifteen minutes, Max was packed and on his way to the airport. He couldn't shut himself of Sin City fast enough. It was an intoxicating temptation that threatened who he was. A few brown liquors and gambling were one thing. The attempted seduction by Taytum was an affront to his memory of Kinsley. And the young girls showing up at his room with a scotch so fine that it might have been the elixir of the gods, well, that was just plain wicked.

He'd planned on showering, but his exhaustion got the better of him. He fumbled his way out of his clothes, the faint scent of perfume still clinging to them, to his body, tantalizing his senses. Once under the covers, he lay rigid for an hour, the torture of sleep escaping him, leaving him to the torment of wakefulness. There was no escaping his demons, only the potential to negotiate an uneasy truce for the time being.

At some point, sleep took him, but the suffering barely shifted gears, his mind a swirling mess of tumblers of scotch, poker hands short of cards and impossibly good, and a wild melee of scantily clad women circling him, calling his name—while from above, Kinsley watched all with interest.

* * *

Rupert was the last one to board the jet. It was just after six p.m. Taytum was waiting for him just inside the door. "Everybody here?" he asked.

"All accounted for. The guests are in the Angevin Suite, and the girls are in the Calliope Suite."

"Ages?"

"They've all been verified to be at least eighteen. Two of them are nineteen, but I'm sure you will approve. They are delicious."

"Wonderful, my dear." Rupert kissed her on the cheek. "Tell the pilot we can take off."

As Taytum went to the cockpit, Rupert moved his way back to the Angevin Suite. The group of men inside was some of the richest and most powerful people in the world. They all had drinks in hand, and there was an excitement to the suite, the anticipation building, the oxygen pumped into the room invigorating, each of them having heard the rumors of the paradise offered by Rupert Hastings, but none yet having been privy to the exotic and erotic Isle of the Holy Grail.

Hudson Ford was an action movie star who dared the occasional comedy but never a serious drama. He'd broken in with some late-night cable flicks that were short on plot and offered flesh over acting. Now, at thirty-four, he was ruggedly handsome and had made four movies, each of which had grossed over a hundred million dollars.

Prince Khalid bin Faisal was Saudi royalty, and while not wielding a lot of clout himself, had all the glory reflected from having been a childhood companion of the Crown Prince. He had more money than he knew what to do with, had attended an Ivy League college in the US, and preferred entertainment over ideology. He had dark eyes and a wide, flashing smile that made people like him immediately.

Senator Todd Dunn was a fierce social democrat—as well as being an actual elected Democrat. He was a family man with a loving wife and two adult children. He believed in money for education, universal health care, women's rights, especially abortion, and was a great supporter of the queer community. What most people didn't know, he also had a hankering for cocaine and a primal lust for young women that he kept tamped down most of the time—except for when he didn't. Sometimes, like now, those base desires got the best of him.

Cole Smith had just finished his fifth year in the NFL, his best yet, and had already signed a salary extension for the next three years that would make him one of the highest-paid wide receivers in the game. His team had been knocked from the playoffs, and he'd finished just out of the voting for the Pro Bowl. He was young, single, and he had money in his pocket. Last month, when his team had gone to Las Vegas for a game, he'd run into Rupert Hastings at the gaming tables, throwing money away in fistfuls. He'd asked the man about how he might find a few young and gorgeous prostitutes and been steered in the right direction. A week later, he got the invite to visit the Isle of the Holy Grail.

Rupert stepped into the suite. "Gentlemen, welcome to the Ninth Crusader, your transportation to the Isle of the Holy Grail. A toast to manhood."

The five men raised their glasses and then drank.

"Are we ready to take off?" the prince asked.

"Maybe this wasn't such a good idea," the Senator said.

"Man, that is some fine whiskey," Cole said.

"This reminds me of one of my early movies," Hudson said.

"Please, my friends." Rupert raised his hands. "Be seated. We should be taking off momentarily."

The intercom rasped to life. "Hello, this is Captain Rogers. We've been cleared for takeoff as soon as we can get to the runway. Buckle up."

Cole was sitting next to Hudson. "You ever been to this place before."

"The first rule of the Isle of the Holy Grail is you've never been, never even heard of it, and what's more, you don't believe it even exists."

Cole grinned at him. "So, you have been there before?"

Across from them, the prince elbowed the Senator. "I don't know what the big deal is. Booze, drugs, and girls. Just another day at the office, am I right?"

The Senator grimaced. He suspected that Prince Khalid bin Faisal had been part of the assassination of that WSJ journalist a few years back, and while his committee had gained enough information to convict in a normal court of law, it had not been near enough to even accuse a future king of the powerful oil nation of Saudi Arabia, of the crime, much less bring charges publicly, or even convict him in the media.

"Rupert Hastings is an important donor," he said. "I do not know of what you speak, but I am here as his friend and his senator."

The prince laughed, smiled broadly, and elbowed him in the side.

The jet engines boomed to life, and the plane began racing down the runway and then lifted off on its journey.

Once the plane leveled off, the girls came in, each of them carrying a bottle of champagne. They paraded past the seated men and then came back, sashaying like they were on the catwalk. They were dressed for the beach, thong bikinis with straps for tops, covered by transparent silk robes.

Five of them chose a man and sashayed into his lap, asking him to pop the cork of the bottle she held as the remaining women found ice buckets for the bottles, all the while cavorting in the aisle with each other, giggling, and play-wrestling, dropping ice down each other's bikini tops.

"Dinner will be served in two hours," Rupert said. "In the meantime, enjoy your cocktails and your appetizers."

* * *

The plan was to meet the merry band back in New York City, but Las Vegas had stained Max's heart and soul, and he needed the replenishment of Long Beach Island to recover any semblance of his bedraggled morality. Thus, he made the call to John Little to round everybody up to be at Teterboro Airport for his arrival. They touched down at the New Jersey airport designed for private jets just long enough to refuel and then off to Wilmington and two SUVs back to his place of solace.

Max would've preferred solitude, but he was on a job now, the first for others, the origin of a new chapter in his life, and he knew there'd be no ease of mind or spirit until it was done. Reward would be had, justice for Sevyn Knight would be achieved, or Max Creed would be dead. There was no middle ground, no grey area, no compromise.

He was surprised and upset that Sevyn Knight was there with the others to board the plane at the airport. John Little shrugged and muttered something about her being a very persuasive lady.

The SUVs were both about fifteen years old, and had several haphazard paint jobs, assorted dents, with the occasional patch of rust decorating their exteriors. Flashy was not the Long Beach Island way, and Max did not want to become a pariah in his new community. The Long Beach Island Max Creed was a laid-back, good ole boy, who, while thoroughly liberal in his politics, was able to blend with the inhabitants of the town with comfort. Las Vegas Max Creed, now that was a far cry from his true self, so different, and a much harder role for him to pull off.

Marian suggested that she was hungry, and others all chimed in with their agreement, so the first stop on the island was the *Lazy Pelican*. It was a dive bar, beach bar, restaurant, and music venue rolled into one. The food was decent, the beer either bottled or canned, and the music was okay. Your feet stuck to the floor when you walked, the table was battered Formica, two of which they pushed together down the side of the room, and the chairs were most certainly suspect.

Max loved the place. He got a cranberry juice and ginger beer. The first night he'd ordered this, the bartender had eyeballed him like he was some freak and might be contagious. The tip had been large enough that Shawn no longer had a problem with his choice of drink. Max figured he could've done one of those light beers the locals seemed to like, but they didn't contain much more alcohol, and tasted far worse.

And he'd made a vow to abstain from gambling, alcohol, and sex, except when working a job. And then only when necessary to fit in.

There was a band on stage, three members on a platform barely big enough to hold them, and less a stage and more a piece of plywood, really. The song was about a Long Beach Island man, and the crowd was hooting and hollering along with it. One man, beer can in hand, stood in the middle of the dance floor, swaying to the music as if he was aboard a boat in heavy waves.

Scads got a Red Bull with a shot of tequila. "You're telling me that two beautiful young women came to your room at four a.m. wearing little, smelling divine, carrying a fifty-year-old Bowmore, and you merely talked to them for three hours and then sent them on their way?"

Max nodded. Smiled. Patted his friend on the back. "They were young enough to be my daughters, that is, if my college girlfriend had gotten pregnant."

"Why didn't you just tell them to go away and close the door?" Scarlett asked.

"Because they were carrying a very expensive scotch," John said.

"Take the liquor and send the young temptresses away," Marian said.

Max chuckled. "My cover would be blown if I turned those two young ladies away, for sure. That'd be the end of the job. Rupert Hastings wouldn't touch me with a ten-foot pole if I had turned those beauties away. No, they were a test from the man, one more call, just to make sure I wasn't bluffing."

"Weren't you afraid that a man like Hastings would have hidden cameras in your room?" Sevyn asked.

Max turned and looked at her, his face impassive, but questions in his mind. "Scads provided me with a jamming device that blocks any video or audio surveillance."

"What makes you think they didn't run straight back and tell Rupert that you didn't want to make yourself into a Max sandwich with them?" Scarlett asked.

"They don't want Rupert to know that I turned them down any more than I did," Max said. "They'd be terrified that he'd be mad, or worse, disappointed. Think they didn't try hard enough."

"Or that they weren't pretty enough," Marian said. "Boom. No more modeling careers."

Max shook his head. "Ten years ago, I wouldn't believe this stuff happened. Then you get Cosby and Weinstein and who knows who else using their power for sex."

Marian snorted. It was a rather loud eruption from such a diminutive figure, but it surprised none of them. She was a snorter of the first class.

"That's because you're a man. Women have known about this since Adam first convinced Eve to take all her clothes off."

"It was Eve who tempted Adam with the whole apple thing," Max said. "Is the way I heard it."

Marian snorted again. "That's just some man rewriting history to make himself look good."

Max raised his hands. "You're probably right."

"Ain't no probably about it," Scarlett said. "That's just a fact."

"What's the next step?" Sevyn asked.

The song ended, the light applause faded, and there was momentary silence in the Lazy Pelican, the question still heavy in the air.

Max shrugged. "We wait."

"Wait? For what?"

"For Rupert Hastings to reach out. I've made contact. I walked away with a bit of his money. Showed that I was a man who liked to have a good time. He'll have his people look into me, and he will find that I am very much his kind of person."

"How's that?" Sevyn asked.

Max chuckled. "What past I do have over the last four years is, how shall we say, checkered? Lawsuits filed against me for unsavory business practices. I like to partake in various drugs, and there are pictures of me stumbling drunk. There've been numerous women who filed sexual harassment charges against me and settled out of court. You name it, I've done it according to the World Wide Web. If he's as perverse and crooked as we think, he'll come looking. Even before my uncle left me a bundle of money, I was a loser of the very first order. Now, I am an obscenely rich loser." He failed to mention that this backstory of Max Creed was a complete fabrication, woven together mostly by Scads with input from them all.

Sevyn looked with wonder at him, and then around the table at the others. "I had no idea," she said.

Chapter Seven

Aldeia Bona, Brazil

Three Years Earlier

T he small prop plane touched down in Aldeia Bona, Brazil. The town had been founded in 1970 as the government attempted to halt the socio-cultural disintegration of the indigenous people of the area. An airstrip had been constructed to aid this effort in creating an access point to the area. Milo Sharp stood and followed John Little off the aircraft.

They'd arrived in Macapá the night before and hired a pilot to take them up to this remote village in the northern region of the country. There was a scattering of thatch-covered structures, peaked and domed, that comprised the tiny settlement. Most of the native population was spread throughout the larger area in conclaves of one or two huts.

John led the way to the Paru River, where he engaged in an increasingly heated conversation in Portuguese with a Wayana man in a loincloth with a long necklace and pendant on the end. His face was like the stone bluffs that could be seen in the distance. Finally, they came to an agreement, and John forked over some cash, obviously regular currency having some clout in this government port, gateway to the northern region.

When Milo asked John what the argument was about, he was told that the man, who was going to take them up the Paru River in a canoe, had feared that this was a bad time for such a journey, as the water beasts were active now. But for a bit more money, he'd agreed to risk the wrath of these ferocious creatures.

They paddled up the river, Milo in the front of the dugout canoe, John in the middle, and Aptuk in the rear. Milo was not concerned about the mythical creatures with multiple heads and fangs that Aptuk claimed resided in the river, but he was concerned about crocodiles, snakes, and other killers on the shore, such as jaguars. This was of particular concern the first night they spent in the brush, and these dangerous cats could be heard just outside camp, their territorial calls sounding like wood being sawed in one direction or an outboard motor trying to start.

At noon on the second day, Aptuk steered the canoe into shore and pointed them to the west. John relayed to Milo that the woman they were looking for was in a remote solitary hut about five miles that way. It took them four hours to traverse the distance through the rugged terrain in the sweltering heat.

The first bullet kicked up rock at John's feet. The second sent splinters from a mahogany tree into Milo's face.

John put his hands over his head. "Amigos."

"O que você quer?" The voice was hard and flat.

"Americanos."

"What do you want?" There was just a hint of a Portuguese accent.

"Just to talk. We are friends."

"Everybody is friends when a .50 caliber pill is about to explode your skull into so many jigsaw puzzle pieces."

Milo stepped forward. "I wish to hire you."

The woman stepped out from her cover. She was dressed in green, head to foot, protection from the brush and the insects, if not the heat. An afro, shaven at the sides, gave her an additional three inches of height to go with her five-foot-six inches or so. Tattoos swirled loose from her sleeves and neckline, and she had a silver nose ring.

"How did you find me?"

"My name is Milo Sharp. This is John Little. I want you to train me."

The woman leaned her head back and laughed loudly. "You came all the way here to offer me a job? Don't you think I might be out here because I don't want to see anybody?"

"John tells me that you are known for your exceptional skills with arms. And that you are currently unemployed."

"Do tell me, my dear John, what is it that you know of me?"

"I am willing to offer you five million dollars for one year of your time," Milo said.

"What is it that you want for that much money?"

"I want you to teach me as much as you can, not that I will ever become an expert in weapons. But I ask that you train me in everything you know, seven days a week, for one year. "

"Where do you wish this to happen?"

Milo spread his hands wide. "Here."

"Why do you wish to become proficient with firearms?"

"Not just guns. Knives. Swords. Axes. Nunchaku."

The woman walked slowly forward. "Why?"

"Let's just say there are too many people in the world for whom there is no justice. We want to help."

"And you know who *I* am?"

"You are Scarlett."

* * *

The next year they spent in the outback of Brazil. Weapons, ammunition, and supplies were brought into Aldeia Bona via plane and then upriver on a motorboat they'd bought.

Weapons training began at six a.m. sharp and went until noontime. Scarlett began Milo with knife training. She instructed him in the proper way to hold the blade, how to make his body as small as possible, the importance of balance, and the necessity of always moving. She drilled him in *capoeira*, the ancient martial art of Brazil, coupled with a blade, before one day tying their wrists together and giving him another style of knife fighting. *Like they used to do in your old west*, she said. That was more about defensive parries than attack and movement. Learning how to throw a knife would not come for seven more weeks.

The first firearm he was introduced to was the CZ 9mm Luger. He would practice with this pistol every day for the entire year. Other weapons he'd become proficient in, from axes to heavier arms, but Scarlett was insistent that the Luger become an extension of his hand as it would be the weapon he'd most likely be using.

Noon to two p.m. was siesta time, to escape the worst of the heat. After siesta, John trained Miles in hand-to-hand combat, and most days, Scarlett joined in as well, as did John in the morning's weapons training. This would go until eight p.m. when they'd break for a meal, followed by meditation until ten. The discipline was almost monastic in nature, and they took no days off.

Milo was driven by the pain of having lost his bride. John and Scarlett both seemed to have demons of their own they wished to exorcise, though neither ever shared what those demons might have been, and Milo never asked. As well, they were both being well-paid, money being little object to a man who'd recently come into untold riches.

None of them spoke of their past. When they conversed about anything other than their training, it was to talk of the future. A shared vision began to develop, shaped around creating a kind of justice that didn't exist in the world. A notion of helping those who had been wronged by the ultra-rich. The wealthy elites of the world to whom the laws of the world did not apply.

One year to the day after Milo and John had found Scarlett in the large nothingness of northern Brazil, they broke camp and set out upon a mission of John's creation. According to John, untold thousands of children a year in Brazil were being smuggled to East Coast resorts in regularly scheduled caravans for the purpose of sexual exploitation.

He'd planned on hitting one of these illegal caravans, in this case a bus filled with young boys who'd been promised work in the cities, with enough pay to send money home to their families. It was a sad enough plight, that these children, all under the age of twelve, were being shipped away by their families, convinced by the *Gatos*, the procurers of this mass of adolescent flesh, that they would be well treated, taken care of, and in return would be working twelve hours a day in a factory. In reality, they'd be forced to have sex with men for those twelve hours and barely be provided sustenance to survive.

The boys were being transported from the State of Para to the resort city of São Luís on the Atlantic Ocean. This was a distance of some 1,500 kilometers and would take them more than a day of straight driving to accomplish. John planned to hit them in the middle of this journey, when the initial excitement of the driver and guards had worn off, and they were not yet primed for the sketchy part of avoiding the authorities as they neared their destination.

On a lonely and remote stretch of road just before dawn, Milo, John, and Scarlett hunkered down on a small knoll looking through binoculars at a deserted stretch of Route 222. John cleared his throat, breaking the silence. "There will be one truck in front and one in back. Four men in each. Driver. Navigator. Two in the back with automatic weapons."

"We've covered that," Scarlett said. "Let's get in position."

The Cobra walkie-talkie crackled to life, John's voice calm but with an edge of excitement. "There is a white truck coming. They are *not* part of the convoy. About five minutes from your position. When it passes, you have ten minutes until the kids' bus. Over."

"Ten-four," Scarlett said. "Over."

"Ten-four. Over." Milo started up the tractor-trailer. And then he waited.

The white truck went past. Milo took a deep breath and put the semi into gear, floored it, and then cut it hard to the left, crossing the road and smashing into a rock outcropping. The trailer effectively blocked the way.

He got out and was rubbing his head facing the truck when he heard the mini convoy approaching. He kept his back to the road until the vehicles behind him stopped. Then he slowly looked over his shoulder as he turned around, still rubbing his head, his other hand at his stomach where he held the Luger inside his shirt with two buttons undone.

There was a pop-pop. Scarlett was up above with a sniper rifle. Milo pulled his pistol out. The two men in the back of the truck were falling backward, already dead, even if they didn't know it yet. Milo shot first the man riding shotgun and then the driver. Crack-crack.

He'd suggested to John that they didn't have to kill the men. John had given him his dead-fish stare and commented that these men were transporting young boys to a brothel to be defiled by other men until they died. And if that wasn't enough, that if Milo didn't shoot the men, they wouldn't hesitate to kill him. Point taken. Still, it was hard to murder a human being in cold blood.

A series of shots rang out from behind the bus. Two more pops came from Scarlett's rifle. Milo ran to the bus as a man stepped out the door. Before he could point the Luger at him, another pop, and the man's face exploded in a shower of blood.

John stepped around the rear of the bus and waved his pistol. The back was clear. Milo went up the three steps into the bus. About halfway to the back of the bus, two men held children in front of them as shields. They were yelling in Portuguese, words he didn't understand. But the intent was clear. Back off, or they would kill the boys.

Milo went to one knee with the pistol trained on them. John stepped up behind him and said, "On three, I got the one on the left, and you got the one on the right. One, two, three—" Crack-crack. Two bullets. Two dead men.

It had been an extremely efficient first operation. They returned to the town of Uruará and put out the word that they had children to return to families. To each family, Milo gave five hundred Brazilian Real, the equivalent of about one hundred American dollars. He thought it fifty-seven hundred dollars well spent.

Chapter Eight

Isle of the Holy Grail

Present Day

Taytum Liu lay in the king bed, luxuriating in the feel of the silk sheets on her naked body. She knew that she was being filmed and that this was little more than a role she was playing. Like that movie, *The Truman Show*, Taytum thought, but unlike the Jim Carrey character, who was unaware of the thousands of cameras filming his every moment, she knew they were there.

It was, after all, she who'd suggested installing the surveillance equipment, both audio and video. Of course, Rupert thought it was his idea, the man never having had an original notion in his noggin, but rather appropriating them from others and making them his own.

It was a man's world, as her mother had told her many a time, but that didn't mean a woman couldn't be pulling the strings and directing affairs as she saw fit. For some reason, humanity had dictated that those with penises were in charge, fit to be kings, politicians, generals, and to rule the world. But that very penis was their weakness, her mother had told her and was but the instrument upon which women could play to manipulate.

Hence, Taytum Liu lay in bed, naked, knowing full well that she was being filmed. Once she'd lain in this very bed and masturbated, the knowledge of those watching, the power she exerted, equally pleasurable to the sensation that built through her body, the climax of mind and body, pleasure and power. Now, she pushed the sheet down and rose from the bed in one flowing motion.

She paused in front of the full-length mirror and studied herself. Pretty eyes, lush black hair, lips that might be too thin, but a body that was full and sensual, even if not as ripe as the young women who by now, no doubt, were at the swimming pool showing off their flawless skin wrapped without a single wrinkle around the elegant bones of their bodies. Liu knew that her boobs now had the slightest sag to them, and there were wrinkles in the corners of her eyes that she worked hard to conceal. Still, not bad for a woman in her thirties, she thought, running her hand over her breasts and across her flat tummy.

After using the bathroom, drinking a glass of water, and getting a cup of tea, she went to her desk and sat down in front of her laptop. Naked. This, she knew, was also monitored. It was important to know what secrets senators, princes, and even celebrities had. Heck, Liu thought, musicians, movie stars, and athletes had more sway over the minds of the population than did congressmen. One simple tweet from Hudson Ford could set off protests and riots if arranged to pop up on the phones of the right people. People, by their very nature, were malleable. None so much as men.

And Taytum Liu meant to wield her power and shape her world as she wanted.

* * *

Rupert Hastings stepped out of the main house and walked the short distance to the swimming pool. There were guest cottages scattered about the island, twelve in all, as well as quarters for the seventy or so servants, cooks, landscapers, and whatnot. There were two trucks and two vans for the workers, but the rest of the transportation was all golf carts.

The island was located south and east of the Bahamas, a spit of land a mile wide and four miles long that he'd bought a few years back and built into what it was now. They'd flown the jet into Nassau and taken two helicopters to the Isle of the Holy Grail, as he'd named it. Officially, it was some Spanish name that he couldn't even pronounce and didn't care to.

This was his pleasure paradise. Secluded from prying eyes, he'd built this to fulfill his own desires, and along the way, come to realize that many other men shared those same cravings. And sharing his salacity with others gave him leverage he'd never known before. It gave him power. Brought him attention. Added to his wealth. All of which titillated his erogenous zones as much as that of the flesh of a young woman.

And they *were* young women and not girls. He made sure of that. Young ladies plucked from his modeling agency, Hastings' Catwalk, a business that focused on young women. Eighteen to twenty-two. Of course, he'd had a few rock stars that he kept on into their mid-to-late twenties, but very few. For the agency was as much for his pleasure, as it was for making money.

Hastings' Catwalk currently had ninety-seven models under representation. Twelve of them had been invited here, which was a huge honor. To be asked to go to the Isle of the Holy Grail with Rupert Hastings was an opportunity for stardom. It was well known that those who gave the greatest effort reaped the largest rewards. Rupert owned three fashion magazines, influenced hundreds of others, and had even got young ladies into the Sports Illustrated Swimsuit issue. One past attendee at the island had recently signed a deal with a major cosmetic company. She was now worth twenty-five million dollars.

Jeffrey Epstein had been a fool, Rupert thought, as he opened the gate to the courtyard and the pool. Eighteen was every bit as nubile as fourteen, and in so many ways, better. And legal. One didn't have to get parental consent to transport the girls halfway around the world. These young women were adults in the eyes of the law, but still, oh so moldable. Their desires and ambitions were every bit as vigorous as his own.

His models want *this*, Rupert thought, taking a moment to appreciate the grandeur of the opulence in front of him. The pool, by no means small, was pear-shaped, sparkling in the late morning sun of the 80° day. There was a fountain in the middle that recirculated the water, bubbling up ten feet into the air before cascading down. The motif was of old Rome, with large stone pillars and a bar that was a mini replica of the Coliseum.

Nine of the girls were present. Rupert noted who was not here. He knew the whereabouts of two of the missing lasses, but not the last one. Three of them lazed in the swimming pool, two of them leaning on the fountain as they talked. Kat was talking with Cole, the football player, giggling at what he was saying, touching his arm as he spoke. Four of the girls were reclined in loungers, tanning, their dark glasses hiding whether they were asleep or awake. Two others sat at stools, one on either side of Hudson, frozen drinks in hand.

All the girls were topless, their ripe skin glowing, bathed in the sun. Miah, basking in the sun, was totally naked, her body smooth, shiny, promising. He hoped that she didn't burn any important parts, but made a positive note in his mind. Flirtation. Willingness. Adventurousness. Graceful nudity. All these things were noted, pluses. Absenteeism. Too many clothes. Reclusiveness. Denial. Drunkenness. These things went into the negative column.

Hence, girls moved up the hierarchy of Hastings' Catwalk, dependent on their performance while attending the Isle of the Holy Grail. And it was a performance. The most important gig of their young lives, thus far. And Rupert reaped the rewards of their efforts. He'd spent the morning with two of the young ladies before sending them on their way. Their efforts were most appreciated.

There was an NFL football star in his pool, having the best time of his young life and eternally grateful to Rupert, as was Hudson Ford, his arm grazing the beauty's breast to his right every time he took a sip of his drink, a motion that he seemed invested in performing repetitively.

Before coming to the pool, Rupert had stopped in the audio-video room located beneath the staircase of the main house. On the screen, he'd watched the prince sitting in his cottage, alone, at a desk on the computer. What he was doing on the computer was being downloaded by one of Rupert's techs. Information gleaned in such a fashion was just as important in creating the dynamics of power as what was being filmed in the Senator's cottage.

Senator Dunn didn't look like he'd slept, his hair tousled atop his head, his glasses missing from his face, his eyes bleary and red as he snorted cocaine from the belly of a young woman who looked as bored as he looked excited. She lay on the table, as if a buffet meal for the Senator, not a stitch of clothing on. The other girl suddenly appeared, standing from where she'd been kneeling beneath the table, and the Senator clapped his hands.

"Roll over," he said to the girl on the table.

Rupert grinned maliciously, thinking back to the recorded video and audio of the esteemed senator, knowing that the man was now in his back pocket. This was not a single chip to be played when needed, but a never-ending bounty of favors. Rupert felt like he'd been visited by a genie and granted three wishes and had had the intelligence to make his first wish that he had an infinite number of wishes.

The trick would be to not push the Senator so far that he retired or killed himself. Even death wouldn't erase the humiliation if the act he was currently engaged in was revealed to his wife and children. No, Rupert had that man firmly in the palm of his hand. Not a bad life he'd made for himself. Here, now, at his pool, luxuriating in the presence of a bevy of beauties, surrounded by celebrities and wealth, he felt like the Roman emperors must've felt at the height of their power.

It wasn't always easy being so much smarter than the rest of the world, Rupert thought, his eyes appreciating Miah's creamy smooth skin, lapping in the other exquisite delicacies in and around his pool like the finest sushi buffet in the world. His girls. His pool. His home. His island. The world was his oyster, and Rupert meant to enjoy his just rewards every step of the way.

His father hadn't understood that. He hadn't comprehended how truly brilliant his son was, how special Rupert was, and how rules and laws didn't apply to somebody who was that incredibly gifted. The same father who let his mother be killed when he was nine, walking right there beside her when the drunk's car veered up onto the sidewalk and clipped his mom clean without so much as touching a whisker on his dad's head. It was Fred Hastings' fault that Rupert's mom was dead.

When his father had tried to preach his morality to Rupert some fifteen years ago, Rupert had finally had enough and told the man what he really thought of him, and then walked away. He'd been embezzling money from the family business for years by then anyway and had a nice nest egg invested in various profitable endeavors and no longer needed the crutch of his father's business.

Then, Rupert had systematically begun bringing financial ruin to Fred Hastings. He'd been patient, and it was quite a bit of money, so it'd taken eleven years. Rupert had not spoken to the man in that entire time, but when he finally drove the last stake into the empire his father had created, Rupert paid him a visit, just to let him know that it was he who'd done it.

"Penny for your thoughts," Taytum said.

Rupert started from his reverie and took in the brilliant number two in all his endeavors. Together, they'd made a lot of money and lived life like a god and goddess. She seemed perfectly happy to fulfill his desires. They'd had a bit of a torrid affair a few years back, but that had waned with the parade of young models offered up to his whims, and now they were partners in life but not in flesh.

"Do you think that immortality exists for people like you and me?" he asked.

Chapter Nine

Columbus, Ohio

"Could be nothing," Max said.

He, John, and Scarlett were sitting in a black Range Rover with tinted windows. They all had binoculars and were looking at a warehouse, a nondescript building that was perfectly innocuous. There were seven bay doors on the side they were facing, with sixteen-wheelers backed up to three of them. There were a couple of hundred cars in the parking lot, or rather, mostly trucks.

"Tucker and Scads have good instincts about this sort of thing," John said. He was sitting in the back, struggling with the binoculars because they were too small for his broad face. "If they say there's drugs down there, well then, I believe them."

"They said there *might* be Iso down there," Max said.

"Never even heard of the stuff," Scarlett said. Her São Paulo accent was only distinguishable by a slight rolling of her Rs. She was sitting in the driver's seat, one of her many talents being that she was an incredibly gifted driver. If she hadn't become a weapons expert and assassin for hire, she always said she would've liked to drive a stock car on the racetrack. "But then again, it's relatively new. Drugs might be the only thing outpacing technology in rapid advancement."

"More potent than fentanyl is all I need to know," Max said. "And harder to detect. One more way for people to die."

"And still legal in China," John said.

Tucker had first come across the fact that the Chinese company, Huang Worldwide, had heavy connections with the 9H Triad, both of which were located in Shanghai. The perfect pairing of organized crime and legitimate business. Huang Worldwide made and distributed Isotonitazene, a synthetic drug new to the market, legal in China but illegal in the US. They also had a flourishing division dedicated to manufacturing children's plush toys. Their best-selling product was the Hug Me Harry teddy bear, and one of the primary importers was Hastings Incorporated.

"Pretty thin, I have to agree," Scarlett said. "It's hard to believe that 9H is in business with Huang Worldwide to smuggle Iso into the US using teddy bears."

"To a warehouse owned by Rupert Hastings." Max was hyped up, feeling the tension climb as they prepared for impending action.

"Scads found some pretty interesting discrepancies in their books when he hacked in," John said. "Large sums of money generated that don't appear in the numbers given to the IRS. If not Iso, there's something fishy going on at Rupert's teddy bear warehouse."

"Well, if there is, let's hope that Dudley can sniff it out."

The three of them looked to the seat next to John in the back. Dudley had a wrinkled face, humongous drooping ears, was liver and tan colored, and was a canine. He was also Canadian, as it was one of the few countries in the world that had revolutionized the training of drug sniffing dogs so they could ferret out incredibly powerful opioids without overdosing themselves.

They'd sure come a long way, Max thought, since the year they'd spent in the jungles of Brazil training with an array of weaponry. Back then, his name had been Milo Sharp, and now he was Max Creed, an identity that he slipped more deeply into with each passing day. But at the same time, little had changed. He'd built a team of superstars in their fields and put in motion the first stages of a plan to exact justice for those who would squash those less fortunate under their feet. But the fact remained that they'd not yet done anything concrete to achieve that goal.

A few minutes later, people began to leave the warehouse, in ones and twos, and then it was like a floodgate had opened. Max looked at his watch. Three-thirty on the button. Good ole Ohio, still working a 7:30 to 3:30 schedule five days a week, maybe overtime to noon on Saturday around the holidays, no second shift, no remote work.

The plan was to go in at ten o'clock, ascertain that there were drugs there, and then make an anonymous tip to the DEA. Max knew some people who would make certain that it would be followed up on, or so he thought, unless Rupert had people in higher places with more clout, which was unlikely.

In the meantime, they went into Columbus to grab a bite to eat at the Wolf Ridge Brewery. Max had the Duck Pot Pie and two IPAs. He figured he was working, and beer barely counted toward his vow of abstinence. He shared some of his dinner with Dudley, having left his dog food back on the jet. The dog made out just fine, as John and Scarlett also shared their dinners with him.

At ten o'clock, they were parked on an access road behind the building, hidden by trees and scrub brush. There was a fence that went around the building with two guards at the front gate. The rest of the security was comprised of cameras, a keyless lock, and an alarm system. Pretty simple. It was a warehouse for teddy bears after all.

Max, John, and Scarlett all pulled on black jumpsuits over their clothes as well as lightweight ski masks in case Scads couldn't knock out the surveillance cameras. Then they all pulled on advanced night vision goggles, giving them added depth perception as well as peripheral view, and were designed to increase their ability to observe, orient, and act.

Dudley wasn't quite sure about the new look, but he was a pretty chill canine and merely looked at them with his mournful eyes, wondering what shenanigans the humans were getting up to now.

Scarlett climbed the oak tree just outside the fence. On her back was slung a Barrett M95, a bolt-action anti-material and sniper rifle, along with a bag containing several of the five-round magazines that went with the weapon. It was capable of wreaking some serious damage as well as being incredibly accurate.

Once she was in place, Max called Scads. "In position."

"Okay," Scads said. "Cameras are now in my control. The last hour will be replayed. All clear. Enter the facility. You have one hour."

John cut through the fence with simple bolt cutters, creating a hole large enough for them to pass through. Dudley began to think this was great fun, but he was a professional and kept his composure. They crept their way across an empty parking lot to a door on the side of the building.

"At the door," Max said into the phone.

"Okay," Scads said. "I'm downloading access to your phone now. Then you have thirty seconds to punch the code I'm texting you to turn off the alarm."

Max looked back over his shoulder. He could see the tree that Scarlett was in about two hundred yards back. He could not see her. He opened the keyless app that Scads had put on his phone and held it up to the sensor. The lock clicked, and Max opened the door, stepping quickly through as he brought up the text code. It was thirteen digits long, and it wouldn't be a good idea to make a mistake. It took him twelve seconds, and then they waited.

"You're clear," Scads said. "Have at it."

Scads had taken control of the side and back cameras, as well as the interior, but had left the ones in front operational, so that he could monitor them in case the guards decided to be curious about something.

"Okay, Dudley, reach," John said.

Dudley looked at him with his mournful eyes and didn't budge. Reach was the command that they'd been told to use to begin the search.

"Reach, Dudley, reach."

The canine didn't move.

Max stepped in front of the dog. "Dudley. Reach, eh."

The dog immediately began his search.

John followed, looking over his shoulder at Max. "Canadians, eh?"

They moved down the corridors of the warehouse, large metal shelving units on either side, filled with boxes, reaching up toward the dim lighting left on at night. The only sound was their breathing and the slap of their feet on the concrete floor.

Max stopped and looked at a box. The outside was marked TB. It had a number on it. 363. He pulled it from the bottom shelf and opened it. It was filled with teddy bears.

He hurried to catch up to John and Dudley, who'd gone around the corner to a new aisle. All the boxes on the row had the same marking. TB.

Max held the phone closer to his mouth. "Everything still good?"

"I'm in the middle of a video game," Scads said. "I'll let you know once it's over."

Max cursed at him.

Scads laughed. "Yes. You are still all clear. I'd let you know if Beavis and Butthead come wandering back. Pretty sure they don't even carry guns, so you should be fine with your hardware."

Max and John both carried the CZ 9mm Lugers, which Scarlett had trained them mercilessly with until it was just an extension of their own hand, arm, and body.

Dudley suddenly hesitated, then darted to the right, pulling John behind him to a box like all the others, and began pawing at it.

Max and John wrestled the box out into the open. It had the same TB on the side. Number 999. They ripped the top off. It was filled with teddy bears.

Dudley certainly seemed to think there was more as he gave a low whine and jumped up, his paws on the edge of the box.

"Down, boy. Sit." John pulled him back from the box.

"Sit, eh," Max said and chuckled.

They tipped the box over, spilling the teddy bears onto the floor. There were four different colors. Brown, white, red, and pink. Nothing else.

Dudley whined low in his throat and scuttled forward.

"Stay, eh," John said.

Max picked up a brown teddy bear. He pulled the knife from his belt and slit it from head to legs down the front. In the stuffing, there was a plastic bag with a white powder in it.

"Max, you got incoming," Scads' voice scratched from the phone. "Coming hot and loaded for bear."

"Ha," John said. "For Teddy Bear?"

"How many?" Max stuffed the bag of Iso into his pocket.

"Hard to tell. Two SUVs out front. Okay, they're getting out. There's eight of them."

"Let's go," Max said, moving toward the side door they'd come in.

They'd only gone a few steps when the front door crashed open, and then the lights came on. They were out of sight, behind the high shelving units, and couldn't see the men, and hopefully couldn't be seen by them.

"Fan out," a voice commanded.

Max and John had their CZs out. Dudley brought up the rear.

They came to the end of the aisle and took the right toward the exit. A man in black stepped around the corner and raised his rifle as they darted behind another shelving unit. The deafening roar of automatic weapon fire split the air. A box just above them was shredded and teddy bears spilled out onto the floor.

"Get Dudley to the exit," Max said.

He stopped, his back to a row of boxes, and then stepped around the corner and fired three times. Pop. Pop. Pop. All three hit the man in the chest and knocked him backward. Another man came from the other direction, and Max went toward the fallen man as bullets rained around him.

A man stepped out in front of him, and Max shot him in the chest. As he passed by the fallen man, he noted the man writhing on the floor, but no apparent blood, and realized he had body armor on. Bullets fanned by his head, and he moved down another aisle. The next man who stepped into view, Max shot in the face.

There was a forklift, and Max jumped in and sent it careening down an aisle toward the exit. Bullets chattered around him as he leaned down low in the seat, snapping return fire out as he went. He heard another pistol and realized that John had opened covering fire from the doorway.

Max dove out of the forklift at the doorway from which John was sending bursts of bullets, and the two men left the building. Dudley led the way across the parking lot. A man came around from the front of the building, and another reached the door they'd just left.

The man in front didn't get a chance to fire as a .50 caliber bullet knocked him ten yards back. Scarlett had begun her covering fire. A second bullet destroyed the man in the doorway behind them.

Then they were at the hole they'd cut in the fence and were through to the other side. Scarlett slid down out of the oak tree. They clambered into the Range Rover and skedaddled.

"Crikey, that was something." Max looked over his shoulder as they sped away from the teddy bear storage facility, doubling as a drug front.

"Crikey?" Scarlett turned from the steering wheel and raised an eyebrow. "You an Aussie now?" They were traveling down a quiet road on a very dark night at a high rate of speed. Luckily, there appeared to be no other traffic.

Max chuckled. Her rolling Rs made the word even better. "It seemed appropriate for a shootout in a teddy bear warehouse."

"Were they Koalas?" she asked.

"You think we should call in the anonymous tip?" John asked.

Max shook his head. "I imagine they'll have it all cleared out of there before the local authorities rouse themselves from bed, if they do at all, based on an unnamed tip about a local taxpayer."

"That wasn't your normal security detail," John said.

"*Caramba*," Scarlett said. "I'd bet my bottom dollar those were mercs."

"Further establishing that there is a major drug smuggling operation happening there," Max said. "At a facility owned by Rupert—"

That's when the truck slammed into the side of them and drove them fifty feet across the ditch on the side of the road and into the trees, which is, in fact, what stopped them.

Max felt like he'd been kicked in the face by a fluffy bunny rabbit, and there was the smell of smoke in the air.

The airbag had deployed, leaving his face razor-burned and stiffness in his chest. He looked sideways at Scarlett. She already had her pistol in hand, pointing at Max, no, past him, pulling the trigger, crack, crack. At the passenger side door, there was a Ford F-150 crumpled up, the heads of two men lolled backward on the bench seat, red splotches in their foreheads.

Max released his seat belt and looked over his shoulder. John was sitting with a dazed expression, and Dudley was on the floor, whining. He climbed over the airbag and out through the opening where the windshield had recently been, pulling his Luger from the holster as he did so. An SUV was coming down the road. As he hopped from the hood to the ground, a man leaned out and opened fire with an automatic weapon.

As bullets peppered the ground at his feet, Max steadied his pistol and shot out the tire. The vehicle skidded to the right, tipped, and then righted itself before coming to a shuddering stop. The man lost his grip on the rifle as he grabbed the door to keep from falling out. Behind him, Scarlett opened fire, sending a wave of bullets cascading into the stopped SUV.

Max went around to the rear door that was not pinned shut by the truck and grabbed Dudley's leash, pulling him from the backseat floor. He seemed to be okay, nothing broken, even if shaken up. John was the same way as he half-fell, half-climbed from the backseat. Blood flowed from his broken nose, and several teeth appeared to be missing.

Rifle fire from behind them pinged into the metal of the SUV like sleet on a tin roof, and Max shoved John the rest of the way to the ground and followed suit. Dudley hobbled off into the darkness. A cloud drifted across the sliver of moon, and everything went very dark, followed by the quiet of rifle fire ceasing.

"Scar, you okay?" Max asked in a whisper.

"Yeah, all good," she replied. "How about John?"

"Looks a bit concussed, but then again, he always looks that way," Max said.

Scarlett chuckled, and John hit him weakly on the arm.

"Dudley?" Scarlett asked.

"He's the bright one and has vacated the premises," Max said. "I suggest we follow him."

He tapped John on the shoulder and began to crawl marine style in the direction Dudley had taken, deeper into the forest at the side of the road. John followed, with Scarlett bringing up the rear.

The going was rough, rocks and brambles littering the ground, but the trees provided good cover. About fifty feet in, there was a small clearing.

As Max went to skirt the edge, the moon came out to reveal a man to their left with tactical gear and infrared goggles taking aim at them.

Max rolled, bringing his pistol to bear, knowing it was too late. A single shot rang out, and the man slowly toppled to the ground.

"Concussed, am I?" John asked, lowering his gun.

"We best move double time," Scarlett said.

Max led the way toward the fallen man. "Let's grab his infrared."

The man was in tactical gear, with infrared goggles on, but unfortunately, they were ruined. The bullet from John's gun had pierced the right eyepiece before traveling through the man's skull. Scarlett picked up the rifle and handed it to Max. "LVAW from Sig Sauer. Might need it. Let's go."

Scarlett led the way. After a few hundred yards, Dudley found them, seeming to think they'd successfully escaped the people shooting at them. Max took this as a sign that they were safe and called Scads. John was the logistics guy, which didn't do them any good, so he thought it best to go to the tech guy and not the lawyer or the financier. Scads' suggestion of a solution was an Uber, not a terrible idea after a moment's reflection, so just after one in the morning, they found themselves on the side of the road waiting for a blue minivan to arrive.

They were forced to stash the Low Visibility Assault Weapon but kept their pistols. The driver looked as if he wished he'd not stopped for them as they clambered into his minivan, a far different fare than the usual late-night drinkers. If they'd at least been drinking, it might explain their presence in the middle of nowhere with no vehicle, ruffled and dirty, and with a dog.

"What happened to your car?" he asked in a tentative Midwestern drawl.

"Got it stuck in the forest," Max said.

"And then we went down the rabbit hole," Scarlett said.

"To the airport, James," John said.

Chapter Ten

Pattaya City, Thailand

There was something calming about riding an elephant, Max thought, as the huge beast lumbered along.

He'd no sooner gotten back to Long Beach Island than he got a phone call from Rupert asking if he'd like to join him for the weekend in Pattaya, Thailand. That gave him three days of restorative calm walking and watching the ocean at his hidden paradise in North Carolina. He walked four hours each day on the beach, the fifty-degree weather ensuring he had the beach to himself, other than the sporadic dog walker who had little choice but to brave the chill for the sake of his beast, whereas Max embraced the bite in the air.

Unbeknownst to Max, John had taken the pinkie finger of the security guard turned assassin for DNA purposes. The results were back, so much quicker when one owned their own lab for that purpose, but they were of no help. The man was ex-military, special ops, out for four years now. So far, they hadn't been able to trace his movements, what he'd been up to, who hired him. He was not employed by Rupert Hastings or the teddy bear warehouse as far as they could tell.

Scarlett was tracking the rifle the man had, which was restricted to military and law enforcement use only, not that that was much of a hindrance to acquiring one. Scarlett was researching who else might have access to weaponry such as this. Max knew that the answer to this was anybody with the money and the need.

Rupert had offered him a ride to Thailand in his jet, but Max declined, wanting to keep his autonomy, gracefully declining the offer of staying at the man's penthouse suite at the Blue Pleasure Hotel & Resort as well. Max claimed to have business to attend to in Nepal, and thus, he'd just meet Rupert in Pattaya City.

When Max landed at ten in the morning on Friday, there was a limousine waiting, which brought him directly to the Pattaya Elephant Village for a trek to the Sanctuary of Truth, the largest wooden structure in Thailand, a building begun in 1981 and not yet finished. John stayed behind to transport their belongings to their hotel, several blocks from Rupert's, and would sweep the room for bugs or cameras.

It was a short trip to the Elephant Village. Max was relieved but not surprised to see that there were no young models. Pattaya City was known as the sex capital of the world, a place where any perversion could be satisfied, and cheaply at that. Why bring your own picnic lunch to the buffet?

The woman from the card table in Vegas the other night was present. Taytum Liu. Scads had dug up a trove of information on her. Her parents had immigrated to the US from China, or rather, stayed, after graduating together from Columbia, where they'd met and fallen in love before eventually marrying. They both came from wealth and continued to build that fortune over the years. Today, while not billionaires, they were easily worth hundreds of millions.

Taytum was born in 1988, an only child, and had been finely spoiled by her parents. She was a black belt in karate, played several sports in high school, and had gone to Harvard. Fluent in four languages, Taytum was widely traveled. She dabbled in real estate, investments, and had been cavorting around with Rupert Hastings for several years now.

"Hello, Miss Liu, I didn't know you'd be here," Max said, nodding to her. The last time he'd seen her, he'd been relieving her of a hefty sum of money, and he wasn't sure what his reception would be. "But it is a pleasure."

She glared icily at him. "I am sure it is Mr. Creed, but forgive me for recalling that the last time we met, you were taking nineteen million dollars from my purse."

"The cards were kind to me," Max said. "Lady Luck was smiling down."

"Tut, tut, tut," Rupert said. "It was only money. Perhaps we will find a use for Max's winnings before the day is done."

Max wondered what he might spend eighty-three million dollars on in Thailand. That was quite a bundle of perversions, he thought, hiding a wry smile. "Hello, Rupert, good to see you again," he said.

"And you, my dear chap." Rupert took his hand and gave an enthusiastic shake. "Max, this is Hudson Ford."

Max looked at the granite jaw of the action movie star. The man's grip was firm. His smile was wide. "I enjoy your movies," Max said. Which was complete shit, as he'd seen parts of two of them, and they were terrible.

And now they were tramping along on elephants. Rupert, Max, Taytum, Hudson, two guides, and three fellows who looked like hired muscle. It was twelve kilometers to the Sanctuary of Truth and well worth the journey. Max's breath was taken away when they crested a hill, and the wooden temple came into view. A spit of land curled out into the Gulf of Thailand, white sand beaches wrapping the Sanctuary of Truth warmly in their grasp.

The building soared over a hundred meters into the air with ornate wooden sculptures adorning every wall, the largest being the gigantic four-faced Brahma, the Hindu deity symbolizing the tenets of benevolence, compassion, empathetic joy, and equanimity, or so the guides told them as the elephants trudged their way out to the peninsula.

Their two guides turned them over to a special envoy of museum guides for a tour of this wondrous building covered in detailed sculptures carved from wood. Max was as impressed by Rupert being here as he was by the temple with all its marvels. The man might be a bully, a pimp, and corrupt as hell, but there was a cultured side to him.

There was a tent set up on the beach for their lunch. The feast began with Bae Mee Kiew, a wonton noodle soup, followed by a meat salad called Laab, and finally, Khao Kha Moo, which was pork leg with rice. It was all incredibly delicious, and Max suspected this was not the normal museum fare.

"This place was built to show that civilization was made and nurtured by religious and philosophic truth," their host said as the last plate was taken away. The four of them, Rupert, Max, Hudson, and Taytum, had lit cigars and were sipping cognac. "It is a place that is home to all seven creators that include the earth, sun, moon, mother, father, stars, and heaven. These are the universal truths of humanity, things to be honored, cherished, and ideas that I believe in."

* * *

Four hours later, the four of them sat in a box seat at Tiffany's, a transvestite cabaret, or ladyboy cabaret as advertised, sipping bourbon, and again sharing a bit of Thai culture as expressed through the dancers wearing extravagant costumes and lip-syncing traditional songs in a mesmerizing show. Afterward, a host of the performers came sashaying into their private booth, offering to pose for pictures, to which Rupert gave an adamant no.

Max briefly wondered if Rupert's sexual predilections leaned towards the world of transvestites, but his interest seemed mostly in the costumes, the songs, and the culture that these performers had shared. Max wouldn't have guessed that the conservative nature of the man would allow him to attend a show such as this and converse with transvestites.

Afterward, the four of them, with the muscle following close behind, went down Walking Street, the most exotic road Max had ever been on. It was a noisy, neon jungle of stimuli. Multi-colored signs blazed brilliantly, advertising everything from dancing girls, men, sushi, and tailored suits. Scantily clad women in uniforms stood outside bars and clubs holding up signs for cheap beer, massages, private dances, and pretty much whatever you could imagine.

Rupert led them into *Lucifer 2.0*, a Hell-themed establishment designed to resemble the interior of an infernal cavern. They passed by the front bar to a raised section and a reserved table in an interior dance club with hip-hop blaring from speakers taller than most people. An enormous disco ball hung from the ceiling, highlighting a laser show that pulsed with the music. A DJ spun the music on stage, mixing songs, beats, and other sound effects as women in string bikinis danced with luminous glittering lights in their hands.

Max didn't recognize any of the music, nor could he understand most of the words, the entire scene overwhelming his senses in a pulsing beat of intoxicating energy. Ladies in elegant, shining dresses brought bottle service, pouring generous amounts of expensive liquor into their glasses, sharing drinks, touching bodies, bewitching the senses.

Taytum Liu seemed to be enjoying herself as much as any of them, unless of course you included Hudson Ford, who'd buried himself in the sinuous embrace of three escorts who writhed around him like snakes tempting Eve in the Garden of Eden. Or was it, Max thought, going back to the conversation with Marian, actually Adam who had been tempted into indulgence by Eve?

Two of the women had pulled up seats on either side of Max and were whispering and giggling, touching his arm, his leg, running their hands across his shoulders, brushing his ear with their lips. If this were Hell, it was not a bad place to be, Max thought, trying to retain his composure instead of caving into the demons of sin, but it was oh so hard.

His mind swirling with liquor, his body teased by sex, Max felt his resolve drowning. Rupert leaned over, touched his arm, and gestured for him to follow. Hudson and Taytum were already on their feet. Max followed through the club as if in a trance, up a circular staircase, down a hallway, and into a private room.

* * *

It was four a.m. when Max got back to the hotel. Zella and Sajja were with him. John was sitting in the opulent living room of the suite, next to the fountain with marble gods and goddesses leaping forth.

"There's coffee in the kitchen," he said. "And a pot of hot water for tea."

"You didn't tell us you had a friend." Zella looked with pouty eyes at Max. "I thought we were going to have you all to ourselves."

"Zell, Sajja, this is John."

"Well, hello, John," Sajja said. "I suppose in our line of work we need to be...flexible."

"A bit of conversation is what I'm into, right now," Max said. "Coffee or tea?"

Max brought them both green tea while he filled the largest mug he could find with black coffee. John was commenting to the two Thai women how impressive their English was.

"In the limousine, you asked me if I'd be interested in klismaphilia," Max said, his eyebrows rising. "Perhaps coupled with electrostimulation with a zapper."

Zella looked wary, but then giggled. "We don't usually call it that, you know. But we can do that," she said.

John looked like he wanted to ask a question. Max raised his hand. "And you suggested that, why?"

"Well, Rupert let on that you might be attracted to that little game, is all," Zella said.

The fictional background of Max Creed included several sexually perverted chapters. "Which he knows from experience?"

Zella stared down at the floor. Then she looked up defiantly. "Yes. On several occasions, he has required this of us."

"What are you talking about?" John asked.

Sajja laughed, a tinkling sound that was a cross between wind chimes and breaking glass. "Klismaphilia is my responsibility. I squirt warm water up his ass, is what I do."

Zella looked pensive. Sighed. "While I use a zapper to electronically stimulate his testicles. A very delicate procedure, mixing electricity to the scrotum while shooting water up a man's ass, as you can imagine. It is truly a skill that few possess."

John guffawed. "Is this service in high demand?"

Sajja snickered. "No, but Rupie certainly seems to enjoy it. The warm water. The shocks. And most of all, the danger."

"Would you be willing to sign an affidavit attesting to Rupert engaging in this activity with you?" Max asked.

"Why ever would we do that?" Zella asked.

"How would you like to emigrate to the US and have a million dollars in each of your bank accounts?"

"What?" Sajja said.

"Two million."

Zella's eyes sharpened. "Two million bahts? Or dollars?"

"Dollars. And I'll get you jobs. Not as sex workers."

"Why?" Zella asked.

"Yes, why?" John asked. "Can I speak with you for a moment?"

"Talk it over," Max said, rising to his feet. "Two million dollars each, and I help you emigrate."

"What if we filmed it?" Zella asked. "Would that be useful?"

She said it in such a way that indicated that they *had* filmed it. Max paused, nodded. "That would be very helpful. Talk it over. I'll be right back."

John led the way into the study. He closed the door behind them. "Four million dollars and jobs for the testimony of two hookers that Rupert has some strange fetishes? Are you crazy? Who cares at the end of the day if the man likes his balls shocked while having warm water squirted up his bunghole?"

"Rupert shared something with me this evening," Max said. "Something that might make this all quite pertinent."

"Yeah? What's that?"

"He plans to run for president. As in, of the United States of America. In 2024. Next year."

Chapter Eleven

New York City

"This is nice," Sajja said.

"It'll do," Zella said.

They both laughed. It'd been decided that they should not return to their apartments in Pattaya City, but rather, go straight to Max's private jet with him and John for the flight back to the States. The film, stored on the cloud, of Rupert Hastings having water pumped up his ass by Sajja while Zella zapped his balls was possibly the most disturbing thing Max had ever seen. That image would more than likely be plaguing his sleeping hours for some time to come. *Get in line*, he said to the image and himself.

The two women had eaten ravenously on the plane, worked their way through several bottles of champagne, and then had slept for the remainder of the nineteen-hour flight. It was hard for Max to reconcile the two prostitutes performing lewd and kinky sexual acts on Rupert Hastings with the two guileless waifs on the plane who chattered away at everything like children on Christmas morning.

Sajja sniffed. "A little dark for my taste."

Zella giggled. "Downright stodgy."

Max shook his head. It was a three-story brownstone on the Upper West Side of New York City that one of his companies had on the market for just under five million dollars. "This is temporary. Of course, once we get everything squared away, you are free to buy it."

"No hurry." Sajja sprawled out on the leather couch and put her feet up on the coffee table. "But I could use a change of clothes."

Max looked at the shiny, very short dress she wore that matched the Jimmy Choo pointed-toe pumps. John had gone straight to the office. Max pulled out his phone and texted him to have somebody come and take their two lady guests shopping.

"What do you like to do?" Max asked.

Zella snickered. "I think we've covered that. Have you changed your mind about having a bit of fun with us?"

Max flushed. "For work. You need jobs. If we can get you employment, then we can apply for a green card and begin the immigration process."

"Doesn't it work the other way around?" Zella asked. "Green card and then job?"

Max shook his head. "Not if you have money."

Sajja shrugged. "Fashion, I suppose."

Max's phone buzzed. He looked at the screen. "A woman will be here in one hour to take you shopping. Her name is Linda Davis. Please keep a low profile and realize that currently you are here illegally."

"What about food?" Zella asked.

"Text me a list of what you want, and I'll see that it is delivered today."

Zella smiled coyly and put her hand on Max's shoulder. "Are you sure you won't stay for a bit?"

Max chuckled. "I believe that you are soon to be in my employ, and that would be unethical of me. I appreciate the offer, though. Please... keep a low profile until we get some things squared away."

* * *

Max decided to walk down to the offices in Bryant Park, where he was meeting the gang to map out a strategy moving forward. He chose to go down through Central Park and escape the city for a brief reprieve, thinking about that Chris Holm book, *Child Zero*, in which this park was used as a detention camp for those exposed to a deadly virus that had changed humanity. Rupert Hastings was a sickness that had to be dealt with before he had the opportunity to infect the entire world with his evil.

Right before leaving Pattaya City, he'd sent Rupert a message that a business crisis had come up, and he regretfully had to leave and would miss the rest of the weekend of debauchery. Except he didn't say debauchery.

As a follow-up to his apology for having to skedaddle, he added that he wanted to get together soon and talk about what he could do to help Rupert in his bid to become president. President. Max shook his head, grimacing, the thought of it bringing bile to his mouth.

That said, there was something intoxicating about the lifestyle. If he was being honest, the girls' offer had been extremely tempting. Just two days ago, he'd been riding elephants, eating lunch outside a temple on the beach, attending a fabulously entertaining cabaret show, and then clubbing and flirting with beautiful women. It was hard to keep one's bearings, he thought.

There used to be elephants here in the Central Park Zoo, Max thought, but no more. He supposed it was inhumane to box up these mammoth mammals in confined spaces. Had it been wrong to ride the elephants in Thailand? What about horses? Eating a steak had become a moral dilemma. Sometimes, it was hard to keep up with what was right and what was wrong.

Before he knew it, lost in his reverie, Max was at Bryant Park and on the elevator going up to the penthouse offices. It was Dale's day off, so there was nobody at the front desk. Max breezed into the boardroom, comprised of thirteen comfortable armchairs, a like number of rolling tables, several television screens, and a bar with beer on tap, liquor, and a vast array of wine.

John Little was watching the news on one of the television sets as he browsed his laptop. "I'll beckon the others. First, I think I've found a good fit for Zella and Sajja. Tony Munday's needs two assistant fashion stylists."

Max grabbed a bottled water and went to sit next to John. "And I own Tony Munday's? That's a fashion line, right?"

John guffawed. "Yes. You are the principal owner, so I imagine that if you put in a good word, the job is theirs."

"What are the qualifications? I mean, are they up to the task?"

"It seems that assistant stylists are merely lackeys for the designer. Follow orders. Fetch coffee. Dress models. That sort of thing."

Max nodded. "If they prove adept at the job, we'll move them up. Let's glorify the title a bit, shall we? It might look a bit odd if we imported two Thai women to be peons. That might raise a few eyebrows."

Marian walked into the room at the last part. "What might raise a few eyebrows?"

"I need you to begin the paperwork to get green cards for two new employees," Max said.

"Sure. Where do they work?"

"Tony something or other," Max said.

"Tony Munday's," John said.

"Nice," Marian said. "Are they designers?"

"Assistant stylists," John said.

Marian exaggerated raising her eyebrows.

"Connoisseurs of style?" Max said.

She snickered. "We'll work on it. This have something to do with Rupert Hastings?"

John handed her a folder. "Everything is in here. Two Thai hookers who we stashed up on the West Side for now."

"Do tell," Marian said. "What is it that they know about our Boy Scout?"

John's ruddy cheeks turned red. "It's all in there."

Marian looked at Max.

He shrugged. "It seems that Rupert enjoys having water squirted up his ass while getting his testicles shocked."

"Doesn't every man?"

John turned a darker red, almost plum.

Max chuckled. "I can't say for all present, but no, I don't believe that I do."

"Does that mean you've tried it?" Marian asked.

Max now found himself flushing at the sharp tongue of his attorney. "Can't say that I have, but I don't have to stick a knife in my eye to know I won't like it."

"Case in point." Marian nodded.

"Although, our flight did have a movie playing, starring our hook...our connoisseurs of style and Rupert Hastings. It was every bit as bad as it sounds. Probably worse."

"I suppose my point is, so what? If it's all consensual, it's not like the man committed a crime. Maybe a small one."

"Might lose the man some votes in his bid for president," Max said.

Marian's mouth made a perfect O, and her eyebrows raised, involuntarily this time.

Tucker had approached during the last exchange and now plopped down in a chair. "Who we talking about?"

"Max just inferred that Rupert Hastings plans to run for president," Marian said.

Tucker nodded. "I've heard rumors out there. He's been putting together financial backing for the play. I was going to mention that today."

Scads and Scarlett came in together, and John updated them quickly on what had been discussed thus far.

"John has found jobs for Zella and Sajja," Max said. "Marian will work on getting them legal."

"You know that you can't fly two Thai women to the US illegally, give them jobs, and then produce a statement from them that Rupert has a kinky side to his sex life, don't you?" Marian asked. "I mean, that'll get thrown out of a court faster than... well, I don't really know, but real fast, okay? Even with a film, illegally obtained, possibly doctored, the defense will shred it."

Max chuckled. "The only court we're worried about is the court of public opinion. We'll leak the girls telling the story to the internet and make sure it goes viral. Scads can you go do the interview with them? Get it on film, but blur their faces. Once the interest of the populace is piqued, boom, we'll flood the internet with the film."

"Gotcha, boss. You want me to do that today?"

"No, how about Tuesday. We'll give them today to acclimate, let Marian work with them tomorrow on beginning their journey to citizenship, and then have you get their story recorded."

"You, uh, got the film? I should probably take a look at it."

Max shook his head. "They're retaining control until my part of the deal is done. Money, jobs, and immigration. The first two are already in the works, but the third might take some time. You can ask them to share it with you on Tuesday when you go over there."

Tucker made a face. "You really think it's a good idea to send Scads over to interview two beautiful escorts?"

"It could be good for him," Scarlett said. "When's the last time you got laid, Scadsy?"

Scads raised his middle finger in her direction. "I don't have to pay for it like you do, Scar."

"Zella and Sajja are no longer escorts," Max said. "They now are—"

"Connoisseurs of style," Marian said.

Max chuckled. "Exactly."

"What's the next move?" John asked.

"More of the same," Max said. "The stakes have risen as now our morally corrupt billionaire seeks to become the most powerful man in the world, which we shall prevent in due course. But the strategy we've devised hasn't changed one iota."

"I meant, what is your next move?" John said. "I know what all of us are doing."

"I'm going to meet with Sevyn Knight and update her on where we stand," Max said.

"She coming here?"

Max hesitated. "Dinner meeting."

Nobody said anything for a few long seconds. Finally, Scarlett said, "She is a fine-looking woman."

"She is a client. Nothing more."

"Sort of like the clients those two Thai women used to have?" Scads asked.

Max stood and walked from the room as his band of do-gooders heckled and jeered him.

* * *

The first course had more flavors than Max had seen on a single plate in some time. He first tried a bite of the Maine Peekytoe Crab "en Aspic", with Satsuma mandarins, horseradish, and kohlrabi. He had no idea what Peekytoe Crab was, but liked that it came from Maine. The waiter told him that aspic meant jellied, and he discovered that the kohlrabi was some kind of cabbage turnip. The horseradish he knew.

His naivete in ordering could've been embarrassing, but Scvyn seemed to struggle equally with the menu. She took a bite of the winter squash velouté, after asking what velouté meant, and was told it was a savory sauce made from a roux and a light stock. After the waiter left, she admitted that the answer had not been very enlightening, but savory certainly sounded promising.

They were at *Daniel* on the East Side, a fancy French restaurant that had come highly recommended by Tucker. Max had sighed in relief when the wine pairing was offered so that he didn't have to admit his total lack of knowledge of wine. That first course had flummoxed both of them, however, and Sevyn laughed with him and not at him, and their shared discoveries bonding.

By the second course, they had covered a bit of the obligatory sharing of life stories. Some of it, Max already knew from the dossier John had put together on the woman, such as her leaving Nebraska behind for Georgetown University before settling in New York City. She had a government job where she input data, pushed papers around, and was paid rather well. Sevyn was thirty-two years old and had recently been in a relationship with a Knicks player, which he knew, but she filled in some gaps, such as that she'd broken it off when she discovered that he had a different woman in most of the towns he traveled to.

She was quite a striking woman, Max had to admit, with her shaven pate, high cheekbones, chill blue eyes, and dragon tattoo rising from her cleavage to wrap around her neck. She was also an inch or two over six feet tall and moved like an athlete. She admitted having planned on playing basketball at college, but, having discovered other more interesting pursuits in life, had decided to drop out of the program. Max gave her time to expand on those other more interesting pursuits, but did not follow up when she chose not to.

"How about you?" Sevyn asked. "Is there a woman in your life?"

"No." Which was a lie. It was not the young models who gave him pause, nor the former Thai hookers living in his apartment on the upper West Side, but a phantom from his past that made his voice choke up. "Once, maybe, there was."

Sevyn looked at him, waiting for more, not pushing. She took a bite of the ravioli with a piece of Nantucket Bay scallop. Chewing slowly. "I was engaged to be married, once upon a time, in a different life," she said.

Max carefully took a bite of the rainbow trout with a touch of wasabi cream and some sort of syrup.

Sevyn took a large sip of her wine, breathed deeply. "Three weeks before we were to be married, we were on our way back into the city from a ski trip to Vermont. We'd rented a car, it was night, and a light snow was falling, icy snow that coated the road. A pickup truck coming the other way on the Merritt Parkway lost control, crossed the median, and smashed into us. I survived. He didn't."

"I'm sorry," Max said. "That is terrible."

"I haven't had much interest in dating since. That thing with the Knicks player was more an exercise in self-punishment than a romance."

"Exercise in self-punishment?"

"I suppose I blame myself for Jonathan's death. If I hadn't been nodding off in the passenger seat? If I'd insisted we stop and get a motel room. I don't know. It just doesn't seem right that I'm alive and he is dead."

Max stared at her. He could certainly empathize.

The waiter came over. "The Day Boat John Dory *Goujonettes*," he said, "in a black truffle 'dashi', with parsley root, and braised Brussels sprouts." He stepped back, nodded, and walked off.

Sevyn looked over at Max and giggled, the somber conversation broken. "I know what Brussels sprouts are."

"Most everything is magnificent, but I certainly hope nobody asks what I had for dinner."

"The place is wonderful, Max Creed." Sevyn took a sip of her wine. "If that is even your real name."

"Max Creed is who I am right now."

Sevyn smiled. "You don't seem to be a party playboy who drinks heavily, dabbles in drug use, gambles, and chases young women."

Max covered his expression with a bite of The Day Boat John Dory thing on his plate. If she only knew how badly he craved a bottle of brown liquor, the adrenaline of betting on the horses, or the touch of a beautiful woman. Just the thought of being touched by Sevyn turned his thoughts to Kinsley, and he found himself shutting down. "You cannot always tell a book by its cover. You might be surprised who I really am."

Sevyn reached across the table and put her hand on his. "You are a good man. No matter what you think, you are a good man."

Chapter Twelve

Long Beach Island, North Carolina

Max sat on the deck of his cottage, sipping a Macallan, the scotch easing his mind, as did the waves dashing onto the sand just a short distance away. He wasn't sure when he'd taken to having a drink, or two, or more, every day. He supposed his vow of temperance had been broken when he'd gone to Sin City and gambled in the Castle Casino for high stakes.

Thus far, he'd given in to two of his cravings, liquor and gambling. As of yet, he'd not succumbed to his desire for sex. That was still between him and Kinsley. But he'd been tempted. Beautiful models. Scintillating hookers. A mysterious consort who gambled and partied side by side with Rupert. And of course, his client, a gorgeous and fascinating woman.

As if on cue, John cleared his throat. "Quiet, isn't it, down here."

When Max had said he was coming down to the cottage this morning for a bit of emotional cleansing, John had invited himself along.

"Simple." Max took a nip of the scotch. "Puts everything in perspective."

Soter sat between their two Adirondack chairs, busy watching an approaching squadron of pelicans, five in number, skimming their way over the waves looking for dinner.

"Probably pretty crowded in the summer."

"Wouldn't know. Haven't been here past March 15th or before October 15th."

"Sounds pretty specific."

"That's the time when the turtles and the people reclaim the beach from Soter. He's allowed out but has to be on a leash. The fellow doesn't much understand the ways of the leash."

John nodded. "Makes sense. Guess that means you haven't seen the hatching."

"Nope. Probably should some time. Those turtles got it made. They got like a hundred siblings to watch their backs when they get born, not to mention a host of humans making sure they're safe. Then they scoot down to the ocean and go chill out in some seaweed for a while before they ride the currents for some thirty years, seeing the world, before coming back home to reproduce. Pretty cool stuff. But Soter? He doesn't care for the leash."

"Sounds like a road map we could all follow," John agreed.

"You ever think about getting married?" The words hurt, coming up from Max's insides and spilling into the air. "Never got much of your past."

John chuckled gently. "No, I suppose not."

"Why not?"

"I guess I've always been an ace."

"An ace?"

John took a long drink of brown liquor. Watched the waves. Leaned forward and scratched Soter behind the ear. "Short for asexual. Never had much desire for sex. Seems like that would hamper a marital relationship."

Max took a long drink of brown liquor. Watched the waves. Leaned forward and scratched Soter behind the ear. "The wanting is not all that it's cracked up to be."

"We done talking about me?"

"Don't know much what I should be saying to an ace. Might be a bit out of my depth."

"Guess I don't know much what to say to a heterosexual sex addict."

Max chuckled. Held out his tumbler. Bumped it with John's. They both took a drink. Watched the pelicans. The waves. Somebody with a dog went by. Soter was very attentive.

"How'd your date with Sevyn Knight go?" John asked after a bit.

"It wasn't a date. It was a client meeting."

"At a fancy restaurant with a beautiful woman."

"Don't think I'm ready for anything like that."

John rustled a couple of ice cubes from the bucket and poured two fingers of brown. "It's been almost five years."

"Time doesn't really matter, now, does it?"

"Can't say that I really know the feeling of missing the touch of a woman, or rolling around naked with one," John said. "But I do appreciate whiskey, scotch, and bourbon."

"What are you saying?"

"So few things in this world to truly enjoy. Why would I punish myself and cease enjoying a fine brown liquor with a good friend?"

"Kinsley is dead."

"Yes, she is. But you are not."

"Maybe my desire for an intimate relationship with a woman died with her."

John scoffed. "Don't lie to me, lad."

Max rolled that over in his head. There was no denying his sexual interest in Sevyn Knight. And he'd connected with her emotionally and intellectually as well. But there was that inner voice that breathed the wrongness of cheating on Kinsley.

"It's complicated," he said.

John drained his glass and stood up. "Life is quite simple, really, when you think about it."

Max sat on the deck for several more hours as the moon rose, the waves crashed, and night descended.

Inside the cottage, John sat in the living room, a book in his hands, held in front of his face, though he didn't see the words. What his mind saw was the recent text message he'd gotten. It was from an anonymous source. He could probably get Scads to look into whether he could track where it came from, but most likely, it was just a burner, and John Little didn't want Scads asking questions about the content of the message.

I know what Mrs. Huffington did to you.

* * *

There is nothing but the best. This was what Scads Miller's dad used to say to him. *There is nothing but the best.* These words reverberated in his mind as he walked to meet the Thai women, former prostitutes, beautiful women— to get their statement about kinky sex with that billionaire pig, Rupert Hastings.

More than anything, the mantra repeated over and over by his dad shaped Scads' life. *There is nothing but the best.* Formed his being. Forged his identity. This was back when he had been called Stanwood Miller. Stanwood, not Stan, had grown up with tutors for everything from science and math to music and sports. But his true passion was computers. Technology. Coding. He was a regular on the Dark Web by the time he was fourteen, not because he was involved in illegal activities, merely because he was interested.

Stanwood grew up in the Hamptons in a mansion on the water. His father was often away on business, and his mother was involved in volunteer groups and cocktail parties. He was often alone, but he didn't become an actual orphan until he was nineteen.

There is nothing but the best. Stanwood went to Phillips Academy in Andover, Massachusetts, where he became Scads. His roommate freshman year asked him one day what he knew about 'all that computer crap', and he'd replied that he knew 'scads of stuff.' The boy had thought that quite funny, whether mockingly or genuinely, Scads never knew, but that became his moniker.

Sports didn't really take for him, nor did the niche of wealthy boys drinking and doing various drugs, but technology continued to grip him. His sophomore year, he hacked into the server for the school and had access to all sorts of private information. He could've parlayed that knowledge into becoming quite popular with the jocks and the partiers, not to mention the young ladies of the institution, but he kept it to himself.

Scads had started Phillips Andover early, and thus, graduated at seventeen and went off to MIT. There, the world of computers, the net, the cloud, and the universe opened for him. He took a summer internship that a professor had arranged for him with a company at the conclusion of his second year. Just before the internship started, Scads went home for a visit with his parents, both of whom he'd become increasingly distant from.

It was May 17th, 2019, when he got off the train, surprised there was nobody there to greet him. He grabbed an Uber for the fifteen-minute drive to the coastal mansion. When they turned into the long driveway, the sight of flashing lights of seemingly every color assaulted his senses.

Scads got out of the Uber and entered a blurry part of his life, his mind initially clouded by the overload of painful information. His parents were dead. They'd been shot and killed along with seven members of the staff, three of whom turned out, were actually bodyguards. The Millers had been killed by a cartel from Mexico.

As the days passed, more information leaked out, none of it, at first believable. Hector and Kitty Miller had been drug dealers, running the operation in the northeast for a Mexican cartel, distributing heroin and then, lately, the same drug laced with fentanyl. Scads was interrogated by a parade of government officials, but in the end, they must've realized his utter naivety. He truly had no idea.

It was theorized that the Millers had skimmed money, product, or were suspected of flipping, even if the DEA claimed no knowledge of any of this. Somehow, they'd operated under the radar from the authorities, their neighbors, their friends, and their own son for years. The negative limelight had driven Scads into a hole in the ground, one from which he'd only recently emerged.

It was the man now known as Max Creed who had brought him back among the living. He and John Little had found Scads skulking in a basement apartment, stealing bits and pieces from various corporate conglomerates in the cyber world. Not much, barely any from any one place, just enough to pay the bills, his one large expense being technology, which he'd immersed himself in ever more deeply with each passing year.

Scads hated the cartel, Los Ceros, who'd been directly responsible for the death of his parents. But he also hated his parents for what they'd done, not only to him, but to an entire population of addicts. Both were forms of abuse of the poor by those with money and power, and thus, when Max had laid out his plan for bringing justice to the corrupt and moneyed elites of the world, his answer was a resounding 'hell yes'.

So far, he'd had a hard time getting to the core of Rupert Hastings. His accounts had some seriously complex firewalls protecting them, and his holdings were hidden in a series of shell companies that was like tracking a tadpole across the Atlantic Ocean. But Scads knew he'd get there. There was always a way. Nothing online could be completely hidden or ever entirely erased.

Scads took a deep breath. The old school method was much harder to trace. A simple piece of paper with four words written on it in black pen. His eyes fluttered to the desk, where that note now lay, retrieved from his door this morning.

You still owe us.

He paused at the bottom of the steps to the apartment in which the two women resided. Scads Miller was the kind of nervous around women that makes your pits sweat through the deodorant and makes you mumble and blurt out stupid things. There'd been a time when he was fairly smooth with the female persuasion. That was before his parents were killed by a drug cartel, and he realized that his entire life had been a lie.

He took a deep breath, climbed the cement steps, and pushed the doorbell on the brownstone on the Upper West Side of New York. After a bit, the intercom rasped into life.

"Who are you?"

"It's uh, Scads, Stanwo…Scads Miller. I'm here about recording a video."

"Who sent you, Scads?"

"Max. Max Creed."

The door opened, and a sprightly young lady wearing a white dress stood there with a sexy, impish smile on her face that matched her equally sassy, pixie-cut black hair. "Well, you are a fine-looking young man. I was expecting some stodgy old fart with mustard on his shirt."

"I'm, uh, well… what's your name?"

"I'm Sajja."

"And I'm Zella." A second young woman, no less sexy and of very similar appearance, but in a yellow dress, came into the vestibule. "Come in, come in. We are so bored being cooped up here. Please, entertain us."

Scads blushed and allowed himself to be pulled inside, a pretty woman on either arm, tugging him along.

"How do you know Max?" Sajja asked. "Isn't he just the sweetest?"

"He's my boss, the one who, uh, found me and asked me to join his band."

"Band?" Zella wrinkled her nose. "Like Bruce Springsteen?"

Scads chuckled. "No, sorry, I mean his group, his team of people."

"Like an entourage?" Sajja pulled him down on a sofa while Zella sat on the other side.

"I guess, yeah, sort of. I'm his tech guy."

"Ooh, so, are you a nerd?" Zella asked.

"What? No, well, maybe…"

Sajja rubbed his knee. "I think nerds are sexy. Did you see that movie, *Revenge of the Nerds*? Is it true that all you ever think about is sex?"

"I'm here, uh, to record you, er, you know, the sort of perversions that Rupert Hastings is into."

"Do you like doing…technology work?" Zella asked.

"Yeah, I suppose so." Scads could feel her breath on his cheek, a deliciously scented puff of warm air. "Mostly."

"Sometimes it is just a job, no?"

Scads hadn't been with a woman since he'd become an adult, some five years earlier. He'd been seeing a girl at MIT right up until almost spring break, and they'd taken every opportunity to get naked with each other. He'd broken up with her before going to Florida for vacation, suggesting they should be allowed to date other people, thinking spring break in Fort Lauderdale was the perfect place to hook up. It hadn't worked out that way for him, and the rest of the semester had been dry, and then he'd come home to discover his parents dead, killed by a cartel they worked for. He hadn't had an erection since.

"Sure," he said.

"Same with us," Zella said. "We work in Pattaya City as escorts because it was a job. Sometimes, the job not so bad, sometime, more difficult, but one does what one must do to get by."

"Do you like sex?" Sajja asked.

Scads squirmed. But he, for the first time in five years, felt a stirring. Two beautiful Thai women, sexy and naughty, were the cause, perhaps the solution, to his problem.

"I like sex very much," Sajja said. "Not always, but yes, often. It feels good. It connects people. What is not to like?"

Zella shrugged. Laughed. "It was even fun electrocuting that prick Rupert Hastings' balls, it was. Zap. Flinch. Zap. Grunt. Zap. Well, you get the picture."

"You had the better end of the deal for sure," Sajja said. "But, as you said, sweetie, we do what we have to do."

"But with a nice young man like you?" Zella leaned into Scads so that her small breasts pushed against his arm, her lips almost brushing his ear, her hand on his chest. "It would be very much a good time."

Scads felt the stiffness.

Sajja ran her hand up his leg from knee to inner thigh, creeping closer, almost touching. "I think you like us, no?" Her fingertips brushed the tip of his erection through his pants.

Scads stood up and walked to the entrance to the dining room. "Maybe sitting at the table would be the best place to get the recording. Once your deal with Max is complete, I'll come back and get you to do, uh, a narration, uh, of the film of you both with him."

"Okay," Zella said. "We take care of business first. And then we have some fun. Okay?"

* * *

For Scarlett, it was a day like any other day. Two hours at the shooting range, two hours at the gym, and an hour run. All by noontime. As Max was at his beach cottage for a couple of days, she'd most likely be doing more weapon training this afternoon, after lunch. After showering at the gym, Scarlett stopped at the bodega on the corner of her street in Bed-Stuy, across the East River in Brooklyn.

It was here that she ran into Jair Otelo. The man who'd caused her to leave Brazil. She was at the counter, waiting for her peach, prosciutto, and Avocado sandwich on whole grain bread when she sensed him next to her. He had a Golden Lancehead snake tattoo wrapped around his left arm, not that she saw it now, underneath his jacket, but it was his kinship to that particular deadly snake of her home that she felt in the suddenly still air of the deli.

Like the viper on his arm, Jair seemed to slither rather than walk and bragged that he could kill much quicker than the hour that the venom of the snake took to kill a human being. He was only about seven inches over five feet and was built slim. His head was shaven, his skin a yellowish shade of black, and his eyes the same.

"What brings you to town?" she asked without turning to look.

"Never could surprise you." His voice seemed to ooze menace. "Hello, Scarlett."

"Hello, Jair."

The man behind the counter handed the sandwich over the deli case. "Made this one special for you, Miss Scarlett."

"Thanks, Izaak." She took the sandwich and walked to the counter. Jair flowed along behind her—a presence that sucked the air dry.

"You on your way home?" he asked.

"Yes."

"Do you mind if I accompany you?"

"Yes."

"Why did you run away?"

Scarlett waited until they were outside on the sidewalk before she answered. "That was over three years ago." Jair and her former boss were the reasons Scarlett had been hiding out in a remote region of northern Brazil when Max and John had come to find her.

"And I have wondered every day since why it was you left."

Scarlett stopped and turned to look at him for the first time. "Because we were going to kill each other."

"I would never harm you."

That was a lie, Scarlett knew, for he'd kill anybody for the right price, her included. "It was the competition."

"The competition?"

"You know what I'm speaking of. Each of us trying to do something even more foolhardy than the other, a dangerous game played with weapons, gangs, drugs, criminals, and the authorities. Who could outdo the other. Which one of us had more balls."

Jair laughed, a low hiss of air, a poof as if out of a toy dart gun. "I think we know which one of us has the balls."

And Scarlett did know. Jair had been the best sex of her life. As the everyday dangers of their occupation as *pistoleiros* for the *donos*, the gang leaders, had ratcheted up, so had the risk and kink of their lovemaking.

"If our job didn't kill us, the fucking most certainly would've."

His laugh was louder, a small explosion of air, the sound like the clatter of pebbles thrown to the sidewalk. "Ah, yes, we were something in the sack."

"It is over now. I have moved on."

"At first, I thought you'd been killed, vanished by some *dono*, fed to the sharks or crocs. When I heard you were still alive, I was angry. Oh, so very angry. But over time, I have come to see that maybe you were right to leave. And that I was the one who was wrong. This has lived with me, hung over me, a doomsday cloud of foreboding. But I was too stubborn to follow you."

"So poetic." Scarlett sighed and rolled her eyes. "Until now. Now you turn up."

"Until now."

"Why?"

"What has made me leave São Paulo and come to New York?"

"Yes. What is it that made you leave the gangs of Christ and cocaine?"

"Would you believe that I am in love with you?"

It was Scarlett's turn to laugh, crystals. "The only person you have ever loved is yourself."

"That is what brought me here. The reason I left? That is because I made a mistake."

"A mistake?"

"I double-crossed *Espada de Deus*."

"You double-crossed the Sword of God?"

"I was paid an enormous sum of money by a new *dono* trying to expand his fiefdom to set him up, but we were ratted out. *Espada de Deus* wiped them out, and under torture, somebody fingered me."

"You are safe nowhere."

"Can I stay with you for a few days?"

Chapter Thirteen

Glendale, Arizona

This was Max's first live Super Bowl. Truth be told, he wondered that it might not be best watched from one's own living room, safely ensconced on the couch, snack and drink at hand, the bathroom close by, and a large screen television in front of him capturing every replay. But he was not in the bleacher seats or with the average rabble, and it seemed to be not half-bad. He was currently inside Rupert Hastings' private loft at State Farm Stadium just west of Phoenix.

Rupert was outside getting photos taken with his celebrity team, Hudson Ford, Senator Todd Dunn, NFL player Cole Smith, and a woman whom Max didn't know. It seemed that the man was revving up the machine to make the announcement that he'd be running for president soon.

A waiter brought him a bourbon. "What is it?" Max asked. He'd just said, 'bring me a good bourbon. '

"It's the Michters' twenty-year-old limited release, sir, a single barrel bourbon from Kentucky."

Max took a nip. "Thank you. Very good."

Taytum Liu sat down in the armchair next to Max. "It looks like we should get to know each other." There were glass windows to the left looking over the field, an enormous television screen to the right, and a scattering of people milling about. "It would seem that we will be seeing a lot of each other."

"Sorry about the straight flush in Vegas," Max said. "That was a gift from Lady Luck herself."

Taytum sniggered. "You did pull that out of your ass."

Max reached over and clinked his tumbler with hers. "To the goddess Fortuna."

"A bit more than luck, or you wouldn't have been able to fill the pot quite so full, Mr. Creed."

"You were the strongest player there."

Taytum smiled, touched his arm. "It was a shame that you had to leave Pattaya City early. I was hoping we might get to know each other better."

"Business called, unfortunately, but here we are."

"Here we are."

"How long have you known Rupert?"

"Ages, I suppose. We met at a charity fundraiser, probably ten years back, hit it off, but drifted in and out of each other's orbits for a few years before reconnecting." Taytum shrugged. "We hopped into bed together for a while, but at some point realized that was not what we were all about."

"And what are you all about?"

"Sucking the motherfucking marrow out of life."

Max forced a smile, taken aback by the intensity, the rawness, of the reply. "And you seem to do that well."

"And you've known Rupert less than three weeks, but already, he has invited you to his private poker game, his exotic playground in Pattaya City, and now this private loft for the Super Bowl, to watch the Chiefs crush the Eagles."

"Chiefs, huh?" Max took a sip. Wondered if cigars were allowed. "Care to place a small wager on that?"

"Straight up?"

"Sure."

"Ten million dollars."

Max nodded. "Sure. How about the National Anthem? You want the over or the under on two minutes and five seconds?"

"I'll take over. Stapleton will probably do a guitar solo that lasts that long.

91

One million."

They might've added another dozen bets, but at that moment, Rupert came in from the outside seats and sat down across from them. "Haven't gotten a chance to speak with you since you bailed out of Pattaya City early," he said.

"Sorry about that," Max said. "There was a bit of a crisis, but I managed to resolve the issue. Pattaya City was certainly magnificent, at least in the short time I was there. First time I've been up on an elephant, and that cabaret was rich."

Rupert cleared his throat. "Tay, honey, can you go check on Senator Dunn? He seemed to be a bit overwhelmed by everything. I don't think football is really his thing." Taytum rose and glided away, leaving the two men. Others milled about, at the bar and the buffet mostly. Rupert leaned closer, conspiratorially. "It seems that you might've had yourself an exquisite nightcap as well."

Max said nothing, just smiled. He'd never gotten himself in trouble by keeping his mouth shut.

"I noticed that you left with two of the young women," Rupert said casually, too casually. "Zella and Sajja, I believe it was."

"They were very intriguing young ladies," Max said.

"Did they go back to your suite with you?"

"Why do you ask?"

Rupert took out a cigar. Offered one to Max. Cut it for him. Lit it. Repeated the process with his own.

"It seems that they've come up missing. The company they worked for contacted me, wondering if I knew anything."

"I hope they're okay," Max said. "We were on our way back to my hotel when I got the message about… well, the issue that had to be handled immediately. I had the driver drop me at the hotel and then told him to take the two…what'd you say their names were? Zelly and Sanja?"

"Zella and Sajja."

"That's right. I might've been a bit overserved at that point, but I had the driver take them wherever they wanted. An hour later, the wheels on my jet were up, and we were on the way back." Max made a note to make sure the driver received a large tip to say that he had, indeed, dropped the two women off at their residence.

"We?"

"National Anthem is about to be sung." It was the woman who'd been outside having photos taken with Rupert, Ford, Dunn, and Smith. "That's something better live than sitting in a lounge and listening on television."

Rupert curled his lip, a hard glint of annoyance briefly traversing his face, before being tucked back behind a broad smile. "Of course. Max, do you know Faith Murray? Faith, this is Max Creed."

And Max recognized the name, if not the face. "Of course, I know of Miss Murray and her lovely voice. I suppose we should follow her out, unless of course she'd rather grace us by singing the anthem to us in here?"

She giggled, and even this had a melody, as if carefully orchestrated. "Today is Chris's day, not mine. Let's go to the balcony."

Max stood, cigar in one hand, bourbon in the other. "Love that song of yours, *I Want to be the Girl in the Back of the Pick-up Truck.*"

"Why, thank you, Max."

The first words of the National Anthem drifted up from the field below as they emerged onto the balcony. Max took off his Eagles hat and held it behind his back. A few people followed suit, but others continued to whisper together, ignoring the song.

As the anthem came to a close, Max put his hands together to cheer for America, for Stapleton, and for the start of the football game to decide the champion.

Taytum sidled over to him. "Two minutes and one second. You won by four seconds, you prick." But she was smiling.

At halftime, with the Eagles up 24-14, Max found himself on the balcony, seated between Rupert and Taytum. People had been milling back and forth throughout, but he'd retained his seat, actually wanting to watch the football game.

"Feeling pretty good about that ten-mil right about now, I imagine," Taytum said. "You do seem to have the Midas touch when it comes to gambling. Maybe some of that will rub off on me."

Max chuckled. "As I remember the story, you don't want to be touched by me at all, or you'll be turned to gold."

"Being gold wouldn't be a bad thing. What's that quote from *The Outsiders*, you know, the book by S.E. Hinton? *Stay Gold, Ponyboy.*"

"Nothing gold can stay," Max said. He wondered about this literary side of Taytum, an interest that didn't fit well with the crassness that was Rupert Hastings.

"What?"

"That line in the movie comes from a Robert Frost poem. Nothing gold can stay. Meaning, I believe, that all good things must come to an end."

Taytum nodded. "That's the truth, sure enough, so we might as well ride the wave as long as we can, don't you think?"

Cheers from the darkened stadiums caused Max to look up. Rihanna, the halftime performer, was suspended on a stage no bigger than a sheet of plywood, slightly elevated from where their loft box was located. She was dressed in red from head to toe, seemingly floating in mid-air hundreds of feet above the football field. There were four other similar-sized stages with white-hooded figures.

Taytum leaned into Max and whispered in his ear. "Red. That gave me eight-to-one odds. I just covered the anthem, *and* if the Chiefs lose."

Max grinned. He hadn't placed a bet on the color of Rihanna's outfit as it didn't seem to be something he knew much about. He preferred to gamble on data, odds, facts, and not on a whim, even if the anthem bet had been a rare whim, if more about building a rapport with one of Rupert's closest confidantes than anything else.

Rihanna began singing as the white-hooded figures danced in perfect choreography. Max realized they were descending to the field where a larger stage held more dancers.

Rupert snorted loudly. "How is that appropriate for national television?"

Max looked at him, taken aback. "What?"

"The woman is dressed like a whore, she's grabbing her crotch, singing *Bitch You Better Got My Money*, while men dressed like sperm gyrate around her."

Max started to speak, swallowed. It was hard to believe that this man, Rupert Hastings, one who pimped out his young models to friends, paid hookers to do perverted things to him—that this man had the gumption to criticize what appeared to Max to be just another spectacle of popular American culture. On his second swallow, Max was impressed that Rupert knew the name of the song that Rihanna was singing.

Rupert did not seem to notice his silence. "There are children watching this. Wives. Mothers. Good Christians. It's utterly shocking."

Max looked around to see if there were some special audience Hastings might be shilling this swill to, but no one seemed to be paying particular attention to anything but the spectacular unfolding before them all, which he had to admit was pretty entertaining. Rihanna was fabulous, the spectacle of stages lifting and lowering inside of the stadium, the entire dance routine— wow. He did have to admit that the dancers did look a bit like sperm and wondered if that was the intent. There very much seemed to be something two-faced about the man, but instead of looking forward and backward like the Roman god Janus, Rupert was a sinner and a Puritan, depending on where he was and who he was with.

Rupert stalked off inside, and Taytum followed to check on him, giving Max a reprieve on how best to answer the tirade about the halftime show. Obviously, an answer suggesting he thought it was terrific was not going to ingratiate him with the target. And Max had to keep reminding himself, the man was a mark, not a buddy to argue with, but a man to smite down and render unto justice, however harsh that might be.

Chapter Fourteen

New York City

"You enjoy the Super Bowl?" John asked as they walked up Columbus Ave on the Upper West Side.

"It was interesting," Max said.

"The game? Or something else."

"The whole thing."

John looked sideways at him. They paused, waiting for the walk signal to change to white. "You getting in too deep?"

"Too deep?"

"You know, in the movies, the undercover guy always has some come-to-Jesus moment as they realize they've become the criminal they're supposed to be getting dirt on. That the lifestyle has wowed them, or some such thing."

The signal changed, and they started to walk again amidst a herd of people. "You think I'm becoming a criminal?"

John shrugged, keeping his eyes straight forward. "Not quite, but you're flirting right up to the edge of it. Gambling. Young women barely eighteen in your room. Escorts. How about drugs? Rupert been sharing some nose candy with you?"

"You know that's not one of my particular weaknesses."

"You know what I'm asking."

They passed a long line of electric bike stations on their right, shops and markets on their left, with apartments on the second and third floors. "Left here," Max said at the next block.

Zella answered the door and ushered them inside. "Oh, thank goodness, live human beings. We're going out of our minds here."

Max chuckled. "Then, I have good news for you."

Sajja came down the stairs to the sitting room as they entered, clapping her hands. "Good news? I think I like good news."

"I believe that asylum will be granted and that your Green Cards will not be that far behind."

Zella folded more then sat on the sofa behind her. "That is impossible."

"Tell us, tell us it's true," Sajja said.

Max sat down in an armchair, and John followed suit. Sajja went over and sat next to Zella on the sofa.

"I have a friend who came to America two years ago," Zella said. "She was detained for six months before being allowed onto the streets, but they told her she had no legal right to work and pay her way. She's been chasing this Green Card for going on two years now, with no end in sight, all the while working under-the-table jobs."

"For almost no money and often for bosses who are pricks," Sajja said. "There is no way that you have bypassed all this American red tape in less than two weeks."

"You met my attorney, Marian Zhang. She is a wizard."

"She came here that first day after we arrived and got us to fill out a whole bunch of paperwork," Zella said. "But told us to not hold our breath."

"I believe she said something about an H-1B work visa, but I'm not quite sure of the exact nature of it all," Max said. "The fact that you had a job waiting no doubt helped speed the process."

John snorted, and both women looked at him. He colored slightly, but then sat up and gathered himself. "And it doesn't hurt to have money, power, and clout."

Max looked at him as if in reprimand, pursed his lips, shrugged his shoulders. "True. That may have helped sway things."

"How much did you give to Mayor Adam's campaign?" John said.

"Not as much as I gave to NICE when Commissioner Castro was the executive director there."

Both men laughed.

"NICE?" Zella asked.

Max looked over, weighed his answer, saw no reason to withhold any information. It was simply a fact. He got his way because he was rich. How he used that power was up to nobody but him. "New Immigrant Community Empowerment. They are a Queens-based nonprofit fighting for the labor rights of immigrant New Yorkers."

"And the new Commissioner of the Mayor's Office of Immigrant Affairs is Manny Castro, who used to run things over there," John said.

"Whatever the case," Max said. "You've been fast-tracked."

Sajja clapped her hands. "We are going to be Americans."

Max held up his hand. "That might take a bit longer. But as soon as Marian gets you to sign a few more pieces of paper, you'll be legally allowed to work here, and the process to citizenship will move forward."

"When will we do that?" Zella asked.

"This afternoon. I am meeting with her after this, and then she should be here by three, if that works with your schedule?"

Sajja snickered. "We'll see if we can sneak it in between bath time and nap time."

"Once that is done, we will proceed on the other matter."

"Proceed?" Zella asked.

Max leaned forward in the armchair. "I will have Scads come by first thing tomorrow morning. You will give him access to the video of the two of you with Rupert, and he will have you…ahem…narrate the scene with his name, the date, the time, the place, and exactly what is taking place in the film."

Sajja fidgeted. Looked down.

Zella stood up, her body suddenly frail-looking, her face tight. "Won't that…won't that whole thing jeopardize our immigration status? I mean, it will show us as prostitutes, rather than fashion designers, and be proof that we are criminals, not fit to be American citizens."

"Scads will blur your faces on the video and alter your voices. Nobody will know that it is you."

"But how will that hold up in a court of law?"

"This is not for the legal justice system," Max said. "It's for what we call the court of public opinion, a much stronger, much less lenient, and far deadlier bench of judges any day of the week."

"And nobody will ever know it was us?"

"My people will know. Me, John, Marian, and Scads, who you've met already. There is also a fellow by the name of Tucker Friedman and a woman named Scarlett. Oh, and yes, my office manager, Dale Allen. That's it."

John shifted in his seat, cleared his throat.

Max looked at him. "And of course, it is more than likely that Rupert Hastings will know it is you."

"Oh, shit," Sajja said.

"We are aware of this," Zella said in a firm voice. "We have talked about this."

Max looked at these two hookers turned fashion designers. Their careers had changed, but they had not. They were just two young women trying to get by. To survive. To live the dream. "You don't have to do this," he said.

"And what? Go back to being whores in Pattaya City?" Sajja asked.

Max looked at John, who nodded. "No. No change. I will still provide you with legal assistance getting citizenship, the promised jobs, and the money."

"And we…can keep this, and not give you the film, not describe what we do, what we did, and not have to put our lives in danger?"

Max looked at her, wondering, not for the first time, if Rupert Hastings was capable of having someone killed. He seemed to be such an affable man. Charismatic. Perhaps he liked his vices a bit too much, and maybe his business practices were abhorrent, but did he actually have what it took to kill someone?

"We will forget there ever was a video," Max said. "It never existed."

"Why is it that you want this, anyway?" Zella asked. "You were drinking and partying right beside the man. Why is it you want to humiliate him in this way?"

"He is a very bad man," Max said. "And the further we dig, the scarier it gets. While in Pattaya City, he shared some information with me that could be disastrous for America, for the world, if it were to happen. I think that this might prevent that particular catastrophe."

"Are we in danger?"

"I have assigned four men, working in pairs, twelve-hour shifts, to watch you around the clock."

Zella nodded. "We have seen them. Gray Chevrolet down and across the street."

Very good, Max thought. These two women were street savvy and smart. "Truth be told, I don't know what Rupert Hastings is capable of. But these men will stick with you until the issue has been resolved."

Sajja looked at Zella, who in turn, nodded. "We are in. The man is a pig. He needs to know that his money doesn't mean he owns the world."

* * *

They were in the war room, as Scads had aptly named it, in the office at Bryant Park. Comfortable recliners, rolling tables, a bar, even if nobody was currently partaking, and televisions now muted.

"Okay, let's get started," John said. "We've had some new developments in our mission. Max, do you want to update us on your activities with Rupert?"

Max shifted uncomfortably. He understood that John had put him on the spot on purpose.

"As you know, I attended the Super Bowl outside of Phoenix as a guest to Rupert Hastings. He has asked me to be a consultant for his presidential campaign, a silent, private, consultant."

Tucker tittered. "Because you are too unsavory for the limelight, Max Creed?'

"A bad boy," Scarlett said. "Best kept in the shadows."

Max noticed a shadow crossing her face as she said this and wondered about it. Mocking him did not usually cause her concern. "Pretty much. I guess the darker elements of the backstory we have created are working their magic. I was thinking that Scads may've buried them too deep, but it seems that Rupert has dug them out."

"And is quite pleased with them," John said. "If his inviting you into his posse is any indication."

"I'm not sure that I'm in his posse," Max said.

John guffawed. "Sure, you are. He's got the bright, shining faces for the camera. Senator Dunn, Hudson Ford, Cole Hill, and I think I read in an online forum that that country singer, Faith Murray, was there. Is that true?"

"She was. I had a nice conversation with her during the second half, after Rupert stalked off pissed about the halftime entertainment."

"Pissed?" Marian asked.

"Something about inappropriate songs, genital grabbing, gyrating, and choreographed sperm dancers."

"Can we just shoot the bastard and be done with it?" Scarlett asked.

"I believe that Faith Murray sings about shooting cheating husbands and leaving immature boyfriends," Marian said. "How does Rupert feel about that?"

"That does not pertain to the stratosphere that he walks in. Lesser mortals, but not him and his ilk."

"What does Rupert's wife think of all of his activities?" Tucker asked.

Max pursed his lips. "He doesn't talk about her."

"I can't imagine she cares too much," Scads said. "Vanessa Pan Hastings grew up poor in Washington State, graduated high school with a GED, and became one of Rupert's models at Hastings' Catwalk at the age of eighteen. On her twenty-first birthday, she married him, and now four years later, has two baby girls."

"And she doesn't care that he's out gallivanting around the world?" Marian asked.

Scads shrugged. "She is the wife of a billionaire. She now has her own fashion and cosmetics company. She still graces magazine covers around the world. Nannies care for the pipsqueaks. She eats fancy food, lounges around the pools of posh hotels surrounded by beautiful people, is driven around by chauffeurs, and lives the life that people dream of."

"Except she has to have sex with a man her father's age who is a disgusting pig," Scarlett said.

"The more he's philandering," Max said, "the less he's around. I get the impression that he's of the old-school principle—wives are for procreating, and sexual fun is found outside of the home."

"I bet she has some dirt on him, though," John said.

"Maybe," Max said. "Maybe not. She might just be a piece of arm candy that he had a thing with, thought that she might make a good mother for his legacy, and then tossed her in the coat room after the family Christmas card was shot."

"Some coat room," Scads said.

"Okay, okay," John said. "Let's move forward. Tucker, what do you got on his finances?"

"Other than the fact that part of his income comes from illegal drugs smuggled through teddy bears?"

Max chuckled. "Yeah, other than that. We seemed to have screwed the pooch on that particular lead."

"Not much." Tucker sighed. And then again. "But he might not be worth as much money as he claims."

"How much does he claim to be worth?" Scarlett asked.

"Nine billion. But it seems that the basis for this might be his branding of the Hastings name. Hotels. Resorts. A wine collection. Casinos. Vodka. Cheese. Shoes. You name it, *his* name is on it, but the kicker is, he doesn't actually own much. How much he does own I can't quite pin down, but certainly not nine billion."

Max nodded. "So, if his name was dragged through the mud, all of these businesses would drop his name like a hot potato."

"Maybe. Just maybe."

"Pour yourself a glass of Hastings Vodka," Scads said in a deep baritone voice, "and sit back and get water jettisoned up your ass while having your balls shocked with a zapper. Hastings Vodka, for the best of times."

The group laughed as one, a bit of the ice broken on what had been an unusually tense gathering. Max was glad to see the lightness return, but wondered about the prior tension. It was unlike this band of people not to make light of even the most serious of situations.

"Speaking of all that," Max said once the laughing subsided. "Marian will be going uptown at three to finish up some legal paperwork with Sajja and Zella, and then Operation Leaked Video will begin."

"Operation Leaked Video?" Tucker wrinkled his nose. "Is that the best you got?"

"Already?" Marian said. "Isn't that jumping the gun a bit?"

"Why is that?" Max asked. "Zella and Sajja have bypassed the asylum holding chambers and have been granted work visas. We'll get them started at…at that fashion company I own on Monday. No sense in holding back. If the video gains traction out there in the viral world, maybe Rupert will back off announcing his presidential bid. Good guys, one. Bad guys, zip."

"When do you plan on…Operation Leaked Video?" Marian asked.

"Oh, come on," Tucker said. "We got to do better than that for the name. How about BASS? Balls and Ass Shocking and Squirting?"

The group again laughed as one.

Max looked at Scads. "Can you get over there first thing in the morning and get the video from Sajja and Zella, have them narrate it for Operation BASS?"

Scads shrugged. A bit too nonchalantly. "I'm happy to swing by there tonight. After Marian is done with them, of course."

Marian snickered.

"You do know," Tucker said, "that you are not reenacting the video?"

Scads was beet red. "I'm just doing my job."

"Are you crushing on both of them or only one?" Scarlett asked.

"They are both—"

Max clucked his tongue loudly. "Scads! You knew that sex was off the table."

"But I didn't do—"

The office manager, Dale Allen, had entered the room, and now he cleared his throat. "There is a phone call for Scads McLovin."

The group went quiet like a candle blown out and then erupted in laughter.

"JK," Dale said, "The client, Sevyn Knight, is here to see Max."

"Show her into my office," Max said. "I'll be there in a minute."

Marian looked at the time. "I've got court, and then I still have to prepare for my meeting with the Thai women at three."

Max nodded. "When will you be done?"

"Two hours max."

"Let them know Scads is going to come by for dinner at six and a movie," Max said with a straight face.

Marian grinned. "Gotcha, boss." She stood and left the room.

"Anybody up for dinner out tonight?" Max asked. "I'm paying."

John shook his head. "Got to catch up on a few things, and then I'm going to a show with a friend."

"Scads isn't the only one with a date," Tucker said. "I'm doing dinner, and then Lang Lang is at Radio City Music Hall."

"Lang Lang?" John said. "Isn't that the pianist who plays the Disney songs?"

Tucker raised an eyebrow. "So, I'm a sucker for pianos and Disney songs. Kill me."

Max looked at Scarlett. "How about it?"

She stared impassively at him for a long moment. "Sorry. Got plans."

Chapter Fifteen

New York City

Marian Zhang strode into the courtroom just as the judge told everybody to be seated. She took her seat in the well, next to her defendant, Jamar Hill. Her co-counsel sat on the other side. There were two prosecutors for the plaintiff, one a young man barely out of law school, and the other a decent enough middle-aged fellow she knew slightly. He wasn't a bad sort, as far as prosecutors went. The judge was soon to become an octogenarian, silver-haired, and white.

Jamar Hill was on trial for armed robbery, a class B felony in New York, and one that could send him to prison for twenty-five years as he'd been deemed a habitual offender. When Jamar was nineteen, he'd been arrested for graffiti. Three years ago, he'd been convicted of selling marijuana, just prior to it becoming legal in the state. Now, thirty-two years old, he'd recently become unemployed and was facing hard times. This was certainly something that he didn't need.

This was the second day of the trial, and her time was now. Marian was not here to beat around the bush and called the primary witness on whom the State's case rested to the stand. Donna Adams had been in her boutique shop just on the edge of the Bowery some three months ago when a man held her up at gunpoint, took the money from the cash register, and walked out of the store.

Donna had followed him to the door, spotted two passing cops, and screamed that she'd been robbed. The two officers, one a white male, the other a Latino woman, came rushing over, just as Donna spotted Jamar walking by. She pointed at him, yelling that he was the bandit, except she didn't say bandit.

When the two officers turned to Jamar, he ran. As the prosecution had pointed out the day before, this was the reaction of a guilty man. He also had escaped detection long enough to have hidden the weapon, ski mask, and stolen money before being captured. For the DA's office, it was an open and shut case, and most likely wouldn't even go to trial.

Then Marian Zhang took the case on, and the DA sent in a second attorney to aid the youngster just out of law school. Marian had cut her teeth working for a powerful law firm in the city, defending wealthy clients before going off on her own and doing the same. An orphan who'd grown up in the system, she was determined to make her 'fuck you' money, enough moolah to tell anybody she wanted where to stuff it. But all along the way, she'd taken on pro bono cases like the one chewing up Jamar Hill. People of color, people of poverty, people whom the criminal justice system didn't care about.

One of Marian's teachers at Big Apple Orphanage had recognized her brilliance when she was thirteen, taken her under their wing, and steered her into a four-year college, where she excelled, and then sent her up the interstate to Yale Law School. She very much wanted to give back to a society that had helped her along the way, but she meant to do it from a position of power, not weakness.

Marian started Donna Adams off easy, walking her through who she was, the day in question, and the events that had led them all here. She called this the Lullaby period. This was followed by the Jolly Chimp period, the mechanical monkey clanging cymbals together.

"Can you tell the courtroom, Donna, what your views on Black men are?"

"What?"

"Objection, Your Honor?"

"Where are you going with this, counselor?"

"Bias is very much a part of the defense, Your Honor."

"Make your point quickly, counselor. We're not conducting a circus here."

"If the plaintiff would please answer the question," Marian said. "What are your views on Black men?"

"I don't have anything against Black men," Donna said.

"No?" Marian raised an eyebrow. She'd already approached the bench. Now, she leaned forward. "Didn't your daughter recently marry a Black man? What was it you called him?"

Over the next hour, Marian shredded the woman's testimony, painting her for what she was, a racist bigot who had walked out of her store after being robbed and proceeded to point out the first Black man she saw, seeing them as all the same—poor, violent, hoodlums with no soul.

Her daughter marrying a Black man had sent Donna over the edge, and Marian called in her family and friends and neighbors and had them repeat under oath the obscene, intolerant rhetoric she'd been spewing over the past year.

The jury took less than an hour to return a not-guilty verdict. It wasn't the magnitude of the work she was attempting with Max Creed. They weren't destroying a billionaire drug dealer who trafficked young women with promises of fame and fortune. A man who destroyed families merely to make a buck, having no idea what waste lay in his wake, nor caring.

All the same, Marian Zhang allowed her heart to fill for the moment, as she watched Jamar hug his fiancée and two young children. She'd done a good thing. The Chrysler Building just down the street was an impressive and awe-inspiring structure, as one of the tallest edifices in the world. But it had been built like so many other things in life, brick by brick, and sometimes you were the architect, and sometimes you were the bricklayer.

Her contentment with a job well done began to spiral, her thoughts turning to her twin brother, one whom she didn't know she had until recently. Marian's mother had left China in 1989, in the wake of the Tiananmen Square protests in Beijing. Her father had been killed in the riots, and her mother had taken young Marian and fled the country, landing in New York City, only to be killed in a shootout between rival tongs in Chinatown three weeks after arriving.

Marian had been thrown into the system without any idea that she had any family left in the entire world. Until this morning, when she'd received the manila envelope in the mail. It held photographs of a Chinese man, along with DNA paperwork attesting that the man was her brother. Of course, the DNA work could be doctored, and the whole story might not be true at all. But what purpose would that serve?

She would investigate the lab from which the DNA work had come, but in her heart of hearts, she knew. That bond people always claim that twins share was the missing link to her entire life, a piece whose absence she'd always felt. Marian had always assumed that it was just that she was an orphan, had no family, but now she knew that not to be true. Somewhere out there, she had a brother, a twin brother.

These thoughts carried her back to her office, where she began preparing the paperwork to take over to the two women Max was hiding in his brownstone on the West Side. That, also, was a good thing. Marian always believed in helping women, especially those thrust into such a difficult situation as prostitution. She had no doubt that with the proper money, influence, and pressure, she could fast-track the immigration process.

After meeting with the Thai women this afternoon, Marian planned to spend the rest of the night, including the morning hours, poring through a roomful of legal documents regarding Rupert Hastings and all his business dealings. Even the smoothest of crooks, criminals, and conmen couldn't hide their iniquitous ways entirely.

If the man's lawyers had missed the dotting of an i, or the crossing of a t, Marian planned to find it and begin building an untouchable legal case against this deplorable mogul. Personally, she hoped that somebody would put a bullet in his head, because prison for the wealthy was a joke.

But at the back of her mind, Marian began to ponder the significance of the presumed threat and blackmail regarding a twin brother she hadn't known she had.

* * *

There were seven of them, as Tony hadn't been replaced yet. Not since he'd been killed in Ohio. Along with four locals hired for their knowledge of the area, if not expertise in weapons and tactics. Here in New York, it was a different operation. Suits and pistols. And everybody was a professional.

They'd been watching the building for three days but had just got the GO command. In a hurry. That's how these things always worked, Jerry thought, sit around and do nothing and then act immediately.

Jerry, not his real name, was the leader of the unit and of the operation. He'd known from the get-go that the order would most likely come to eliminate the targets. He'd hoped that they'd be allowed to go in at night, at the witching hour, sometime between two and four in the morning, when the city was asleep.

As was so often the case, the optimal time was not to be. Instead, the window was at five p.m., the busiest part of the day, their risk of exposure at its highest. No matter, he thought, that was the job, and they were well paid for their efforts. There were not many places paying top dollar for doing what Jerry liked most in the world. Killing people.

The pay sure beat the thirty thousand bucks from the US government to shoot *hajis* in the desert. Three stints and he hadn't been promoted once. *It wasn't your fault,* Jerry said under his breath. No, it wasn't his fault that his commanders had been weenies and did not have the sack to do what it took to defeat the enemy.

His options were limited. He couldn't see himself enjoying anything else. Even if the pay was shit. But then Biden had shut down that shit show, ending the war, pulling everybody out, not that Jerry cared much about the fact that the friendlies were now being killed by the Taliban. He did care that his license to shoot *hajis* had been revoked. But he wasn't going to take the shit pay just to go stateside and be yelled at by pricks.

Luckily, his term was about up, and he separated from the lame duck military service, not giving much thought to the next step. Which was a mistake. Turns out he wasn't good for much more than digging holes for minimum wage. Until he met a guy, who put him in touch with a guy, and next thing you know, he was making a shit-ton of money for killing people. Turned out his commanders appreciated his zeal, and here he was, just a year in, commanding a unit of his own.

The Asian lawyer lady came down the steps of the brownstone and walked off in the opposite direction. Jerry looked at his watch. Five o'clock. They had less than an hour. With a nod to Marc, not his real name, Jerry began to walk down the sidewalk. They timed their approach to the car for the least possible traffic, vehicular as well as pedestrian, slowing their pace to let a couple and two cars go by.

The windows were cracked on the Chevy. The two men were smokers. This had been noted and appreciated. A man came towards them, walking a dog. Jerry paused, took out his phone, and faked a call until the human and canine were past, Marc seemingly waiting for him to continue walking.

There were still people in sight, but there would never be a totally open window at this time of day. Jerry nodded. Go. He stepped off the sidewalk behind the Chevy as if to cross the street while Marc continued. They removed their pistols with the sound suppressors already attached from the slings inside of their overcoats, tilted the barrel through the cracked open window, and shot the two men in the head, twice. Pop. Pop.

The single dame in the unit, Lola, not her real name, went up the steps of the brownstone and rang the bell. Jerry knew that she was going to pretend to be the lawyer, saying that she'd forgotten a folder. The place had an exterior door and an interior door. The hope was that she'd be buzzed through the first door and that one of the Thai women would open the interior door before realizing she wasn't Marian Zhang.

Lola opened the outer door, dropping a rolled-up newspaper in the crack to keep it ajar. Things were going perfectly, Jerry thought with a smile, as he approached the steps to the brownstone. There was the muffled pop-pop of Lola's pistol, also with sound suppressor. Jerry and Marc went up the stairs, past the other mercs standing guard outside, two others at either end of the street.

That's when the plan hit a kink. Lola was in the vestibule, her arm reaching inside the shattered glass of the inner door.

She looked over her shoulder. "She ducked away before opening the door. I missed."

Then the door was unlocked, and they were inside. Jerry led the way. There was a sitting space to the left, stairs to the right. He motioned for Marc and Lola to go up.

The living room was clear. He went down the hallway, his eyes on the back door that was still creaking back and forth, left ajar. Jerry pushed open the door and stepped onto a deck. A tall fence enclosed the backyard. A woman was pulling herself up, having pulled a chair over to reach the top. He shot her in the back. Her body went slack, but she clung to the pointed top of the boarded wooden fence.

Jerry went over, put the sound suppressor to the back of her neck. Pop. She fell. Tumbled over onto her back. Face up. Eyes wild in her head, mouth open but making no sound, body paralyzed.

He looked around for the other woman. Didn't see her. Looked up. A man was standing at a window across the way, staring at him. Jerry waved. Then he shot the woman between the eyes as sirens began to sound. It was time to get out of Dodge.

Chapter Sixteen

New York City

Max was at the Igloo Bar on the rooftop of 230 Fifth with Sevyn Knight, having a whiskey cider, when his phone vibrated. The private phone whose number only the band knew. He'd promised himself he'd only have one drink. He was on his second. Even though the private igloo they were in was heated, they'd also been given red Snuggies for warmth.

The screen said it was from Scads.

"Sorry, I should take this," he said.

"No problem," Sevyn said.

"What's up, Scads?"

"Police. Everywhere. They've cordoned off the brownstone Sajja and Zella are staying at."

Max looked at the time. Six. "Find out what you can. I'll be right there."

"Where are we going?" Sevyn asked.

"I am very sorry, but a crisis has come up, and I gotta go."

"Related to my case? Something to do with Rupert Hastings?"

"Um, yes." It'd been almost a mile walk to get here from the office, Max was thinking, in the wrong direction from reaching the Upper West Side.

"I'll go with you."

He could call for a car, but Uber was probably faster. "I'm not sure what's going on. Best if you didn't." Five minutes for the Uber to arrive.

"I can be of help. I'm more than just some lame government paper pusher."

"We are playing a very dangerous game here." Max stood, put a hundred-dollar bill under his glass. "And you shouldn't be involved."

Sevyn followed him to the elevator. "I am involved."

* * *

It turns out the band did get together for a late dinner at a Korean barbecue by the office at Bryant Park. The place closed at eleven, but Max knew the owner, and the owner knew Max was a generous tipper.

Max and Sevyn had arrived at the scene as the police were discovering the two dead men in the car, both double-tapped in the forehead. That caused the entire street to be closed down. A uniform, for a Benjamin, told Max that there was one dead body in the courtyard behind the brownstone. That's all he knew.

And then they'd assembled at the restaurant to try to figure out what had happened.

"Okay, John, we're all here. Sorry about interrupting your show."

"This is a fitting second act for Sweeney Todd." John was picking at a shrimp chive pancake, absently dipping it in the sauce, and then taking small nibbles.

"How about you bring us up to speed on what you found out from your source in the police department?"

"Professional hit. Our two guys were executed before they went in. Looks like the assailants got buzzed in the outer door but had to break into the inner door. Seems that Sajja tried to escape out the back but was shot three times and killed. Guy across the way saw the whole thing, called it in. The police are getting a sketch, but my guy says he doesn't hold much hope. Too far away."

Max rubbed his hand across his eyes. "Where'd we get the security detail? BeSafe?"

"Yep. One fellow was an off-duty cop. That's going to galvanize the department to find the sons-of-bitches who did this."

"Married? Family?"

"Don't know."

"Make sure they are well-compensated...." Max's voice trailed off, and he rubbed his face with his hands again. What was good compensation for a husband, a father, a son? "Goddammit. We shouldn't have been protecting them with rent-a-cops."

"Don't beat yourself up," John said. "We thought that Hastings was corrupt. Not a criminal mastermind with soldiers of fortune on the payroll."

"No more security details," Max said. "From now on, while we're on Hastings, we hire out only to private firms with ex-military backgrounds."

"I can reach out to some people," Scarlett said.

"Do it. Just feelers for now. But I'm sure we'll be needing them before long."

"Gotcha, boss."

Max turned back to John. "Sajja is dead? How about Zella?"

"They found her passport and IDed her that way. Probably be best if one of us did a positive identification, as we're the only ones in the US who knew her."

"I'll do it. Text me who to contact." Max was picking away at short ribs in a savory sauce, but that night, was taking little pleasure in the delicious Korean dish. "And Zella?"

"My source didn't mention a second woman."

Max sighed. "They don't even know she was there. I guess I should update them on that as well. I do own the building, and they were almost employees of mine as well. I guess I'm the closest thing they got to next of kin in New York."

"What do...what do we think happened to Zella?" Scads asked. This is the first time he'd spoken in hours.

Max looked at him sadly. The poor kid, he thought. It was probably eerily similar to finding his parents killed by a drug cartel, out of the blue, showing up at a crime scene where a girl he was sweet on was dead, and the other missing.

John cleared his throat. "Either they took her, or she escaped."

"So you think she's still alive?" Scads said.

Nobody said anything. Max picked at his short rib. Scads took a sip of his Shirley Temple.

Tucker broke the silence after a long minute. "We have to go on the assumption that she is still alive."

"Which means we have to find her," Marian said, "before the bad guys do."

"Or rescue her before they kill her," Scads said. "If they did, indeed, take her."

"Any more information on that fellow whose pinkie you took out in Ohio?" Max asked, directing the question at John.

"He's been getting monthly payments from a company in the Seychelles."

"Shell company?"

"Yep. P.O. box in a building with a thousand others."

"Can you trace it back?"

"I can try."

"Okay, then," Max said. "You, Scads, and Tucker work that angle. That pinkie is likely to lead us directly to these mercenaries who killed Sajja and may have Zella."

"I'm sure my Valentine's date will understand," Tucker said.

Max raised an eyebrow. "Your Valentine date was going to have a nightcap after the kids' concert?"

"Lang Lang is not..." Tucker took a deep breath. "He was very funny. We talked about a drink at my place. And then you called."

"Sorry. Once you track down whoever these soldiers of fortune work for, we can reprimand them for the indecency of killing and kidnapping on Valentine's Day."

"Duly noted," Tucker said. "My love life takes a backseat."

"Probably not the first time that your love life has been in the backseat," John said.

The mood was too somber for this to elicit any more than a few muffled chuckles.

"Scarlett, make your connections with some heavy-duty protection, and then spearhead the search for the missing Zella. If she is on the run, she probably doesn't have anything but the clothes on her back and doesn't know anybody. She's a stranger in a strange place. Where would she go to ground?"

"One would think she'll reach out to you when she's able, then," Scarlett said. "Or maybe Scads."

Max turned to Marian. "Anything come up when you were there getting the paperwork done?"

She shook her head. "No. Took care of business. Left them promptly at five."

"The eyewitness called in the shooting at ten minutes past five," John said.

Marian's bronze skin paled slightly.

"Good thing they weren't fifteen minutes earlier," Tucker said.

"Thanks, Captain Obvious," Scarlett said.

Max smiled. "Did you notice anybody on the street who looked suspicious?"

Marian sighed, shook her head. "No. My mind was busy making sure that I'd dotted the I's and crossed the T's."

"Well, for several reasons, I think it'd be best if you come along to give a statement to the police," Max said. "Being the last person to see Sajja alive and Zella there, as well as being my legal counsel."

"Billionaires don't go to the police station," John said. "I'll arrange for them to come to the office building."

"Okay, then." Max stood up. "I'm going to take a walk the long way back to the office. I'll see you all there in an hour."

* * *

Max walked west into Hell's Kitchen. Realtors had been trying to change the name of the neighborhood for some time now to Clinton, or Midtown West, or even, the Mid-West. He mused about the need to put a good face, or title, on a place to make it enticing to those with money. The gentrification here was interesting, though, as it was money, but also very artsy, with a strong LGBTQ presence.

His thoughts trailed their way to the dead Sajja and the missing Zella. Two women whom he'd put in harm's way and then not sufficiently protected. Not to mention the two men on the security detail. To a certain extent, they knew what they were getting into, but not really. They didn't have the training, expertise, or firepower to combat what had most certainly been an efficient black ops mercenary extermination team.

Sajja. She was like a young girl in her innocence, her infectious smile, her giggling, which was hard to reconcile with the fact that she was a prostitute who was used by men for their, sometimes perverse, sexual pleasure. At the base of it all, we are all just human beings, Max thought, as he turned left on 10th Avenue.

Not so many years ago, Hell's Kitchen got its nickname for being such a terrible and dangerous place to live. Now, the streets were lined with trees, wrapped in lights, and it seemed quite festive, even as light snow began to fall from above.

The avenue was chockablock with an incredible array of diverse, ethnic restaurants. In just a few blocks, Max passed by Ecuadorian, Mexican, Korean, Peruvian, and Thai restaurants. This last one giving him pause, turning his thoughts back to Sajja, but only now, her face was replaced in his mind by Kinsley. Not the dying bride of their wedding day, but the one of the caustic wit, sarcastic and wry grin, and contagious laughter.

He missed her so much.

Chapter Seventeen

Daytona, Florida

Max watched the start of the Daytona 500 from the outdoor patio, but after several laps, most of the guests of Rupert Hastings' High Banks Suites moved back indoors. The race was going to last approximately three-and-a-half hours after all, and there were many tasty morsels of food and fine cocktails to slake the appetites of the hungry guests.

Rupert had filled half the suite with various celebrities, politicians, athletes, and musicians. As far as Max could tell, the only guest who was not male was Taytum Liu. Unless you counted the other attendees as guests rather than from the service industry, as they were all female. Max guessed that there were ten or twelve young models from Hastings' Catwalk, but it took him longer to place the rest of the women as porn stars.

It seemed that whereas the Super Bowl was considered more of a family event, that the gloves were allowed to come off at the racetrack. Max had taken pictures of several of these women and texted them to Scads, who quickly relayed back that they were also movie stars, albeit the kind that wore little clothing and didn't fake their sex scenes like Hollywood actors.

Max was on his second *Daytona 500 Rolling Thunder*, a mixed bourbon drink with peach schnapps with a few dashes of juice. He thought it quite tasty, as were the Maine oysters, the South Carolina barbecue, and the New Orleans gumbo. He'd already had a nice conversation with a pretty young lady who'd recently starred in *Sexy Teacher*, *Top Guns*, and *Doctor Strange in Love*. As a matter of fact, her call sign in *Top Guns* had been Tasty, and that was the name she now went by, Tasty Williams.

He hadn't yet had a conversation with Rupert. Max wasn't sure he'd be able to pull it off, not with the knowledge that the man had most likely ordered the execution of Sajja and Zella. There was still no sign of Zella. If she'd escaped, she wasn't calling in to get help from Max or the band, not even from Scads, who she seemed to have an affinity for. Not that they'd done their due diligence in protecting her, Max thought grimly, his emotions veering between sadness and rage.

If Zella had been taken, that left two possible scenarios. One was death and the other was life. If she were alive, then it was possible that Max could learn something from Rupert that would help them find her. That was priority one. But he also didn't want to destroy the overall mission in the process.

As if sensing his thoughts, Rupert sat down next to him in the front of the stadium seating overlooking the racetrack behind the thick glass window. The man was wearing his typical blue blazer, what he wore to ride elephants in Pattaya City, to the Super Bowl, gambling in Vegas, and apparently, to a NASCAR race. His tie was red, and his shirt was white, possibly to give him an American flag look here in the heart of flag country.

"Nice turnout," Max said, nodding over his head. "This could be a People Magazine cover."

Rupert laughed. "People mixed with Hustler, sure. Now, that'd be something. That could be big. Real big. I'll put my people on it. If you don't mind?"

Max shook his head. "All yours. How do you come up with your guest list?"

"Taytum takes care of everything. She knows how to make things happen, and it's like I have direct communication from my brain to hers. She knows exactly what I like."

Max hid his smirk. Hard to figure out what the man liked, he thought— blonde hair, big boobs, mixed in with lithe, athletic, yet curvy, young women.

He wondered if Rupert had a preference between the two. Of course, he also seemed to enjoy the attention of Thai women. Perhaps he was a man of eclectic taste in women.

"Something wrong?" Rupert asked.

"Just got an issue I'm working through."

"Yeah? What's that?"

"Been refusing payment to a company down in Texas for some work they did for me." Max picked his words carefully. Words he and John had devised. "And they're suing me."

"Ha," Rupert said. "That's not an issue, that's just business."

"What do you mean?"

Rupert popped a slider into his mouth. "My brand gets invoiced for hundreds of millions of dollars a year. You know how much money I can make if I just refuse payment for six months? A year? More than most people make in a lifetime. Then, when push comes to shove, I pay them." He shrugged. Slid another slider into his mouth. "Or don't."

"Doesn't that catch up to you?"

"Nah. Once they get paid, they agree to drop the lawsuit. If they don't, I refuse payment, drag things out in court, until they cry *no mas*."

"How about ongoing? Doesn't the word get out that you often don't pay, and then you can't find people willing to work for you?"

"Ha. There's always somebody willing. It's like women. They think they can fix you. Up and coming businesses are like that. They're so hungry, they think it's going to be different with them. That all the others did something wrong, but they are special. When, really, they are just blinded by the size of the job and the money they think they're going to make."

Max nodded. "My legal team has told me roughly the same thing. But there's something they don't know."

"Yeah? What's that?"

Max shifted in his seat. Looked around the room. Leaned closer. "They claim to have a video of me acting inappropriately with a female member of their staff."

Rupert leered. "How inappropriately?"

Max sighed. "It was not my finest moment. I was heavy into the sauce. She was a knockout. She'd been flirting with me and I... well, as I said, let's just say I let my urges get the best of me."

"How'd they obtain video?"

Max squirmed. "It was in her office. Which, apparently, has video surveillance. As I said, I'd been drinking, and did not make the wisest of choices."

Rupert nodded. "It's hard to be a man these days, especially a white man. Things have changed." He leaned even closer to Max. "Talk to Taytum. She handles that sort of thing for me."

With twenty laps to go, the group went outside to the patio for the finish. Paunchy politicians mixed with handsome actors and fit athletes, all sidled up with beautiful women and gorgeous young ladies, the fine food and flowing alcohol, and possibly some other chemicals, having loosened everybody up. All, on the surface, appeared to be having a grand time.

With eighteen laps to go, there was a huge pile-up, knocking out many of the contenders for the win, and the race resumed with fourteen laps to go. With four laps to go, it looked like Kyle Busch had it locked up, but then a spinout between two cars led to a flag and then overtime. Max had no idea what overtime was, other than it now appeared it'd no longer be the Daytona 500, but instead would add laps to the end. With a roar of the engines, they resumed the race, only to have another big pile-up on the last lap, and a second overtime was called for. After the restart, barely into the second turn, the third big pile-up occurred, and NASCAR awarded Ricky Stenhouse Jr. the win.

Max thought that this might be because he was the only car left driving out there, or that he won merely because he had the necessary racecar suffix of Jr. to his name, but an offensive tackle for the Texans explained to him that it was decided enough was enough, and that they'd gone to instant replay to see who was leading at the moment of the final crash. Seemed like a helluva way to gain a victory, as far as Max was concerned, but a win was a win.

Tasty Williams sat down next to him with a tall tumbler of brown liquor, which she handed him. Her other hand held a fruity-looking drink. She reached out and clinked glasses with him. "I love crashes," she said.

* * *

Tucker Friedman had been orphaned at the age of three. His parents were returning from a weekend in New Orleans when their airplane crashed. That was forty-eight years ago.

It was not easy being a queer Jew in Queens and being raised by an aunt and uncle who didn't understand him. They had five of their own children and liked to point out that none of them were as odd, loud, or peculiar as he was.

When he was five, they gave him the book *Where the Wild Things Are* by Maurice Sendak. They thought it was a commentary on his wild and unpredictable behavior. He felt it was an explanation of everything that he was feeling, but couldn't put into words and pictures. It was the sixth book of the Torah of his childhood.

It wasn't until he was in his mid-twenties that Tucker came to realize that Maurice Sendak was queer and that the book was an attempted explanation of the jumbled emotions within him that he couldn't express.

Tucker quit school when he was sixteen. Got his GED. Briefly dabbled in drugs. They weren't for him. Was homeless for a bit, more by choice than necessity. Met and had a secret fling with a married man, a relationship that got his foot in the door to become a bond trader. And found his passion. Money made sense to him like nothing ever had before.

The romance with the married fellow fell apart, but not before the man had gotten him a job with an up-and-coming corporate bond trading company. He worked for them for three years, until he'd developed a nest egg big enough to branch out on his own. He had a true feel for how to work with money and investments, but it was tough to make money without having money. It also proved hard to get people willing to invest in a man who hadn't graduated high school.

Still, things had been going in the right direction, even if more slowly than he wanted, when he was conned out of his money by a lover. This was a low moment in his life, and he went into a deep funk for several years before he once again stood up, dusted himself off, and began again.

Tucker looked at the photograph that had arrived in the mail the day before. It was of his aunt, uncle, and five cousins, who were his adopted siblings. It was recent and appeared to be the first day of Hanukkah, as a solitary candle in the menorah was lit in the background. A bit more than a month ago. Most likely, it'd been taken by his cousin Nathan with a selfie-stick, as he was slightly distorted, as if extending a camera in front for the photo.

They looked good, Tucker thought, even though he hadn't seen most of them for over thirty years. They had somehow learned that he was not just an odd duck, but was queer, and his uncle had disowned him and forbid anybody in the family to see him. This had been fine with all of them, except for Abigail, who'd always had a fondness for Tucker. She'd followed her father's ban, but, though she hadn't seen Tucker in person since the decree, she had emailed him every week. For thirty years. And he'd replied. The only family that he had.

The photograph had a red swastika drawn upon it, and there'd also been a note. Tucker sighed, thinking of the note, thinking of Abigail, and wondering about the evilness of mankind.

About two years ago, Max Creed came into his office and changed his life. He'd been put in charge of a billion dollars to invest as he saw fit— and quickly made a healthy percentage gain by making the most of an opportunity in a turbulent market. Like an oracle, Tucker seemed to view the future and get in and out of investments at the perfect moment.

In the last couple of years, he'd doubled Max's money and made a good chunk of change for himself. More importantly, he felt that he'd been given a higher purpose for the first time in his life. He was an important part of a team, where each was an expert responsible for bringing their own pieces of the solution to the problem at hand. Max had gathered them, trained them, and now, they were on their first adventure, their first mission, their first crusade to bring redress to the inequalities of the world.

Tucker had done his part in creating Max Creed, giving him backstory, depth, a financial history to follow. In truth, the man didn't exist, and with a few strokes of the keyboard, would vanish as if he'd never been, which he hadn't. This was important, because when you struck the wealthy where it hurt, in their pocketbook and personal lives, they tended to lash out like a cornered black mamba.

The trick was to not allow the wealthy gulls to know anybody but the front man, Max, and then to make Max disappear after the scam had run its course.

Tucker was currently at work creating a series of shell companies that would be the basis of the bait offered up to Rupert Hastings. That was one segment of the plan that had begun with the simple case of Sevyn Knight's father being bankrupted by an obscenely wealthy man. Now, after Sajja's brutal murder, the caper had escalated into total war, for Rupert was worse than corrupt. He was evil incarnate.

Chapter Eighteen

New York City

Zella spent the first night in the area of Central Park called the Ramble, a large, wooded tract of land straight across from the brownstone she'd been staying in. It was cold. So cold. She had no jacket but found brush to pile over herself as she sat hidden between two large rocks. She had no jacket. No phone.

She'd been coming down the stairs, having heard the buzzer from the front door, when Sajja had screamed that there were assassins there to kill them. Zella had fled down the hallway with Sajja right behind her, out the back door, across the small yard, and flung herself at the fence. She'd gotten her hands over the pointed tops of the solid wooden fence and was trying desperately, but fruitlessly, to pull herself up, when Sajja had boosted her from below, and she toppled over to the far side.

Zella had seen Sajja's fingers curl over the top of the fence, but she couldn't reach to help, and she'd been looking for something to pull over and climb atop to aid her friend, her only friend, when the gunshot had rung out. Zella watched in horror as Sajja's fingers stiffened, the knuckles turning white with strain, and then a second shot, and those fingers had released their grip. Zella was halfway down an alleyway to the next street when the third shot had rung out, and she knew that Sajja was dead.

Sajja, who had saved her life, had boosted her over the fence, and now was dead. The same girl who was the first person she met when she arrived in Pattaya City. Fresh from the countryside, wanting more glamour and excitement in her life than her small Thai village offered, Sajja had taken her in. The same woman who'd had her back for the past seven years. Her housemate. The only person she'd ever really cared about. Dead. Murdered. Why?

It had to be Rupert Hastings who was behind this. It was possible that their pimp, Frog, had put out a bounty on their head for leaving, but his reach was not this powerful. Back in Pattaya City, Zella would've thought that it was possibly just bandits, but not here, not on the Upper West Side of New York City in America. No, it had to be Rupert, that pig, who was responsible for killing Sajja.

Through that first night, teeth chattering in the Ramble of Central Park, Zella considered her options. She could go to the police station, but she understood that against the incredible wealth and power of somebody such as Rupert, the police offered no real protection. Chances are they'd deliver her to the assassins, dead or alive, it didn't matter, not for the right price.

That fellow, Max Creed, meant well, but he certainly hadn't proven up to the task of protecting them. Perhaps, he was overmatched in his clash with Rupert. Zella had seen plenty of men who talked a better game than they performed. It was the most common male trait, as a matter of fact, this confusion between reality and their perception of themselves.

The only other people she knew worked for Max. Marian Zhang, the lawyer, with her no-nonsense and practical let's take care of business approach. John Little, the hulking bear of a man with the kind eyes. Scads, the young and handsome computer nerd, was the one that Zella contemplated the longest, but no, his loyalty would be to Max, and not some Thai whore, even if he seemed quite smitten with her.

There was one other choice. She knew of a former client, a Thai businessman, who'd emigrated to America about two years earlier. He said that he was going to open a restaurant in some place called Queens. She did not know any more than that, but she knew somebody back in Pattaya City who might. She just needed the use of a telephone.

Zella waited until the sun was a quarter of the way into the sky before she eased from her hiding place, straightening herself as best she could. The sun warmed her skin somewhat, and, though it was probably not much more than ten degrees Celsius, the daytime was better than the cold night and the dark. She kept her head down, walking through the paths of the Ramble, until she found what she was looking for, a solitary man reading a newspaper, a cup of coffee on the bench next to him.

She sat next to him, struck up a casual conversation, and asked if she could use his phone. He squirmed, agreed to let her use it for a blowjob, and then walked away after getting his jollies without sharing the cell phone. The next two men were strikeouts from the get-go, but the fourth was promising, and she agreed to go back to his place. He was a fine-enough-looking specimen, well-dressed and spoken, and it was easy enough to trade sex for a phone call.

This fellow, named Harold something or other, was good to his word and gave up his phone after four minutes of romping in the sheets. Unfortunately, the contact in Pattaya City didn't answer the telephone, and she had to leave a message for him to call her back. Which she was not sure that he would do.

Zella spent three days hiding out with Harold in his apartment, leaving numerous messages for her contact. Finally, he answered, and she was able to get the name of the restaurant that Fat had opened in Queens. She kicked herself when she heard the name of the eating establishment—*Walking Street Thai* on Little Thailand Way in Queens. She probably should've realized that was the place, as it was named after the epicenter of Pattaya City's red-light district.

At this point, it was a dilemma, as Harold had treated her well, and his was most likely a good place to hide out. But then Harold resolved the issue, telling her he had to go back to work, and he wasn't comfortable leaving her in his apartment while he was gone. This was done in a very earnest manner, the young man telling her that she was welcome to come back and spend nights with him.

Zella figured she could've twisted the boy's arm to allow her to stay, but he'd served his purpose, so on Sunday morning, she bid him farewell. He gave her fifty dollars and called her an Uber. Chivalry was not totally dead in New York City, just cheap. She gave Harold a false address about a mile from Walking Street Thai for the Uber, just in case somebody came looking for her, or he realized that he'd just let the best sex of his life drive away.

As Zella walked down Little Thailand Way in Queens, a wave of emotion rolled through her like a tsunami making landfall. It shook her to the core, and she stopped, bent over, gasping for breath. It wasn't until now, the familiar sights of Thailand all around her, that the totality of Sajja's death and the last few days caught up with her.

A man stopped, touched her arm, and asked if she was okay. *"Khuṇ s̄bāy dī h̄im?"*

Zella gasped at the familiar tongue. She nodded and told him that she was fine. *"Chạn s̄bāy dī."*

And then she saw the sign. ถนนคนเดินไทย. And underneath, in English, *Walking Street Thai.*

Fat was sitting at a table in the back with some papers spread out in front of him. When he saw Zella, a broad smile spread its way across his face. At just five feet tall and ninety pounds, he did not live up to his nickname, but his grin was quite fat.

"Zella! What are you doing in Queens?"

What indeed, she wondered, was she doing in Queens? "I have left Pattaya City behind and come to America to find my dreams."

"With the blessing of Frog?"

Zella felt the storm cloud cross her face, unable to stop it. "I do not want that life anymore."

"Of course not, my dear Zella. Of course, you don't. We speak no more of Frog."

She wondered how true that was. Back in the day, Fat and Frog had been quite tight. But that was eons ago and thousands of miles away. "I am excited that your dream to open a restaurant in America has come true."

"The timing was not good, right at the start of the pandemic, but we managed to stay afloat, and now? Business is booming. I am thinking of opening another location in Manhattan."

"*Yindī dwy*," Zella said. "Congratulations."

"How did you get here?" Fat asked.

"A wealthy man offered to take me on vacation here. I told him that I'd never been, and he was only too happy to make the arrangements. But he was not a very good man, so I just walked away from the hotel early this morning and came looking for you."

"What are you hoping for?" Fat's emotions crossed his face. Hunger, curiosity, and calculation. Zella could feel the gears clicking as the man plugged figures into an expense profit worksheet. "What can I do for you?"

"I need a place to stay and a job. A real job. Not what I did before."

"You have no papers?"

Zella shook her head no.

Fat nodded, rubbed his hands together, and looked her over. "I am sure that we can work something out."

Chapter Nineteen

New Orleans

T he day started early for New Orleans. Rupert had moved his retinue from Daytona to the Big Easy for Fat Tuesday celebrations. It seemed that the celebrations had barely waned when they began again.

Not the entire entourage made it over from the Royal Sonesta Hotel for the morning parade hosted by the Krewe of Rex, but Max had never experienced it before, so he took Rupert up on his offer to have breakfast at the Z Lounge on Canal Street overlooking the end of the parade route.

Senator Dunn was sitting back in the corner, staring down at the pastry in front of him. Faith Murray, the country singer, sat across from him, looking slightly less worse for the wear. Hudson Ford was holding court with two attractive women at the table next to Max, overlooking the parade route. Max was sitting with Taytum Liu. He didn't recognize anybody else. Rupert, even after having rented out the café/bar for the entourage to enjoy, seemed to be bypassing the morning festivities.

Okay, Max mused, they'd caught just the end of Krewe of Zulu and were now watching the beginning of the Krewe of Rex, King of Mardi Gras, and it was now past noontime. Marching bands and floats, all brightly colored with plumed feathers, passed by underneath their vantage point, with dark-faced skeletons interspersed throughout, weaving in and out like the lost ghouls they were.

"Those two women are missing, you know," Taytum said.

Max started, his attention drawn back to the lady across from him, away from the celebration below. "What two women?"

"Those two escorts you took back to your hotel room after the club in Pattaya City."

"What? Pattaya City? I don't….we did not go back to my hotel room. I had my driver take them home."

Taytum nodded. Took a sip of her Mimosa that had been listed as a Bugsy Fizz. "It seems that you were the last person to see them. That is, according to their boss, a fellow who goes by the name of Frog."

"Did you speak with the driver?"

"He seems to have disappeared, according to Frog. Came into some money and upped and left."

"I certainly hope they're okay. That nothing bad has happened to them." Max pinned Taytum with his eyes.

"I am sure that they will turn up, one way or another. That sort of person often disappears for a bit, only to resurface later, or not, I suppose. Who knows? Maybe they are here in New Orleans."

A group of men paraded by who looked like the Blues Brothers, only their suits and fedoras were purple, to match the traditional colors of the festival. They were throwing beads and candy to children. This was the family time of Mardi Gras; as day wore into night, the scene would change.

"How well do you know them?" Max asked.

"Me?" Taytum raised her eyebrows. "Not very well. I arrange for them to be there when we visit Pattaya City."

"You mean they are regulars? Does that make them favorites of Rupert?"

"Why do you ask?"

"I, well, I just wasn't sure if I should've left with them in the first place. I didn't want to be infringing on the hospitality of my host."

Taytum laughed loudly. "That's rich. You didn't want to be infringing on the hospitality of your host by fucking his whores?"

Max kept his face steely but was rocked backward mentally by Taytum's sudden coarseness. "Well, you said they were regulars, and they spoke fondly of him."

The New Orleans Baby Dolls came past, dancing in single file, looking like little aqua teapots with painted faces and poofy skirts.

"What did they say about him?"

"Only that he was a generous man."

"Mm." Taytum took a bite of a beignet. A bit of powdered sugar remained on her nose, and Max reached across and wiped it free with his napkin.

"What is... what is your relationship with Rupert?" he asked.

Taytum licked sugar from her lips. Looked at Max with her dark eyes. "We were lovers once upon a time, but one woman will never be enough for him. The man knows how to have fun though." She waved her hand around, encompassing the café, the parade below, the sky above. "So, I stay for the excitement. But I do not know that anybody has ever called him generous."

"No? He has barely allowed me to pay a dime in all the time I've spent with him. This café, the hotel, all paid for by him. That seems very generous, to me."

"It is not for free, my dear Max. Nothing is ever for free."

* * *

After the parade, they went back to the Royal Sonesta. Rupert had rented out the entire third floor, and the balcony was filled with his retinue in full revelry. Max found himself drinking Manhattans, Old Fashions, brown liquor on ice, neat, and even a few shots. There was such an excitement in the air that it was intoxicating, like the casinos in Vegas that pumped oxygen through the gaming rooms and brought all your senses to life.

As dusk approached, Rupert led a group to a jazz club, a darkly lit room with an array of horns blowing to a drumbeat with a female singer belting out tunes. Max found himself sitting at a table with Tasty Williams.

"I didn't even know you were here," Max said. He had to lean close to her to be heard. Her scent sent tremors through his body. "This is the first I've seen of you."

"I got in late last night and slept in this morning, well, actually, until mid-afternoon."

Tasty wore a satiny dress of various blue swirls that was really two pieces, held together by strings. From her right breast to her right thigh in a crooked J shape was bare skin, the ties barely holding the material together.

"I'm glad you made it."

"Well, I wasn't going to come, wasn't initially invited, actually, but Rupie came by my room yesterday in Daytona and said that I had to come. So, here I am."

Max remembered vaguely having a long talk with Tasty on Sunday night after the Daytona 500. She seemed to be a bright young lady. He'd asked her why she made porn movies, and she'd laughed, and told him for the money, of course.

"Rupie said you were asking about me."

Max took a deep breath. "I enjoyed our conversation."

"They sure can blow those horns."

* * *

In what could've been an hour or minutes, Rupert roused the group from their seats, saying there was one more stop on their individual parade before returning to the Royal Sonesta to enjoy the nighttime revelry of Bourbon Street below.

There was a gentlemen's club just around the corner that he herded everybody into, where they were led up to a private room on the second floor, where one main stage with three poles held the entertainment. Their group was about forty people. Max thought that perhaps they'd picked up a few pedestrians as they wound their way from jazz club to strip club, caught up in their wake like pilot fish to a whale.

The music started, the famous Mardi Gras refrain spilling from the sound system, *If I Ever Cease to Love*, the adopted song since 1872 when Rex utilized it to mock the Grand Duke of Russia who'd become infatuated with a burlesque dancer, Lydia Thompson, who incorporated the tune into her erotic operetta, *Bluebeard*. Three dancers sashayed their way out onto the stage, colorful boas wrapped around their bodies.

Max was sitting between Tasty Williams and Cole Smith, who was waving his fist overhead and hooting and hollering. They sat with their arms on the stage. A tumbler full of brown liquid that tasted like candy water was thrust into his hand. Flashing lights pierced the otherwise shadowy room.

Tasty leaned into his side. "They are beautiful, aren't they?"

Max looked up. The three women were now topless, perfect breasts exposed as they shimmied up and down and around their poles.

"It is not so easy to be a stripper," Tasty said. "It's a job of work like any other. You must work hard to make money."

"Like making adult films," Max said.

"Hard work, and a bit of luck," Tasty said, laughing lightly, her hand on his leg, her lips close to his ear. "I'd been in the business four years and was thinking about quitting, as I was going nowhere. And then I got cast into *Top Guns*, these being my guns," she hefted her breasts in either hand to showcase them, "and my call sign in the movie was Tasty. That seemed to stick. Ever after, if I mentioned that I was Tasty in *Top Guns*, I was given the role. Three years back, I had my name legally changed. Things have been going marvelously ever since."

"We all need a bit of luck in life."

Tasty kissed him on the cheek and stood up. "This is my request." She stepped lithely up onto the stage from the stool as *Moneymaker* by Rilo Kiley began to play. She sauntered over to the center pole, gave the lady there a long kiss on the lips, and began to sway, wrapped herself around the pole, climbed it, turned upside down, and slid back down, spinning all the way. Her blue patterned short dress threatened to burst loose, but never did, and she didn't disrobe any farther than the scant outfit she already wore, but the group went wild with applause when she was done.

Afterward, they went back to the Royal Sonesta. Out on the balcony, men and even a few women threw beads up to Tasty, and she undid the collar that was the only thing holding the dress up, and flashed her perfect boobs to the crowd below, as Max stood in awe next to her.

At midnight, the mounted police of New Orleans came out and cleaned the crowds from Bourbon Street, the official end of Fat Tuesday, Mardi Gras, and the advent of Lent. Max and Tasty went back to his room for a nightcap. He was not sure that he was giving up anything for Lent.

Tasty fell asleep on his bed, and he pulled out the sofa sleeper for himself. He may've gambled, drank obscenely, and done drugs, but at least he hadn't cheated on Kinsley. Even though Tasty had greatly tempted him and had seemed game to get physical if that was what he wanted. As it was, neither of them had made the first move, and both seemed okay with that.

Chapter Twenty

New York City

John Little lived in a studio apartment in Hell's Kitchen. His criteria were that he wanted ceiling height, an ample bathroom for his enormous frame, and doorways he didn't have to stoop to get through. He didn't care that his bed and living room were the same space, or that there were no guest facilities. John did not have visitors.

Most of his fifty years of life, he'd been a nomad. Wandering the world, looking for enlightenment, understanding—a sliver of comprehension on a level hopefully deeper than the fact that humans lived and then died. He'd started with the Abrahamic religions of Christianity, Judaism, and Islam.

When they were found wanting, he'd traveled to Nepal, climbed Mount Everest, meditated in the hills' region for six months, but his salvation was not to be found there. He gave Hinduism a whirl, but it was much like Buddhism, and his only takeaway was that there were several Hells.

About ten years ago, John had bought this apartment in Hell's Kitchen, figuring if he was going to end up in Hell, this was the best of all of them. This was but a home base for his travels. He'd been in a dive, about four years back, when he noticed a man, drunk at the bar. The man was a mess, disheveled, eyes red, voice slurred. But through all that, John sensed an energy emanating from the man. Even if he did knock the fellow out cold.

John wouldn't go so far as to say that the man, now known as Max Creed, was a god on earth. Far from it. He was a complete walking mess. But whenever in his presence, John felt a crackle of something, a hint of some promise, some potential, something to be achieved with him that might leave Earth a better place. That first day, John had shaken his head, finished his one scotch, and left the man bloody on the floor of the dive bar. But the next day he went back, and the man was there again, in no better shape, but that rippling verve prickling his skin forced John to approach him.

He went back five days in a row, having long conversations with the man. After a week, they left the dive bar behind and met at a coffee shop. When the man learned that John was proficient at various forms of hand-to-hand combat, he offered to pay lavishly for training. It wasn't until weeks later that John learned the drunken bum was a billionaire.

There was a knock at the door. This was unusual. John did not have visitors. He considered getting his Walther from the gun cabinet but decided against. He was more efficient in hand-to-hand combat, especially in these close quarters.

There had been no buzzer, so chances are it was just one of his neighbors, perhaps dropping off mail that had been delivered to the wrong box, wanting to borrow a cup of sugar, or some such thing as that.

John looked through the peephole. All he could see was a floppy-white-wicker hat adorned with fresh flowers perched upon the head of a diminutive figure.

He opened the door.

It was Mrs. Huffington.

The woman who'd groomed him at the age of ten, and then, when his parents died, sold him into a life of prostitution for filthy pedophiles who liked to molest young boys.

* * *

Tucker Friedman considered himself a cultural Jew but not a religious one. That had ceased long ago with the disappointment and banishment by his uncle.

Cousin Abigail had taken a more cautious escape route from the strict household of his uncle, her father. Tucker had followed her through the years. She'd attended Brooklyn College, married another Jew, and the two of them now lived in Williamsburg, in the north, not in the southern section where the Hasidic Jews made their home.

She tread cautiously, seeming to be unwilling to offend her father. Tucker knew long before he did that her daily prayer service appearances began almost immediately declining upon marriage, going from daily attendance to weekly and then monthly. Now, Abigail and her husband, with no children in the house any longer, were lucky to make Passover Seders or the lighting of the Hanukkah candles.

Still, she had not gone against her father's orders that she would not see Tucker, even though she kept up correspondence with him. Tucker wondered if, after the old man died, he was in his eighties now, Abigail might finally break down, and they might be able to reconnect face-to-face after all these years.

Tucker had no such allegiance to the old man's prohibition. Thus, for some thirty years now, as long as he was in the city, he tried to see Abigail, even if from a distance. For the past year now, that took place on Tuesday nights, as she was taking a ceramics class up in Greenpoint, just about a mile from her home.

The studio was in an old department store, the front was glass windows from top to bottom, and the students would sit on their stools and create their pottery pieces using either hand-building, mold casting, or wheel-throwing techniques. There was a bar across the way with outdoor heated tables. Here, Tucker would order a martini and watch Abigail like he was a part of her life.

As far as he was concerned, she was the only family he had. Halfway through his martini, the vase that Abigail was spinning began to take shape, a spirited and challenging shape for her level of development, he thought, wishing her the best.

That is when the man came down the sidewalk from the far side. He wore a long black coat and had a bowler pulled low over his face. He looked across the street and waved. There were only two other people sitting outside on this chilly night. Tucker half-raised his hand to wave back.

It was hard to tell, but the man might've smiled, a flash of teeth in the shadows of the early winter evening. Then he pulled a shotgun from under his jacket and aimed it at Abigail from a distance of no more than a foot from the window, another ten feet to where she sat.

Tucker rose from his seat, spilling his drink in turn, his voice caught in his throat, a warning that would be unheard anyway, a noise lost in the hum of the city. The man held the shotgun pointed at Abigail with one hand, his other making a pistol, which he pointed at Tucker.

Then, as suddenly as he'd appeared, the man walked on past the window, turned left into a side street, and was gone.

Tucker knew not what to do? Chase him? He was no tough guy. Go warn Abigail and let her know he'd been stalking and spying on her for years?

He sighed. Sat back down.

* * *

Marian Zhang knew that she was being blackmailed with the life of her unknown twin brother. She just didn't know what for. As an orphan growing up in the city who'd gone on to become one of the most feared litigators in the state, if not the country, she knew a thing or two about manipulation, leverage, and power.

She sat at the copper-topped counter of a martini bar on the Lower East Side of the city. Even at one inch under five feet tall and not more than ninety pounds, there was a chill to her dark eyes that steered the men away from her before they could start some desultory conversation or offer to buy her a drink.

First, the picture of a man who was her twin brother had arrived in the mail, along with the DNA tests proving that he was her brother. Not an identical twin but a fraternal twin. Plus, she knew in the core of her being that it was true.

A video came today. It was the same man from the photo. Her twin brother. He had a grain sack over his head at the start, a spotlight shining down on him as he sat tied to a wooden chair. It looked to be a dirt floor. Nothing else could be seen until a man in a ski mask with a hood stepped to his side and yanked the sack off before stepping back into the shadows.

"What do you want?" her brother asked. His voice was controlled, but his eyes betrayed his fear.

"Tell the camera who you are."

"I am Wen Zhang."

"Tell us about your family."

"I have a wife and two children. Twelve and nine."

"Who were your parents?"

"My father was killed in the protests, and my mother abandoned me when I was three weeks old."

"To go to America."

"That is what I was told. I was left with an uncle, but he died when I was a year old. I then went into the orphanage."

"Why did your mother leave you?"

"I don't know."

"Did you know that you have a twin sister?"

Wen Zhang's eyes fluttered in surprise. "A twin sister?"

"Your mother chose her over you and brought her to America. She is a wealthy lawyer. And if she does exactly what we ask of her, you will live."

"That's a lie."

The man stepped back into the video and replaced the sack over Wen Zhang's head. He turned to face the screen, his face covered by a black ski mask underneath a red hooded sweatshirt. "If you mention this to anybody at all, we will know, and we will kill him. That is a promise. We will be in contact."

The video ended there. It crossed her mind to ask Scads to see if he could track it in any way, but Marian was pretty sure she knew that it would be untraceable. And she wasn't sure that she wanted to let the band into her secret, that she had a twin brother, and that he was being held hostage. Marian was not somebody who ever let anybody else fight her battles. Never.

Because she had no idea who was making this play against her. Sure, she'd pissed-off quite a few powerful and wealthy people over the years of her career. Three people came to mind as having the money and reach to discover and kidnap her twin brother, and then blackmail her with a video from China. She would see that the two men and one woman who had that kind of hatred for her and clout were investigated. No need to include Max Creed and gang in this. Not yet. Also, she'd recognized the honesty in the masked man's voice. One word, and her brother was dead.

* * *

Scads was pretty torn up by the death of Sajja. If he'd just gotten to the brownstone early, maybe he could've saved them, he thought, but in the back of his head, he knew that he would just be dead as well. He was no fighter. That was the role of Scarlett, and to a lesser role, John and Max.

He probably should be spending his time digging into the intricate trail of Rupert Hastings' unethical and possibly illegal business practices. Perhaps he should be trying to find out more about that drug, Iso, that was being smuggled into Hastings' warehouses. Or his modeling agency for young women, Hastings' Catwalk. The list of things he could be trolling through the cloud to find was endless, but he was preoccupied by the missing Zella.

And he was able to rationalize that his interest in her tied in nicely with bringing down Hastings. The audio of Zella and Sajja was useless without the video, something that would be laughed away as a poor Thai woman trying to shake down an upstanding American billionaire.

If Zella could be found, they could still get the video. He could clean it up, have her narrate the weird kink taking place, and they'd release it to the world, besmirching Hastings' reputation, ruining his presidential ambitions, and severely hurting his brand, and therefore, his wealth. And Scads would be a hero. Then he and Zella would take a long vacation in a Caribbean paradise, just the two of them.

Scads had agreed to come to work for Max a few years back, intrigued with the idea of bringing justice to the world. He had little need for money, other than for computer equipment. And this, Max had supplied him with. Max also had an apartment building in Bushwick, remodeling the two ground-level units into one, so that Scads could live on one side and have his toys on the other side.

Between Zella and bringing Hastings down, Scads was a bit preoccupied when he took a break from his, so far, fruitless search, and decided to walk up to the corner bodega for some junk food and a liter of Dr. Pepper. He passed up the first corner market to go to the one on Knickerbocker, primarily because they carried Hostess Snoballs, the chocolate cakes coated with marshmallow, rolled in pink coconut, and stuffed with crème filling, being by far his favorite food in the world.

He came out of the bodega on Knickerbocker Ave just before midnight with a Snoball already in his mouth when he saw the two men. He'd seen them before outside of his apartment. One fellow was Asian, a stocky man with short-cut black-hair and dark glasses on even though it was night. The other was a tall and angular Mexican with a hooked nose and a scorpion tattoo on his forearm.

These things Scads noted right before he turned and went the other way. The two men were loitering on the corner of Hancock, the street that Scads had come down. He had a pretty good idea they'd been following him. He risked a look over his shoulder. They were coming his way. He quickened his steps. Stuffed the second Snoball in his mouth. Shook up the liter of Dr. Pepper.

"Stanwood Miller."

Scads picked up his pace.

"The Headless Rooster has a message for you."

Scads had a good notion that the cartel that had killed his parents was Los Ceros. Now he was certain, as the Headless Rooster was the top lieutenant of that particularly brutal gang of drug-dealing thugs.

That's when a man stepped in front of him with a knife. He hesitated, paused. A hand grasped his collar from behind. He was jerked around.

"You shouldn't run away from us." It was the Asian doing the talking.

Scads knew that Los Ceros had aligned with a Chinese Triad to open up new drug markets and possibly increased potency of product. This man, then, must be one of the Chinese operators.

"The Headless Rooster says that you still owe."

"The man who killed my parents says that I still owe *him*?"

"Much like our parents are responsible for us, we are responsible for them."

Scads figured if push came to shove, Max might be good for a payment to the cartel. "What is it that the rooster guy wants?"

"He has two options for you."

"Yeah?"

"We kill you here and now."

"Or?"

"There is a man you know who calls himself Max Creed."

Scads grasped the top of the Dr. Pepper liter. A twist of the cap, spray the two men in front in the eyes, turn and dash before the fellow behind him could stick him with his blade. Easy Peasy, he figured.

"The Headless Rooster would like you to set up a meet with the man."

"A meeting?" Scads asked. "That's it?"

"That's it. But you can tell nobody about it. Not even Max Creed."

"What? How is that supposed to work?"

The Chinese triad gangster reached out and cupped the side of Scad's head. "It will be here in the US. We will let you know when and where, and then you get Creed there under some other pretext. *Jiǎndān de.* Simple."

* * *

Scarlett had a pretty good idea that if the Thai woman, Zella, was alive, she'd have sought out her own people. That was what people did in times of crisis. Of course, this put their family and friends within the crosshairs, too, but it was a natural human instinct to seek the comfort of those you know.

Zella had no family that Scarlett could ascertain. She had not flown back to Thailand from any Eastern seaboard airport. It was unlikely that the woman had the contacts to obtain false papers. She did not yet have access to the five million dollars promised by Max once the compromising video of Rupert Hastings was turned over.

Thus, it was most likely that if the woman was still alive, she was hiding out in the Thai community in Queens, by far the largest group of Thai people outside of the Kingdom of Thailand, many of them concentrated in a three-block stretch of Woodside Avenue. It was a delicate manner, nonetheless, to search for Zella in this protective Thai community.

If Scarlett was perceived as a threat to one of their own, doors would close, and the woman would be shuttled out to safety somewhere else quicker than one could say scat. Chances are that whoever had tried to murder her—and succeeded in killing Sajja—was also looking for Zella, and Little Thailand Way in Queens was the obvious place to search. This endangered not only the prey, but the hunter, if these other operatives thought it necessary to remove her.

This was her second day of visiting shops, restaurants, and bars. At each place, Scarlett showed the picture of Zella that Scads had procured, and on the back, Scarlett's phone number, a cell dedicated to this line of search. Also, she wrote Max=5M, a reference to what the search was about. She told each place, each person, to just please hand the message on.

She'd also developed a network of informers, all well-paid, who were to keep a lookout for Zella. Two bartenders, three prostitutes, and a few homeless men. All who'd been promised handsome rewards if they supplied information that led to the finding of the missing woman.

It was close to ten at night when Scarlett walked up the stairs of her apartment building with a mixture of excitement and dread. Jair Otelo was the thing in life that thrilled and terrified her the most. She loved him. She hated him. He made her feel alive. He was going to get her killed. His sex appeal rocked her world. Who he was made her skin crawl. It was a strange dynamic that unsettled her to the core.

She probably should not have allowed him to seduce her, but oh, it was so good. Scarlett had lasted a week before she tumbled into bed, well actually a bathtub, followed by the dining room table, a kitchen counter, and the balcony, with Jair. He was lying low, hiding out from the Sword of God, and seemed truly contrite. He made wonderful dinners every night for her. Slept on the couch until he didn't.

Scarlett opened the door to the smell of *Feijoada*, a rich, hearty stew consisting of black beans cooked with different cuts of pork, supplemented with tomatoes, cabbage, and carrots to round out the flavor. It was her favorite and made her homesick for Brazil. A place Max was on his way to right now, to enjoy Carnival in Rio, while she stumped around Little Thailand in Queens looking for a woman whose life he'd endangered.

"I'm glad you're home," Jair said. "I am not sure that I could wait another moment to eat, what with the beautiful smells."

"It does smell delicious," Scarlett said.

"Did you have any luck today?"

"Not yet."

"What is it that you are doing? Did you say you are looking for a missing woman?"

Scarlett took her jacket off and hung it on the wall. Walked to the Dutch oven, took a spoon, and eased just the right mixture of meat and vegetables onto it, holding it in her hand to cool for a few seconds. "I don't believe I said."

"Yes, yes, of course. This morning you complained that to find her would be like finding a needle in a haystack." Jair laughed quietly. "And I asked what this meant, to find a needle in a haystack, before realizing of course, that it meant it would be very difficult."

"Ah, yes." Scarlett shrugged, took a bite. "Mm. This is wonderful."

Jair handed her a bowl. "Let us eat then, and you can tell me all about this missing woman."

Chapter Twenty-One

New York City

"How'd you like Carnival, boss?" Scarlett asked.

"Missed it." Max's eyes were deeply etched in blood-red.

"You missed the parades, but how were the parties?"

"Not sure I saw much of Rio. We flew in, took a limo to some resort where we stayed. They had music and Samba dancing there the first night and a masquerade ball the next. In the morning, a limo took us back to the airport."

"Who was there?" John asked.

"The regulars. Same group pretty much that went from Daytona to New Orleans and then on down for Rio."

"That Faith Murray singer there?" Tucker asked. "Not much of a country fan, but I do like her."

"Yeah, she was there."

"How about that porn star you were hanging out with at Daytona?" John asked.

Max turned wearily with a wary mask to his features. "Porn star?"

"Scads found video footage of you at the racetrack." John stared him in the eye. "You seemed to be pretty tight with that large-bosomed blonde, who, upon further investigation, turned out to be one Tasty Williams, star of quite a few X-rated flicks and a headliner at strip clubs."

Max turned to look at Scads, who shrugged and turned away.

"Then in New Orleans, he found footage of you and her wrestling on a balcony, or it looked that way, anyway." John spoke in a monotone. "And then the two of you stumbling into your private suite. As far as we could tell, she didn't leave until morning."

"Yeah," Max said. "She went to Rio as well."

The band had gathered at the Bryant Park office. The televisions were off, and nobody had so much as given the bar a perusal. Max, through his fog, began to recognize the mood in the room. Somber. Edgy. Rankled.

"What's up?" he asked.

Scarlett snorted.

John cleared his throat, started to speak, stopped.

After a bit of silence, it was Tucker who broke the ice. "Did you have a good time on your whirlwind tour of pit crews, parades, parties, and porn stars?"

Marian snickered. "Nice alliteration."

"It just came to me, like a Diva singing in my ear." Tucker smiled broadly.

"Look, guys and gals, this is the mission." Max sighed, rubbed his hand over his eyes. "I earn Rupert's trust. Get dirt on him, whether of social failings, business transactions, or illegal activities, and we bring him down."

"Seems like maybe you *are* in too deep," John said.

"What's that supposed to mean?" Max stood up and walked to the window looking out toward the Hudson River and New Jersey.

"Sort of like *Serpico*," Tucker said.

John scoffed. "Pacino was on the up and up in that one. More like that Scorsese flick, *The Departed*."

"Which character is Max?" Scarlett asked. "Damon or DiCaprio?"

"Let's hope we're not the mob," John said. "So, I'm going to go with Billy Costigan, played by DiCaprio."

"Can we stay on topic here, please?" Marian said.

"Yes, please," Max said. "And enough with the cliché movie references."

"Would you say that you remember everything over the past week?" John asked. "Or were you blackout drunk at points?"

"I'm playing a role," Max said.

"You are an addict who has been given the keys to the liquor cabinet," John said. "I thought you were ready to handle it."

"Are you having sex with Tasty Williams or is that just an act for Rupert's benefit?" Scads asked.

Max turned to face the band. "Look, if I'm going to gain Rupert's trust, he has to believe that I am a billionaire playboy just like him. Booze, drugs, and girls. Yes, I've been hitting the sauce pretty hard. I did not have sex with Tasty, but it can only help if it looks like I did. I can only avoid sexual relations for so long before he gets suspicious. So I might have to engage in fornication at some point. Better with Tasty than some eighteen-year-old still in high school."

"I'd say he is already on to you," John said. "It had to be him that sent the team that killed Sajja and made Zella disappear."

Max nodded. "And I was the last one with them before they disappeared from Pattaya City and reappeared in New York City."

"In a building you own," John said.

"What's he playing at?" Max asked.

"Maybe he doesn't know," Marian said. "All he knows is that you took a liking to two Thai prostitutes and put them up in a building you owned so that you could visit them when you liked."

"It is something that Rupert would do," Tucker said.

"Why kill them, then?"

"Because he couldn't chance them sharing his weird sex kink with you," Marian said. "He does want you to financially back his campaign."

Scarlett nodded. "And getting your scrotum shocked while having water blown up your ass might be one fetish too far even for a fellow pervert such as you. He couldn't chance that."

"You should say something to him," Tucker said.

"What?"

John rubbed his hands together and stood up. "Yes. Exactly. Tell him that you brought those two… escorts home with you, hope he didn't mind, but one was killed and the other is missing. Confess. If he has any doubts, that'll clear things up."

CHAPTER TWENTY-ONE

Max nodded. "Smart. It might do the trick."

"And back off on the booze," John said.

"Noted."

"That Tasty is one pretty lady," Scarlett said.

"Adult lady," Max said. "Who has sex for a living. I don't think hooking up with her would be all that ethically wrong." He seemed to be trying it on for the room.

"Only a little bit," Marian said.

"Let's move on," Max said. "Enough about me. What progress have you made here?"

"No hide nor hair of Zella," Scarlett said. "I figure that if she is alive, she'll be somewhere near Little Thailand Way in Queens. Got eyes on the street, pictures in the businesses, and reward money offered, but nothing. I've expanded the search, but…." She spread her arms wide, shrugged. "I think she might be dead."

"I don't think so," Max said. "Call it a hunch, but she's a survivor. Keep looking."

Chapter Twenty-Two

Long Beach Island, North Carolina

T he tide was coming in, causing the waves to pound the shore, the pelicans skimming their way between the rise and fall of the ocean, finding the valleys in their search for dinner. The sun was a fiery orb of gold descending to the horizon, yet another hour from slipping into the ocean.

Max was barefoot, the sand cool on his feet. He had on cargo shorts but wore a fleece over his shirt as there was a chill to the end of this March day in North Carolina. Soter was unaware of this nip in the air or the bite to the water as he had trotted out knee deep into the swirling ocean waves to eyeball the passing pelicans more than once.

There were few people on the beach, one family of four digging holes in the distance, a woman and her dog passing by on the dunes. This was the sweet spot, as far as Max was concerned, the men fishing having gone in for the day, their coolers empty of beer, and the sunset peepers not yet arrived.

A pod of four or five dolphins cruised along in the opposite direction, fins arcing their way into the glinting sun, up and down, their precision finely tuned and in sync with each other. Nature, Max thought, is in balance, unlike my life. It was hard for a man with an addictive personality to be forced to periodically immerse himself, and deeply and convincingly, into Sodom and Gomorrah and come out unscathed. And scathed he was.

The band in the office had been spot on the previous day, he mused, calling him out for diving too deeply into the excesses of the Rupert Hastings lifestyle. Last week had been a swirling maelstrom of human baseness capable of sinking the most seaworthy of crafts, and he was far from unsinkable. He did not know if he could withstand the temptations offered. With booze, he could go cold turkey, but if he partook of sensual delights, he was one and gone, unable to stop.

And hooking up with Tasty Williams or some other woman seemed inevitable if he wanted to get and retain Rupert's trust. It raised too many red flags if Max was abstemious. Hopefully, it would help once to guiltily share with the man that he'd brought the Thai hookers back to New York. Of course, as far as the man knew, he and Tasty had hooked up, too.

He'd been able to come to agreement with the young ladies in Vegas to keep a secret from Rupert, it being in both of their best interests, his because it was wrong to copulate with women less than half his age, and theirs, well, because they were being pressured to do it for their careers, and he was more than twice their age.

Whisking Zella and Sajja away from Thailand to the US provided two solutions, one being their keeping quiet about the fact that Max had not engaged their services, and two, building the campaign that would tear down the brand, wealth, and prestige of Rupert. That had not worked out as hoped.

Tasty Williams, on the other hand, was a full-fledged adult who had sex for a living, and also, it seemed, for pleasure. And he assumed that sex with her would be pleasurable. If not enjoyable. Max understood the distinction between these two adjectives. The idea of sex with Tasty had piqued his physical senses while distressing his emotional state of being.

Kinsley still reverberated in his heart. Married for one second, married for a lifetime.

"I, Milo Sharp, take thee, Kinsley Bishop, to be my lawfully wedded wife, for all of eternity."

"I, Kinsley Bishop, take thee, Milo Sharp, to be my lawfully wedded husband, for all of eternity."

As the ring slid onto his finger, Milo looked in confusion at the red dot on the

151

breast of Kinsley's wedding gown that had not been there a split second earlier, a dot that swirled and grew and became a swirling pool of blood.

"Kiss me."

Milo looked up to his beloved's eyes, which were a mixture of love, tenderness, bewilderment, and dawning comprehension that the end was nigh.

He stepped closer, bridging the gap between them, his lips finding hers, trying to breathe life into his bride, preserve their love, bind them together for all of eternity.

It was not to be. Milo laid the lifeless body of Kinsley gently to earth, his emotions a queer mixture of love, heartbreak, and igniting rage.

"I am sorry, my love," Max said.

He realized that he was knee deep in the water, staring out at the vastness of the ocean, and wondered how nature could be so in sync, and he was so far from that balance.

* * *

When Max got back to his cottage, there was a woman on his deck. For a moment, he thought it was Tasty Williams, then he realized it was the taller, less voluptuous, and more athletic form of Sevyn Knight, her shaven head glinting in the setting sun on the deck of his cottage overlooking the dune, beach, and ocean.

Soter ran up the stairs and went in for a good head rub. Man's best friend, Max thought, had certainly seemed to give her his stamp of approval.

"Hello, Miss Knight. What brings you to my humble abode this evening?" He wasn't sure what he thought of her visit. His mind was in chaos already, and to add the alluring presence of his client to the mess seemed a bad idea.

"Why, Mr. Creed, I was hoping to get an update on where we stood."

This seemed to be an open-ended statement, Max thought, regarding *where they stood on what?* "Can I get you something to drink?"

"If I could use your bathroom, that would be wonderful."

Max nodded to the door. "It's not locked. Bathroom on the left."

He sat down, back to the sliding door, and contemplated the waves. Such a simple thing, really. Steady. Consistent. Like a heartbeat. Soter sat next to him, and then slumped to the floor as Max absently rubbed his butt.

"John told me you were here," Sevyn said, rejoining him on the deck, sitting next to him, with Soter in between.

Max nodded.

"I hope it's okay that I just showed up. John said you have a new cell phone number, but he wasn't comfortable giving it to me."

"How'd you get here?" He understood not everybody had a private jet, a thought that almost made him grin, but he fought it back.

"I've been at Camp Lejeune the past few days. Japanese envoy came to visit. The powers that be sent me down to make sure everything went smoothly."

Max nodded. He had, of course, done his background on Sevyn. Her job was slightly more involved than the glorified paper pusher for a government agency, she had said. In fact, she worked for the CIA in the Directorate of Analysis. He supposed that that could be considered the same thing as a glorified paper pusher.

"Didn't know that you went out in the field," he said.

Sevyn shrugged. "I'm one of the Japanese experts in the office."

"Have you eaten?"

* * *

A glass of cabernet and one of pinot grigio sat on the table to go with the crack garlic bread. Since his first visit to *Catch 22*, up on the main road of Long Beach Island, Max had always ordered this delicious appetizer when eating here. Sevyn seemed to be enjoying the mix of cheeses, garlic, herbs on croustades, her eyes were currently closed as she chewed while mmm leaked from between her lips.

"They got the name right when they called it crack." Max wondered if this had to be added to his list of addictions. Perhaps the healthiest of all of them, he figured, taking another bite.

Sevyn opened her eyes. "Tell me about the girl who was killed and the missing one."

"They were Thai prostitutes from Pattaya City who had—have—video of

Rupert engaged in some extremely kinky sexual behavior."

"I won't ask what that might be or how you found them. Do you have the video?"

Max shook his head no. "Scads was on his way to the townhome when the assassins struck. We had an agreement, I kept my end of the deal, and they were about to make good on their promise and share it with us."

"Assassins?"

"Yes. Mercenaries almost certainly sent by Hastings."

"How did Hastings…the mercenaries know where to find them?"

"I don't know. Maybe one of them contacted a friend from back in Pattaya City who spilled the beans as to their whereabouts. No knowing unless we can find Zella."

"I have certainly stirred up the hornets' nest."

"Rupert Hastings is a terrible human being." Max said this aloud, almost trying to convince himself. "We have evidence that he was smuggling Iso, a synthetic drug ten times more powerful than fentanyl, in teddy bears of all things."

"You have proof?"

Max shrugged. "Nothing that would hold up in a court of law. And even if it would, it'd be almost impossible to connect it to him. I'm sure he is legally about as far from being associated with it as you can get."

"So, nothing tangible yet?"

"We are working several angles. Helping perverted sexual acts go viral on the web to destroy his public image, which should damage him as a credible candidate for president." He shook his head as if to clear it. "Of course, it's hard to tell in this crazy world we live in, but hopefully it will negatively affect him. Connecting him to distributing illegal drugs, again, hard to prove in a court of law, but should help put the kibosh on his POTUS dreams. These two things will also bruise his brand, hitting him where it hurts, in the wallet."

The waitress approached with their plates. An eight-ounce center-cut filet mignon for Sevyn and herb Romano horseradish crusted salmon for Max. Both had ordered mixed vegetables in lieu of a salad.

The restaurant had a rustic décor, wooden beams, solid tables, with a fireplace across the room from them. The waitstaff was incredibly friendly and seemed genuinely happy, making Max think they were well paid and treated with respect. And the food was incredible.

He watched as Sevyn cut into her steak, again closing her eyes, appreciative noises escaping from her mouth every other bite. He took a forkful of his salmon, which melted in his mouth in a savory bliss.

"How far is the drive back to Camp Lejeune?" he asked once he'd satisfied his initial hunger.

"Almost two hours." Sevyn tipped a bit of wine into her mouth. Arched one brow. Smiled coyly. "But I'm not sure if I'm driving back tonight or in the morning."

Max took a sip of his own wine as he contemplated the fullness of that statement. "I have a spare bedroom if you'd like to stay."

"Hm. I wouldn't want you to have to make up an extra bed."

Max decided to move the conversation back to firmer footing. "Hastings has proven to be very slippery so far. And deadly."

"How about non-payment of bills for work done?"

Max nodded. "We are creating a dossier on his business dealings that should damage his reputation when we share it with the media."

"But, so far, there is nothing illegal that can be tied to him directly?"

"Nothing that will stick."

"What about his modeling agency? Hastings' Catwalk? Didn't you mention that he tried to push two young girls on you for sex?"

"Two young women. We investigated, and Hastings doesn't employ anybody under the age of eighteen."

"You still can't pressure women to have sex with promises to advance their careers. Look at Harvey Weinstein."

"So far, there have been no complaints."

"Have you spoken to the parents of any of these girls?"

Max stopped, a bite of asparagus partway to his mouth. "No. That's an excellent idea."

"Did you know that Hastings owns an island in the Caribbean?"

"Just east of the Bahamas, actually."

"He goes there for privacy. For the real debauchery. And he brings an entourage only too happy to experience the forbidden—and very illegal—pleasures offered there."

"That's the rumor anyway."

"Has he invited you to go yet?" Sevyn set her fork down and leaned forward slightly, much of her steak having disappeared. "Seeing as the two of you seem to be all buddy-buddy."

Again, Max thought, there was a lot to unpack in that seemingly innocuous comment. "No. I haven't been invited yet."

"It must be tough."

"What?"

"The temptation of sin swirling all around you when you are off partying with Satan. Which seems to be pretty often." She took a slug of wine and looked at him inquiringly over the rim.

"I spent most of last week with an adult film star." Max wasn't quite sure why he blurted this out, only that he wanted to make sure that all his cards were on the table with Sevyn. It was a difficult balance being a moral and honest person when half the time you were playing the role of an amoral miscreant.

"What exactly are you saying?"

"I am saying that to gain the trust of Hastings, I have partaken of things and acted in a way that I believe to be out of character for me." He squirmed in his seat, feeling as awkward as the words sounded.

"You've been having sex with this adult film star?"

"No."

"Is that the truth?"

"Yes. But I can't rule out that possibility in the future. To convince Rupert that I am the bad boy he thinks I am."

Sevyn nodded. Then shook her head. Took a gulp of wine. "A very difficult position, I'm sure." He looked up sharply, looking for the sarcasm in her eyes.

The waiter came and took their plates. They declined dessert, and Max gave him his card.

"I am not interested in having a relationship with Tasty."

Sevyn snorted into her hand, stifling a guffaw. "Her name is Tasty?"

Max nodded. "She is a very nice woman, actually, and quite beautiful. But I am not interested in her."

"Nobody ever wants a relationship with a beautiful porn star." Sevyn scoffed. "They just want to fuck them and then go home to the docile wife."

"I loved a woman once. And when we made love, it was better than I could ever imagine. I'm not sure that I can ever have that again."

"What happened to her? I know there was one that got away, but what happened, actually?"

Max breathed in deeply through his nose. He rather liked Sevyn Knight. And didn't want his interaction with a porn star to ruin the accord they'd developed. "She was shot and killed on our wedding day."

Sevyn's mouth made a perfect O. Her eyes softened. "What? How?"

"A man whom I had investigated and had indicted arranged to have her killed. He was very wealthy and walked out of court on a technicality. And then hired a man to kill the one person I loved to inflict pain on me in a way that shooting me would not."

"You are...Milo Sharp."

Max had figured that sharing this information would give away his true identity. It had, after all, been on every media outlet in the country. BRIDE MURDERED AS SHE SAYS, 'I DO'.

"Do you want to talk about it?"

"Not yet. Maybe one day, though."

"I'm so sorry."

"I suppose that is why I so badly want to bring down men like Rupert Hastings, who trample the liberties of others in their desperate attempts to grab the meaningless things they mistake for happiness."

"No matter what the cost." Sevyn nodded. "I understand."

The waiter came back with the card and bill. Max signed. Looked at Sevyn. "So, would you like me to make up a bed for you at the cottage?"

Sevyn stood, and Max followed suit. "I think I'll drive back tonight."

"If that works best for you."

"I would like very much to spend the night with you…Max Creed. Just not tonight. I think perhaps it is best to wait until our business with Hastings has been completed. And then we will, both of us, be able to see more clearly what might lie ahead."

"I understand."

Chapter Twenty-Three

New York City

Jerry only knew of the contact as Forge. Forge was not very happy.

"Maybe I made a mistake putting you in command."

"I will rectify the situation."

"Trailblazer is not happy."

Jerry wasn't sure what there was to say. Having only ever spoken with Forge, he didn't even know who his employer was, only someone referred to as Trailblazer. "We will find the woman."

"Before Max Creed and his merry band of fuckups do, I would hope."

They were sitting on a bench in Central Park in the area known as the Ramble. Just to the west was the brownstone where the hit had taken place. The March sun was warm, and the paths through the woodlands were busy with walkers, joggers, and idlers.

"You gave us a tiny window at the busiest time of the day to kill the bitches. It was a shitshow order, and we did the best we could."

"You have one week to get your shit in order. One week to find the girl. And if Creed finds her first…."

"We have a lead that she may be hiding out in Queens. In Little Thailand."

"Find her. Kill her."

"Will do."

"I have something else for you as well. We are going to clean something up for Los Ceros."

"What the fuck is Los Ceros? Some kind of cereal?" Jerry sometimes had a hard time keeping his mouth shut when funny tidbits like this popped into his brain. He tried not to, but smirked, and then snorted.

Forge gave him a look that could crack nuts. "A Mexican Cartel. Their don has asked us a favor. He is sending one of his lieutenants to New York to oversee the operation. The Headless Rooster."

Jerry tried. He really did. But funny was funny. "Does he want us to choke his chicken?"

Forge sighed. "Stanwood Miller. He is one of Creed's band. Goes by the name of Scads. I will text you his address. Put a scare into him. Don't kill him. We might need him."

"Why are we doing work for a Mexican drug cartel?"

Forge smiled. And then pressed a sharp blade to Jerry's neck and another to his forehead. He never even saw her move. "Do not make the mistake of thinking that because I am a woman that I am weak, my dear Jerry. These are deer horn knives, sometimes called crescent moon, or duck blades. Can you feel their sharpness? Blink twice if you can."

Jerry could feel the sting of the keen blade and knew that he was one twitch away from death. He blinked twice. He wanted to swallow but feared that would mean bleeding out.

"You are paid to provide a service. Not ask questions. Not make stupid jokes. And certainly not to fail. There are many more ready to step in if you cease to exist. Blink twice if you understand."

Jerry blinked twice.

And then the blades were gone. He never even saw them. It was like it never happened. But a trickle of blood ran down from his forehead onto his nose, and he could feel the slice on his neck.

Forge stood. "Kill the whore. Scare the preppie geek. Or pay the consequences."

* * *

Rupert walked into his New York City residence in Hastings Heights. It was his building, of course, and he lived on the top three floors of the sixty-floor structure. Well, Rupert thought with a wry smile, technically, the staff lived on the very top floor of the building. The maids, cooks, cleaners, security, and chauffeurs.

The fifty-eighth floor was the living accommodations, and the floor in between was a room for his wife, Vanessa, another for him, a room for the babies, and four guest rooms, not that they were often used. As was his room. It was hard to find fun in New York City like it could be found in Vegas, Monaco, New Orleans, Rio, Pattaya City, and oh so many other places.

He grimaced slightly as the maid took his jacket. She was a dog, probably not even a five on a scale of ten, but he'd allowed Vanessa to pick the staff. She, after all, lived here mostly, or at least when she wasn't in Paris. That was another reason not to come home, he thought grimly, for he had to put up with ugly. The only member of the staff with any sexual appeal was the cook, who was at best an eight, and in her thirties to boot.

"Vanessa," he yelled. "I'm here."

There was no answer. Rupert shrugged his shoulders and went into his man cave, a large room with a wall of panoramic flat screens, a poker table, and most importantly a bar. He waved the maid away, the beast, and poured himself a whiskey. He put the Arnold Palmer Invitational on the biggest screen. He pecked out a Tweet regarding the recent SpaceX rocket launch sending astronauts to the International Space Station.

SpaceX is peanuts. Hastings Patriot plans to put men on Mars by 2025.

Rupert smiled happily. It was complete bullshit, of course. Which didn't matter. People would believe it. When he announced his presidency, he was planning on being the candidate who promised to take America to space, cut taxes for the middle class, support the Evangelists, and protect women's rights. All bullshit, of course, but who was to know better?

"Rupert. I didn't know you were coming home."

Vanessa swept into the room wearing a floor-length gold sequined dress with cut-outs exposing a fair amount of flesh. Her hair was blonde, straight, and held flat to her head with spray, pulled back to expose her Greek-goddess chiseled features.

"I texted you."

"Oh, you know I never know where my phone is."

Rupert knew that to be a complete lie as she spent the majority of her day with her nose buried in TikTok, Instagram, and other sites. Why couldn't she just use Twitter, he wondered, like a normal human being. Especially now that Musk had loosened up the restrictions.

"Are you going out?" he asked.

"Yes, I am finally making it to the *Couturissime* exhibit of Thierry Mugler at the Brooklyn Museum."

"What the hell is that?"

"He is an extremely edgy fashion designer from Paris."

"Is he going to be there?"

Vanessa snorted. "I certainly hope not, as he died two years ago."

"Why don't we spend the night in, honey? I don't really want to go look at a bunch of mannequins in dresses tonight."

"You are in luck. Because you are not invited. I am going with Jacques Rochefort."

"Who the hell is that?"

"Oh, he is a wonderful and dashing artist who is also a Count, well, if they still had aristocrats in France, then he would be, I suppose. He has the sexiest mustache and is built like a bullfighter."

"What?" Rupert was riled, another reason never to come home, as Vanessa had that effect on him. "You are going on a date to a fashion show with a bullfighter?"

"It's not a date, silly, as I am married to you, but he has been gracious enough to offer to escort me this evening. I had no idea that you'd be around."

"But I texted—"

"I have to be going now as I'm already terribly late. Jacques rang up from the lobby ages ago, and he does hate to leave his Lamborghini with the valet as those boys just aren't very trustworthy, now, are they? Remember that old movie, Ferris Bueller. Terrible."

Vanessa kissed him on the cheek and flowed toward the exit.

"Are the girls still awake?" he asked her back. "I'd like to at least see them."

Vanessa paused at the door and half-turned. "I don't know. You will have to check with the nanny."

And then she was gone, and Rupert was left with his whiskey, a houseful of ugly servants, and two baby girls.

Chapter Twenty-Four

New York City

"You look better," John said.

It was six a.m. and they were in the Bryant Park office in New York City.

"Long Beach Island does that for me," Max said. He took a bite of bagel. "But they don't have BB & C kettle-boiled bagels there."

"That was a masterful decision picking those up on the way in."

Max nodded. His plane had landed at five, and he'd had the limo driver swing by to pick up bagels, coffee cake, and plenty of coffee. Now, they were sitting in two recliners looking out over the East River, watching the sunrise emerge from Long Island.

"You all were right, you know, calling me out about…living the high life," Max said. "Booze and sex are too easy when you're a billionaire."

"Oh, fucking woe is you." John grinned. "It must be tough to be a billionaire playboy."

It is, Max thought, but kept that thought to himself. When you have money, all those desires in life are attainable, and it is far too easy to go over the edge and slide into oblivion. "I think I can turn Tasty."

"Turn Tasty?" John smirked.

"She made a few snide comments regarding Rupert, and his sidekick, Taytum. I don't think she's a big fan. Just along for the party."

"That's probably true for quite a few of his posse." John nodded. His

164

eyes were faraway, lost in thought. "That'd be a great angle to follow up on. Who else might not actually care for the prick that much? How about that, Senator?"

"Dunn. Haven't spoken with him much, but I'll see what I can do on my next adventure, if there is one."

"Oh, he'll have you back. You have too much money to walk away from."

"Unless he knows we were trying to turn Zella and Sajja on him. His suspicions might be up."

"That's why you need to do damage control like we said. Next time you see him, confess you brought the two Thai prostitutes to America because they did things for you nobody ever has before. Hint at some weird kink of your own, and then lament that they were killed in a home invasion."

"One killed. One missing."

"Out of sight, out of mind. Don't let on that you are looking for her."

"Let's say it was Rupert who sent that team to kill them. How'd *he* know where they were?"

John shook his head. "Good question."

"You think they told somebody back in Thailand? Somebody who passed that information onto Rupert?"

"Could be." John shifted his feet. Took a sip of coffee. Stood up and went closer to the window. "Gotta tell you something."

"Yeah? What's that?"

John cleared his throat. "You know how I told you I was an ace?"

"Sure." Max spoke gently. "That you were asexual."

"That might not be absolutely true."

Max pursed his lips but kept his mouth shut. John Little's broad back faced him from the window. The orange tip of the sun had just emerged to the east, illuminating Brooklyn and the river in its glow.

"Aces have never had an interest in sex. My issue might be more psychological. When I was ten, I gained the attention of a neighbor lady. My parents were drug addicts living here in the city. I was an only child and would be left home for days at a time on my own. On one of those occasions, I started knocking on doors in my apartment complex. There was no food, and I was starving. After five or six attempts, one of those doors opened. A woman, Mrs. Huffington, invited me in and fed me. This became a regular pattern. When my parents disappeared, I'd go to her house, and she'd feed me."

There was a pause, and Max realized that John was getting choked up, something he'd never seen or heard from this seemingly impervious man.

After a minute, he continued, "One day she insisted that I use her shower to clean up, and rightfully so, as I was quite dirty. This, too, became a pattern. Eat, shower, scrub with soap. At some point, she started coming into the shower with me to help me clean."

Max imagined the ten-year-old boy in the shower with a grown woman and wanted to ask her age, but didn't want to interrupt.

"And of course, one thing led to another, and I began to engage in sexual acts with Mrs. Huffington. When I was ten." John turned from the window and stared Max in the eye. "This went on for more than a year, less than two, because when I was twelve, my parents died in a drug deal gone bad, or so Mrs. Huffington told me. She hid me from the police so that I wouldn't be taken into foster care. Then one day we went to a place in the Bronx where she left me for my own safety, or so she said. I now realize that she'd sold me into sexual slavery as a plaything for male pedophiles who liked little boys."

This, then, Max thought, was why John had targeted two human trafficking rings for their first two missions. The one in Dhaka with just the two of them, and then the one in Brazil with Scarlett. "Why are you telling me this now?"

"The other day, Mrs. Huffington came to see me."

"What?"

"She is a little old lady now, with white hair, and frail of body."

"What did she want?"

"To have tea."

"What did you do?"

"I served her tea while devising schemes on how to kill her and dispose of the body."

CHAPTER TWENTY-FOUR

"And?"

"We had tea, crackers, and then I let her walk out."

* * *

"Got a minute to chat, Tuck?" Max had lightly knocked on his office door just after nine.

Tucker looked up with surprise. "Hey, I didn't even know you were back from Long Beach Island."

"Flew in this morning. There's bagels and coffee in the conference room if you want any."

Tucker patted his ample belly. "No to the bagels, but once that morning smoothie works its way through my system, I might hit up a cup of the java."

Max sat down across from him. "Any more from Mr. Right? The fellow that I ruined your date with...after the girls were attacked."

"You sure they didn't just take her, boss? I mean, why do we even think she escaped? That's she's alive? Scarlett hasn't turned up any trace of her. They probably took her somewhere to torture her to find out what you know, and now they know, and you are up shit's creek."

"You seem to be avoiding talking about Mr. Right."

"We have a date tonight. Frankly, I'm surprised he agreed to see me."

"You didn't tell him that a mercenary team killed a woman you were helping to hide out, now, did you?" Max smiled wryly.

"I probably should have. No. I told him that my mother was in a car accident." Tucker raised his hands in despair. "Now, if things go well, and we hit it off, how do I explain away the fact that my mother is dead?"

Max grinned. "I guess with a tear in your eye, you tell him that she didn't survive the car wreck."

"And studiously ignore that this happened some forty years ago." Tucker nodded. "I like it. A relationship built upon a lie is a sure-fire bet for success."

"Once we exact justice upon Rupert Hastings, you can come clean about everything. He'll think you are a hero and will forgive you for everything."

Tucker sighed. "I think I found some dirt on Rupert. He pays quite a bit of money for NDAs. Women. Employees. Payoff to keep their mouths shut. As well as settlements out of court for non-payment of goods. But the thing is, there is no record of where this money comes from. Meaning he isn't paying taxes on it."

"Tax fraud."

"Tax evasion. Slightly different. More intent. Higher conviction rate. If proven, he'll likely face a fine and three to five years in jail."

"That's a great start. Put it all together, and we'll cobble it with a few other things and send the bastard off for an extended vacation on an island slightly less of a paradise than the one he owns."

Max stood up and started for the door.

Tucker cleared his throat.

Max paused and turned back.

"Can you close the door?" Tucker said. "I have one more thing to speak to you about."

Max shut the door and came back to sit down.

"Somebody is threatening my cousin," Tucker said. "The only family that I care about."

* * *

Max had just gotten back to his own office when his cell phone buzzed. Rupert Hastings.

"Rupert."

"Max. You got a second?"

"I was meaning to call you, anyway. Something I have to tell you." Max shut the door and went and sat down at his desk. "But I can get to that after you say your piece."

"No. Go ahead." Rupert's voice had a tinge of arrogance, mixed with condescension, even when he was placating. "What's on your mind?"

"You know those two Thai women I left the club with in Pattaya City?"

"Sure. You know they were whores, right?"

Max gritted his teeth. "Yeah, quite an interesting pair, actually. They were really something."

"Ah, I thought there might've been a bit more than you were letting on. You didn't just send them packing with the driver after all, did you?"

"No. As I said, they were quite the adventurous pair. So much so that I brought them back to New York with me."

Rupert made a sound between a scoff and a snort. "Ha. You brought two Thai hookers home with you. That's rich."

"I, um, put them up in one of my properties so that I could visit them and, well, you know..." He cleared his throat awkwardly. "Only, the shit hit the fan. The worst of bad luck. They were victims of a home invasion."

There was silence on the line. Then Rupert cleared his throat. "A home invasion? Were they hurt?"

"One was killed, and the perpetrators took the other one, Zella, with them."

"That's terrible."

"You don't think that it could've been their...pimp, do you? Angry that they left him?"

"Frog Boon-Nam? No, I don't think he'd do that. Or have the reach overseas to be able to, even if he wanted. I can ask around, though, if you want. Don't imagine Zella would do you much good even if you find her. The talent of those two was in their being two of them." Rupert laughed loudly. "If you know what I mean."

Max underlined the name he'd written. Should be easy enough to track down a pimp named Frog Boon-Nam. "No, don't worry about it. Just want to make sure she doesn't pop up, as I had the fellow in charge of my rental and sale properties tell the authorities that the two must've broken in and were squatting. Wouldn't want her showing up and wrecking that."

Rupert laughed again. "Doubt anybody cares much about a couple of whores anyways."

Max winced, ran his tongue over his teeth. "What'd you have on your mind?"

"Was wondering if you might want to get away to a tropical paradise for a few days next week."

169

"Where'd you have in mind?"

"I own an island that I escape to every once in a while. Bring a few friends. Plenty of poontang and good liquor. Sit by the pool and enjoy carnal pleasures. You up for it?"

"Absolutely."

"Great. I'll text you the details."

The phone went dead just as there was a knock on the door. It opened, and Marian popped her head inside.

"Max. You got a second?" she asked.

"Sure. Come on in. You just getting here?"

"I had court this morning."

Max nodded. She was the only one of the band who still had a day job. "You win?"

"Not yet, but I will." Marian plopped into a chair across from Max. "I just wanted to update you on my investigation into Hastings' legal cases."

"What do you got?"

"Currently, there are five suits being brought against him. Three businesses that claim he hasn't paid them for work done, and two women who say he pressured them into performing sexual acts. I have contacted their attorneys and offered them support in the form of a team of lawyers and researchers dedicated to the cases. So far, four of them have agreed, and the other one should be back to me today."

"Winnable?"

"The non-payment to the businesses should be easy enough, but we will also be attaching a huge figure for emotional damage caused, and that might be a bit of a stretch. It will at the very least be an irritant to him. The two women? Tough to tell. Classic case of he said she said. And he's a billionaire, and they're...well, one is a stripper and the other one is a B-list actress in late-night cable shows."

"Tucker has a lead on Rupert evading taxes with payoff money to various women to keep their mouths shut about...well, most likely, sexual indiscretions of some sort. We package that together with their legal claims, it might give it some more credence."

"Great. I'll get together with Tuck and see if we can't stitch something together that sticks."

Marian stood up and walked out the door.

*　*　*

It was almost eight o'clock when Scads barged into the office.

"I think I got something, boss."

Max looked up, his eyes bleary from the computer. "Like a cold or some kind of virus?"

Scads looked confused, shook his head, muttered something under his breath. "No. A lead where Zella might be."

"Yeah? Where?"

"I hacked into the computer of that Thai pimp you gave me. Frog Boon-Nam. Not easy, mind you, but people are idiots. I did a—"

"I don't need the computer mumbo jumbo," Max said. "Let's skip right to what you found."

Scads looked hurt, but apparently his news was too exciting to sit on. "Frog kept a record of all the men who were clients of Sajja and Zella. There were several regulars, but one lives here now. And has a business, a restaurant. *Walking Street Thai*. In Queens. On Little Thailand Way."

Max nodded. Scarlett had been on the right trail. If Zella was truly still alive and on the run, this must be where she was. And she must be keeping a real low profile for Scarlett not to have found her.

"What's the fellow's name?"

"Fat Thong Di."

"Excellent work."

Scads fidgeted in the chair.

"Is there something else?" Max asked.

"It's, uh, well, you know how my parents were killed?"

Max nodded. "Yes."

"It's, um, believed by the feds to have been the Los Ceros cartel. A lieutenant in the gang that goes by the nickname the Headless Rooster."

"Yes. I know all that." Max shifted with guilt. Perhaps, he thought, he should've been using his vast wealth to track down the man responsible for killing Scads' parents. But a Mexican lieutenant in charge of an incredibly powerful cartel was in a different league than a billionaire playboy. Or so he'd thought, until a professional team of killers ended Sajja's life so violently. "Go on."

"They contacted me."

"Los Ceros?"

"A bit back there was a note on my door saying that I still owed them, and then, just recently, well, more like a week, or maybe ten—"

"Who contacted you, Scads?"

"It was an Asian guy who did the talking while another held a knife to my throat."

"A Mexican?"

Scads nodded yes. "I've been digging into Los Ceros. They have teamed up with a Chinese triad, 9H in Shanghai, to combine their heroin with the synthetic Iso that the triad manufactures in Asia."

Max drummed his fingers on the desk. "That's the triad associated with Huang Worldwide that was sending stuffed toys full of drugs to Hastings' warehouse in Ohio?"

Scads nodded. "The same."

"So, what makes you think that this Chinese fellow was working for Los Ceros?"

"Because he wants me to lure you into a trap so that the Headless Rooster can kill you. And then my parents' debt will be paid, and they'll leave me alone."

Chapter Twenty-Five

New York City

"What's the play here?" Scarlett asked. They were sitting at an outdoor table on Little Thailand Way in Queens, just down from the restaurant, Walking Street Thai, owned by Fat Thong Di.

Max took a sip of tea. What was the play, indeed, he wondered. "We try to talk to her. Let her know that we can protect her. Apologize for our lapse."

"We don't always get second chances in life, do we?"

"As long as we survive, the opportunity of a second chance always exists. We are both living proof of that. We must impress upon Zella that we are her best chance at survival."

"Are you sure that she's here?"

Max shook his head. "No. The owner is a former client from Pattaya City. Seems like a connection she might run to if in trouble."

"Speaking of connections that people return to when things go to shit," Scarlett said, pausing to take a sip of her tea. "I got something to tell you."

It had been a day of revelation, Max thought, wondering what was to follow.

"You know what I did in São Paulo before emigrating to the States, right?"

Max nodded. "You were an enforcer for a don down there. The Sword of God. In the land of Christ and Cocaine."

"I did some pretty bad things. Certainly nothing that I'm proud of. And I

had one other *pistoleiro* that I worked very closely with. We were a team."
Scarlett cleared her throat. "We were lovers."

"Jair Otelo."

The normally passive face of Scarlett winced slightly. "I never told you
his name."

Max said nothing. It was his business to know. And she should know that.
She did know that.

Scarlett nodded. "Yes. Jair Otelo. Well, the thing is, he is here. Staying
with me. Hiding out from the Sword of God, who he double-crossed."

"Is this a problem?"

"I don't know."

"Two people. Man and a woman. Ten o'clock." Max spoke in a hushed
whisper. "Do they look out of place?"

Scarlett turned her head. A man with a buzz cut and in a cheap suit and
a woman in a jumper were coming down the sidewalk. They turned into
Walking Street Thai, disappearing through the door. "The Boy Scout had a
pistol in a shoulder holster."

"They look like mercs to you?"

"Yep."

Max stood up. "Let's go." He dropped a twenty on the table.

It was hard to be inconspicuous, Max thought, if you were two tall people,
one very white, and one very Black, in Little Thailand. Especially if you
were walking with purpose.

They reached the front of the restaurant. Scarlett pulled the door open,
and Max went through. Even at this late hour, there was a good-sized crowd
eating dinner. A man was standing at the host podium with a worried look
on his face, looking toward the back of the room. Max followed his eyes
and saw the two mercenaries pushing a man in front of them through a
pair of swinging doors. He recognized the man from the picture Scads had
texted him. It was Fat Thong Di.

He turned partially to Scarlett to point them out and saw a man step
behind her with a pistol pointed at the back of her head. Max's eyes going
wide was all the warning that Scarlett needed as she wheeled around, leading

with an elbow into the solar plexus of the man. His gun went off into the ceiling as he gasped and bent over.

Several people screamed while others looked confused at the loud bang. Scarlett drove the flat of her hand into the man's neck, and the gun fell from his hand.

Max, realizing that she had the situation well in hand, sprinted across the room as diners dove to the floor, stood to flee, or just milled about in utter confusion. He had to force his way past people in the bedlam of the dining room, fighting his way to the back of the room, his gun in hand, yelling at people to get down, to move, to get out of the way.

He barged through the swinging doors, pausing with his Luger in both hands in front of him, crouched, the pistol sweeping across the kitchen. Cooks, assistants, dishwashers, waiters, and waitresses looked at him and screamed, some dropping to the floor, while one woman pointed to the corner of the room where there was another door.

The door led to a set of stairs and Max went up them two at a time, his head up, his pistol leading the way. He went through the door on the second floor, pushing the heavy door open and slipping through. To the left was a man lying in front of an open doorway. It was Fat Thong Di. He was blubbering and sobbing but appeared unhurt.

Max stepped over him and into the entrance. It was an apartment. Not very big. A small kitchen to the right and one big room with a dining table and living area. There was a doorway to the back left corner, but more importantly, outside of the window on the fire escape was a man pointing a gun downward.

Max snapped a shot at the man. Due to the angle, the window exploded, but the bullet deflected ever so slightly, just clipping the side of the man's head. A cloud of minuscule glass debris rained over him as he clapped his hand to his ear, turning and returning fire. Max dove to the side, rolled, and came to a prone firing position, but missed as the man lunged to the side.

A woman stepped into the bedroom door with a gun, and Max rolled away again as a bullet grazed his side, buzzing and stinging like an angry bee.

Scarlett stepped in from the hallway and took a shot at the woman as she dove out through the shattered window. The man on the fire escape came to one knee, his head just over the window, and took a shot, the bullet plowing into the doorframe next to Scarlett's face. She dropped to the ground and scuttled across behind the sofa.

Max pulled the trigger twice as the man ducked back down.

Then it was quiet. Max did the Marine crawl across the living room floor, looked over his shoulder at Scarlett, who was on one knee, with her pistol leveled. She nodded.

Max came to one knee, gun at the ready, but the fire escape was empty. He poked his head through the open window, not the shattered one that he'd shot. There was an alleyway below, and he saw the two soldiers-of-fortune fleeing. Before he could bring the gun to bear, they turned a corner.

He jumped through the window and took the fire escape ladder to the ground two steps at a time, landing in a rolling crouch, coming back to his feet in one smooth motion.

The alleyway led to a side alley and then back onto Little Thailand Way. It was crowded with people, nobody knowing where the gunfire had come from, everybody hurrying in different directions to escape whatever danger there was.

There was no sign of the assailants nor of Zella.

Scarlett stepped up next to him, her pistol at her side, and then back into the holster underneath her black leather jacket. "Any idea?" she asked.

Max shook his head. "No. How about the fellow at the entranceway?"

"He should be just lying around over there," Scarlett said. "Taking a bit of a nap."

"Let's go have a chat with him before the police come."

But the man was gone. Zella was gone. The soldiers of fortune were gone. And then sirens rang through the air. It was time to get out of Little Thailand.

Chapter Twenty-Six

Isle of Holy Grail

Max got off the jet in Nassau and was led to the private helicopter, the rotors already whirring into life, whipping wind through his hair as he ducked to climb in, even though he knew that he didn't need to bend over and that there was a good five feet from his head to the blades.

He slid into a seat on the Sikorsky S-92 next to Rupert on one of the leather two-seat sofas, facing Senator Dunn, who was sideways to them in a single recliner across from Prince Khalid bin Faisal of Saudi Arabia. A man who might've been a butler handed them two cocktails from the bar. It seemed that this helicopter was for the men, and the girls were being transported in a second whirlybird. There were six others besides Rupert and Max, not counting the pilot and the bartender.

He guessed there were double that many young ladies culled from Hastings' Catwalk, eighteen-year-old beauties hoping to make it in the modeling profession. Max did not see the two young women from the Castle Casino in Vegas.

"I didn't see those two young ladies that you sent up to my room in Vegas with the bottle of good liquor," Max said. "Are they still with your agency?"

"No." Rupert pursed his heavy lips. His eyes squinted slightly more than normal on his florid face. "I had to let them go."

"What? Why?"

"Because they lied to me."

"About what?"

"About their experience with you, of course. You think that I don't pay attention, Max?"

Max winced. He'd been caught in a lie by a man who had in his employ covert mercenaries, and now he was isolated on an island with the man. *Was it possible that he'd been brought here to be killed and disposed of?* "What... what did they say?"

The helicopter suddenly rose in the air, and then forward. Max was quite impressed with how smooth this luxury chopper was.

"How did they lie?" Max reiterated.

"They said that they... pleased you."

"You fired them because they didn't have sex with me?"

"They did not have what it took to become successful runway models."

Max knew he was on delicate ground here. On the one hand, he was appalled to think that he'd gotten those two young ladies fired by not having sex with them. On the other hand, he was in danger of letting the shark slip the hook. And truth be told, weren't they better off having cut their ties to Hastings' Catwalk?

"It was me who turned them down," Max said. "I...well, frankly, I am uncomfortable, well, I just, uh, wasn't able to—"

"I understand," Rupert said. "You like a more experienced woman. I wondered about your rejection of Gina and Darcy at the time, but then when you came clean about your enjoyment of those two Thai hookers, especially after your tryst in NOLA and Rio with Tasty Williams, well then, I understood that your particular taste," Rupert laughed loudly at his joke, "ran more to a woman well versed in the art of pleasing a man in bed instead of the more virginal variety. So, don't worry, I have got you a special treat for the next couple of days, let us say, that it will prove to be quite...tasty."

Max breathed shallowly through his nose. He was off the hook, and it seemed that Rupert was still on the hook. "When do you announce your presidential candidacy?"

"Next week, Fox Nation will be running a documentary on me. It is a five-part series detailing the tremendous successes of my life, and which, in turn, will be the basis for laying out my platform. Coinciding with that, we will leak my intention to declare my candidacy for the Republican nomination and let my social media influencers promote that for a few days."

"And your actual declaration date?"

"March 20th. The first day of spring. The spring equinox. The National Day of Happiness. And from that day forth, Rupert Hastings Day. A day when prosperity returned the US to the prominence—and dominance—we once commanded."

Max shook his head. "All the power to you. I'd never want to be president."

"Those of us with superior genes and intellect have to step up when called upon. My name has been chosen, and I must stand for the sake of my nation."

This, as well as the previous statement, Max thought, had the tinge of memorized sound bites. "The day following your announcement I will publicly announce my support of your presidential bid and announce the creation of the Super PAC, American Phoenix, and will seed that with an initial donation of fifty million dollars."

"That is greatly appreciated." Rupert smiled widely, his lips stretched far into his wide face, his teeth bared. He nodded across the aisle. "The next few days, you should speak with Prince Khalid. He cannot legally donate to a Super PAC fund, but there are many ways to… circumvent that silly rule. He has a bottomless wallet and is a huge supporter. I think that the two of you will hit it off quite well. Even if he prefers a younger lady, and you a more experienced woman."

* * *

Rupert arranged it so that Max and Prince Khalid were sitting next to each other at the dinner table. The eight men each had been awarded a beautiful young model as their dinner date—the young ladies resplendent in what Rupert said were replicas of 18th-century French ball gowns. The corsets gave the girls tiny waists, the corresponding plunging necklines above accentuating their bosom.

The remaining models had been given the job of servers. They wore abbreviated pink outfits, the skirt barely covering their derrière, the top so tight their boobs burst out, with a matching pink cap, and black stockings held up by a garter belt. Max figured that these were the ladies low on the totem pole who were being motivated to work their way higher in the rankings, to gain the eye of Rupert, and in turn, be made famous.

The first dish consisted of escargot, stuffed mushrooms, and bruschetta. Max left his scotch untouched on the table and sipped a glass of white wine. He had plans for the evening and would need his wits about him. The young model who was Max's date had given up trying to flirt with him and was now pouting as she poured wine and snails down her throat.

"Rupert tells me that you have formed a Super Pac," Prince Khalid said. His English was quite good, his accent a bit clipped.

"Well, no, not me, technically." Max took a sip of wine. "I am involved in a foundation, a non-profit, that benefits veterans, and this will be the official host of American Phoenix."

"Ah, even better. Dark money from a non-profit. I will look into making a donation to benefit this charity for American vets."

"There will be a particular channel to funnel gifts such as yours. I will make sure to share those details with you before the announcement on March 20th."

"He will make a fine president, I think."

Max nodded his head. "He will be a refreshing change."

"The alliance between the US and Saudi Arabia will be stronger than ever. We will open up our country to American businesses and work to keep oil prices reasonable."

"And how do you benefit from this alliance?"

Prince Khalid looked surprised. "We will get American offensive weaponry that will finally allow us to end the war in Yemen."

"I thought that peace talks have been very favorable, and a resolution without further violence with Yemen might be reached."

"Ha. Yes. Unless, of course, we get the weaponry to end the war on *more favorable* terms to our interests." Prince Khalid laughed loudly.

"And Rupert has promised this to you?"

"Rupert hopes to build three enormous Hastings Hotels as well as other businesses in Saudi Arabia. Plus, his options with several weapons manufacturers are bound to make him a huge amount of money. No, my friend, we are all on the same side."

It was all Max could do to get through the dinner. He ate only about half of his ribeye and passed on the dessert. He introduced the young model to the prince and suggested she move over next to him. She was happy to be given an opportunity to impress Rupert, the prince was happy to have a beautiful young lady on either side, and Max was ecstatic to escape his role as minion to an egomaniac.

The operation to find and secure Zella had been a failure, but at least she was still alive, having seemingly escaped the mercenary team who had arrived just before Max and Scarlett. They were no closer to finding the identity of this soldier of fortune team or who they worked for, but it seemed a sure bet that Rupert Hastings was the one pulling the strings. The same man who Max was now on a journey of debauchery with—him and his hangers-on taking their fill of young models, illicit drugs, the whole watered with copious amounts of expensive booze.

As everyone else was partying in the dining hall, he took the opportunity to step out and peruse the main building, which consisted of a bar, a kitchen, a game room, and multiple locked rooms whose use was not obvious. On this wander, he saw two security guards go down a hallway, and shortly after, two different men in gray uniforms emerge from that hallway.

The interesting thing was that there were restrooms down that particular hallway and nothing more. When Max poked his head into the men's room and then the ladies' room, he discovered them to be quite empty. There had to be a hidden entrance to a covert room, likely a guardroom, Max figured, which is exactly what he was looking for.

There were no visible cameras, but Max knew that they were there, so he used the restroom, washed his hands, and stepped out the door. There was a bookcase at the end of the hallway, and he stepped over and pretended to look at the titles. This had to be the way in, he figured, if into what, he didn't know. Max turned to go, stopped by a potted floor plant, bent to fix his sock, reached slightly to his left, and clipped a tiny camera to the stalk of a tropical leaf the size of his hand.

As Max emerged from the hallway, Rupert hailed him from across the room. "Max, my lad, there you are. My surprise for you has arrived and is in your room. I can assure you that the treat will be quite *tasty*." He laughed coarsely. "Can I interest you in a nightcap first?"

* * *

The nightcap turned into a two-hour affair, and it was close to midnight when Max begged off, suggesting he was interested in getting a *taste* of his surprise. This bawdiness proved the correct button to push, as Rupert laughed loudly and slapped him on the back in good humor.

When Max walked into his room, Tasty Williams lay on the bed, reading. She was dressed in jeans and a teal T-shirt, her hair tousled on her head.

"Why, hello, Mr. Creed." There was an impish grin on her face. "Where *have* you been?"

Max chuckled. "There was a rumor that you might be visiting the island. What are you reading?"

Tasty held up the cover. "*The Female of the Species* by Mindy McGinnis."

Max took the book and looked at the back cover. "Any good?"

"It is aimed at a young adult audience, but I believe that I will find it very satisfying."

The gist of the back cover suggested it was a book of revenge for a wrongful death, and then a further balancing of the scales of justice. Much like Max was doing. Interesting, he thought. "I have to admit that I am a bit puzzled that you are here."

"You don't like being with me?" Tasty smiled wickedly.

Max flushed. "Yes, I do. But I believe there is more to you…that perhaps I should not judge your book by its cover."

Tasty grabbed his hand and pulled him down onto the bed. "Don't you like my…cover, Mr. Creed?"

Max rested his hand on her stomach. "You are a beautiful woman, for sure. I'm just wondering what plot twists might lie within."

"What are you suggesting?"

"I have seen the way you look at Rupert."

"And how is that?"

"As if he were a lecherous toad who only can ever see a woman as one thing."

Tasty pursed her lips. "We'll get to that, but first," she paused and looked around the room. "You know, I get paid to be filmed having sex," she said finally.

Max nodded.

"And you know that Rupert most likely has video cameras hidden in here. As he did in New Orleans and Rio. And therefore, he knows that you and I have never had sex. Yet, for some reason, he keeps inviting me to keep you company."

It was time to roll the dice, Max knew. He decided to ease his way in. "I have a whiz kid on my payroll. He has given me a device that blocks all audio and video waves, not that I understand it. Long story short, we cannot be seen or heard."

"Why, Mr. Creed, aren't you the savvy fellow? So, as far as Rupert Hastings knows, we have been having sex?"

"I believe he thinks that, yes."

"And why, pray tell, Mr. Creed, are we not having sex? I know that you are attracted to me. After all, who wouldn't be? I paid enough for this body to make any man combust in lust."

Max chuckled. "Maybe I'm not the person you think I am."

"I certainly know that you're no drunken playboy like you've been pretending."

"No? Perhaps you give me too much credit."

"You are a gentleman, and I have seen how you look at Rupert, as well."

"And how is that?"

"As if he were a lecherous toad you'd like to crush underfoot."

Max laughed. Waved his arm around to indicate all directions. "The whole kit and kaboodle of them. Using their money and power to corrupt the world they live in."

"Is it not the world you live in?"

This was the final call, and there was rarely anything such as a sure thing in gambling. "My goal," he said plainly, arms spread and palms up, "is to destroy Rupert Hastings and bring down as many of his whalesuckers in the process as I can."

Tasty flinched at his intensity. Looked away. And then her eyes locked back onto his, blazing with ferocity. "Well, then, I believe we may just have some common ground."

"Why?" he asked.

"My younger sister was one of Hastings' Catwalk models. Half-sister. I don't know what he did to her, but I have a pretty good idea. One day, not long after coming to this island for a long weekend, Bev killed herself. I think she was so ashamed, she couldn't live with herself, or even look our parents in the eye."

"I'm sorry."

"It's not your fault. It is the fault of the bastard who owns this island. And he is going to pay for what he did. What is your part in this? Why do you hate the man so much?"

"The woman whom I loved some years ago was gunned down at our wedding by a man much like Rupert Hastings."

"Aren't you chasing the wrong man?"

"That asshole has been dealt with. But I still have a hunger to right the wrongs inflicted on others by pricks like Hastings. And I plan on sating my appetite."

"How do you plan on doing that?"

"By refusing to accept that there are two sets of laws that govern the US, one for the ultra-wealthy and another for everybody else. A miscreant is a miscreant no matter how much money they have. And if that means redistributing a little—or even all—of said miscreant's wealth along the way and leaving them behind bars for the rest of their natural lives, so much the better."

Tasty smiled, then burst out laughing. "Jesus, what we have here folks is a fucking modern-day Robin Hood."

Chapter Twenty-Seven

Isle of the Holy Grail

Max and Tasty spent the night together cementing their shared vow to demolish the life of Rupert Hastings. She told him about her half-sister, Bev, same mother, different father, who'd been a precious child eight years her junior. Tasty had been a cross between aunt, mother, and sister to the girl, who, when she was thirteen, fell in love with her own looks and began to pull away.

Tasty had no proof that Rupert Hastings himself had done anything to her sister that led to her committing suicide. But her investigation had discovered plenty about what happened here on the Isle of the Holy Grail, the place Bev had come to just a week before she killed herself. Something had happened to the girl, either with Rupert, or after he pawned her off to one his parasites, some man given a license to abuse by the evil incarnate that was Rupert Hastings.

"Tell me about your bride," Tasty said gently.

Max's mind stalled, his mouth opening and closing. Where to start? He related how he'd been a PI and amassed enough evidence against a drug-dealing billionaire to put the man away for several lifetimes, but how his corporate team of lawyers had allowed him to walk free on technicalities, perhaps after paying bribes and calling in chits from powerful friends. He decided that he was not ready to tell Tasty about Kinsley, but could relate the facts surrounding her death.

"After he walked out of court a free man, I shrugged my shoulders and thought there was nothing to be done." Max stared at the ceiling for a few long moments. "That was the way of the world. The rich do as they want with no repercussions. And then he paid a man to kill my bride, on our wedding day, just as we were pronounced man and wife."

"So you decided to take justice into your own hands? Bring the rich fuck down?" she asked.

Max appreciated that she didn't push him to talk about Kinsley. He was not ready to speak of his bride to anybody as of yet, certainly not to the woman in bed with him at the moment. Even if they were sharing it platonically.

Instead, Max skipped the details of the murderous wedding and instead told how he'd hunted Winthrop Gould like he would a coyote with a taste for human blood. The first step had been to pen him in, attack his prestige, or what was left of it after his trial for drugs. The mogul had been exonerated after all, and human memory can be short, especially with celebrities and the wealthy.

Max had spent his life savings destroying the reputation of the man. He pulled a trick from Gould's own playbook, funding the attacks through shell companies that couldn't be traced back to Max. The brand began to falter. Gould's wife left him when Max plastered the internet with pictures of the man at strip clubs, in bed with prostitutes, sometimes having sex with several women at once. His children disavowed him. Cheating spouses had been the foundation of Max's PI business, after all, and he knew how to get the dirt.

Day by day, he tore down the world of Winthrop Gould, making him suffer, even if only inflicting just one-tenth of the pain that Max felt every day. And then Max abducted the man. It was all over the news, but as the human attention span is short, people no longer cared what happened to Winthrop Gould by the time Max was done with him. It took months, but Max gained access to the man's hidden dirty money.

Gould, pleading for his life, had shared that he had offshore accounts holding over a billion dollars that he'd secreted away, profits from selling drugs legally and illegally. Max had agreed to let the man live in exchange for access to this money.

"Holy shit," Tasty said. "And then you killed him?"

Max shook his head. No, Winthrop Gould was still very much alive. Max had addled the man's brains with heroin laced with fentanyl mixed with the legal painkillers his company had been pushing before dropping him off at an insane asylum in Uzbekistan with a monthly stipend to ensure he was fed, kept alive to endure the horror of each day.

"With money," Max said, "almost anything can be accomplished."

* * *

In the morning, Max turned off the blocking device so that they could access the camera he'd hidden in the plant by the bookshelf. They fast-forwarded through the footage, pausing to note a change of personnel at four a.m. For this graveyard shift, there was only one guard who checked in, replacing the two Max had seen go through the bookcase at ten p.m. Behind a book on the second shelf, it appeared there was a panel that popped open, and a keypad. The code the guard keyed in, however, was not visible.

"That's it, then," Max said. He wore shorts and a T-shirt while Tasty sat next to him at the desk in a silk kimono. "We have to access that room while there is only one person on duty. That's our best bet."

At just after ten in the morning, they strolled arm in arm to the dining room where a buffet brunch was set up. To all appearances, they were lovers who couldn't get enough of each other, even after a blissful night. The main lodge consisted of three rooms, Max had ascertained, a grand suite for Rupert, a guest suite for Max, and another for Taytum Liu, who now sat alone at a table, laptop in front of her, picking at a bowl of fruit and yogurt. She did not seem inclined to be social, so they sat at a table in the corner.

Afterward, they spent several hours at the pool, but left as the young models came drifting in in various stages of undress. The clincher was Senator Dunn in a Speedo in the company of a sullen blonde girl.

They retired to their room, put on an amorous act for the camera, and then blocked the audio and video so that they could speak freely, planning for the night, as well as talking about their lives. Max told her about his work as a PI, she related how she had become a porn star. Daddy issues, social media addiction, stripping—and the final step was but one small piece of the journey. Not that she minded it all that much at first. It sure beat working as a waitress or a checkout girl at a grocery store for fifteen bucks an hour.

But, Tasty concluded, she'd done well in the business of sex. She'd moved up the ladder, slowly taking charge of her gigs as a stripper, and after the success of her pornographic movies, becoming a director, and eventually a producer, of those movies. She was a brand. Much like Max Creed was a creation for specific purposes, Tasty Williams was the embodiment of the ideas and dreams of others, a person who didn't really exist.

When Max asked her what her real name was, she merely smiled, and said she didn't know anymore. But, she added mischievously, if she were to rediscover it, he would be the first to find out.

Max had moved the potted plant with his secret camera inside to a new angle, hoping that nobody would take notice of the adjusted placement, and when the security guards changed details at the four p.m. shift change, they were able to home in on the keycode that gave access to the secret room behind the bookcase.

At five, Rupert gathered the men, along with Taytum, together for a brief talk about his presidential campaign, replete with cocktails and cocaine. As far as Max could tell, the strategy was simple and straightforward. Protect guns, ban abortion, undermine the opposition, and mock the liberals.

Again, the group gathered for dinner, followed by cocktails and a jazz band, an eight-piece group flown in just for the gig. Liquor flowed, but any drugs of a more serious nature were hidden behind closed doors.

Max found it easy to appear more loaded than he was, as the criteria seemed to merely be louder than normal, find everything funnier, and have fewer inhibitions. Not that he was able to keep up with the debauchery blossoming around them. At one point, Cole Smith was getting a blowjob at his table while Hudson Ford seemed intent on drinking a shot of tequila from the belly button of every woman in the room. Tasty and Taytum were the only two who declined.

When Max and Tasty slipped away just after midnight, nobody seemed to notice, and it was very doubtful anybody cared.

Back at the room, they prepared for the four a.m. outing by drinking copious amounts of coffee and going over their plan one last time.

Scads had also provided Max with a device that made him partially invisible to cameras. "He tried to explain it to me," Max told Tasty. "But the only part I got was that it was like the background screen on a Zoom call, you know, where sometimes things disappear from view. Or if you are on a green screen and if you have on green pants, then your legs are gone? Well, it has something to do with that. It can be any color, really, so I will be wearing skin-colored clothing, a hat, and the device will make me invisible. In theory, anyway."

At ten minutes after four in the morning, having watched the lone security guard passing through the secret bookshelf to replace the team of two, Max slipped out of the room with the device turned on. The main lodge was quiet, the others having returned to their cottages to pass out or continue their depravities behind closed doors. Of course, unknown to them, on camera.

Max passed nobody in this witching hour as he worked his way to the bathroom near the bookcase, entering a stall.

A few minutes after he was settled, Tasty emerged from their room, stumbling. The makeup on her face was streaked and smudged. Her left boob had popped out of the confines of her dress. Just around the corner from the corridor leading to the secret bookcase door, she fell, her dress hiked up around her waist, as she lay on her back. The freed boob, silicone gel doing its job, pointed straight up.

This was the tipping point of the plan. Max was betting that at this hour, there'd be nobody for the security guard, presumably watching the cameras, to call. He certainly wouldn't bother Rupert. But, at the same time, he couldn't leave a guest passed out in the hallway.

Max looked at his watch. One minute past go time. Then two. He heard a rustle in the hallway, the sound of a bookcase on well-oiled hinges swinging open, a muffled footstep, the click of the door shutting, and then the pad of steps down the hallway.

Max left the stall, went to the door, cracking it in time to see the guard turn the corner at the end of the hallway. He slipped out, pulled the correct book, tapped on the panel behind like he'd seen done, and a cover popped slowly open to reveal the keypad. He punched in the number, and the secret bookcase doorway clicked and snapped ajar. He swung it open, slid through, and shut it behind him.

He was in a room with at least a hundred computer screens, alive with blinking lights, whirring noises, muffled audio, and devoid of human presence. In the center of the room was a raised stage and the most impressive of the computer hardware. The mainframe.

It was to this that Max went. He took the two steps up, sat at the desk, and called Scads, who talked him through the process of inserting the device into the guts of the machine.

"Okay, it's sending," Scads said.

"How long?"

"A lotta shit here."

"How long?"

"Twenty minutes."

Max hoped that Tasty could keep the guard occupied for that long, but he was certain that it wouldn't be a problem. She was built like a goddess and had proven to have an agile mind to match her fantastic looks. He had underestimated her at the beginning, taking her stunning looks, large breasts, and chosen profession to mean she was just a bimbo. Max was finding more and more that assumptions based on appearance were ingrained cultural mistakes that he had to overcome.

On careful count, twelve of the computer screens were dedicated to the Isle of the Holy Grail, each with twelve smaller screens. Max assumed this meant that there were twelve cameras in each for a total of 144 cameras throughout the compound. The only person who appeared to be still up, according to the cameras, was Prince Khalid, busy at his laptop.

Then, Max caught sight of the security guard, supporting a very limp and incoherent Tasty, struggling with her on the way down the hallway back to their room. His right arm fondled, more than supported, her breast, and his face was flushed. Tasty leaned into him, her lips mumbling into his neck, the audio not clear enough to hear what she said.

Max grinned. The man was no match for Tasty Williams. The other computer screens caught his interest. It looked to be transcripts from phone text, social media messaging, emails, and more. There seemed to be flagged words in red that appeared. Sex. Drugs. Adultery. Pedophile.

Before Max could ascertain more, Scads spoke over the phone. "Done. Take the transmission stick and get out."

Max looked back at the camera covering Tasty and the guard. Only they were no longer there. He'd either gone in the room with her, which was blacked out due to the blocking device, or was on his way back. Max grabbed the device from the mainframe and went back to the secret doorway, just as it swung open, causing him to scuttle sideways and behind a computer screen.

The guard came through the entranceway, paused, sighed loudly, and muttered something that could've been 'holy shit.' He walked right past where Max was pulled into a corner, but his attention seemed on the screens in front of him, rather than the room.

The man went to a computer, tapped away at the buttons, and an image of two of the young models applying sunscreen to each other appeared, apparently from earlier in the day.

Max crept out from his corner, and when he realized the man had unzipped his pants and snaked his hand inside, moved quietly to the exit. He eased the door open, slid out through it, and fast-walked down the hallway.

Chapter Twenty-Eight

Miami

Max stood at the window of the Gondek Hotel in Miami Beach on Biscayne Bay. Mainland Miami was directly across, but he was looking to the left at about ten o'clock, his binoculars focused on the marina. Behind him in the suite were John, Scarlett, and Scads.

"I'd be much more effective back in the city with my equipment," Scads said. "If you want me to decipher the download from Hastings' mainframe in the Caribbean."

"Don't really feel safe leaving you behind with no protection," Max said. "Not with some dude called the Headless Rooster after you."

"What about the mercs?"

"The very definition of mercenary is a soldier of fortune who sells himself to the highest bidder." Max lowered the binoculars and turned from the window. The hotel suite was nice enough, and more in line with Max's character when he wasn't trying to impress a billionaire playboy. "And therefore, not trustworthy with your life."

"I can take care of myself," Scads said, but it didn't sound like even he believed the words.

The initial report from Scads had suggested that the computer system on the Isle of the Holy Grail was used for more than just keeping tabs on the guests at the island. It appeared that they'd hacked into thousands, perhaps millions, of people's text messages, emails, social media posts, and much more. The system was, in fact, monitoring these online correspondences and flagging keywords. The words in red. Sex. Drugs. Adultery. Pedophile. And hundreds more.

So far, Scads had identified seven U.S. senators, forty-one congressmen, a multitude of judges, businessmen, celebrities, military, and police. Not that these powerful people had been necessarily compromised, but the keywords had flagged their computers, which had been hacked into for blackmail. And, though the team's examination had barely scratched the surface, it seemed that plenty of dirt had been exposed.

"We'll get you back to your metaverse paradise soon enough," Max said. "But first, we have to strike a blow at Rupert's drug-smuggling operation."

"I could've asked Jair to protect him," Scarlett said. "Then we wouldn't have to listen to the little bitch whine."

Scads snorted. "You mistake the tone of my voice. I am R2-D2, silently doing all the work, and you all are wasting my time with your action figure heroics."

"Well, keep the beeps and whirrs down while us flesh and blood super-heroes save the day." Scarlett grinned. The banter between her and Scads was brutal, but also bordered on the flirtatious.

Max chuckled. Then his face grew grim. There'd been something he'd been wanting to broach with Scarlett, and this seemed to be the opportunity he'd been waiting for. "Have you, uh, considered, Scarlett, that Jair is not to be trusted?"

"That's rich." Scarlett scoffed. "I have. As a matter of fact, not once since I've known him, have I ever considered the possibility that he *is* to be trusted."

"And this is the person you suggest protecting me from the baddies?" Scads asked in mock outrage.

"Well, if he lets them kill you, then we'd know if he was to be trusted, wouldn't we?"

Max chuckled grimly. He'd gotten Tucker to convince his cousin, Abigail, to take a trip to Jerusalem on Max's private jet while he was on the Isle of the Holy Grail. A detail of men had accompanied her, unbeknownst to her, as protection. A manhunt had begun for the mysterious Mrs. Huffington, who'd turned up in the life of John Little after so many years of absence, presumably to mess with the man's stability. And he was keeping close tabs on Scads, ensuring that the Headless Rooster didn't get his talons into the young man. But, this is the first that he'd broached his concerns about Jair suddenly reappearing in Scarlett's life.

"Yet, you sleep with the man," Scads said.

"He is staying with me." Scarlett glared at him.

Scads smiled slyly but kept his eyes on his laptop.

"You are playing with fire," Max said. "The man is dangerous."

He, of course, had done his homework on Jair Otelo. His background was much like that of Scarlett, but didn't suggest he had the innate moral fiber that she possessed, nor the burning desire for redemption.

"What's the plan?" Scarlett asked. "I take it we're not just in Miami to go to the beach."

"Blow up a boat." Max turned back to the window and raised the binoculars.

"When?"

"Very soon." Max watched as coolers were being carried onto the *Red Lotus*, a ten-million-dollar yacht. "How many coolers does it take to carry 300 pounds of Iso?"

"Four, maybe," Scads said.

"What's its street value?" Scarlett asked.

"Three hundred million dollars."

Max grimaced as three couples walked down the dock and onto the *Red Lotus*. White suburban yuppie types. He did not take them for drug runners. He figured them for patsies, part of the camouflage.

* * *

Two hours later, they cruised out of Biscayne Bay into the Atlantic Ocean on an Outerlimits offshore power boat with a Mercury 565 sterndrive motor.

But instead of bearing left and going up the eastern seaboard as Max thought, the yacht in front of them bore to the right in the direction of the Florida Keys.

"This baby is sweet." Scads was at the wheel, his face plastered in a huge grin. Growing up wealthy on Long Island, he was comfortable with boats but had probably never driven anything this fast. "I bet you this thing flies."

Max was next to him in a bucket seat while John and Scarlett were shoved together on the bench seat behind. The boat was made for speed, not comfort. "We're going to give you a chance to find out."

"You think that guy who is threatening me is part of this drug operation?" Scads asked. They'd picked up speed, and the two in the back had a hard time hearing.

"You're the one who connected the dots between Los Ceros, the 9H Triad, and Hastings. If I were to guess, I'd say...." Max stopped speaking, a faraway look on his face.

"What?"

"I think we may have a change of plans."

"Why's that?"

"I was wrong about where this shipment of Iso is going, but I'm betting I now know."

"Yeah? Where's that?"

"Somewhere in the Everglades."

Scads looked perplexed. "Does Hastings have a warehouse in the Everglades?"

Max chuckled. "No. Well, not in his name, but yes, I do believe he does."

"What are you thinking?"

"My guess is that the Iso delivery from the 9H Triad to Miami is now on its way to meet up with a whole shitload of heroin from Los Ceros, to be combined, packaged, and shipped."

"In the Everglades?"

"Yep. Once they have combined and packaged it, they will probably ship it up to Tampa, or maybe even New Orleans, hell, possibly Houston, put it on trucks, and flood the Midwest with it."

"Hastings has a shipping company in Mobile," Scads said.

"That's it, then. Who would ever suspect Mobile as the gateway for one of the largest drug operations in the western hemisphere?"

The yacht dropped the three suburban couples off at the Sunset Grille in Marathon overlooking the seven-mile bridge. John and Scarlett stayed with them while Max and Scads followed the crew of the Red Lotus to Burdines Waterfront to fuel up, where they also grabbed a bite to eat. It looked like the patsies had been dropped off for a night or two in the Keys while the yacht delivered its valuable cargo. Max guessed that it'd be back after two nights to pick them up.

They followed the *Red Lotus* through the night, keeping the blinking dot of the tracking device about a mile in front of them. As the sun peeked up over the Everglades, Scarlett joined Max at the helm. John and Scads were draped on the deck, sleeping.

"Ten Thousand Islands," she said.

"What?" Max asked.

"They're going into the Ten Thousand Islands. Really, just a labyrinth of mangrove forests between Everglades City and Marco Island. A haven for smugglers."

"Mangroves?"

"The bad asses of the tree and shrub world. Twisted and gnarled roots that grow in saltwater that periodically tries to drown them."

The beeper on the tracking display stopped moving. "Wake the other two up. It looks like something is up." They rounded an island, and there was a point of land ahead with a small marina. The *Red Lotus* was obvious among the fishing boats it was berthed alongside.

"Chokoloskee Island," Scarlett said, looking at a map she'd pulled from a compartment. "Had to go old school. No internet." She stepped down to the deck and shook John awake, and then kicked Scads lightly in the side. "Rise and shine, boys."

The four-man crew of the *Red Lotus* was transferring the coolers, presumably containing the Iso, onto an airboat.

"We might have difficulty following them where they're going," Max said.

"And we won't have the benefit of the tracking device."

The airboat came across the bay past them, the *Lotus'* crew, now in the airboat, stared openly at Max's sleek racing boat as they went by. It was not exactly low-profile, and there would be no opportunity to follow them without being made at this point. Not that it would've been possible as the airboat disappeared into the mangrove like a crumb swallowed by a kraken. The twisting mangrove forest was like a maze, filled with secret passageways and dead ends.

"A smuggler's haven," Scarlett said.

The airboat, its crew, and the Iso had disappeared as if they'd never been.

Chapter Twenty-Nine

New York City

Max was at a diner in Hell's Kitchen as the sun slowly illuminated the city for the day. He was drinking his coffee black this morning, sitting alone in a booth, as he stared out the window, his gaze empty and turned inward, trying to process everything that was going on.

The airboat carrying the Iso had disappeared into the Ten Thousand Islands region of the Everglades, a dense maze of mangrove islands and narrow waterways bisecting them in a convoluted path. Somewhere, out there in that uninhabited territory of southern Florida, Rupert Hastings had a drug processing facility.

Scads had continued to uncover the names of powerful figures in America who'd been compromised. Whether access was gained through phishing scams, data breaches, unsecured networks—it didn't really matter. Rupert Hastings had leverage on a chunk of society, men and women who wielded power, had wealth, fame, and could sway the laws and minds of America.

Not to mention the visitors to the Isle of the Holy Grail. Men such as Senator Dunn, whose political career was based on being a staunch family man, filmed more than once committing acts of lechery while abusing drugs. And there were many others, the stars of their own movies, unbeknownst to them, acting out their perversions and gluttony on the silver screen.

Then there was the missing Zella. Scarlett was in charge of a massive manhunt for the woman to bring her back into the fold, but obviously, she did not want to be found. And Max couldn't really blame her, for he'd failed miserably in protecting her once already, with her only friend, Sajja, dying as a result. Zella was on the run and might be safer on her own, he mused, no matter how much he wanted her to share the compromising videos of Rupert Hastings. It'd be interesting how his base of supporters would react to that image when it was shared across the internet.

And then there was Hastings' Catwalk. The modeling agency of women barely of a legal age, pressured to become the playthings of powerful men just to earn their shot at fame and fortune. Girls who'd watched *Jersey Shore* and *The Bachelor* and wanted their chance at unlimited partying, good-looking men, and luxurious living. And were willing to do anything to achieve what they perceived as paradise on earth.

The two girls who'd come to his room in Vegas had been let go from the agency, and they might be willing to point a finger at the institution, if not the man, who was pressuring them into sexual acts to enhance their careers. Perhaps Marian could get them to share their ordeal. More than likely, the girls had signed some sort of NDA threatening them to stay quiet, but Marian would know how to circumvent that and alleviate their anxiety.

"Hello, Milo." Sally Blum sat down next to him. She had frosted yellow hair, mostly covered up by a floppy hat. He knew her eyes were a chill gray underneath the designer sunglasses covering them. "Funny running into you here."

Sally Blum was the administrator for the DEA, reporting directly to the attorney general, and had many thousands of agents working under her supervision.

"Hello, Sally. Good to see you." It was strange, Max thought, to be called Milo again. It was almost like the man he had been no longer existed.

"Always a pleasure, Milo. You're the only man I know who could get me into a Hell's Kitchen diner at the crack of dawn."

"It's important to get out from behind the desk." Max grinned. "See the little guys you've been arresting and throwing in prison."

A waitress came by, and Sally ordered a cup of coffee. Also black. "Not fair, Milo. Not fair."

"If I thought that was true, I wouldn't have called you."

"If I thought you thought that was true, I wouldn't have come."

Sally was from Maine and had been the attorney general there when Max had been assembling the drug case against Winthrop Gould. Even though the tycoon had eventually gotten off on appeal, she'd built a strong case against him, and this national spotlight had garnered her the position of DEA administrator with the current administration.

"How's the husband and kids?" Max asked.

"Adapting to life in DC."

"Long way from Maine."

"Too far to commute." Sally shrugged. "Life is sacrifices."

"Yep."

Sally looked him in the eye. "What have you been up to?"

"Well, for one, my name is Max Creed now."

Sally nodded. "I heard that our friend, Winthrop Gould, ran into some financial and legal troubles, and then disappeared into thin air. Probably living life large now on some South Pacific Island."

Max kept eye contact. "Or in a psychiatric institution in Central Asia." He shrugged. "Broke and doped up on his own shit."

"I'd like to think you are right."

"Got something else for you."

"Yeah? Let's hear it?"

"Big drug operation. Iso being shipped into Miami, transported to a facility off the coast of Everglades City, where it is being mixed with heroin from Mexico, repackaged, and delivered to a shipping operation in Mobile."

"And where is this facility in Florida?"

Max shook his head. "Hidden away in the mangrove forest of the Ten Thousand Islands, a smugglers' haven going back to the pirate era. But...the shipping facility is easier to find. Put surveillance on it. Keep an eye out for boats coming up from Chokoloskee Island or Everglades City, swoop them all up in the big net you've been given."

"Earned," Sally said. "Not given."

"Yes. Absolutely."

"Who's behind all of this?"

"I believe the Iso is coming in from a triad in China called the 9H, and the heroin is coming from Los Ceros."

"I've been after that bastard, Don Blanco, and his top dog, the Headless Rooster, since I took office," she said. "Who is the American contact?"

"The shipping facility is owned by Rupert Hastings."

"Holy shit."

* * *

Scarlett was sitting in the driver's seat of the SUV with tinted windows just up Stanhope Street from where Scads lived. She smiled, thinking about how the putz had chosen to live on a street that incorporated his given name and the word hope. He was a good kid, even if a bit dorky and a weakling, she thought, now chuckling out loud. That was not his strength. Technology was his muscle, and Scarlett would pit him against anybody in a computer cage match, if such a thing even existed.

John Little was riding shotgun with her today, but had gone down the street to find them some lunch. Scarlett had been doing stakeouts and protection services since she was a teenager and could be more patient than a frogfish if necessary. If there was food, she would eat, but if there was none, that was fine as well.

They could be sitting inside comfortable protecting the lad, Scarlett thought, watching television and munching on snacks. Max had thought it best if they watched from outside. If they could get the drop on any thugs who came to rough Scads up, a bit of questioning might illuminate who exactly was pulling the strings.

A man was coming down the sidewalk from behind her, sliding along, a hat pulled low over his face, collar turned up against the chilly New York day. He had a pair of coffees in his hands and looked quite familiar.

"Oh, Christ," she said and rolled down the window.

"Scar! Funny running into you here," Jair said. "And me with an extra coffee."

"What the fuck, Jair? You followed me?"

Jair grimaced. "I was worried about you, *minha linda mulher.*"

"Don't call me that. I'm not your beautiful woman."

"But you are beautiful. And you are my woman."

"I am not your woman, Jair."

"But we have the sexy time together."

"And I like chocolate cake, but it doesn't own me."

Jair smiled broadly. "Mm. You compare me to chocolate cake. That must be a good thing."

"I'm working, Jair."

"That's what I need to talk to you about. Your boss. Max Creed."

* * *

Jerry wasn't happy that Forge had ordered him to bring the Asian and the Mexican dudes along as observers. What was this, he asked himself, fucking show and tell? At least he had Lola along, which smoothed the irritation a bit. Not for the first time, he wondered how she'd be in the sack. Lola was a real bad kitty, in the finest sense, and Jerry could feel himself stirring as he waited.

The diversion came along, and it was go-time. Lola went first, Jerry watching her ass as she went down the two steps and began fiddling with the lock. It took her less than a minute, and the dumb broad in the car never looked over once. Lucky for her, Jerry thought, because he would've shot her right between her pretty eyes.

They found the computer nerd in a roomful of computers with headphones on and his back to them. To get his attention, Jerry whacked him hard across the back of the skull with the barrel of his pistol. The boy tumbled to the ground like he'd been deflated, and Jerry worried at first that he might've hit him a bit too hard. Luckily, the kid started flopping and gasping on the floor. He grabbed the punk by his hair and hauled him back into the roller-chair. Lola stepped behind him and wrapped her arm around his neck, her breasts pressed to the back of the kid's head.

"These hombres here tell me you owe them something," Jerry said.

"Who are you?" Scads blurted out.

Jerry punched him in the nose, just a jab really, but enough to get the blood flow going. "I asked you a question."

"What was the question?" Scads' tone was even now, as he apparently recovered his composure.

The kid wasn't the little pussy Jerry thought he was. "Do you owe these hombres something?"

Scads twisted his head to look at the two fellows. "Ran into them the other day. Don't believe I owe them a thing."

Jerry laughed. Slapped the boy hard across the face. Lola shifted but held him intact in the chair. "They tell me that your mommy and daddy stole a whole bunch of money from their boss, and he expects you to make it right."

Scads scoffed. "Guy's name is the Headless Rooster. Can you honestly take him seriously?"

Jerry thought the kid had a valid point there, but punched him in the eye anyway. He was a professional, after all, and he had a job to do. "Tomorrow. Two o'clock. Bring Max Creed. I will text you where."

"How am I supposed to get Max there?"

"Tell him that the Headless Rooster has info about a certain somebody. That'll do the trick."

"A certain somebody?"

Jerry jabbed him in the mouth and split his lip. "This Mexican hombre wants to cut a deal with Creed to save your life. I don't care how you do it, but get him there. If you don't? Next time ends up with you dead."

Lola released her hold on Scads. Jerry walloped him a final good one, sending him toppling to the floor. Then the four of them walked out the door.

Jerry fully expected the kid to blab to Creed. But the man would still come. That was all part of the plan.

* * *

"You need to break all ties with Max Creed." Taytum stood in Rupert's office as he sat behind his extremely large walnut desk.

He thought that she was looking pretty good in her black jumpsuit, even if she was dressed like a man. "What?"

"You heard me."

Maybe it was time to give her another whirl in the bedroom, he thought, his eyes appreciating her thin waist, full bosom, and flashing eyes. "Why would I do that?"

"He is not who he says he is."

"What are you talking about?"

"Those two Thai women from Pattaya City? He brought them back to the states to leak information about your... sexual proclivities."

Rupert colored slightly. Felt himself stir. They were very good at what they did. "That's nonsense. Max told me he brought them back here because he enjoyed their company so much."

"He has been seen associating, perhaps romantically, with a woman named Sevyn Knight. Her father committed suicide a bit back after going bankrupt when you refused to pay his company what you owed them and then sued him into the ground."

"Knight? I don't even know the name."

"She happens to work for the CIA."

"I can't be responsible for other people's mistakes." Rupert was growing irritated. Like he had done anything wrong? It was just good business. It wasn't his fault if other people were jealous of his success."

"I think they may be working together to—"

"Ha. Max and the CIA? Trying to do what? You are wrong about him. He's a good fellow. I was a little concerned when he didn't bop those models I sent to his room, but he had himself a good time with the Thai women and then Miss Tasty Williams."

"Speaking of that porn star. Did you know that her half-sister was a model for Hastings' Catwalk?"

"Williams?"

Taytum shook her head, a look of patience on her face. "Different father.

205

Her name was Beverly Johnson."

Rupert smiled, a fond memory tickling his mind. She'd been a very feisty romp. "Huh. Tasty is Bev's sister. Didn't know that."

"Was. Bev is dead. She killed herself."

"What? Why?"

"Not clear, but it wasn't long after parting ways with the modeling agency."

"That's a shame. She was a mighty fine girl. Had fun with her, I did."

"I am not sure why, but I believe that Max Creed is trying to destroy you."

"That's ridiculous."

"I'm afraid that he may've hacked into our computer system last week at the Isle of the Holy Grail."

"Why would you think something like that?"

"Between four and five in the morning, our security guard manning the cameras left his post to aid an apparently extremely intoxicated Tasty Williams. He helped her back to Creed's room. He was gone from his post for seventeen minutes."

Rupert shook his head. What in hell was Taytum talking about? "She wasn't the only one who got lit that night. That's the whole point of going there is to get fucked up and do whatever you want."

"Our cameras picked up an odd shadow. The secret doorway swung open, apparently on its own, and closed again, but there was a flicker of something. I think it may have been Creed using some sort of techno cloaking device."

"What is this? Harry Potter?"

"Max Creed is not who he says he is."

"He is a fine fellow who happens to have a great deal of money. Hell, he's going to create a super PAC to back my campaign, and he's just plain fun to be around."

Taytum nodded. "Okay, then. Of course, you are right." She turned and left the room.

Rupert scowled as the door closed behind her. Taytum Liu seemed to be getting a bit big for her britches, almost like she didn't know who was in charge. It might be time to make some changes, even if she had been a fine lay, introduced him to his wife, had suggested the idea of his own island, as well as many other things.

Taytum, for her part, left enraged, but by the time the elevator reached the ground floor, was back in control. Of course, the man was just a buffoon. An idiot. A puppet, always ready to have his strings pulled so that Taytum might achieve her goals, the only important ones. He truly thought that he was in charge of his own destiny. It was up to her to clean up the mess and make sure that none of it touched the golden boy, the shining star, the man who had the face, the skin color, the charisma, and the money to open the doors to the White House.

Chapter Thirty

Port Richmond, Staten Island

"You know the plan is to kill you, right?" Scarlett said. "And Scads, too."

"That does seem likely," Max said.

"Yet, you're going to walk in there?"

"Not in. I will agree to meet them in the auto yard. You will have my back from the boat. I'll make sure that we are visible to the water. And John will lead the hired guns into the fray at the first sign of trouble."

The message sent to Scads' phone one hour earlier had ordered them to meet at a deserted junk yard between Richmond Terrace and Kill Van Kull, the strait of water between Staten Island and New Jersey. Rusted-out junkers littered the fenced-in area. A crane with a clawed pincher looked poised to pick up a car, arrested in motion for perpetuity, never to complete the task of transferring the automobile to the crusher.

As soon as the text message had come, John secured a forty-three-foot cabin cruiser to provide cover and possibly escape options if necessary. They had a mercenary team of twelve on standby. Three of them would be on the boat with Scarlett, six of them would be on the perimeter, and the last three would be with John, breaking down the front gate.

"Ready for this, Scads?" Max asked.

"Yep."

The young man's face was tight, but determined, as evidenced by his Thor

T-shirt, the Marvel superhero standing with crossed arms, one hand holding his hammer, with a dogged expression to his countenance. Max knew it was the shirt that Scads wore when he wanted to look and feel powerful.

"What are you hoping to gain here?" John asked. "Risk versus reward. To me, this is a huge risk, and I'm not sure what the reward is."

"Well, for starters, we're going to get some payback for what these dirtbags did to Scads yesterday, and on your watch." Max put a bit of snap into those last words. He had been furious that John was off getting food while Scarlett had let herself be distracted, allowing four people to break into Scads apartment and knock him around. "And secondly, we got to shake the branch and see what falls out. We let Sajja get killed and lost Zella. Twice, we've allowed drug shipments to get away. We're playing a very sophisticated game and getting our asses kicked."

John looked grim, knowing full well that he'd let Scads and Max down the day before. "You're the boss."

"Get out on the boat," Max said to Scarlett. "We'll give you ten minutes to get set up, and then we're going in. I'll steer things to an open spot by the water. You see anything odd out there, let me know immediately."

Scarlett left to join the three soldiers of fortune already on the cabin cruiser. The six men containing the perimeter were grouped into pairs and already posted at the east, west, and south sides of the junkyard. The last three mercenaries were in the SUV in the parking lot of the park, a few hundred feet from the entrance to the junkyard.

"Go make sure your guys are ready," Max said to John. "In nine minutes, we'll walk past you and access the junkyard through the fence on the east side."

"Aye, aye, sir." John gave a mocking salute and walked off.

"You all set with the pistol I gave you?" Max looked at Scads. "It's not all that easy to shoot a human being."

"If I get a chance to pull the trigger on the prick who killed my parents, you can be sure that I won't hesitate."

"Point and squeeze. Easy-peasy."

Scads gave a tight grin that didn't reach his eyes. "Let's do this thing."

Max nodded.

The two of them strolled out of the park and past the parked SUV with John Little and three heavily armed men. Right before they reached the fence of the junkyard, they passed the eastern perimeter of two men, standing and smoking cigarettes, a ruse to cover why they were standing around outside.

They'd come prepared to cut an opening in the fence but had already discovered several possibilities for passage. Max pulled a section of fence back and let Scads pass through before following. They made their way cautiously down a row of junked vehicles.

A movement in the window of a rusted-out white panel van caused Max to pull his pistol. He stepped past Scads, one finger raised, gun out in front of him. The sliding door was missing, and he stepped into the opening with the weapon leveled.

Looking back at him with wide, frightened eyes was a ragged-bearded man who'd apparently taken up residence in the van. Max put one finger to his lips, and they continued on their way.

They went past the crane and the main building to a small grassy area on the tidal waterway, Kill Van Kull.

From across the way, four people stepped out from behind a pile of wrecked automobiles.

"That's the four who came to my place yesterday," Scads said. "That white asshole seemed to be the one in charge."

Max nodded, and they moved forward several steps before stopping, about fifty feet away. "Where's the boss?"

Jerry nodded his head, and out stepped a wiry Mexican man dressed in tight clothing with a thick gold chain that drew attention to the scar that circled his neck.

Perhaps, Max thought, whence the nickname the Headless Rooster came from.

"You're the bastard who had my parents killed," Scads said.

Max put a calming hand on his elbow. "Easy," he whispered.

The Headless Rooster smiled broadly. "They were pieces of shit who thought they could steal from me. And now you owe me. But you have done your part. Go ahead. Walk away, and I will let you live."

"You said you had something of interest to me," Max said.

"Yes, yes, that I do." The Headless Rooster smiled lazily. "Today is the day you die. You see, you have been a problem for some associates of mine. Your death will greatly increase my value."

Max hoped that John and Scarlett were catching this on the two-way transmitters. He risked a look out on Kill Van Kull. The cabin cruiser was out there about two hundred yards, rocking gently in the waves. He scanned the immediate area, looking for more gunmen.

"What associates?" Max asked. The Headless Rooster cackled. Max thought he sounded more like a chicken than a rooster.

"Let's just say that with your death, I will cement the backing of the most powerful man in the world, well, soon enough, he will be. With my relationship with the United States and the Chinese, I will become the most powerful cartel leader in Mexico."

"I thought you answered to Don Blanco?"

"Don Blanco is old. The world is all about change. And the wind is blowing."

"How do the Chinese come into play? You mean the 9H Triad who supplies you with Iso?"

The Headless Rooster cackled again. "If you only knew who is in charge of 9H. Never mind. It is time for your death. It appears that Thor there has decided to die alongside you. Loyalty is a mighty fine thing. Very admirable."

"I am not scared of you," Scads said. "Not anymore."

"You should be. Things are not going to turn out like you think they will."

Several gunshots rang out over the Kill Van Kull, and all eyes swung to the cabin cruiser dancing on the waves. Max shoved Scads behind a rusted-out Chevy sedan and tumbled down next to him as an SUV came barreling through the gate at the front.

* * *

Scarlett was prone on the top deck of the cabin cruiser with a tripod set up for the Barrett M95, a bolt-action anti-material and sniper rifle. The weapon was effective up to 2,000 yards and was capable of piercing armor or rusted-out automobiles, as necessary. She watched as Max and Scads approached the clearing, having already spotted the men they were meeting.

Her thoughts were a whirlwind. Jair had betrayed her. The man she'd been sleeping with had been sent to play her, and yesterday, had caused her to drop her guard, and a close friend had been beaten. Scads was like a younger brother to Scarlett, and she felt both mortified and infuriated at her blindness.

She listened to the two-way as the flunkies came out first, and then the Headless Rooster. She had the white guy in her gun site, pegging him as the most dangerous. First him, and then the cartel leader, perhaps dissuading the others from having anything to fight for. It was a salty group, Scarlett thought, noting that the woman and the Asian both looked extremely badass.

Scads was proclaiming that he wasn't scared of the Headless Rooster, and Scarlett was about to take out the white merc dude when one of the hired guns came up the deck behind her.

"What are you doing?" she said without turning to look, her eyes glued on the target. "Your position is down below."

"That's the thing," the man said. "I have a new mission."

The tone of his voice gave away more than his words, and Scarlett rolled over, pulling a pistol from her side as she did so. He opened fire with his M4, the deck where she'd been instantly shredded as the hail of bullets tore it apart. Wood splinters and fragments exploded into her face, but she was oblivious.

Scarlett squeezed her trigger, the bullet low, hitting him in the tactical body armor vest instead of the head like she was aiming for. As he swept the rifle barrel toward her, Scarlett tumbled over the side and landed on the lower deck. The two soldiers of fortune there brought their weapons to bear. She shot one in the head and felt a jolt in her bicep before diving over the side of the boat as a curtain of lead ripped into the space behind her.

* * *

Max risked a look over the dented trunk of the Chevy at the water. He could see two figures scrambling around the boat, but couldn't tell if one was Scarlett.

The SUV came to a skidding halt in the open ground between them, and four men tumbled out. John was in the lead, carrying a Kel-Tec P50 submachine pistol with a 50-round magazine. It was a short and ugly weapon and one that John preferred for close work.

The Headless Rooster put his hands up with a mocking grin on his face. "An ambush? How clever."

"Hands away from your weapons," John said as several hands started to creep into jackets, presumably hiding guns. "On the ground. Get on your knees."

Max came to his feet as the soldier of fortune directly behind John raised his own pistol and shot John in the back of the head.

Max, in turn, shot that man in the head, and then the other two mercenaries who were in the process of double-crossing them, bang-bang.

A hail of bullets filled the air as the Headless Rooster and the four assassins with him opened fire. Max dropped to the ground next to Scads.

"They shot John," Scads said, his face white.

"I think they might've gotten Scarlett as well," Max said as a barrage of fire erupted from the cabin cruiser on Kill Van Kull, the rounds plowing and tearing into the steel automobiles around them.

"What are we going to do?"

Max had his phone in hand. He dialed the cell phone number Sally Blum had given him earlier. Luckily, she answered on the third ring.

"Max?"

"Need a favor, Sally. I'm pinned down in a junkyard in Port Richmond on Staten Island by the top lieutenant of Los Ceros, the Headless Rooster. Several people down. Automatic weaponry. Send the cavalry, not just the local police department. And ambulances."

Chapter Thirty-One

New York City

The sirens had scared the baddies away. Max had been at John's side when the first blue uniforms came bursting in upon the scene. Somehow, the man had still been breathing, even if that breath was labored, with the back of his head mush.

The boys in blue had cuffed Max and Scads, but when they'd gotten to Central Booking in the 120th Precinct, the feds had been waiting, agents for Sally Blum with the DEA. Still in handcuffs, they'd been transported to the DEA office in Chelsea, overlooking the Hudson River.

It took another three hours for Chief Blum to arrive. Time in which Max tortured himself over what had happened. John barely hanging onto life. Scarlett missing, most likely dead. Scads locked up in a separate room.

They had been double-crossed by the hired mercenaries, Max realized, not just one of them, but the entire team of twelve. But how? Max had kept it very hush, paid very well, and yet, somebody had found out and gotten to them with a better offer. Who had leaked the information?

This entire mission had been nothing but a shit-show, Max thought, his soul burning in embarrassment, anger, and contrition for having fucked up so badly. The previous missions had gone smoothly, first in Dhaka and then again in Brazil. There had been more over the past two years as they flexed their muscles and brushed up in preparation. But that had been the minor leagues, Max realized, and they were now in the majors, and the fastballs were coming at a hundred miles an hour.

Still, he couldn't get past the thought that it was highly unlikely that all of this was being orchestrated by Rupert Hastings. The man was a dolt, a dunderhead, a dunce. I mean, Max thought, he was of average enough intelligence, had charisma, and a buttload of money—but could he really have the chutzpah, never mind the contacts, to find and bribe the covert soldiers of fortune to betray the man paying them? That just seemed to be far outside Hastings' expertise, which leaned much more to attack by ferocious attorneys and death by the slow torture of endless litigation.

The door opened, and Sally Blum came in. "Hello again, Max. Just what are you up to?"

She was calm, hell, she had always been calm, even when he'd been with her after the death of his wife. "Hi, Sally."

Sally told the agent guarding Max to uncuff him and leave. Then she turned back to Max. "Heard you were in the middle of a firefight on Staten Island."

"I believe I was the one who called and told you that."

"Three dead crew-cut fellows who looked like they were on the last plane out of Afghanistan. Would you know who shot them?"

"I did."

"Care to share the details?"

Max sighed. "I hired them and nine others to provide support for a meeting with the Headless Rooster. Somebody got to them. The one fellow shot John Little in the back of the head, and the others were turning their weapons on me when I shot them."

"John Little is your man?"

Max nodded. "Have you...heard anything about his condition?"

"He's still alive. So, you, this John Little, and the computer nerd, Stanwood Miller, in the other room, were meeting with the Headless Rooster. Why?"

"There was a fourth. Scarlett was on a cabin cruiser in the Kill Van Kull. I believe she was also a victim of the double-cross."

"Scarlett who?"

Max shrugged. "I believe she has only the one name."

215

Sally scoffed. "Okay. Whatever. What were you doing meeting with one of the most vicious cartel leaders in all of Mexico?"

"Can I fill you in later? After I check on John Little? What hospital is he in?"

"You just killed three men, Max. You're not going anywhere. Not unless you can convince me otherwise."

Max rubbed his knuckles over his eyes. Tried to clear his thoughts. Everything had gone to shit, he thought, and he couldn't quite see a way out of it. "Did you find a body in the Kill Van Kull?"

Sally sighed. "No. No cabin cruiser with double-crossing soldiers of fortune manning the vessel, either."

Max picked his head back up and looked at Sally, thinking that maybe they'd just taken Scarlett, and she was still alive. "Nothing?"

"We're interviewing the captain of a pleasure cruiser who heard the gunshots and put the glasses on the boat. Said some lady got shot and fell overboard. But we've found no body. Tidal water, Kill Van Kull is, so that doesn't mean there isn't one."

"You gotta let me out of here."

"And you have to give me a good reason."

Max cleared his throat in frustration. "As I told you at the diner, I have come across information linking a Mexican Cartel, a Chinese Triad, and Rupert Hastings' business empire. I am investigating that further, mainly because, as you may know, Hastings is planning on running for president, and if he is truly a crook, I'd like to expose him before... well, just before."

"Late this morning, we tracked a ship from Everglades City to Mobile. It made a delivery to Hastings' shipping company there. We went in full force and raided it."

"And?"

"Nothing. Unless you count the total embarrassment we experienced, the threat from Hastings to sue our department, and the flak I'm getting from the DOJ."

"Who owned the ship?"

"A Chinese Company. No overt links to the 9H, but there was enough suspicion to give the go signal, after what you'd told me. Not my finest hour."

Max opened his mouth, shut it, and allowed himself to silently fume for a moment. They'd tracked a yacht from Miami carrying Iso to a mangrove area off Everglades City a few days ago, and then today, a Chinese ship came out of Everglades City and went to Hastings' trucking company in Mobile. Too many coincidences. There should've been drugs in massive quantities. Unless, of course, they'd been tipped off.

Sally gave him a moment before continuing, "So, Max, I'm going to need more from you if you want to walk out of here today. Otherwise, I'm going to leave you locked up."

"What do you want?"

"The kid in the other room? Stanwood Miller says his friends call him Scads. He happens to be the son of Hector and Kathleen Miller, who were killed out on Long Island a few years back in an assassination that was attributed to Los Ceros. Do you want to explain that?"

"Remember how Winthrop Gould walked free on all charges even though we had him dead to rights? And then he sent a sniper to kill Kinsley?" Max stood up from the table and began to circle it as he spoke. "Well, I wasn't going to allow that to go unavenged. I tracked the man, irritated him, cajoled him, and finally relieved him of a large sum of money. I walked away from that a very wealthy man and created a new identity for myself."

Sally nodded. "Very impressive credentials, back story, and all. It took my people quite a bit of digging to make the connections, even after you told me that Milo and Max were one and the same."

"Money greases the wheels, for sure."

"I suppose I shouldn't ask you how you obtained this money?"

"Winthrop made some financial mistakes, and I reaped the benefits." Max paused across the table from Sally. "I'll be honest with you. After the death of my wife, everything fell apart. And then John and Scarlett helped to put me back together. Along the way, I realized there was more for me to do in life than catch cheating spouses and slacker employees. Winthrop's money, that gave me a chance to make a difference on a grander scale. I took that chance. I went big. I have decided to bring justice to those who are untouchable and assembled a team of experts to help."

"You, and this so-called team of experts, are single-handedly going to bring down the likes of the Rupert Hastings of the world. That's rich, so to speak. And illegal."

"Yes. But you, of all people, know that the government stands almost no chance of convicting a billionaire of wrongdoing. That is where I come in."

"Judge. Jury. Executioner."

Max nodded. "The goal is to find evidence of wrongdoing so concrete, so monumentally fucking concrete, that no team of lawyers can let the son-of-a-bitch walk away."

"And if that fails?"

"You know that I am a man of principle." Max sat back down and leaned forward over the table.

It was Sally's turn to nod her head. "Hence, the new name."

"You got it."

Sally sighed. "You know that if I let you go out that door and you fail, that I will lose my job, and most likely be brought up on charges. I'm not really made for prison, my friend."

"Do you think that you can stop Rupert Hastings? Working within the justice system?"

"Why do I need to stop him?"

"Because I fear that he, not totally of his own volition, is going to destroy America, if not the world as we know it."

"You are suggesting that you are more capable than I to stop this from happening."

Max stood up. "You have one problem, Sally. You are bound by the law. I am not."

* * *

Sally cut Max loose with the promise that he would notify her if he were to move past investigation towards final resolution. She did not have to be convinced of Rupert Hastings' poor moral character or the inherent evils of Mexican cartels and Chinese triads infiltrating the US and operating quasi-openly on the streets of New York City. Or that, in many ways, her hands were tied and unable to combat any of it.

With Scads at his side, his white Thor T-shirt slightly worse for wear, including several smudged bloodstains, but a determined look on his face, they left the building for an awaiting limousine. The traffic across town was a bear, and Max finally grew impatient and dragged Scads from the car to walk the two miles to the Mt. Sinai Beth Israel Hospital, where John had been taken.

They found Marian and Tucker in the waiting room. John was in surgery.

"What in holy Moses happened?" Tucker asked.

"Somebody got to the protection we hired, and they double-crossed us," Max said. "They knew we were coming. What's going on with John?"

"They're putting a plate in his head as we speak," Marian said. Her face was white. Strained. Her voice was barely a whisper.

"Mistake to shoot that lug head in the skull," Tucker said. The remnants of tears streaked his cheeks. "Probably just cracked his noggin at the most."

"Is he going to be okay?" Scads asked.

Marian looked at the boy. Shrugged.

"Doctor says he's got about a twenty percent chance of living," Tucker said. "But he doesn't know John Little like we do."

Sevyn Knight came striding across the waiting lobby, people parting in front of her. "I just heard. Is he okay?"

Max licked his lips. "Don't know. How'd you hear about this?"

Sevyn waved her hand impatiently. "I might just be a pencil pusher, but I still work for the CIA."

"Where's Scarlett?" Marian asked. "You heard from her?"

Max winced. Shuffled his feet. "Not sure."

"What do you mean by that?" Tucker asked.

"Like I said, we were double-crossed. Somebody got to our hired guns, and they turned on us. Scarlett was on a boat in the waterway off Staten Island, the Kill Van Kull, along with three of those bastards. There were shots. Then the gunfire turned on us."

"They killed her?" Marian's voice was like coarse sandpaper.

Max looked at her, his eyes hot with pain and anger, but didn't say anything.

"We don't know," Scads said. "She's a tough cookie."

"I'll find her," Max said. "If it's the last thing I do."

"I'll pray for her," Sevyn said. "And for John Little."

Marian turned her head and glared.

"Now that'll help," Tucker scoffed.

Scads spit on the floor of the lobby.

"What?" Sevyn looked from face to face before settling on Max. "Prayer can't hurt, certainly?"

Max cleared his throat. "Praying for somebody is sort of like saying fuck you, we don't care enough to do anything to help you."

"If there is a God," Tucker said, "he believes in those who help themselves."

* * *

Max stepped out of Mt. Sinai Hospital, and Dale Allen, the office assistant, was standing there next to a Harley-Davidson Sportster. He was also holding a leather jacket for him to exchange for his Armani suit, which was bloodstained and ruined. Once Max put the jacket on, he handed him a pistol to replace the weapon taken by the police as evidence, which Max slipped into the empty shoulder holster.

"How is John?" Dale asked.

"He's in surgery. Getting a plate in his head. Marian, Tucker, and Scads are in there. Go ahead in." Max put his leg over the bike.

"Where are you going?" Dale asked.

"Looking for Scarlett. Thanks for bringing the bike."

"You want me to come with?"

Max looked at the young man whom he barely knew. "You know how to operate a boat?"

Dale shook his head. "No."

"Go inside and get Scads. Don't tell Tucker, Marian, or Sevyn Knight what you are doing. Then go find a boat to rent, or hell, buy the fucker, and the two of you search the Kill Van Kull between Bayonne and Staten Island. Start there and work your way out further. If you spot Scarlett, the cabin cruiser called *Golden Cloud*, or any suspicious characters, you call me immediately. Do not put yourself in harm's way."

Dale nodded. "Gotcha."

Max nodded back his appreciation, started the Harley, and sped off into traffic.

He thought about Scarlett and what she would have done in that situation. Returned fire as best she could, before saving herself however she could, if he knew Scarlett. There was a minuscule chance that the duplicitous bastards had taken her alive, but that was highly unlikely. There was also little reason to cart around her dead body in a boat when the authorities were swarming both land and sea.

Therefore, more than likely, dead or alive, Scarlett had been in the water of the Kill Van Kull off the junkyard in Richmond Terrace since the shooting began. If she was alive, well then, she must've gotten ashore somehow. That was where he meant to look, the places where he might find Scarlett still breathing. Dale and Scads would look for the alternative, her lifeless body floating in the water.

Max took the Sportster zipping across town, weaving through the cars, knowing this was irritating to the automobile drivers, but at the time, not giving a shit. With the throttle open, he descended into the Holland Tunnel, weaving in and around cars like a video racer in an Atari game come to life.

The tide had been coming in at two p.m., which meant that it was most likely Scarlett had drifted or swum west toward New Jersey. As he came over the Bayonne Bridge, the last glimmer of the sun slid over the horizon. It had been just a bit more than five hours ago that he, Scads, John, Scarlett, and the twelve traitors had come over this same bridge on their way to the ambush. Those men knew then what was going to happen, that treachery was afoot, but had given nothing away. In just five hours, Max thought, everything had changed.

He got off Exit 13 and reversed directions on Morningstar Road, back up to Richmond Terrace, where he took a left to begin searching the shore of the Kill Van Kull. All the while, he pushed one thought from his head, but it tickled the edges of his consciousness, teasing and tantalizing like the itch of poison ivy.

Was it possible that Scarlett had betrayed them? Knowingly or unknowingly? At one point in her life, Max knew she'd been a hired gun, paid to kill. Did she still have a price? Max banished that thought from his mind, unwilling to entertain the notion. He trusted Scarlett implicitly. There was a connection between them, a desperate need to right their own wrongs, change the universe, and fight for moral worth. Scarlett would not have turned her back on all that, on them, for money.

The thought that dogged him was that she had been spied upon by Jair Otelo. Max did not believe that this man, who he'd had checked out, had any morals whatsoever. Yet, Scarlett seemed smitten with the fellow. Love was blind that way. Lust more so. Both equally powerful.

Max cruised the bike in and out of small peninsulas, stashing it in scrub to make forays out to the beach, stopping to scout hiding places where a wet and exhausted—and possibly injured—Scarlett might hide herself. A concrete supply company, warehouses, car dealerships, all perched on the edge of this tidal waterway between Staten Island and New Jersey. Deserted buildings, junk heaps, men and boys standing in groups who eyed him suspiciously as he trolled his way past. As he parked his bike by an abandoned building to walk around searching for Scarlett, four or five Mexicans approached and began to accost him. Max pulled the Glock out, and they backed off right quick, confirming they were just locals, and not part of Los Ceros looking to finish Scarlett as well.

* * *

At ten, he called Scads, confirming that the two lads had procured a boat and were trawling the busy waterway of Kill Van Kull looking for Scarlett's body. The junkyard was off limits for search, still teeming with local police, federal officers, forensics personnel, and who knew what else. Surely they would have found Scarlett if she were there. Max drove up and down the riverbank, offering rewards to anybody and everybody, sharing his phone number with bartenders, dogwalkers, gangbangers, and homeless people as he traversed Staten Island.

It was almost midnight when he got the call. A gruff, coarse voice, slurred with alcohol or some other chemical, possibly glue, rasped into the phone that he'd found a woman. He wasted ten minutes getting assurances that the caller would be paid his money before sharing the location, Arlington Marsh Park.

Max's GPS led him down a dirt road that was no more than a path, dodging random trash and navigating the bumps on the Sportster. It was more a marsh than a park and, at the end, when he came to the water, Max parked the bike and continued on foot. The man had told him that he'd been bedding down by the Kill Van Kull at night near a pile of debris that allowed him a small fire at night. It was here that he'd found the woman.

It was Scarlett. She was semi-conscious. Her lips were blue. There was a bullet hole in her arm, part of her shirt ripped off, and tied around it to staunch the flow of blood. Max pushed a wooden container crate from the top of her and knelt next to her.

Her eyes fluttered, opened. They were hot with fever, ignited by anger, drilling their way into a soul he hadn't been aware he still possessed.

"Some people are going to fucking die," Scarlett said.

Chapter Thirty-Two

New York City

They were quite the bedraggled group, Max thought, looking around the circle of the band, minus John, who had gathered at the Bryant Park office. It was hard to believe, but he was quite sure that one of them had double-crossed the group, and he had a fairly good idea of who it was. A betrayal that had left John Little clinging to life in the hospital.

Scarlett had her arm in a sling, the bullet having creased the flesh above her bicep, various scratches on her face from splinters spit up by the deck of the cabin cruiser raked by automatic weapon fire, and then crawling onto shore from the Kill Van Kull. There were shadowy smudges around her eyes from pain and lack of sleep, but the dark orbs of her irises shone forth fiercely.

Max had put his coat around Scarlett the previous evening, and she'd clambered aboard the Sportster behind him. She'd resisted the idea of going to the hospital, and instead, Max brought her back to the office building and then had called in a favor from a very prominent surgeon. Of course, the woman was very well paid for the somewhat unusual house call, and then Scarlett had napped in one of the recliners for a few hours.

The first order of business for Max, after making sure she was okay, had been to clear her of any suspicion in their betrayal. It wasn't a very good sneak who sold you out and then was almost killed, but Max's concern was not that Scarlett had purposely betrayed them, but more that she might've

224

let something slip to her lover, Jair Otelo.

Scarlett had been quite clear that she sent Jair packing after he distracted her from keeping watch on Scads. As a matter of fact, Scarlett had pointed out, she'd told Jair that if she ever saw him again, she'd put a hatchet between his eyes. And, she had most definitely not let on to him that they were setting up an ambush for the meeting with the Headless Rooster. This she was sure of, because she'd sent him packing before she knew that they were setting up said ambush.

"What's the latest on John?" Scads asked.

"Marian spent the night at his bedside," Max said. "Found her there this morning when I stopped by the hospital."

Marian did indeed look like it'd been a sleepless night. Her hair was askew, and her pantsuit rumpled. "He is in an induced coma."

"What does that mean?" Tucker asked. "I mean, I know what it is, but what are the chances of recovery?"

Marian shuffled her feet under her chair. "Only twenty percent of patients put in an induced coma fully recover. The doctors aren't quite that hopeful in John's case, seeing as he was shot in the head."

"They don't know John," Scarlett said. "What's the plan, boss?"

All eyes turned to Max. How had he become the leader of this group, he wondered, looking around, knowing that he was responsible for their lives. That it was he who'd gathered them together with the purpose of bringing justice to the most powerful people in the world. And neglected to think too deeply about the possibility that some of them might be casualties. Had he bitten off more than he could chew, as Kinsley liked to say?

So far, they'd been stymied at every turn. If this were a chess match, they'd be a few moves away from check and with one important piece missing. It was time to turn the tide of the game. Time to stop playing defense, but to attack. That had been the original plan, to charge forward and topple their opponent before he knew what had hit him, but several blows had set Max and the band back on their heels.

"Okay, here's the thing," he said. "This has gotten epic in proportion, and by that, I mean incredibly fucking dangerous. Anybody who wants to walk can do so now."

"We're here for a good time," Tucker said. "Not a long time."

"Is that some country music shit?" Scads asked.

"Trooper. Canadian Rock Band from the '70s. Before your time."

"Let me know when the good times begin," Scads said.

"As soon as we start getting some payback," Scarlett said. "So, let's have it, boss. Nobody's walking. What's the plan?"

Max cleared his throat. "As I see it, we have four things to follow up on, all of which will create huge public discomfort for Rupert Hastings, quite possibly put him in the crosshairs of the law, and at the very least, destroy his bid for the presidency."

"But not make a pauper of him," Tucker said.

"Nor put him six feet into the earth," Scarlett said.

"Okay, so what are they?" Dale asked. "I'm in the dark about a lot of this."

Max held up a single finger. "One. We find Zella. If we can convince her that we can provide for her safety and get her to share the video, the public humiliation will shatter his reputation, especially with his strong fanbase of blue-collar rural supporters."

"She's the Thai prostitute?" Dale asked. "Heck, those people will just think he's a stud and wish they could be like him, getting exotic escorts and all of that."

Scads snorted. "He's supposedly on video having Sajja squirting water up his ass while Zella shocks his balls with a zapper, or vice versa, I forget."

Dale looked like he wanted to ask a question, opened his mouth, shut it, nodded his head, and remained quiet.

"I will find her," Scarlett said.

Max looked at her. "We are out of time. Get it done. Now."

Scarlett nodded.

"Second," Max said. "Sexual harassment and possibly assault of the models that are part of Hastings' Catwalk. Young girls being pressured into...well, into terrible things by that pig. How none of them have come forward is beyond me, but we need to get somebody willing to go on the record about it all."

"Awful hard to make that sort of public mind-bending career and social cluster-fuck decision in your life," Marian said. "I mean, their career as models will be effectively over, their visions of grandeur dashed, and they also have to go on the record admitting they allowed themselves to be sexual toys for perverts to further their career?"

"They are victims," Tucker said.

"Of course, they're fucking victims," Marian said. "But what will the modeling world say? They will be outcasts. What will other women their age think of them, the goody-two-shoes who already think their shit doesn't stink? They'll be shunned, and not just by their mothers and their fathers."

"Can you run with this one, Tucker?" Max asked. "The two models he sent to my room in Vegas were named Gina and Darcy. And he let them go, most likely effectively ending their careers anyway. See if you can get them to talk, go on the record, bring charges. If this is like the Weinstein thing, once one or two women show their mettle, others will be inspired to follow."

"On it."

"You convince them to come forward, we'll sit down together," Marian said. "And I'll get the paperwork drawn up, and we'll burn that bastard to the ground."

"Before you get started, come on back to my office," Max said. "I have some information that will help you track them down."

"Gotcha, boss."

"Then we got the hacking operation he's running from the Isle of the Holy Grail," Max said. "There must be something illegal about all of that."

"Unethical, yes," Scads said. "Illegal enough to implicate a billionaire in a crime? Doubtful."

"How about the people he's hacked?" Dale asked. "Who are they, and is he blackmailing them?"

Scads scoffed. "Only the most powerful people in the country, heck, in the world, and yes, he is most certainly blackmailing them, but there is no proof, and well...."

"Well, what?" Marian asked.

"If word gets out that we are privy to information about who Rupert Hastings is blackmailing, we'll be arrested, no, we will be whisked away in the middle of the night and find ourselves victims of the Patriot Act, sharing a cell with Middle Eastern terrorists in Guantanamo Bay, Cuba."

"Anything you can do about that, Marian?" Max asked.

"We can...well, not really. I mean, not necessarily under the Patriot Act, which has technically expired and was aimed at immigrants and not citizens—"

"Bullshit," Tucker said. "It was aimed at anybody they thought was subversive."

"The intent was... oh, whatever. Yes, if certain members of the government and/or federal authorities want to detain you and make you disappear, you will be gone. And there's not much I'll be able to do about it."

"To Gitmo," Scads said. "Maybe we can all be cellmates."

"Even though the prison there has been called a violation of international law by the United Nations, the International Red Cross, and Human Rights Watch," Tucker said.

Max held up his hand. "See if you can figure out an angle that helps destroy Rupert Hastings and doesn't end up with all of us disappearing to a black site."

"Easy Peasy," Scads said. "Maybe a little blackmail of our own. I'll get on it."

"You working here or in your apartment?"

"No offense, but I think I'll stay here. Not sure I feel all that safe in Brooklyn on my own."

"What do you want me to do?" Dale asked.

"You're command center. You don't leave here until this thing is done. All communication goes through you."

"Can't we just contact you directly, boss?" Scarlett asked.

Max shook his head. "I might be busy, and this way we can all access the latest updates by checking in with Dale."

"Is that thing number four?" Tucker asked.

"Yes. I'll be handling that one personally."

"How about me?" Marian asked. "You want me to just keep digging away at the lawsuits pending against Hastings?"

"I got something else for you. Let's go back to my office. Once we're done, I need to see Scarlett and then Tucker. I'll find you in your war room, Scads, after I talk to the others."

Chapter Thirty-Three

Chokoloskee Island, Florida

After Max had private conversations with the band, giving explicit instructions on their particular mission and stressing that they were, in fact, not supposed to communicate any of this with Dale Allen, but to Max directly, he went straight to the airport. Just over three hours later, he landed in Miami to find a waiting Mustang Convertible. Where he was going, a driver would only be a liability and an inconvenience. This was a task he would be doing on his own.

At ninety miles an hour, it took him just over an hour to get to Chokoloskee along the Tamiami Highway, the road whose name was a combination of Tampa and Miami, the two cities it connected to each other. He was more worried about gators crossing the road than police, but completed the trip without running into either aggravation.

The pleasure yacht, the *Red Lotus*, was in the slip at the marina on Chokoloskee Island, and the bearded fellow who'd met the drug runners a few days back was finishing up cleaning the exterior of the vessel. Max thought of confronting the man then and there, but figured a commotion in public was less likely to achieve the desired results. So he waited until the man left in an old, beat-up pickup truck, and then followed him.

He had no chance of finding the drug operation hidden inside the Ten Thousand Islands. He needed intel from somebody, and this man was the likeliest choice. Chokoloskee Island was connected to the mainland by a causeway to Everglades City, and it was this low-lying stretch that the man led Max to in his rattling and rusted-out truck. Chokoloskee Island itself towered a full twenty feet over sea level, primarily due to Native Americans depositing their shellfish there for 2000 years, but this spit of land appeared approximately just feet above the level of the bay.

The truck took a right and clunked its way behind an outdoor bar called the *Gator Hole*. Max parked in the far corner of the largely deserted lot. It was the shoulder season in the Everglades, he reasoned, that time between the arrival of the snowbirds who come south for the winter and the influx of those migrating to the water in the oppressive summer months.

Max wasn't sure what his plan was, but he followed the man into the thatch-covered bar. There was a mix of picnic tables and wicker settees, a bar wrapped around one side with maybe sixteen stools, facing a makeshift stage in front of the boxed-in restrooms that bordered the front parking lot and road. On stage were three fellows playing guitars and a sign that proclaimed them to be the *Hot Country Band*.

Fake gators, huge and small, adorned the walls, stood upon the bar, and hung from the ceiling. The bearded guy shaped like a Coke bottle settled his way onto a barstool, and the bartender poured a Bud Light for him without asking. Max figured the guy either was more enlightened than he looked or hadn't heard about the scandalous Bud Light promotion featuring the social media influencer Dylan Mulvaney.

Max sat down next to him—a three-foot-tall gator perched on the bar to his right with a mounted deer head above. It was cool under the thatched roof, the band was pretty darn entertaining, and the vibe of the place was just people out to have a good time. He tried to order a Manhattan, was met with a blank stare, and settled for Jack Daniels on the rocks.

"Band's kicking it pretty good," Max said to the bearded man.

"They're regulars." The man turned his thin neck and head to look at Max. "You're not."

"Came down from Charlotte to do some fishing," Max said. He was glad that he'd had the thought to change from his expensive suit into his Long Beach duds, board shorts that went to his knees, and a T-shirt with the

Carolina Panthers logo. "Just got into town."

"Panthers, huh? You know, we got some of them down here. They estimate six of them pussycats running 'round in the Glades." The man cackled, took a drink, laughed again. "Was seven up 'til last year, but a buddy of mine shot one of 'em. Made some money selling that pelt, he sure did."

Max eyeballed the man, trying to distinguish if the man was threatening him or just making small talk about friends poaching endangered animals. He decided it was the latter. "Not much of a hunter, but I sure do like going out fishing."

"Good place to come to, this is."

"You know what's running now?"

The man turned the rest of his rotund body so that he was facing Max. "You looking for a boat and a guide?"

"Sure am. You know of somebody with a boat who knows his way around?"

"Snook. Snook is heading out to find cooler water. You ever fish for snook?"

"Can't say that I have."

"Well, if you like sport, there ain't nothin' better. Son-of-a-bitches get up to be over forty pounds and put up a helluva fight."

"Sounds like you're a man who knows what he's talking about." Max held out his hand. "Rob Hode."

"Snapper Brown. And I sure as shit know what I'm talking about, and I got me a fishing boat I can take you out on."

* * *

"Well, you sure made a mess of this," Forge said. Her eyes were hidden behind black Cartier sunglasses with gold frames. "And after I made it so easy for you."

"The men on the boat have paid for missing the broad." The Headless Rooster had his own dark glasses, Ray-Ban Aviator Classics, just like Tom Cruise wore in Top Gun. "Right before I shot them in the back of the head, they swore that they got her, and she's most likely floating on the tides out into the Atlantic Ocean."

"It's not her that I care so much about."

"Cops showed up a lot faster than I thought they would. Didn't really want to stay around and find out if you have enough clout to get me out of jail or not."

Forge lowered her dark glasses to reveal eyes blacker and colder than the sunglasses. "You are lucky that you are still alive."

"Cool your jets, *muchacha*. I said I'll take care of it, and take care of it I will."

Forge wondered about cutting the man's neck with her Crescent Blade. He was so cocksure, and it would be so easy and satisfying at the same time. Then, just get up and walk away from their sidewalk table at some anonymous Hell's Kitchen café as if nothing had happened. And she'd finally know the answer to whether roosters really continued to run around after having their heads chopped off.

"You had seventeen professionals, and you couldn't finish off one playboy billionaire and his nerdy gamer accomplice?" She scoffed. Ran her tongue over her lips. "That's what happens when you send a man to do a woman's job."

The Headless Rooster smiled lazily. "Creed's righthand man is dead."

"In the hospital. Still, very much alive. But out of play."

"I have a man on it. Consider it done."

"I am glad you feel comfortable handling the man in a coma. Very brave of you."

"It was mostly your people at the junkyard," the Headless Rooster said. "Not mine. It is more your failure than mine."

Forge nodded. "But you will correct the situation?"

"We will find the woman and finish the job as well. Jair Otelo will reach out if she surfaces, and then she, too, will be corrected."

Forge flicked her wrist, and the curved blade was at the Mexican's chin. "Max Creed. Dead. You have forty-eight hours. After that, you will be answering a question I have long had, and I will resolve the matter on my own."

"What is the question, muchacha?" The Headless Rooster smiled and winked at her. "Do I have magical beans in my pecker?"

"Kill the Brazilian woman. Find Creed. Kill him as well."

"His private jet is gone. He flew to Miami."

Forge winced. "Miami?"

"Yes."

"Do you know why?"

"I am concerned."

"Concerned?"

"That he may know of the facility in the Ten Thousand Islands."

"Find him. Kill him."

"I have people looking for him."

"Get there. I will ask my source where he has gone and let you know."

* * *

Half an hour before sunrise, at seven a.m., Max was sitting on a bench swing by the marina waiting for Snapper to show. He had a cup of Colada, a Cuban coffee, in his hand that he'd gotten to go after having a pretty good breakfast at the *Havana Café* just around the corner. They hadn't been open yet, but had gone ahead and seated him on the patio and whipped him up a Havana omelet.

He wore jeans with his CZ Luger shoved down into the back, covered up by his long-sleeved shirt from The Lazy Pelican in Long Beach. Snapper had said that it was still too early for bugs to be much of a nuisance, but Max wasn't buying it. He also had a baseball cap pulled low, but instead of a fishing rod, he carried a briefcase. In the Mustang, there were ten five-gallon containers of gasoline.

Snapper's truck rumbled up, and the man clambered stiffly out, his eyes looking for, and finding Max, sitting on the porch swing looking out at Chokoloskee Bay.

"Where's your fishing gear?" Snapper asked as he walked over to Max.

"Slight change of plan."

"What's that? You wasting my fucking time, is you?"

Max tapped the space next to him on the bench. "Sit."

"You gonna have to pay me even if you don't go out fishing, you is."

Max pulled out the Luger, lazily waved it at Snapper and then tapped the bench with the pistol. "Sit."

"Look, man, I don't want no trouble. I can't get in no trouble."

"Sit."

Snapper said. "Look, man, I'm on probation. I'm not going to do any smuggling for you. I'm all done with that."

Max had found Wi-Fi and done his homework last night. Snapper had been scooped up in one of the largest drug busts in US history back in 1983, when eighty percent of the adult male population of Everglades City had been arrested on drug smuggling charges. It seemed that the town as a whole was smuggling seventy-five tons of marijuana from Colombia a week through the Ten Thousand Islands.

"I'd have to say you got a raw deal," Max said. "Forty years for moving a bit of pot."

Snapper sank into the bench seat. "Who are you?"

"Served thirty-two years and got released on probation for good behavior."

"There's fucking rapists and murderers that serve less than ten years, and I got forty big ones for transporting some Mary Jane."

"Government took everything you had, I assume," Max said. "No nest egg stashed away?"

Snapper shook his head. Sighed. "I was twenty years old and had just got married. Fucking government took away all the fishing out there." He waved out toward the mangrove islands. "Couldn't make a living no more. And then opportunity came. Fellow asked me if I wanted to make some money being a bale hopper. One night, hell, part of one night, unloading the product from boats into trucks, and I got paid twenty-five grand. Twice what I made in a whole year fishing."

"How come you're dipping your toes back in? I mean, on probation and all, you get caught, you spend the rest of your life in prison."

"What are you talking about?'

Max nodded his head at the dock slip. The sun behind them had risen far enough to begin illuminating the marina. "That's a pretty nice cabin cruiser. The *Red Lotus*."

Snapper looked nervously from the boat to Max. "What are you talking about?"

"I spoke with a few of the locals. They think of you like a hero. You did what you had to, moved some marijuana that isn't even illegal now in most states, Florida excepted. You refused to give any names, and the feds threw the book at you and gave you forty years in the big house for it."

"Wife didn't think so. She divorced me and got remarried, some asshole up in Copeland."

"And, it seems, the people in Everglades City pride themselves that they never dipped into smuggling cocaine, which was big in the '80s, but a whole different ballgame than pot."

"Nothing wrong with smoking a bowl or a joint."

"How come you're now involved in smuggling heroin mixed with Iso, which is extremely lethal and is killing thousands and thousands of people every year?"

"What? Iso? Heroin? I'm not. No fuckin' way."

Max pointed the pistol at the Red Lotus. "That's what they're doing. And you're helping them. You know as well as I do that when you get rung up for being an accomplice, you're done."

"I don't know nothing about that, man. I just get paid to moor their boat, clean it, give them an airboat to go out in."

Max shook his head. "You know better, Snapper. You aren't stupid."

"What do you want?"

"I want to help you."

"Help me?"

"Bring me out to where the people in that boat go, and I'll make sure you stay out of what happens next. Which is likely to bring some attention from certain government authorities."

"I don't know. I just trade out boats with them."

"You're not stupid, Snapper. You know those islands. And you're a curious fellow. You know."

"They'll kill me."

"They'll all be in jail by the end of the day."

"Not the big bosses. They'll put out a hit on my head."

Max nodded. No need to mention the Chinese Triad or the involvement of a candidate for president whom Snapper would most likely support. "The Headless Rooster is going down soon. Until then, you might need to lay low."

"Lay low?"

"Disappear into the Glades."

"I got bills, man."

Max nodded at the briefcase at his feet. "There's a hundred grand in there. You take me out and help me do what I'm going to do, there's another fifty grand in it for you. I suggest you hide it and use it sparingly. Not like back in '83 when you all were buying yourself new flashy cars, homes, swimming pools, and whatnot. Be smart."

Chapter Thirty-Four

Ten Thousand Islands, Florida

They cruised across the bay on Snapper Brown's fishing boat. Max had thought they would take an airboat to navigate the narrow passages of the Ten Thousand Islands, but Snapper had scoffed at him, telling him that the noise alone would get them shot before they were within half a mile of the facility. Instead, the plan was to moor off Buzzard Key and take the rowboat up Lostman's River before diverging onto waterways without names.

Snapper had not been happy to guide Max into the mangrove maze, but also did not want to go back to prison, liked the idea of the money, but most of all, was aghast that he'd been helping in the smuggling of hard drugs. It appeared that, while the population of Everglades City and Chokoloskee Island still embraced the romance of being gentlemen bandits helping others bliss out on pot, the notion of being associated with heroin, much less Iso, a drug which the man had never even heard of, was repugnant.

Once off Buzzard Key, the two of them stacked the ten containers of gasoline in the aluminum skiff, and Snapper manned the oars. Max sat at the front to warn of jutting rocks, tangled roots, and other impediments to their progress. He could feel the Luger at his back, and his senses tingled the deeper into the mangrove they went. It really wasn't like islands at all, but a labyrinth of passageways into a jungle.

Within minutes, Max was lost, knowing that he might never find his way out of here if left to his own devices. Snapper told him that the warehouse facility was built into an islet that the locals called Pirate Key. It was about four acres in size, was nestled into the center of the Ten Thousand Islands, and as desolate and unapproachable a place as could be found.

For the occasional kayaker who strayed into the area, the smugglers had lookouts that would dissuade them, words and the wave of an automatic weapon usually sufficing to scare them off right quick. But Snapper knew a route that was not watched, as far as he knew. That last part is what made Max's neck tingle every time they eased around a bend, wishing he had more firepower with him than just a pistol.

Snapper stopped rowing, and they snuggled into a small indentation in the gnarled and twisted mangrove vegetation, the trees ranging from a few feet off the ground to twenty feet in height. The mangrove is the only tree that is capable of having its root system submerged in salt water and survive, even thrive, in the loose soil and changing tides. Max looked to his right, expecting to see snakes and alligators ready to pounce.

"What are we stopping for?" Max asked.

"The Kraken Cave is in there." Snapper nodded to the thick mangroves. "We're on the backside of the entranceway."

"The Kraken Cave?"

Snapper snorted impatiently. "That's what us locals call the warehouse the Mexicans built there. But we just thought it was weed, man, not hard stuff."

"You're doing the right thing here, Snapper."

"We don't got all day."

"You say the building is built down into the ocean floor and only protrudes up about five feet?"

"Yep. If you ain't gonna do your thing, let's get out of here."

"Are there alligators?"

Snapper shook his head. "Unlikely. Too salty for them. Possibly some crocs. Maybe a python."

Max nodded. Stepped from the boat into the tangled limbs of the mangroves. He was immediately entangled as if snared in a spiderweb.

It was only fifty feet or so to the back of the sunken concrete building, but it took them over an hour to transport the ten containers of gasoline through the twisted labyrinth of jungle.

It was a square building, approximately seventy-five feet along each side, to Max's best guesstimate. The top was a bed of loose saltwater and dirt dotted with mangrove trees as camouflage from the air. Without a guide, it'd take the authorities a long time to find this place, and there apparently wasn't anybody willing to face the wrath of the populace by ratting to a government who was the sworn enemy, especially since that infamous raid that had resulted in so many of their young men ending up in prison.

Snapper handed the containers up onto the roof, a height of only about five feet, and then retreated to the skiff. Max thoroughly doused the mangrove trees. He was not too worried about setting the concrete warehouse on fire and destroying the drugs within or injuring the workers presumably inside. It was going to be more like a flare gun, sending a signal into the sky for the Feds to see.

When he was done, Max built a small pyre of cut vegetation in the center of the roof, dripped the last of the gasoline onto it, lit a cigar, took several puffs, and then cast the stogie into the middle. By the time he reached the edge, the fire was beginning to ripple out like spreading cracks in a windshield.

The heat of the fire was similar to opening a hot oven door by the time he got back to the rowboat. There were yells of alarm from the far side of the building where the entrance was located. As Snapper put his back to the oars, Max took out the satellite phone and called Sally Blum.

"Look for the flames and the smoke. Somewhere in the middle of the Ten Thousand Islands region. The Kraken Cave is lit."

"The Kraken Cave?" she asked.

"That's what the locals call it." Max hung up and looked back over his shoulder. Thick, dark smoke billowed into the sky, and flames could be seen dimly crackling in their midst.

"That the Feds?" Snapper asked, breathing heavily.

"Yep."

They reached the fishing boat as the first of the helicopters came in from the northeast, flying low in a direct line for the capacious clouds of smoke. Max sincerely hoped he hadn't set the entire Ten Thousand Islands on fire, but was fairly certain that the fire would quickly burn itself out in the sodden terrain.

Max scrambled aboard the fishing boat and tied off the line thrown to him from the rowboat by Snapper, and in seconds they were swinging wide through the mangroves to return on the Turner River side of Chokoloskee.

"We'll dock at the Smallwood Store and walk back to our vehicles," Snapper said. "I imagine the bayside is filled with federal boats looking to sweep up any crooks on the run."

"How long?" Max asked.

"This is the Chokoloskee Pass we're going through now. Should be there in about half an hour."

As they rounded Rabbit Key, two airboats suddenly whined into life and came shooting out from cover at them.

"Shit," Snapper said. "Are those Feds?"

Max had the binoculars on them. He recognized the Headless Rooster and the tall Mexican who'd been with him at the junkyard a few days back. There were four other Mexicans he didn't recognize.

"Nope." Max pulled his Luger. "Worse. It's the bad guys. This thing have any giddy up?"

The airboats were a hundred yards out when the first shot cracked out. Snapper began swerving in a lame attempt at evasive maneuvers. To be fair, the fishing boat was in no way constructed for dipping and dodging. The man was cursing, a string of obscenities, something about trying to outrun airboats in the mangrove islands being about as useless as a screen door on a submarine.

The shots from the careening airboat didn't seem all that accurate, even though Max heard several bullets thud into the hull, and one splatted into the helm, inches from Snapper's face. To his credit, the ex-smuggler and convict didn't flinch as he tried to maneuver the bulky fishing boat through the mangrove keys.

The distance between them was steadily closing. The airboats were only about thirty yards back, and Max could clearly make out their faces. A huge bear of a man was at the wheel of the boat with the Headless Rooster and his right-hand man. The other boat carried shorter, wiry men who had the look of *pistoleros*. That meant there were four rifles shooting at them, and the range was closing steadily.

"Cut the motor when you go around this key," Max yelled.

Snapper looked at him like he was crazy, but as the fishing boat rounded a key that was no more than an acre in size, he pulled the throttle to neutral and cut the helm to the right, avoiding the wake from swamping them and turning them sideways to the incoming airboats. He also had the foresight to drop to the deck and lie flat.

Max steadied himself on one knee, the pistol out in front of him in a two-handed grip. As the first airboat rounded the corner, cutting the wheel to miss hitting them, Max fired three shots. The first hit the pilot in the mouth, exploding teeth and blood all over the wheel. The second shot hit the tall right-hand Mexican in the chest, and the third scratched the face of the Headless Rooster.

Then the second airboat came around the key and slammed into the fishing boat, knocking Max tumbling. He came back to a crouch and pulled the trigger at point break range, the bullets ripping into the pilot and another man on the second boat before the third man, apparently having lost his grip on the rifle, leaped into the boat and tackled Max.

Max was already rolling before they hit the deck and slid from the man's grasp on impact. He went to bring the Luger to bear on the man, just as a gunshot rang out from the first boat and a bullet hit his pistol, his hand going numb with the impact, the weapon knocked from his paralyzed fingers.

Max rolled as more shots followed. With his left hand, he drew the *bo-shuriken* from the scabbard at his ankle. He palmed the six-inch Japanese double-ended blade, hoping that his endless training with Scarlett in the jungles of Brazil had paid off, but before he could come to his feet, the man who'd leaped into the boat lunged at him. Max hooked his foot behind the man's ankle and toppled him to the deck.

Before the man regained his wits, Max plunged the blade into his neck, severing the carotid artery, spraying blood like an erupting volcano, drenching Max. His eyes clouded in a red haze, he looked up to see the Headless Rooster standing in the bow of the airboat, rifle pointed down at Max on the deck of the fishing boat.

With a demented grin of enjoyment, he pulled the trigger to send a burst of automatic rifle fire to riddle Max's body with lead. But, in the sudden stillness of the day, only marred by the gurgling of the man who'd just had a major artery severed, all that could be heard was the click of an empty chamber.

Max rolled, his arm sweeping over his body, as he let the *bo-shuriken* loose, the Japanese throwing knife hissing through the air of the Everglades, planting itself in the Headless Rooster's cheek. The man screamed in pain, dropped the rifle, and clawed at his face. As Max looked for his own pistol, the airboat suddenly roared into life, and as he looked over his shoulder, Max saw the tall right-hand man turn the wheel and send the craft skimming away over the water. He must've been wearing body armor, Max thought with chagrin.

Snapper poked his head up from under the wheel of the fishing boat. He looked at the man bleeding out first, then at the floating airboat with two bodies on it, then at the other disappearing airboat heading back into the mangrove forest of the Ten Thousand Islands, and finally, his eyes came to rest on Max.

"Not sure a hundred and fifty grand is gonna be enough," he said.

Chapter Thirty-Five

Thai Town, Los Angeles

Max was sitting on a bench on Hollywood Boulevard in the middle of Thai Town in Los Angeles. Tasty Williams sat on his left, and Scarlett on his right. He thought that they probably made quite the trio in the six-block neighborhood of Thai Town. Busty, blonde porn star, middle-aged white-male billionaire, and sleek Brazilian assassin.

While Max had been down in the Everglades doing some boating, hunting, and starting a campfire, as Scarlett put it, she had had the great idea to tap into Tasty's knowledge base. Having worked as both a stripper and in the pornographic film industry, she had more connections to Zella's world than all the rest of them put together.

"I been asked to do a lot of funky shit in the movies," Tasty said, stifled a laugh, and choked, which led to a fit of coughing. "But...never anything as freaking deviant as what Rupert likes his lady friends to do to him."

Max looked at Scarlett. "How much did you tell her?"

Scarlett shrugged. "Everything. You're the one who brought her on when you were hacking the computers on that island of misfit toys. Figured half in, might as well be all the way in."

"That's what she said," Tasty said.

Max tried to smile but couldn't quite do it. John was in the hospital. The entire mission was up shit's creek. "Zella is the key to bringing the man who killed your sister to justice."

Tasty nodded and said nothing. Message received.

"Before we go any further, are you sure that we're not leading the baddies right to Zella?" Scarlett asked. "I mean, they seem to be one step ahead of us all the way. Especially bribing those mercs to change sides. When did we hire them? A few hours before they turned on us?"

Max stared at the blue sky that seemed to belie LA's reputation for smog and wildfire smoke. He thought that he had a good idea who the snitch was. But now he wasn't so sure. He'd made sure to keep the plans from her, instead, meeting with her one-on-one so as to give her a busy job to perform that didn't overlap with the work being done by the rest of the band.

Still, the Headless Rooster had been waiting for him in the Everglades. It was possible that it was just a coincidence, and the Mexican don had been at the warehouse facility when Max set the roof on fire, and then had come after him and Snapper. But it didn't feel that way.

"Somebody in the band is selling us out," he said.

"Who?"

"I don't know," he said. "I thought I did, but now I'm not so certain."

"You thought you knew what?" Scarlett asked. "Who do you think the snitch is?"

Max's reverie was interrupted by this comment, and his eyes turned to Scarlett. "I'm still working on it."

"Here she comes," Scarlett said.

Zella came out of the Crispy Pork Gang Thai Restaurant, looking both ways before slipping dark glasses on and walking quickly up the street. Tasty had tracked her down with the help of the producer of several of her movies. This gent also owned several strip clubs and was the money behind a string of pimps in Central Los Angeles.

Max was not sure of the relationship that Tasty had with the guy, but he put the picture out to his people in Thai Town, and a hit had come back. Zella had come into town two weeks earlier and turned some tricks working solo before the pimp in charge of the Thai girls paid her a visit and told her to stop or join his stable.

She stopped, but Scarlett had come to town, shared her picture around, and found that she worked at the Crispy Pork Gang Restaurant as a waitress, under the table. The manager had tried to say he didn't know her, but Scarlett caught his hesitation, and could be quite persuasive when she wanted to be. Her next shift, the manager told Scarlett, started at noon today, and so, she and Tasty had been here watching when she showed up. Max had rolled into town just about an hour ago.

Scarlett followed behind Zella at about twenty feet, Max and Tasty giving her a head start before standing up to amble along. Zella was a bit skittish and circled down and around the block, and Scarlett called to hand the pursuit to Tasty, in case she'd been seen following. Max made sure to stay within a block of Tasty as they followed down Hollywood Boulevard. He caught up to Tasty, standing in the shade of a large billboard proclaiming the Songkran Festival for the Thai New Year coming up in a couple of weeks. Scarlett slid up next to them.

"She went in the motel," Tasty nodded her head across the street. "Room 29."

"What's the plan?" Scarlett asked.

"I suppose I'll go knock on the door and talk to her."

"Tasty, why don't you go out the back and make sure she doesn't climb out the bathroom window and make a run for it," Scarlett said. "And I'll stand guard out front in case we've been betrayed."

As Tasty walked off, Max turned to Scarlett. "Who do you think the fink is?"

Scarlett shrugged. "I was talking about that with Marian the other day in the office. No idea."

Max froze. "Did you tell her about me going to the Everglades?"

"Yeah, I guess I…" Scarlett's face flushed. "Wait…you think?"

Max nodded. "That's why I told you all to not share anything with anybody."

"But Marian?" Scarlett grabbed Max's arm and clenched. "Shit. I told her about this, too."

Max handed her a set of keys. "Black SUV down that way in front of Siam Book Center. Call Tasty, pick her up, and then get me and Zella in front of room 29."

Scarlett took off down the sidewalk, and Max jogged across the street to the motel and then walked briskly through the parking lot to room 29 and knocked three times on the door. There was no answer. Twice more. He saw the curtain move.

"Zella, you're in danger. We have to leave right now."

The door opened, but the chain remained in place. "How did you find me?"

"It doesn't matter. We must go."

"Why should I trust you? You got Sajja killed."

A white Chrysler sedan careened into the lot and skidded to a stop. The passenger-side window rolled down, and a woman leaned out with a submachine pistol, and Max shot her in the face. It was the woman from the junkyard. Her fingers convulsed on the trigger, and bullets sprayed into the air, some of them thudding into the eaves of the motel.

A man got out of the far side back door of the car with an automatic rifle, and Max put his shoulder into the motel door and burst through, knocking a shocked Zella to the floor underneath him as lead tore up the interior of the room. Max rolled to the side, grasping Zella, who weighed almost nothing, by the arm and pulling her along behind and out of the open doorway.

There was a screeching of tires outside. It seemed quick for Scarlett to be back already, but Max risked a look out the window. A second sedan had pulled up, and Max recognized the white flattop mercenary from the junkyard who'd been standing next to the Headless Rooster. He was one of seven men with weapons leveled at the motel, and then a thunderous eruption broke the momentary silence as they all opened fire on the motel.

Max pulled out his phone and hit Scarlett's name. "Change of plans. Back window. Now."

Zella was staring at him wide-eyed but far from scared. Max supposed that the woman must've seen a lot in life if being trapped in a motel room by a bunch of soldiers of fortune firing automatic weapons didn't send her into a panic.

Max pointed to the bathroom, then to Zella, and began to slither across the room on his stomach. He reached the door and was happy to see her right behind him. There was a window to the left of the toilet that had just a few shards of glass left under the fusillade of bullets.

The firing eased up and then stopped completely. Max stood, smashed the last of the glass with his pistol barrel, picked up Zella, shoved her through the opening, and then clambered through behind her.

A black SUV came to a shuddering halt on the side street. Scarlett leaned out the open window. "C'mon. Over here."

Max grabbed Zella by the hand and ran down the alleyway toward the vehicle. Tasty was ahead of them, proving quite fleet of foot. As they reached the open back door of the SUV, shots erupted behind them. Max turned, aimed, and fired, his shot taking off part of a man's face.

A sedan came screeching down the street, and Scarlett stepped out of the SUV, pulled a Mac-10 submachine gun from under her jacket, and opened fire. The windshield exploded first, and then the front tires, and the automobile veered into a lamppost. Three men tumbled out as Max leaped into the back of the SUV, pulling Zella behind him, and then they were off, screeching down the side street.

As they reached the crossroad, the second sedan suddenly blocked their way. Scarlett cut the wheel to the right. For just a second, Max was face to face with the white flattop mercenary who appeared to be the leader. It was no more than four feet, and Max shot him in the nose. Then they were gone, racing down the road.

Max looked over his shoulder. There was no pursuit. "Let's get to the airport," he said.

Chapter Thirty-Six

New York City

The text was simple. *I found Berta Huffington.*

Max had just woken as the jet made the approach into Teterboro Airport in New Jersey. It was from Dale Allen. He texted out his reply. *Where?*

"What's the plan, boss?" Scarlett asked, plopping down in a bucket seat across from him.

"Dale just sent me the address for the woman who took John Little's virginity, sold him into sex slavery, and then popped up on his doorstep a few days back."

"Sorry about spilling the beans to Marian. Shit. *Pisar Na Bola.* I'm sorry I let you down. How did you know it was her?"

Max yawned. Pressed a button and asked for coffee before replying. "You all came to me with something going on. The enemy was pushing on pressure points. You having Jair Otelo show up on your doorstep. They were threatening Tucker's cousin. Scads was being pushed by a Mexican drug cartel."

"And this woman who scarred John's life."

Max thought about the fact that John was now asexual, an ace by psychological circumstances. "Yes."

"All of us were being scammed, intimidated, or threatened in some way. All except Marian."

"I imagine that Marian has been pushed in some way. I don't know how, or in what way, yet. All I know is that she didn't come to me with whatever it is."

"Meaning she'd been conscripted."

Max nodded. "That's why I told you all to keep your plans to yourself. My bad, I should've been more explicit."

"But you weren't a hundred percent sure yet."

"I had to be certain it was Marian. She deserved every shred of doubt possible."

"And then I spilled the beans and told her about you going to the Everglades and shared with her that I'd found Zella in LA. Shit."

"Take Zella back to the office. Get her to share the video with Scads and do the voice-over thing. Do not leave her side for one second. I have promised her that she will be safe, and I mean to honor that bond."

"I won't let you down, boss. What are you going to do?" Scarlett smirked. "I promise not to tell Marian."

"Tie up some loose ends. Pay John's tormentor, Mrs. Huffington, a visit. Meet with Marian. Check on John in the hospital. And then I'll come back to the office, and we'll unleash our final crusade."

"What about the porn star?" Scarlett blushed. "Not meant in a derogatory way, boss. She's one bad-ass lady. We all do what we must do in this world."

Max looked to the back corner of the cabin where Tasty was sprawled out fast asleep. "Send her home, I suppose."

"You said she had a vendetta against Hastings, too, didn't you?"

"Yeah. Her half-sister committed suicide after being assaulted by Hastings, who then had her fired from the modeling agency for non-compliance."

"And she helped you get into that mainframe on that island that houses all of Hastings' dirt, didn't she?"

"That she did."

"She was a big help in locating Zella. Didn't shirk from any of the nasty stuff, either."

"What are you saying?" Max asked.

Scarlett pursed her lips. Sighed. "She deserves to be in on this until the end. See the fruits of her labors."

Max stared at the cynical Brazilian assassin and smiled. "Sure. Bring her along with you."

* * *

Max stared at the body of the dead woman on the kitchen floor. She had been strangled, her face purple and mottled. Rats had begun gnawing away at her flesh. They had scurried away when Max broke down the door, but were starting to creep back, angry at the intrusion on their meal. There was the stench of death in the air, but also that of rotting food, and something else that clung to the fabric of the apartment that couldn't quite be described.

Mrs. Huffington lived, had lived, in a fifth-floor walkup in Hunts Point in the Bronx. She was one of a very few white people in the neighborhood, Max guessed, as it seemed to be mostly Hispanic, partially black, and totally poor. His driver had seemed nervous as Max had exited the limousine to climb the stairs to the apartment over the corner bodega.

Out the window, Max could see Rikers Island, the holding grounds literally built on ashes by convicts, and the place that many of the local inhabitants of Hunts Point would most likely pass through at some point in their lives. Max felt sympathy for poor Mrs. Huffington living in such squalor, strangled, and being eaten by rats. Even after what she'd done to John Little.

There was nothing to be done about it. He stepped out into the hallway where a cluster of people had gathered, having heard him bust down the door. One man brandished a knife. The butt of a pistol peaked from another man's waistband, gold chains dangling from his neck, while a woman cowered behind him. Max suggested that somebody call the police to report a dead body, but nobody seemed much interested in the idea.

The limo driver, a fellow by the name of Dave, seemed quite relieved when Max slid back into the car. Mt. Sinai Hospital seemed to be more to his liking when told where to go next. To his credit, there was a group of teenagers gathered around the car, wondering if they should mess with the guy, but fearful that it was owned by some violent drug dealer.

251

Somehow, the death of Mrs. Huffington, that vile woman, made Max think of Kinsley. Perhaps it was because they were polar opposites but shared similar endings. It was, as Dorothy Parker said, "I know this will come as a shock to you, Mr. Goldwyn, but in all history, which has held billions and billions of human beings, not a single one ever had a happy ending."

And to her credit, Kinsley, that is, Max thought, she wouldn't want him moping around about her death. If she were able, she'd grab him by the shirtfront, pull him close, and exhort him to embrace life, enjoy each day's tiny miracles and pleasures, and dance at midnight with a beautiful woman.

Which, Max supposed, he had been doing—if not letting himself savor the moments. He'd convinced himself that drinking expensive liquor and cavorting with nude women was but a role he played, and like actors in movies said, the nude scenes were all work and far from sensual elation. The sights of Vegas, Pattaya City, Daytona, New Orleans, Rio, the Isle of the Holy Grail—these he had seen through a haze and not lived and experienced them as himself.

It could be that he dove so deep into character, becoming Max Creed, that he no longer had the ability to taste the nectar of life. He chuckled silently to himself at his inadvertent use of the porn star's name, but in reality, she was a mighty fine lady, if not the one for him. He had finally realized that this was not out of regret for his own murdered bride, but just a fact as he felt the ties to his dead love loosening.

"We're here, sir."

Max looked up to see Mt. Sinai Beth Israel Hospital looming over them. "No more than an hour. I'll text you."

John was alone in his room, hooked up to various IVs pumping medications, as well as multiple monitors, the dim light broken only by the blinking lights of various machines. Max realized that his friend, his mentor, his righthand man—had grown old. Lying there in a comatose state, he looked every one of his fifty-seven years.

Max pulled a chair close, sat down, and grasped John's hand. "How are you, buddy?"

There was no answer. The man was in a coma.

"The doc said your head must be made of concrete to take that round and not explode like a pumpkin dropped from a high-rise on Halloween night. As it is, you got a plate in the back, some sort of metal shield for the next time somebody tries to blindside you from behind."

There was the tiniest flicker of John's eyelids, his body functioning while his brain slept.

"I got some news for you. We found Mrs. Huffington. Or, rather, Dale found her, and I just came from visiting her. She was dead. Somebody strangled her, and the rats were eating her. She was living in a dump up in Hunts Point. I'm thinking being murdered might've been a respite for her from this thing called life."

John's eyes opened wide, wider than normal, the lids peeled back as if trying to expose his entire eyeballs. His lips moved as if trying to say something, but no words came out.

Max pressed the button for the nurse.

John's hand tensed in his pocket, but did not move otherwise. He took a gasping, hoarse breath, and then his eyes closed and his hand relaxed.

The nurse came in, and Max told her what had happened. A doctor came. Vitals were taken. Reports were looked at. Tests were done.

After a bit, the doctor pulled Max aside and told him that it appeared that John was fighting to regain consciousness, and that this often took time, even when the news was good. He suggested that Max should leave now, but the doctor promised to call him with any and all updates.

Max texted the driver. *Pick me up now.*

Max texted Marian. *Meet me for a drink?*

Max texted Sevyn Knight. *Dinner tonight?*

Chapter Thirty-Seven

New York City

Max met Marian at a dive bar sandwiched between SoHo and Greenwich Village. She'd just come from a meeting at the executive office of the immigration court and had twenty minutes before she had to skedaddle across town to another pro bono case.

She was all business in a black pantsuit and white shirt, her leather briefcase on a stool next to her, a shot of tequila, untouched on the bar. Max took the stool on the side not occupied by the briefcase.

"Heard you been busy," Marian said. "Had yourself a little dust up down in the Everglades, did you?"

Max ordered a Jim Beam on the rocks. He doubted the place had anything better for brown liquor. "Who'd you hear that from?"

Marian smiled wearily. "I have my sources."

"I haven't had a chance to touch base with you," Max said. "Everything good?"

"Jesus Christ. You do think I'm the snitch, don't you?"

"What?"

"Oh, give it a fucking rest, Max. I thought it odd that I heard from Scarlett that you were going down to torch one of Hastings' drug warehouses. I thought it might've just been an oversight, or a need-to-know basis, but you think I fucking sold you out."

Max took a slug of the Beam. Shrugged. Not a lot less tasty than a bottle ten times as much. "Did you?"

"Why do you think it was me? Why *would* you ever think it was me?"

"Everybody else on the team has been harassed, threatened, blackmailed, someone trying to get them to turn on me. They all came to me and told me about it."

"You're fucking kidding me, right?" Marian tossed back the shot and slammed the glass back down on the bar. "Okay, Max, here it is. I got pictures of my twin brother, a brother I didn't know I had, but at the same time, I knew, because, you know, we're twins and have that special ESP connection or some such shit like that. He was left behind in China when my mother took me and fled to the US."

"Threatening pictures?"

"Yeah. Video, actually, of him with a bag over his head. Proof of life. Proof of blood."

"I'm sorry. I could've helped."

"Jesus Christ on a fucking popsicle stick, you goddamn nitwit." Marian pushed the empty shot glass at the bartender. "I took care of it."

"You what?"

"I extracted him. He's staying with me now."

Max finished his drink and pushed it to the bartender. "Why didn't you say anything?"

"I'm a big girl, Maxie, and I clean up my own shit." Marian tossed back the second shot, stood up, grasped her briefcase, and turned to stare him in the eye. "And you're a real shit for thinking I turned on you, that I got John almost killed, Scarlett shot, tried to have you assassinated—all because I didn't come crying to you about something in my personal life."

Max watched as she walked out. She was right. He was a real shit. He wondered if she would ever forgive him. Not for quite some time, he guessed, if ever.

* * *

Max was back in the open conference room of the Bryant Park Office. Scarlett, Tasty, and Zella were slouched in chairs. Dale Allen was on his laptop. Scads sat across from him.

On the way back, he'd spoken with Scarlett on the phone and confirmed what he'd guessed. That there'd been another person present, in the vicinity, if not in the conversation, when Scarlett had told Marian about the Everglades and California. Somebody who was always around, lurking on the fringes.

"I've uploaded the video from Zella, and she's done an audio monologue to go with it," Scads said. "When do you want me to flood social media with it?"

Max steepled his fingers under his chin. He was still processing his wrong and hateful intuition that Marian was the betrayer. "Let me think about it."

Scads nodded. "How about all the dirt we hacked into from Hastings' mainframe?"

Max looked at him. Stared out the window. What indeed, he wondered? The scandal would be epic in proportions, maybe powerful enough to topple the government, destroy America. At the very least, it was deadly poison for anybody involved. Very powerful figures would move to quash, discredit, and quiet anybody involved in their quest to prevent their perversions from seeing the light of day.

"It's a real Catch-22," Max said. "We take the chance we'll bring down America, or we get killed."

"We have to do something with it," Scads said.

"I suppose we all have secrets that we don't want aired in public," Max said.

Snippets of things floated through his mind. Young models in his room, the temptation, Thai hookers, one who was dead because of him, Tasty Williams, putting Kinsley's killer into a middle eastern insane asylum, his brain addled by the drugs he'd been selling.

"What are you saying?"

"Can you destroy it?"

"Destroy it?"

Max stood up impatiently. "Put a virus in and shitcan the whole mess. We don't have it. Rupert doesn't have it. Everybody keeps their secrets."

"Some of it is freaking morally total bankrupt," Scads said. "Illegal. Illicit. An offense to humanity."

Max sighed. "Can you shitcan it or not?"

Scads stared angrily at him. "Of course, I can computer herpes the whole thing. Are you sure that's what you want?"

Max nodded. "Make me a hard drive of the worst of it. Then send in the virus."

"You're the boss." Scads stood and stalked off to his office.

Max's phone buzzed. The burner that only the band knew the number. He walked to the far corner of the spacious room before hitting the answer button. "Tucker."

"Max. What's better than two birds in the bush?"

Max could hear the brindling excitement in the man's voice. "A bird in hand?"

"Even better. Both birds in hand."

"Are you telling me the two models are ready to bring charges against Hastings?"

"Yes, they are."

"Where are you?"

"Turns out Gina and Darcy are best of friends and live together in Denver. Both work at the same Hooters."

"You're in Denver?"

"Nope. Just landed at La Guardia. I'm bringing them to the office. You there?"

Max paused, looked around the room. "I am, but don't bring them here. Things are heating up. It's not safe."

"What? Where then?"

"Get a hotel. Not in your name. Just for tonight. I think everything is going to shake out by tomorrow."

"How am I supposed to get a hotel room not in my name?"

"You're the financier. We must own a place that is unoccupied where you can stay. I'll call you when I know something."

Max made a mental note that they needed to develop some safe houses if they ever engaged in another mission. But, he mused with a detached air, that was only if he lived, which at this point he very much doubted would be the case.

* * *

At five o'clock, Scads came into Max's office and set a stick down on his desk. "It's done. Right about now, somebody is pulling their hair out, wondering what the hell happened to the computer. If they're smart, they'll walk out the door, quit, and disappear."

Max nodded. "Shut the door, would you?"

Scads shut the door.

"Sit," Max said.

Scads sat.

"It's for the best," Max said. "This footage would be like trying to douse flames with a hydrogen fire extinguisher."

"Explosive, I know."

"Extremely. And, more than likely, will get us all killed, so we will never know if the entire shitshow burns down or not."

"I'm not afraid to die."

Max shook his head. Just barely into his twenties and not afraid to die. At least Max had gotten into his late thirties before his embrace of death. Perhaps tonight would be the night that the last dance would sound, and he could exit the stage, but not Scads, not this brilliant young man before him with so much to live for.

"At nine tonight, release the footage of Rupert with Zella and Sajja," Max said. "Make it go viral. I want the whole world to have seen that by nine tomorrow morning."

"I can do that. What are you going to do?"

"In five minutes, I'm going to leave and walk out with Dale Allen. As soon as I'm gone, you, Scarlett, Tasty, and Zella will go down the back service elevator. There are maintenance uniforms for you in the copy room closet. There is a white panel van outside the service garage doors. The keys are under the mat. Here is the address where you'll go. Tucker is there. Wait for word from me as to the next step. Do not contact anybody."

"Where are you going with Dale?"

"Nowhere. I'm just making sure he leaves the building before you do."

"Why?"

* * *

"Where you off to?" Dale asked.

Max paused at his desk. "Long Beach."

"Really? All the shit going down, and you're going to disappear to some barrier island in North Carolina?"

"That's where I do my best thinking." Max tapped the memory stick on the desk in front of Dale. "Gotta decide what to do with all of this."

"What about the others?"

Max shrugged. "I told Scads to spend the night here with Scarlett, Tasty, and Zella."

Dale nodded. "How about Tucker and Marian? Where are they?"

Max mentally kicked himself. His contentious conversation with Marian had caused him to forget about her safety at this dangerous time. "Between you and me, I have split ways with Marian Zhang. We no longer see eye to eye."

Dale nodded. "She's the mole."

Max didn't respond.

"How about Tucker?" Dale asked.

"I believe he is in Colorado or some such place searching for those fired models. No word from him, and he's not answering his phone."

"What are you going to do about the footage on that memory stick?"

It was a gamble, but then again, Max was a gambler. "Perhaps you should spend the night here with the others. For your own safety."

"I, uh, I'll be fine. I'll go stay with a friend of mine up in the Bronx. You think this whole thing will be over soon?"

"One way or another, it will all be over by tomorrow." Max turned toward the door, paused, and looked back at Dale. "Walk out with me. I'll give you a ride, make sure you get someplace safe."

Dale looked down at his desk, looked like he wanted to say no, thought better of it. "Sure. Just let me close down my computer."

Chapter Thirty-Eight

A Jet in the Sky

Max had his driver take Dale up to the Bronx before bringing him to Teterboro. The snare had been set, and he, Max Creed, was the bait. It was time for Max Creed to die, anyway, or at least Milo Sharp, his thoughts shifting from his upcoming death to the last details of what needed to be set in place before he joined Kinsley in the afterlife, or more likely, merely became ash blowing in the wind, floating in the ocean, mixing with the earth.

Once on the jet, Max called Sevyn.

"Hello, Max."

"Hello, Sevyn." Max cleared his throat. "I'm sorry, but I'm going to have to cancel our dinner plans this evening. Something has come up."

"That's too bad. I was looking forward to seeing you. I think we have unfinished business."

Max thought of the dinner in Long Beach he'd shared with Sevyn, the promise that perhaps there might be more to their relationship than just shutting down Hastings. That this stunning woman might be interested in—Max cut his thoughts off there. There was a very good chance that there would be no tomorrow for him, and therefore, no future.

"I'm sorry," he said. "Unforeseen circumstances, and I have to go out of town."

"Regarding Rupert Hastings?"

"I believe that we are on the cusp of resolving the Rupert Hastings case."

Sevyn laughed. "Resolving? What does that mean? A slap on the wrist and a slight public embarrassment?"

"Hopefully, if all works out, it will be much more substantial than that."

"Where are you going?"

"To a place of solitude so that I can think and connect all the pieces and make sure nothing has been forgotten."

"Call me when you come back to the city?"

"Goodbye, Sevyn."

Max hung up the phone just as the jet roared down the runway and lifted itself into the air away from the tarmac. It wasn't that he wanted to die. He just was not afraid to do so. And there was that one missing piece to the puzzle that eluded him.

Rupert Hastings was a billionaire playboy, arrogant, narcissistic, egotistical, sure, but was he really a stone-cold killer? Max understood how a man like Hastings might rationalize dealing lethal drugs to the population of America, well, not really, but he knew what the argument was. The drug users had the choice: take the drugs or don't take them. What right did the government have to take away the choice to ingest whatever drug you wanted? In the world of Rupert Hastings, there were no repercussions, nobody to tell him no. His wealth and power made him untouchable, and if he could make a bundle selling illegal drugs, why not?

The same twisted logic Hastings applied to engaging the services of prostitutes; that this should be illegal was just ridiculous in this seemingly free country of America. If a man had the money and wanted to hire a woman who was willing to take the money for a service, why should that be wrong? Max winced as he thought about the human trafficking he'd witnessed over the past few years and the perverted logic espoused by people like Hastings.

Max's phone buzzed. He hit the accept call button. "Sally Blum. Good to hear from you. Good news, I trust?"

"Max. Can you talk?"

"Yes."

"The warehouse facility was a gold mine, or rather, a drug mine."

"Can you link it to Hastings?"

"Everybody was claiming ignorance, but then we happened upon a Mexican fellow in Everglades City trying to get a knife removed from his cheekbone. Had a tattoo on his back of a rooster with no head. Stupid fucking tattoo if you ask me."

Max grinned. "Was he willing to talk?"

"He shared plenty before he realized he should save his cards for some sort of plea deal, not that we'd ever give that piece of shit any latitude."

"Did he implicate Hastings?"

"Yep. Connected the warehouse to the shipping company to an offshore shell account that we've discerned is owned by the Hastings Corporation. We're going to arrest him tomorrow."

"You're not going to get him to turn himself over to authorities? Isn't that the normal rich person procedure?"

Sally snickered. "Not in this case. We're going to walk into his home and cuff him in front of his wife and kids."

"His place in New York? Are you sure that he'll be there?"

"Yep. His wife, Vanessa Pan Hastings, has agreed to cooperate. She says that they are going to have lunch at home to 'discuss' some things. Seems Rupert is a bit worried that a few things might leak out that would tarnish his reputation, perhaps negatively affect his marriage."

"You're going to arrest him at noon tomorrow?"

"Yep. Just thought I'd give you a heads-up, as you served him up on a silver platter. Thanks, Milo. Max. Whoever you are. You *are* a modern-day Robin Hood."

The phone screen went blank, Sally having hung up. A modern-day Robin Hood, Max thought, shrugged, and accepted it as his due. He'd gone to bat for the disenfranchised to fight the rich, starting with Sevyn Knight's father, who had committed suicide after being driven into bankruptcy by Hastings' sketchy business practices. He made a mental note to make sure that the Knight family received the money due them, and then, realizing that for him, tomorrow was unlikely to come, decided to call Tucker.

The entire case had morphed into something even more insidious and complicated, but it was winding down now. There were just a few more boxes to tick, and then Max would be done, having brought justice, at least in this one case, to a world often lacking in that ideal.

Max dialed the number for Tucker Friedman.

"Hello, Max. You'll be happy to know that the band is all here. All except John."

Max again wondered about John's safety. He was showing signs of coming out of his coma, but still resided in the darkness. Max had considered moving the man, but his condition was too fragile, and the move would more than likely kill him.

He'd considered asking Sally Blum to put a detail on his room to protect him, but that opened a can of worms that might prove worse than helpful. There were certainly people in the Department of Justice who could not be trusted, and by putting the safety of John Little on the agenda, it might suggest to certain parties that he was a threat. Better for the enemy to think that he was on his deathbed in the hospital and posed no threat.

"Max? Are you there? Is this you?"

"Yeah, it's me. I'm here. How is everybody holding up?"

"A bit tense here, to tell you the truth. I got two eighteen-year-old prima donnas who insist on watching *The Bachelor* nonstop, a Thai prostitute terrified that she just signed her own death certificate, a porn star who wants to go shopping because she's been stuck in the same outfit for two days, a computer geek who's pissed at you for not having the gonads to expose the sordid underbelly of America, a lawyer who you accused of being a traitor, and a Brazilian assassin itching to kill somebody."

Max chuckled. "Sounds like you have your hands full."

"Well, between you and me, I kinda like *The Bachelor*. The outfits are pretty chic, and the bachelor is absolutely smoking hot."

"But, by definition of the show, straight, right?"

"This chap is most certainly not straight. He might be fooling the producers and America, but he's not fooling me."

"Get an early night. Tomorrow morning at nine, you and Marian need to be at the courthouse with Gina and Darcy to file charges of sexual assault against Rupert Hastings."

"Will do. Are we taking him down for good?"

"Scads should be going ahead and blitzing social media with the video of Rupert getting voluntary enemas while getting his testicles shocked, the whole narrated in Zella's dulcet tones, as we speak."

"You know that neither of these things will stick. His people will discount the video as AI-generated Chinese propaganda, or some such thing, and his lawyers will dodge and evade Gina and Darcy until they decide to settle for a nice chunk of change outside of the courts to drop the charges."

"The third piece of the trifecta is that the Department of Justice is going to arrest him tomorrow at noon for smuggling and selling drugs."

"Holy shit on a pancake. That's fantastic."

"Meanwhile, you will keep building a case against him for tax fraud, Marian will continue to dig into the pending court cases against him, and we will make every effort to ensure that he doesn't walk free."

"What about the footage that Scads hacked from Hastings' mainframe?"

"I can't see how releasing that will do any good."

There was a pause on the line. A silence that ticked away heavily. "Why does it sound like you're saying goodbye?"

"One last thing? Can you make sure that the Knight family gets what they are owed and then some?"

"What's going on?"

"Gotta go. The wheels are down."

"That's not what I mean."

"Make sure you get those papers filed first thing in the morning."

"I'll give you a call tomorrow to give you an update."

Max hung up the phone.

Chapter Thirty-Nine

Long Beach Island, North Carolina

Max drove himself from the airport. Along with the SUVs, he kept a ten-year-old Jeep in a garage next to the airport in Wilmington. It was like he was shedding his billionaire persona and becoming a real person as he opened the gate of the banged-up Wrangler. No matter how hard he tried, he was just not a billionaire playboy who ate in thousand-dollar-a-plate restaurants and flew in private jets, not that both those things weren't nice. No. Who he really was, well, he was just a humble fellow from Maine playing a game that had gotten him in over his head.

One last chance to salvage the mess, he thought. There was a duffel bag in the back with cargo shorts, T-shirt, and sandals. He changed out of the Armani suit and shoes, leaving them in a pile on the cement floor of the garage/storage facility.

Halfway to the cottage, he stopped and bought a bottle of Jack Daniels and a bag of pork rinds. By the time he crossed the bridge onto Long Beach Island, the bag was half gone, and the bottle of brown liquor had been breached. He figured that it might be important to have his wits about him tonight, but a few nips certainly wouldn't hurt, and might even bring clarity to the muddle of his thoughts.

It was late to pick up Soter, and it wouldn't do for the dog to be around tonight, anyway. It was safer for the dog to stay with his caretakers for the evening, especially as there was a good chance that they would be his owners going forward.

It was a still night, wind and traffic activity both in a lull, the town of Long Beach Island having gone to bed, only a few lights indicating any signs of life as Max turned left onto Beach Road. The stars pierced the sky like scattered diamonds as there was a new moon, the lack of light allowing the jagged astronomical objects to shine clearly in their perch in the velvet background.

Max parked underneath the cottage and went up the stairs to the back deck, unlocking that door to enter, used the bathroom, filled a bowl with ice, grabbed two tumblers, and carried them, the bottle of JD, and the pork rinds back onto the deck. He pulled a chair across from his so that he could sit and put his feet up as he waited.

There was more of a breeze here, the wind coming from the south, off the ocean, a cooling waft of salty freshness. This caused the waves to crash onto the beach a bit more violently than normal, a steady pounding of ocean onto earth. He was on his second snifter of whiskey, and the pork rinds were nothing more than crumbs in the bottom of the bag, when he heard the stairs creak.

Taytum Liu stepped onto the deck, pausing briefly, before sitting down in the chair next to Max. He nodded to the tumbler, ice, and whiskey. She nodded, poured herself two fingers neat, swirled it slightly, and took a nip.

"Not the highest quality," she said.

"Nope. But it has taste and does the job."

Taytum nodded. "That's what I like about you, Max Creed, or should I say Milo Sharp. You are no American snob."

"I've been playing the part of one," Max said. "Can't say that it suited me."

"You looked like a little boy in a play-acting like an adult. A fish out of water."

"How long have you been on to me?"

"How long have you been on to *me*?" Taytum took another sip of whiskey.

Max shrugged. "Not long. You played your role well. Spoiled wealthy American heiress. Sucked onto the charismatic Rupert Hastings because it was just good fun."

"We all play a role. Me, you, even Rupert."

"How much do you have on him?"

Taytum smiled, her face glowing slightly in the amber turtle lights on the deck, giving her a satanic appearance. A real devil. "Enough. He would've been my puppet as President of the United States. A marionette for my government. But you have ruined that, Max Creed."

"How is it that you came to be an agent of the Chinese?"

"I was raised to be who I am, educated in diplomacy, trained in warfare, carefully cultivated so that when my time came, I would be ready. I have been an ambassador of my country since my birth."

"And your government recognized the charisma and the weaknesses of Rupert Hastings and sent you in to get close."

Taytum nodded, baring her teeth again, her eyes glinting red. "Sex was an easy introduction to the man who has the appetite and discipline of a teenager. I was his toy to be used as he pleased. Then I started to introduce him to other women, younger girls, more nubile, but professional women trained in the art of pleasure—I plucked them from every area of the spectrum and titillated him and kept him happy, and gradually I was no longer forced to be his plaything."

"And you began grooming him to be a candidate for president."

"Not a candidate. Without your interference, Rupert would've been the next president, without a doubt. Americans are so stupid. You all want what you can't have, and when you hold up some buffoon who has everything that your peasant population dreams of, they piss their pants and idolize that fool."

"He doesn't even know I'm his enemy. It was you who bribed those mercs into turning on me. He had no idea."

"The man is a buffoon. But a buffoon who captures the imagination. He would've been the perfect patsy."

Max finished his glass. "But I have ruined that."

"My sources tell me that Rupert will be arrested tomorrow for drug smuggling."

"Does he even know that his warehouse, his offshore account, his shipping company—are being used to smuggle drugs?"

"It was but a step in the process of converting Rupert into a man who would listen to anything."

"You introduced him to the Mexican Cartel and the 9H Triad and suggested that they could make him enormously rich, not just a billionaire, but a wealthy billionaire."

"Ha. I like that. A wealthy billionaire. Yes, it took some time, but when the recession came, he saw the advantage of diversifying into illegal activities."

"That's why he and his father split?"

Taytum shrugged. "I couldn't say. Take your pick. His father saw what Rupert was becoming and cut ties with him. Made my job so much easier."

"But don't you work for the Chinese government? Why would they allow you to deal with a gang of drug smugglers like the 9H Triad?"

Taytum snickered. "The Chinese government runs the 9H Triad, my dear Max. It seems that the two entities share a common interest. Making money and destroying America."

"But now you're on the run from the American authorities. I imagine that the dragnet will be wide enough to scoop you up as well."

"I will be long gone by then."

"But first, you want the memory stick I possess. With that, you can control American government. Heck, maybe you can groom Senator Dunn to be president."

Taytum scoffed. "He doesn't have anywhere near the magnetism that it takes to hoodwink the American peasant class."

"One of the others, then? There are plenty of governmental figures on display. Doing all sorts of things. I can only imagine they desperately want to keep their debauchery and criminal activity from the public, from their spouses, from their kids, and from their mothers."

"Oh, I am sure we will find somebody, but it will take time. You have no idea how long it took to groom Rupert to a point where he was willing, electable, and pliant to our demands. You, Max Creed, have put us back to square one."

"What if I have already thrown the memory stick into the ocean or buried it in the sand, never to be found?"

Taytum laughed loudly, a melodic sound like wind chimes, pleasing to the ear but worrisome to the soul. "Oh, Max, you are priceless. Do you not think that I don't have all the video and audio footage that has been gathered at that silly island? Putting the cameras and microphones in was my idea. Adding computer hackers to search, analyze, sift, and gather incriminating intel against powerful American figures was my idea. My idea. You don't think that the buffoon, the child-man, the idiot who thinks with his wang—you don't really think that he was the one collecting the information, do you?"

"Why are you here, then?"

"Two reasons, Max Creed. I am here for two reasons."

"Care to share?"

Taytum snickered. "I have come to make certain that the information on your memory stick has been destroyed. Your fellow, Stanwood Miller, what is it you call him? Scads. He has corrupted the system, so luckily, the feds won't be privy to any of the secrets. As of now, there are only two backup files in existence. Mine and the one you possess. I have come to destroy it."

"How did you get to Dale Allen?"

Taytum shrugged. "It is not difficult to make a young man pliant. Sex. Love. Secrets. Money. You Americans do not understand the concept of principles. Of honor."

"And you were the one behind blackmailing my people with threats and intimidation? Rupert knew none of it?"

"That buffoon?"

Max took the memory stick from his pocket and handed it over. "I have already erased it. They were not my secrets to share."

"You are a strange American, Max. I am sorry that it must end this way, but I see no other course of action."

"You said that you came here for two reasons."

"The second motivation of my being here is to kill you, of course."

Max nodded. "Why?"

"Why?"

"Yeah. The memory stick is erased. I have no backup. I think you believe that. The wheels have been set in motion for the public and official destruction of Rupert as a presidential candidate, and will almost certainly end up with him in prison. You will disappear into the night. What reason is there for you to kill me?"

Taytum smiled wickedly. "Because you have been a serious thorn in my side."

"This is personal, then? Not the machinations of the Chinese government but a matter between Taytum Liu and Max Creed?"

"I plan on killing you with my bare hands."

"Should we go down to the beach?"

"You lead the way."

Max grasped the bottle of Jack, took a slug, stood, and went to the stairs. He could hear Taytum's light steps behind him as he went down, turned, and followed the path through the dune to the beach. At the top of the dune, he removed his sandals and continued barefoot. The tide had receded, and he walked down to where the ocean pooled in the glint of the starlight, before stopping and turning around.

Taytum had also removed her shoes. She stood about ten feet to his side, the cool Atlantic swirling around her toes. "You have not seemed surprised by my arrival, nor by my pronouncement that I planned to kill you with my hands just for my own sheer pleasure," she said. "Why is that?"

"I knew you'd come."

"Yet, you did not bring any soldier friends? Or try to flee. You knew Dale Allen was the stool pigeon, yet you told him where you'd be. You expected this, and yet here you stand, unarmed and unaccompanied."

"Here you are, unarmed and unaccompanied as well. Perhaps we were made for this moment. Each step leading us closer to the beach, the surf, and death."

Taytum smiled. Took a few steps closer. "I have been training in fighting methods since before I could walk."

Max chuckled. "I grew up in a redneck town in Maine fighting bullies every day at recess. I'm sure that's not something you experienced in your

271

private school days. Tell me, have you ever truly been in a fight?" He didn't mention his training of the last four years with John and Scarlett.

Taytum wheeled on the ball of her foot and drove the other one, crashing into the side of Max's head. He staggered a couple of steps and regained his balance. "Was that a ballet move?"

Taytum dropped to a crouch, her hands out in front of her, revolving, extending, retracting. Max stepped forward and threw a punch which she deflected, her palm coming up under his chin, clamping his teeth together with a snap. He brought his elbow down on her shoulder, driving his weight behind it, but she twirled away.

Max took a step further into the ocean so that it was now at shin level, rising to his knees with the current, receding to his feet as the tide ebbed. The water would take away the nimble edge that Taytum possessed, evening the odds with his sheer brute force.

"Come and get me," Taytum said from the beach, a few feet away, a ferocious grin plastered to her face.

"You came here to kill me," Max said. "C'mon and do it."

Taytum eased forward, and then charged, arms and feet windmilling in front of her like a snowblower gone mad. Max slapped away a punch, took the brunt of a kick on his bicep, and then drove a punch into her nose. The cartilage screeched in complaint under his knuckles, and she hissed in pain and surprise, then fury.

Max went to grab her in a bear hug, but she spun away, her foot kicking backward, catching his knee, which buckled, toppling him into the surf. He raised his face, gasping from the water, only to be met by the solid chop of a cupped hand to his eye. Again, he went down under the water.

She grabbed him by the hair and dragged him above water. He took the opportunity to grasp the back of her head and slam his forehead into her downturned face. And then they were at it, punching, kicking, twisting, wrestling, gouging eyes, each looking for any advantage possible.

Taytum slammed Max on the side of the head with a rock plucked from the ocean floor. As he fell, he grabbed a handful of her hair and pulled her down with him. One hand found her throat, but before the other could follow suit, he felt his manhood grasped and twisted, and he lost his grip as he twisted free. They both came to their feet in the shallow water and began to circle each other.

She came at him again, a whirling dervish of spins, kicks, and punches. He gave ground before her attack, drawing her in, until he saw his opportunity and drove his fist into the already mashed nose of her face with a good deal of shoulder behind the punch. She stopped, paused as if in thought, and he hit her with a left-right combo, pop, pop. As her eyes glazed over, Max put all his weight behind a right-hand wallop that came all the way from his toes, and she flipped over backward into the surf.

Max stumbled after her, his guard ready, but she was sinking into the knee-deep water, her body serene, like seaweed returning to its home. He reached down and grabbed a handful of her hair, wrapping his hand in like tying himself to the horn of the saddle of a rodeo bull, and pulled her from the water. Her body was completely limp. She was out.

He turned and dragged her from the ocean, out of the waves, away from the tide, and up onto the sand of the beach, where he dumped her unceremoniously. Only then did Max realize there was a man standing there with a rifle held casually in his hands. It was too dark to see what the weapon was, but Max was betting it could put fifty holes in him in a minute.

It was the Asian man who'd been at the junkyard with the Headless Rooster and also present when Scads had been beaten. Max figured him for the 9H Triad connection.

"You stupid Americans. Do you ever consider a backup plan when going into battle? Of course, Colonel Liu had a plan in place in case you proved more formidable than she thought. Now, you will feed the fish."

The man raised the rifle, and a shot rang out. Most of Max's body hurt with bruises, scratches, and cuts, but he didn't get the impression that he'd been shot. He ran his hands down his chest and abdomen, feeling for the burning pain of a bullet wound. Nothing. He looked back up.

The Asian gangster had dropped the rifle and was staring at Max with a confused look on his face, possibly due to the round red hole pierced directly between his eyes. Without a sound, not even a gurgle, he fell forward on his face in the sand.

Sevyn Knight stepped from the shadows. "Thought I might come down and give you a bit of backup."

"So, you're not just some paper-pushing desk jockey for the CIA, are you?"

"I was until a year back when I was pulled for a special assignment. Let's just say covert political action."

"They wanted you to bring down Rupert Hastings."

"Yes."

"But we checked your story out. Your father really was screwed over by Hastings. He did commit suicide."

Sevyn nodded. "That's why they thought I might be ripe for recruitment for their special assignment."

"You used me. Us. As a tool."

"We had the same goal in mind. And it has been achieved. Let's move on."

Chapter Forty

New York City

It was just after ten in the morning on the Upper East Side of New York City. Max gave the man at the desk a hundred dollars to let him go up to Rupert's suite at the top of the building without being announced. The night before, three SUVs had pulled up, loaded the body of the Asian man into the car as well as the unconscious form of Taytum Liu, and then sped off. Sevyn had gone with them, leaving Max to make his way back into his cottage, clean the blood, sand, and saltwater from his body, grab the bottle of JD, and return to his private jet, where he slept until dawn before flying back to the city.

Rupert opened the door himself, a look of surprise on his face. "Max? What are you doing here?"

"I've got something I need to show you."

"What happened to your face?"

"Rough night at the beach."

Rupert shrugged. "It's not a real good time."

"You're going to want to see this." Max stepped past him into the room.

"Well, come in, then," Rupert said to his back while shutting the door. "Let's go to my study."

Perfect, Max thought. A fitting place to destroy a man's life. He followed Rupert down a hall and back to the study. Rupert offered a scotch, and Max agreed, even though it was almost two hours before noon. This might be his last drink, for all he knew, because his excuse for alcohol and gambling was about to end, as was his life as Max Creed.

He walked to the desk, pulling the laptop from the briefcase, setting it down.

"Try that, my boy, just give that a go." Rupert handed him a tumbler with a generous two fingers of brown liquor.

Max took a nip. It was very smooth.

"That is the Macallan 1926," Rupert said, gesturing for Max to sit. "It's called the holy grail of whiskey. Apropos, don't you think?"

"Of what?"

"As smooth as the skin on the models on my private island. The Holy Grail."

"Heard you've run into some problems."

Rupert waved his hand and laughed. "Nothing at all, my boy. Somebody created a fake video of me online, probably using that new AI stuff. You know that artificial intelligence is going to be a game-changer. If you're looking to invest. I know I plan to do so." Rupert pulled a chair next to Max at the desk and sat down. "What do you got here?"

"As a matter of fact, I know that it is you. And those two women are the Thai prostitutes you introduced me to in Pattaya City."

Rupert's eyes narrowed. "What are you saying?"

"I heard that assault charges were filed against you in New York District Court this morning."

"First, I've heard of that, but somebody is always looking to make a buck with some trumped-up charges against me. You must know how that goes."

"Funny thing is, these are the two girls you sent to my room in Vegas that first night we met."

"What two girls? What are you talking about?"

Max couldn't quite believe it, but it appeared as if Rupert were truly disbelieving that these charges were anything but contrived by a jealous world to bring down a god among mortals. That he would brush off the unpleasantness of it as if crumbs from a sandwich before continuing his parade through life as the center of his own making.

"Did you hear about the drug bust down in Florida?" Max asked.

"Drug bust? Florida?"

"Seems the feds raided a warehouse facility down there where they were combining heroin from Mexico with Iso from China to be distributed throughout the heartland."

"I don't watch the news or read the newspapers," Rupert said. "Bunch of baloney is all it is. Who cares about some drug bust down in Florida? Probably just something made up by the fake news."

Max struggled to keep the shock from his face. Rupert had no idea what was coming down the pike for him. He was so far removed from his business dealings that nobody had informed him of the bad news yet. More than likely, the contact person had been Taytum, and she was not currently answering her phone.

But that is why he'd brought the laptop. He wanted to spell it out for the man-child.

First, he brought up the video of Rupert having Sajja and Zella squirt water up his ass while shocking his testicles.

"Pish posh," Rupert said, but his voice was a bit strained. "Any kid with a spate of computer knowledge could photoshop that."

Max held up a finger and let the video play. The last part was a close-up, zoomed-in look at Rupert's face as he orgasmed. His cheeks had bypassed ruddy and were red and pudgy, his eyes rolled back in his head, teeth bared in a churlish manner, giving him the appearance of a demented and evil Shrek.

"That's not me. Where'd you get this filth?" Rupert slammed his hand down on the desk, but his voice had spiked to a high-pitched screech.

The video transitioned to one of Sajja and Zella. Their faces were not blurred. Zella had decided to go on the record, admit to her own transgressions, and make a statement to the authorities. It was her belief that Sajja would've wanted that, and she wanted to honor her friend by destroying the man who'd used them poorly. They introduced themselves and gave details of being hired by Taytum Liu on seven occasions to have sexual relations involving the twisted sexual perversions shown on the video with Rupert Hastings.

"Where'd you get this. This has not... what the hell are you doing?" Rupert turned his eyes from the screen and glared at Max.

Max reached up and grasped the jowls of the man in his hand and turned his face back toward the laptop. "Just watch."

The video transitioned to just Zella. "It is March 22nd, 2023. My name is Zella Shinawatra. On Valentine's Day, February 14th of this year, my best friend in the whole world, Sajja Ngam was killed by assassins hired by Rupert Hastings in hopes of silencing this video and our story. I will not be gagged or suppressed any longer. My voice, and the words of my dearest friend, Sajja, will be heard. Rupert Hastings is a vile pig, and I want the world and the authorities to know this."

"I thought that you..." Rupert trailed off, coughed, choked, and spat a glob of phlegm on the hardwood floor.

"Zella is currently giving her statement to the authorities." Max's voice was calm, level, but tinged with the disgust he felt for this man.

The video transitioned to Gina and Darcy, the two young models who'd come to Max's room in Vegas with the marker for his winnings, a gift of expensive scotch, and an offer of nubile carnal delight.

They introduced themselves and shared how they'd both been promised successful modeling careers in exchange for 'playing the game.' And how that game began with having sex with Rupert Hastings and then agreeing to be chips in his game of power, to be traded to other players to perform erotic and animalistic acts in exchange for favors owed to Rupert.

"This was just the summary," Max said. "Gina and Darcy are currently sharing a much greater detailed litany of transgressions with the authorities."

"What are you doing? Why are you doing this?" Rupert spluttered and spat again. Sweat ran in rivulets down his splotchy face.

The video flickered to a new face. "Hello, Rupert. My name is Tucker. I have uncovered three different shell corporations and have connected them to you. There is clear evidence of tax evasion, such infraction each coming with a jail sentence of three to five years. More importantly, the Feds will be seizing this money and freezing all your other assets. The good news is that you seem to have very little liquid money. It appears that most of your declared wealth is attached to the branding of your Hastings name. Which, as of today, is shit, and less than worthless. I hope you have a good day."

Rupert grasped Max by the shoulder and spat out incoherent words. Max knocked his hands free. He stood up and grabbed Rupert's hair in one hand and his neck in the other, and turned his face back to the screen.

"One more video to watch. This one is live."

Max reached forward and connected the laptop to a Zoom link. It took a few moments, and then two figures in the cockpit of a helicopter came on the screen.

"Hello, Rupert. My name is Scarlett."

"And I'm Tasty. You took poor young girls here and abused them. One was Bev Johnson. She was my sister."

Rupert tried to stand up, turn, twist—but Max held him firmly down.

The video tilted, turned, and then pointed down.

"That is an island below. It is Isla de Barro. I believe that you have nicknamed it the Isle of the Holy Grail."

The video zoomed in. "This is the swimming pool replete with Greek and Roman statues."

An explosion boiled forth, water shooting upward in a geyser, marble statues splintering to dust, flames shooting forth in a rolling wave, and then everything caving back into nothing but a crevice of burning rock marred by, and then blocked by, black smoke.

The camera shifted. "Your residence, also home to your network of surveillance technology."

Another explosion. Fire and brimstone. And then a crevice.

There were five more explosions.

Scarlett's face appeared. "There were no models, workers, or other abuse victims hurt in the making of this video."

Max released his hold, and Rupert stood up.

"I thought you were my friend."

"You are a soulless scumbag, Rupert. You have no friends. Only parasites hoping for a handout and people that you pay. And if you're wondering why your wife never showed for your important discussion, it's because she is currently giving a statement to the Feds."

"You lie. I am loved. People love me. I am going to be president. You'll see. None of this matters. Don't you see? I am rich. I am good-looking. I am smart. I am likeable. People love me. You'll see. You're just jealous. I am Rupert Hastings."

Max chuckled. "You're a piece of shit who is about to be arrested, and you're going to rot in jail for the rest of your time. More than likely, you will be introduced to a new sexual practice, most likely not something that you will enjoy."

"Get out of my home."

Rupert swung a looping roundhouse punch at Max.

Max casually knocked it aside and drove his right fist into the man's nose, the cartilage squishing and splintering before the more satisfying cracking of bone. Blood spread down his face but Max was busy sinking his left fist deep into the man's belly.

Rupert gasped loudly, spraying blood, and bent forward in pain, his face meeting Max's rising knee and flipping him over backward into the middle of the floor in the study, where he lay blubbering and crying in a pool of blood.

Max winced as he looked at the bloody face imprint on his trousers.

There were three sharp knocks on the door.

Max looked at Rupert. "Just so you know. I am not you. I never was you. You are everything that is wrong with the world."

He walked out of the room, down the hallway, and opened the front door. Sally Blum stood there with a host of federal agents and local cops.

"You'll find presidential hopeful Hastings in his study. He is reflecting on his mistakes."

Max stepped past them and went to the elevator.

When he stepped out of the building onto the curb, Milo wondered what was next.

Epilogue

Long Beach Island, North Carolina

Soter was sitting attentively next to John Little on the deck of the Long Beach Island cottage. Milo grinned. John had made the mistake of giving the dog a chip and was now being implored for more. Once successful, the canine would be relentless with his begging.

John had been released from the hospital three days prior, and Milo had brought him down to the beach for his recovery and rehabilitation. He still moved stiffly, and sometimes forgot things, but he was slowly coming back.

He had fared better than Rupert Hastings, who'd been found dead in his jail cell less than twenty-four hours after his arrest. The official ruling was that he had had a stroke, brought on by the stress of his arrest and demise. Milo knew better. He had too much dirt on too many people. He'd most certainly been assassinated.

It could've been any number of people. Perhaps the rumor had come out that he'd been videotaping and hacking the secrets of many a powerful person for several years now. The murder could've been ordered by a senator, a judge, a federal agent—the list went on and on. Powerful people with money and a motive to kill.

Or it could've been the Chinese, making sure to muzzle one source, all the while wondering what had happened to Colonel Taytum Liu, who'd been a top undercover asset for them and had disappeared into thin air. Did the Chinese possess the dirt gathered by Rupert's people, or had it disappeared with Taytum? Milo supposed that time would tell. Or not.

Dale Allen had been arrested and was being held for conspiracy against the US government. It seemed that the boy, under the thrall of acrobatic sex, had fallen in love with a beautiful Chinese girl who'd clouded his mind with lies about Milo. Poor Dale was devastated. Max wasn't sure if it was because he'd been a traitor to his friends and country or because the girl was gone in the wind.

Scads was still angry with Milo for not releasing the smut of the rich and famous to the world. Max assumed that he'd relent as he realized that the murderer of his parents and threat to his own existence, the Headless Rooster, had been taken off the board due to Milo's efforts. Life was a series of compromises, and this was just one more.

Marian had verbally forgiven him for doubting her, but there was still an iciness between them, one that might never melt.

Scarlett was missing, and Milo suspected she was hunting down Jair Otelo, the man who'd shared her bed and then double-crossed her. Milo did not envy the man when she found him.

Tucker seemed to be the only one of the band largely unscathed. He was even dating the fellow whom he'd gone to see Lang Lang with, a date that had been interrupted by the death of Sajja.

Their first mission together had shaken them to the very core of their existence. In the end, the bad guys lost, but at what price?

Sevyn Knight came up the deck stairs wearing a white tank top and tight jean shorts, her athletically fit body prominently displayed. Her shaven head gleamed in the sun, and she positively glowed with health.

"Good night for a barbecue," she said. "After a swim."

He hadn't seen her since the night she'd saved him by shooting a man in the head and then disappearing into the night with the dead body and the unconscious Taytum.

"The mysterious government agent," Milo said. "I thought you'd be done with us now that the case is closed."

"I was talking to the boss yesterday about something that might interest you."

The boss, Milo wondered, almost speaking his thoughts aloud. Would that be the Director of National Intelligence? Or maybe even the President himself?

"You want something to drink?" he asked.

"Chardonnay would be fantastic." She looked at him and laughed loudly. "You should've seen your face. I'm joshing you. I'll take a couple fingers of that bottle of fine Jack Daniels you got open somewhere, I'm sure."

Milo got a glass from inside and put two cubes in. Came out. Poured her some of the brown and sat back down.

"What were you and the *boss* talking about?"

Sevyn grinned wickedly. Took a healthy swallow. "We might have something for you. Off the books, of course. How do you feel about getting the band back together?"

A Note from the Author

Justice is a right and not a privilege.

Ackowledgements

If you are reading this, I thank you, for without readers, writers would be obsolete.

I am grateful to my mother, Penelope McAlevey, and father, Charles Cost, for raising me with a love of books.

Much appreciation to the various friends and relatives who have also read my work and given helpful advice.

I'd like to offer a big hand to my wife, Deborah Harper Cost, and children, Brittany, Pearson, Miranda, and Ryan, who have always had my back.

Thank you to Level Best Books and the amazing duo of the Dames of Detection, Verena Rose and Shawn Reilly Simmons, for giving me the opportunity to present this book to the world.

About the Author

Matt Cost (*aka* Matthew Langdon Cost) writes the Goff Langdon Mainely Mysteries, the Clay Wolfe Trap Mysteries, the Brooklyn 8 Ballo Mysteries, The Modern-Day Chronicles of Max Creed Thrillers, and three works of historical fiction. Cost was a history major at Trinity College. He owned a mystery bookstore, a video store, and a gym, before serving a ten-year sentence as a junior high school teacher. In 2014, he was released, and he began writing. And that's what he does: he writes histories and mysteries. Cost now lives in Brunswick, Maine, with his wife, Harper. There are four grown children: Brittany, Pearson, Miranda, and Ryan. They have been replaced at home with four dogs. He now spends his days at the computer, writing.

AUTHOR WEBSITE:

www.mattcost.net

SOCIAL MEDIA HANDLES:

Facebook: https://www.facebook.com/MattCost8

Instagram: https://www.instagram.com/mlangdoncost/

Also by Matt Cost

The Mainely Mystery Series
Mainely Power (2020)
Mainely Fear (2020)
Mainely Money (2021)
Mainely Angst (2022)
Mainely Wicked (2023)
Mainely Mayhem (2024)

The Clay Wolfe Trap Series
Wolfe Trap (2021)
Mind Trap (2021)
Mouse Trap (2022)
Cosmic Trap (2023)
Pirate Trap (2024)

The Brooklyn 8 Ball Series (Historical PI)
Velma Gone Awry (2023)
City Gone Askew (2024)

Historical Fiction
I Am Cuba (2020)
Love in a Time of Hate (2021)
At Every Hazard (2022)

www.ingramcontent.com/pod-product-compliance
Lightning Source LLC
Chambersburg PA
CBHW020602110726
47899CB00002B/341